IN THE
STILL OF THE NIGHT

ALSO BY DAVID L. GOLEMON

IN THE
STILL OF THE NIGHT

THE SUPERNATURALS II

David L. Golemon

St. Martin's Press ≈ New York

IN THE STILL OF THE NIGHT. Copyright © 2017 by David L. Golemon. All rights reserved. Printed in the United States of America. For information, address St. Martin's Press, 175 Fifth Avenue, New York, N.Y. 10010.

www.stmartins.com

Designed by Omar Chapa

The Library of Congress Cataloging-in-Publication Data is available upon request.

ISBN 978-1-250-10310-9 (hardcover)
ISBN 978-1-250-10311-6 (ebook)

Our books may be purchased in bulk for promotional, educational, or business use. Please contact your local bookseller or the Macmillan Corporate and Premium Sales Department at 1-800-221-7945, extension 5442, or by email at MacmillanSpecialMarkets@macmillan.com.

First Edition: October 2017

10 9 8 7 6 5 4 3 2 1

For my family—
Life Begins Anew

PROLOGUE

OUR TOWN, USA

Like a rubber ball I'll come bouncing back to you . . .
—Bobby Vee, "Rubber Ball," *Billboard* #89 Top Hits of 1961

GEORGETOWN, WASHINGTON, D.C.

The gathering consisted of the elite of governmental society. Some would say the real power brokers of that elite. That power being the wives of senators and House members.

For the guest of honor, there were whispered innuendos about her own motives in attending, but not one of the women present this night would be caught commenting on it. The guest in question used the occasions to conduct business without the prying eyes of the media or the security elements that constantly surrounded her.

The blond woman eased past her security team with a raised hand as she approached the hostess. She would leave them behind for her clandestine meeting. The lead security man nodded as she passed, and the agent spoke softly into the hidden microphone.

She smiled as she was greeted by the hostess. "You have a visitor. I have shown him into the study."

"Thank you," the woman said and then was shown in. The double sliding doors were closed as the man stood from a chair at a small table.

"I was expecting you forty-five minutes ago, Mr. Webber," she said as turned and faced the smaller man.

"It took more time than expected to get the request from Mr. Avery to myself. Then it took more classified digging than I had originally thought it would take."

"Do you have the information?" she asked impatiently.

"Yes. And if I get caught, it will be no less a charge than treason. This is beyond classified. If the assistant director ever got wind—"

She held up a hand. "From what Mr. Avery has told me, you're good at your job. So, instead of assisting my husband, you'll be assisting me."

The man sat down in the Queen Anne chair and then placed his briefcase on the table. He opened it and produced a thick file. Her brows raised when she saw the TOP SECRET stamp printed onto its front. Then the embossed departmental seal for the Central Intelligence Agency. Then he placed another, even thicker file on top of the first. This one had emblazoned in bright red lettering the seal of the United States Army. Then a third file was placed on the first two. This was from the Department of the Air Force.

"All three confirm what you suspected. Your father-in-law was involved to the top of his head and was the main participant in all three after-action reports from 1945, by the army, the U.S. Army Air Corps, and the old OSS, the precursor to the Central Intelligence Agency. How your husband would be involved, there is no mention, considering at the time the boy was only three months old and living at home with his terminally ill mother."

"Have you and Mr. Avery come to any conclusions about the town? Is there any financial connection to Moreno by either my husband or his father to the corporation—a paper trail, perhaps?"

"If the town is connected in any way to your future holdings, it's buried so deep in the company's financial infrastructure that you'll find out in ten, maybe fifteen years of reading the fine print on thousands of deeds of ownership documents on what you own or do not own. I, as well as Mr. Avery, suspect that the corporation has no direct ties with Moreno."

"Okay, what did you find?"

"I would rather place my findings in a written report to you, which I have already completed. I don't relish the opportunity to revisit that damnable military operation."

"Perhaps that's a good place to start. My husband has dreams and nightmares about something that he never actually witnessed, but is so traumatized by it that it invades his sleep. So, start with the operation, and tell me why he's haunted by something committed when he was but three months old."

Webber swallowed and then pulled out that written report. "Operation Necromancer, conceived by Dr. Jürgen Fromm, from dates 1941 through 1945. Captured by special operation in Yugoslavia on June 13, '45."

"Read my father-in-law's entry on that last day once more," she said, wanting to hear the gruesome details again. Webber swallowed and took a sip of water. He picked up his report and found the day in question.

"June 13, 1945, 0240 hours," Webber read. "Low-altitude jump was completed with the only casualty being Sergeant Leach, who sprained his ankle severely in the landing. Proceeded to the bunker complex fifteen miles outside of Belgrade with the assistance of the Slavic underground forces in the area. Attempted to contact by radio for verification of initial radio communiqué received two weeks ago in London by Major Dietz. Radio contact with German SS security unit was established with Major Dietz—"

The night was overcast when the gray-uniformed man stepped from the deepest shadows of the demolished structure that had been hit by no less than four Royal Air Force bombing missions over the area in the last year of hostilities. The Americans stood in a group with weapons raised. The members of the Yugoslavian underground stood aloof of the group. They had done what the Allies had asked of them and guided the soldiers to the underground complex. The Yugoslavian resistance melted into the shadows. The SS officer faced the men in front of him and in the waning moonlight started to raise his right arm in the air until he saw the American colonel raise his left brow. He lowered the hand.

"I take it you are Major Dietz?" the tall American colonel asked.

The German clicked his heels together in answer. He then reached for his sidearm. This brought an immediate response from the men attached to the Office of Strategic Services. Five Thompson submachine guns were raised. The major held his left hand up as his right withdrew the Luger semiautomatic from its holster. He offered it to the colonel, who took it and tossed it back to Captain Frank Perry, who caught it in turn and ejected the clip and then discharged the chambered round.

"My men will be taken into your custody, and our deal will be intact?"

"They will receive the treatment my superiors promised," the colonel lied. He knew that every SS officer and enlisted man would face warrants for war crimes. "Just as long as you were truthful about this little camp you have here."

The German major bowed his head and then gestured for the team of commandos to follow him. "All of my men, except for Fromm's guard detail, have been disarmed. I do not wish them shot," he said as he stepped into a battered and crumbling doorway.

"Goddamn Kraut speaks better English than I do," Sergeant Leach said as he limped but followed the team onto a lift that had survived the bombings.

"When I produce Fromm and supply his journals and notes to you, I have your word as an officer that my men will——"

"Major, let's not get into whose word is good while we stand in the middle of a city that is lying in ruins because of you. This is not a negotiation. If what we find is useful to us, you will be treated accordingly."

The lift continued deep into the earth.

The major raised the gate when the lift came to a stop. He stepped out, and the commandos immediately saw the twenty SS personnel standing at attention. Their weapons were placed on the floor in front of them.

"Sergeant Leach, sit these men down and disable those weapons," Captain Perry said as he followed the German major and his commanding officer, U.S. Army colonel Robert Hadley. The farther they traveled, the more oppressive the air became.

The major came to a large steel doorway and he stopped. He knocked three times and the doors opened. The Americans were greeted with the muzzle of a German Grease gun. The automatic weapon's barrel was lowered by Major Dietz, and the SS sergeant holding the weapon saw his and then backed away, offering Captain Perry his weapon as he did so. The other two SS guards did the same. When the guards stepped away they saw a small man with graying hair and white coat sitting in a rolling chair. He was handcuffed to the chair's arms. His glasses were askew. He spoke rapid German at the major, the goatee-style beard moving rapidly up and down as he sprayed spittle in his anger. Colonel Hadley looked at Captain Perry, who knew German from his college days.

"Our friend here is quite angry at his perceived betrayal," Perry translated.

"I speak English very well, Captain . . . Perry, is it?" the small man in the chair said. "Whatever this fool has promised you, it will do you no good. The information you will seek is in my head and mine alone. Even if this traitorous pig gives you my journals, I am the only one who can interpret them."

"Okay, you've demonstrated your ability to speak English; now shut the hell up," Hadley said as he stepped past the chair and examined the large enclosure in the middle of the hidden laboratory. "Is this it?" The colonel moved to the front of the giant vaultlike structure and looked closer. He saw lines of rubber and metal running in and out of the steel like snakes emerging from holes in the ground. He saw viewing ports that had slide shutters on them, and then he saw the most outstanding feature was on the top of the vault—two large steel tanks that fed the lines running into the container.

"This looks like the pressure chamber we saw in the States, all right," Captain Perry said as he too examined the vault. "Except for those tanks up there, almost identical."

"And you have all the high-altitude experimental data, Major?"

"Well-documented data, Colonel. It's all there."

"High-altitude data—is that the goods you are selling the Americans, Major?" The small scientist laughed from his chair a few feet away. Dr. Jürgen Fromm used his feet to turn in his wheeled chair.

"Explain, Doctor," Hadley said.

"I would not have contacted your organization, Colonel, if I did not have more to trade than high-altitude experiment results that the Allies have not previously discovered. That alone would not have saved the lives of me and my men."

"You are not qualified to explain what happened. No matter what you study or even reverse engineer, you Americans will never grasp what I have discovered," Fromm said confidently from his chair.

The German officer turned away and then angrily stepped toward the vault and up on a small platform that lined it for viewing purposes.

"Captain, behind you you'll find a small switch on control panel B. It says viewing port, chamber one. Throw that switch, please."

Perry looked at Colonel Hadley, who nodded that he should do as asked. He did. There was the sound of an electric motor, and then the viewing port in front of the major and colonel began to slide into the side of the thick steel. The major reached out and turned on the light inside.

"What in God's name is this?" Hadley said as he turned angrily to face the seated scientist.

"That is high-altitude experiment 1193-A, oxygen deprivation at fifty-six thousand meters, the result of well over a thousand attempts to understand oxygen deprivation and its effect on pilots at altitude," Fromm said with a satisfied grin that froze Perry's blood as he too stepped onto the viewing platform. He turned back when he saw what that was inside. He looked at Fromm with murder in his eyes.

Arranged in a circle where each had died a horrid death were the sludge-like remains of many people. They could see that some were men and others women. From what they could see of their expressions, they had succumbed to a death that sent them to the afterlife screaming in agony.

"What in the hell did you do to these people, you son of a bitch?" Captain Perry said as he turned away from the horrid scene and faced the grinning doctor in his chair.

"By happenstance—sheer luck, really—the men and women you see in that section of the vault were from the same small village near the town of Sarajevo. We were lucky to have entire families involved that proved crucial to our inevitable result. It was a godsend for our accidental discovery."

Major Dietz turned and walked to the control panel and hit another switch. Fifteen feet away, toward the back of the vault, another viewing port opened. The two Americans moved farther down. Perry did not want to see any more, but Hadley looked far more intrigued as he viewed the room through the reinforced glass.

"Not that I would not like to see all of you killed for the fools you are, may I suggest you flood the vault sprinkler systems with M-12, Major."

Dietz looked at Fromm and then turned the opening valve on the mixing chambers on the top of the vault. The automated safety system kicked in with a hiss of flooding chemical rushing into the steel and rubber lines.

"Oh," was all Captain Perry could get out of his constricting throat as the lights came up.

They were all layered in a pile in front of the wall that separated the two different sections of the vault, which they now saw was two rooms. The wall had windows almost exactly like the viewing ports on the outside so each could view the occupants of the opposite side. Hadley turned silently and looked at Fromm before turning back.

"As I mentioned, the last high-altitude test conducted for, and sponsored by, the German Luftwaffe, did not have the result we initially intended."

"Fucking children?" Captain Perry said, sorely tempted to open fire on any German he now saw. He would start with those available, Dr. Fromm and Major Dietz.

"Yes, children. The children of the subjects you have just observed inside section A. Purely an accidental discovery because we were running low on slave labor, so we used the children to fill the role of adult subjects.

It was just a lucky circumstance, as I said, that we had nothing but families left. That was the turning point on the initial discovery."

"What result?" Hadley asked, staring at the moldering bodies in their small pile of humanity. None of them could have been any older than sixteen years of age. "All I see here is cold, calculated murder, the same things we are finding all through the eastern countries. Just more mass murder."

"Yes, mass murder, but for a cause, Colonel, a cause. You will receive your high-altitude results from my files; you may even learn something new from them. But the discovery you are about to see is the real miracle here. What I have proven in this cesspool of a bunker is the very secret that all of mankind has wondered and dreamed about throughout human existence. The power of the mind and what it is capable of."

Hadley and Perry stood before the madman in silence.

"Now you will see who holds the real bargaining position here. It's not this fool with his Death's Head cap on; it is I, a mere doctor of cardio and vascular theory. Now lower the chambers lights and watch the magic."

Hadley nodded to Dietz. The lights, not only in the bunker but the vault itself, turned low.

"Examine chamber A, please, gentlemen," Fromm said.

They both looked inside. Nothing had changed; the bodies of the parents were still arrayed in a semicircle against the wall of the vault.

"And now the children in chamber B, please," Fromm said, watching the men move down to the next section and look inside as the metal lines above them hissed with pressure.

"If we did not have containment security, this experience would surely be your last, Colonel Hadley. It was too late for sixteen of my colleagues and twenty security men before we found the chemical makeup to contain them, weaken them."

Once they saw inside, both Americans knew their lives had changed forever. Hadley's eyes widened, and then Captain Perry felt his heart race to dangerous proportions.

"God Almighty, look at them all," Hadley said.

"This is not God's design, Colonel, it is mine." Fromm laughed.

The view inside had affected Hadley for no other reason than he saw a way for him and his small team to benefit from, and in turn take something more than just honor out of this war. His mind began racing.

"Now shall you deal with the author of this amazing discovery, or do you wish to deal with the fool Dietz? Because without my knowledge, the experiment can never be duplicated."

With his eyes locked on the activity inside the steel vault, Hadley flinched when something came at him at the viewing port. He heard the hiss above his head and a fine mist of something heavy and silver in color fell from a small shower-like head in the ceiling of the enclosure. He finally tore his eyes away and faced Captain Perry.

"Free the doctor, Captain."

The CIA researcher placed the file report on the top of the pile of three folders, and then he looked at the back of the woman at the window as she finally turned and smiled.

"Thank you. And this has been verified as actually having taken place?"

"By no less than three agencies that do not falsify reports, ma'am."

"Did you get the photos that I requested?" she asked.

"Mr. Avery has them. I also have an item that was found in a very old safe-deposit box account of your husband's that even you knew nothing about." He reached into his coat pocket and brought out a small wooden box and placed it on the table.

She reached down and, with her expensively manicured fingernails, opened the box. She smiled; this time, the gesture reached the cold eyes.

"These are hers, you're sure?"

"The only thing that your husband had safely hidden. Now you have them. The only thing physical that remains of the person in question." Webber stood and replaced the stolen files that he had to return and put them back into his briefcase.

"Tell your Mr. Avery that I will await my payment."

She held the item a moment longer and she didn't notice Webber leaving. Once the sliding doors were closed, she placed the dark-lensed glasses back into the box.

MORENO, CALIFORNIA

The town was incorporated and designed like most small towns in America— four main streets that formed a square with a small courthouse, police department, and general civic center at its middle. The park surrounding these grounds was now overgrown to the point that most of the playground equipment was hidden from view by the dense cover of weeds and grass. Of the few businesses still operating in the once-thriving town, only the used record store operating out of the old K-Rave radio station on Main and

Cypress was making anything close to a living. This was only because of the current trend of collectors buying up old-fashioned vinyl records.

The houses, once perfect little homes produced after World War II, were now shells of their former selves. Of the nearly 612 homes built from old aircraft parts and into prefab housing, over half of them were now scorched reminders of the industrial accident that happened in Moreno in the fall of 1962.

Of the old factory overlooking the town, all but two six-story brick walls had been knocked down during the explosion of that eventful year. The old Spanish mission and winery on the opposite end of town high up on the hill was still there. The winery was built next to the crumbling Spanish Santa Maria Delarosa mission. The winery itself had succumbed to the elements about 150 years after the mission's own destruction by an earthquake in 1821. Both ruins overlooked the town as if in guardianship of what had once been, but never would be again.

The news camera was set up in front of the old Newberry's Department Store, one of the tallest buildings inside the deserted town. Standing tall at four stories, it seemed to tower over the next-largest building, the old Grenada Theater, two blocks down. The young reporter was a smallish woman who was currently trying her best to cover her growing frustration toward the old man she was interviewing. It was for a throwaway piece for the eleven o'clock broadcast for the local ABC affiliate in Los Angeles. The old man was a cook who still operated the lunch counter inside the old sectioned-off area of the department store, which had been officially closed since the death of the town. Newberry's, despite the disaster, kept operating for two more agonizing years before finally succumbing after the disaster. The man was frustrating for the mere fact he didn't, or claimed at least not to, fully understand what happened that night in October 1962. Out of the thirty-three current residents of Moreno, the stories were familiar in their telling— that either they weren't alive at that time, or they lived in some other part of the country when the events in the small, hidden town in the hills happened. The young reporter knew this was a story that would never make the news cycle even as a throwaway piece leading up to Halloween.

"Since the evacuation of the town fifty-five years ago, many had decided to stay even though the contamination unleashed that night threatened their very health and life. You were one of these people who chose to stay. Why, Mr. Leach?"

The old man wiped his arthritic hands on his filthy apron and looked at his watch as if to say she was taking up his valuable time, even though it was clear the lunch-hour rush inside the dead town was fifty-five years into the past.

"My father, Roland Leach, was one of the original five investors in Moreno." The old man turned and gestured toward the four-story department store behind him. "Newberry's was his crowning achievement. To have a department store in a burg this small was a gamble at the time, but the town was bustling back then, and it gave him and my mom the means to raise three children. Let's just say I'm attached to the property and have chosen to finish my life here." A sad look flitted across his old features as he turned back to face the reporter and her intrusive camera.

"So, you aren't afraid of the groundwater here due to the factory explosion in 1962?"

"I'm still breathing, ain't I?"

"Mercury poisoning doesn't scare you?"

The man didn't respond, looking at the reporter as if he were about to say something but held back.

"Mr. Leach, thank you for your time."

The old man nodded and then turned and opened the once-proud double doors of Newberry's Department Store whose name was etched into the once-stainless steel handle.

The woman lowered her microphone and then hissed a curse at the old man's retreating form.

"How in the hell am I supposed to make this into a story?" She handed her microphone off to her soundman and then faced the deserted street called, of course, Main. "Mayberry, the ghost town, is not a very good pitch."

"Yeah, right, at least Mayberry had Don Knotts; we have only Goober inside an old department store cooking greasy burgers for all four operating businesses. Hell, it's not even an empty ghost town. And did you see that couple running the record store? Can you say Haight-Ashbury and the Grateful Dead?"

"Yeah, hippies in this day and age, that's what's creepy, not the deserted town."

It was the hundredth time news organizations tried to get a firm story on the old town and the hundredth time the footage wouldn't air on television. Outside of the disaster in October 1962, there just wasn't an angle for a good story anymore.

The news van left and drove back to the real world.

The young face vanished back into the boarded-up front of the old theater. He took a deep breath, and then the brightness of a flashlight lit his face. He leaned against the old and cracked plywood and breathed heavily. He reached out and pushed the brightness away along with the offending hand.

"Damn, I thought that camera guy saw me when he got into that van."

"Take it easy. Even if he did, do you think he's going to go snooping around here in the dark looking for us? The only people we have to worry about are those security guards up at the mission and the idiots who live here. If we can't dodge a few morons, we deserve to get caught."

The boy leaning against the plywood barrier looked over at the girl standing next to his brave friend who seemed to fear nothing. He and the girl were a different story. They feared everything, including the ridicule they received from the asshole holding the flashlight. Dylan was a bully of the first order, and he did things according to how he was taught by his brutish father—ruthlessly and absolutely.

"Trespassing is trespassing, no matter how you look at it," the emaciated, frightened girl with the arm-length tattoo of a twisted vine said to assist her boyfriend and let him know she shared his fear of this place.

"You both agreed. Those posters are worth a small fortune. On eBay, you can get as much as seven hundred dollars per print. There has to be at least a hundred posters down there."

"What if they're not there?" the boy asked as he finally moved away from the front windows.

"Look, my grandfather once lived in this dive and was the theater's projectionist, and he swears they took nothing out of this place but a few dead bodies, and then they sealed it up for good. The only people inside this place are county and state inspectors—those environment assholes, checking for chemicals in the water. The damn posters and even a few old film prints are down there. That's where everything was stored."

The young thief wannabe leading them was intent on following through with his little heist of movie memorabilia, but the vision of riches was not transferring well to his two companions.

The light caught the left side of the twin sets of winding stairs that led to the upper balcony, which was mostly gone now. The fire in 1962 had spread quickly to the upper reaches of the Grenada, and that was where most of the young bodies had been found after the total collapse of the balcony itself.

The flashlight moved, and they saw the two sets of double doors that led to the first-floor seating of the theater on either side of that snack bar. Two of these doors, old Naugahyde-covered wood that had lost most of the golden tacks that had once given them beauty and that tuck-and-roll look, were now hanging on by a screw or two, and the view beyond these doors was dark and foreboding. Then Dylan's light moved to the office of the theater manager, where they had already looked, and next to that, the door that led downstairs to the basement, where the real treasure was awaiting them.

"Well, let's do this and then go make some money."

The boy and his girlfriend looked at each other and knew in their silence both would indeed follow. As the door to the basement was opened with a loud creak, the musty air from below wafted to their nostrils and forced the three treasure seekers back a step. Most unsettling was the plaster art deco gargoyles looking down upon them from the ornate wall sconces that once circled the lobby. The beastly eyes looked as if their sculpted and very scary faces were happy for their visit.

"Smells wet," the girl said as she tugged on her boyfriend's arm.

Dylan stepped through the door and started down the wooden stairs. "There's probably been water down here since the fire. Let's just hope those posters were stored off the floor."

The large circular beam of the flashlight finally settled on the lowest part of the basement. There was water. So much so that they could see small ripples as a rat or two scurried away from their sudden intrusion.

"Water *and* rats?" the girl said squeamishly.

The boy took her hand, and they continued down to the bottom.

"Is that a vault?" the boy asked. "Maybe the posters are in there?"

"Nah, my grandpa said that when the new Moreno National Bank was built in 1960, they moved the old Savings and Loan vault to the basement here in the theater. He said it was the only place in town big enough to store it and had a lift with enough capacity that could lower it down here. So, no money or anything worth anything is in there. What we're looking for is right here." The light settled on six steel cabinets that looked as if they rose above the one foot of water in the basement. They were school locker–style, and they were covered in dust and rust. The light played over them, and the anticipation rose. "Let's just hope the tops of these things didn't rust out."

The two boys examined the locker-style cabinets as the girl stayed in place far behind them. She was looking at the old, rusty, iron-and-steel-framed vault before her. She reached out and felt the coldness of the iron and steel and then remembered she had a lighter in her pocket, which she reached for. Both boys turned when the lighter flared to life.

"I told you, there's nothing in there," Dylan said, giving her boyfriend a dirty look as if blaming him for not keeping the girl on point. He turned his attention back to the unlocked cabinets before him.

The girl kept her free hand on the coldness of the vault's door. The flame from the lighter showed condensation on the facing of the vault's door and a funny, silverish smear across the door's seal. She ran her hand through the moisture and then smelled the wetness that was gathered. She recoiled as if smelling something dead. She quickly wiped the water and funny-feeling paint away and then stepped back as she though she felt the door vibrate before her.

A yelp of happiness filled the darkened basement as the first locker was opened.

"I told you!" Dylan said, not so carefully sliding the large rubber band down on the rolled-up print.

He handed the flashlight to his friend and then unrolled the old movie poster. Even the girl wandered over through the foot of water. She saw the poster, and even she had to smile.

"Unbelievable!" said Dylan. The light caught the colored print and all their young mouths fell open. "The very first one we come across!"

The poster was a famous one from the golden age of Hollywood. The block lettering was wide and bright at the top as the light caught the lithographed rendition of Lon Chaney Jr. in his role of the original Wolf Man. The paper it was printed on was thick, just like Dylan's grandfather had said to look for.

"It's was what was known as a four-ply, thirty-two by forty-four print."

"What does that mean?" the girl asked, moving closer to the beautiful poster as the light played over Lon Chaney's fierce makeup.

"It means it's real. Original and one of the most valuable posters in existence. Get it now?"

The girl shot Dylan a dirty look as he let the poster roll back into itself as he reached for another after handing off the Wolf Man once again to the boy staring wide-eyed at the locker, awaiting more great news.

"Whoa, look at this!" he exclaimed as a full-view photo of a helmeted John Wayne met their astonished gaze. *The Sands of Iwo Jima.* Can you believe it? Mint condition and dry as a desert sand dune." He turned and looked at the two. "We're going to score big on these." He shoved the poster into the boy's arms and then jerked the flashlight from his fumbling hand and then shined it into the cabinet. "Look at these! Let's just hope we can get them in one load."

The girl gave Dylan's back a scowl and her boyfriend a shake of her head as she turned back to the vault and struck her lighter once more.

She moved back and examined the door again. For reasons she couldn't figure out, she was curious beyond belief about this old vault. She tilted her head and looked it over. Her hand holding the lighter moved to the stainless-steel handle on the door. She smiled and reached out for the handle and turned it. To her surprise, it moved as if greased just the day before. It made a loud clack as it was turned to its stops. A loud bang sounded from the inside.

"Would you leave that damn thing alone?" Dylan said. "What did you do?"

"N-n-nothing," the girl stammered as she stepped back from the heavy iron-and-steel door. The lighter in her hand flickered as if a cold breath of air had struck it. "I . . . I . . . turned the locking handle, that's all."

The bright light moved to the vault as both boys stepped toward it. Her boyfriend had an armful of rolled-up movie posters. Dylan moved next to the girl as the flashlight examined the vault's door. He touched the strange silver paint.

"What is it?" the boy asked as he fought to hold all the posters.

"Damn mercury!" Dylan said louder than he had wanted to.

"Mercury? I thought you said that those old stories were just made up," the boy said as he stepped back from the vault.

The girl was furiously wiping at her pant leg.

Dylan smiled. "I told you not to touch anything."

The loud bang sounded again, shaking the very foundation they stood upon, enough so that the stinky water that covered their feet and ankles moved in ripples. This time, the light as well as their eyes went to the thick door. The sound had come from inside the vault. They looked from one to the other as they realized for the first time just how dark the basement truly was.

From the high vantage point above the town, the old mission and winery sat in abject ruin. While an historical eyesore to some, the two buildings had their own aura about them. When viewed, they seemed just two crumbling buildings, but inside, there was a totally different vibe as the cameraman had earlier stated. This vibe was one that few visitors could describe. But one thing they did feel that they knew to be a fact was one of being watched.

One mile away and farther down the hill known as Drunk Monk's Road, the trespassing trio had just started feeling the strangeness of the steel vault inside the basement of the Grenada. Inside the collapsed building, the winery came alive.

The thirteen tons of roof debris that had collapsed the remains of the old winery in 1962 after the explosion of the factory on the opposite hill moved, and dust swirled in the flow and ebb of the draft that reached the lowest section of the ancient ruin. In what was once the root cellar, where barrels were once made by carpenters, there was another vault. This one was six times the size of the smaller version inside the burned theater, only this vault looked more like an old steel box. The debris covering the steel suddenly burst up and out, uncovering the hiding place. The welded-shut double doors of the vault bent outward, creating a crack in the seal, and what was once designed to keep the beast imprisoned failed as it had many, many years before.

As the sun went lower in the west, the darkness once more shot toward the world of the living.

The beast discovered the town had company, and those visitors threatened the one thing it ever cared for.

The boy nervously moved posters to his other arm and then reached out and pulled his frightened girlfriend away.

"Something just shifted inside is all," Dylan said as he moved closer to the door. He listened.

This time, the bang was so loud that Dylan fell backward and splashed into the foulness of the rotten wetness. As he spat out the terrible-tasting water from his mouth, the handle on the vault spun crazily. Their eyes widened, and the movie posters, the treasure they had sought, fell from the boy's arm as the girl flung herself away from Dylan and the vault.

"Let's get the hell out of here," the boy said as he turned away with the girl.

"Not without my—" Dylan began.

The crying sound was unmistakable. It started slowly at first, and then the sobs became deeper, more frantic. They all turned to the vault's door once more, and then they knew that something was indeed inside.

The air turned foul as the light from the flashlight in Dylan's hand slowly died. The heavy crying continued.

"Hey, turn that back on!" the girl cried out. "We have to get someone to help. That may be a child trapped in there."

Dylan was hitting the flashlight with all the strength he could muster as the smell was also starting to consume his own senses. The beam flared to life and then went out. It came back on and then just as quickly died. He gave it another good whack, and then the light illuminated briefly just as the door at the top of the basement stairs burst open and then flew off its hinges. They all turned and looked up into the blackness as their hearts leaped from their chests. As the light moved upward toward the door, they saw something standing there as if it were looking down upon them.

The blackness at the top of the stairs didn't move. Dylan backed away from the staircase, and then his legs gave out as all thoughts and dreams of money escaped him. As he fell, he moved the beam of light up and then his eyes widened as he caught the darkness start to move down the stairs. They heard the crying as it became louder and fiercer. Then the crying went from sorrowful to one of screaming anger. The change had come when whatever was at the top of the stairs made its presence known. Then the darkness started down, cracking the old wood as it moved.

The darkness stepped from the last stair riser. Dylan felt the water rise and then settle as something heavy added its weight to the sea of debris and filth floating in the basement. He backed away on his palms and heels. The light never left the darkness stepping from the now-broken stairs. Dylan started to shake as the darkness moved toward him. Again, he tried to move away, splashing as he did. Between the darkness walking toward him and the screaming anger seemingly soaking through solid steel, Dylan heard his two friends making a run for the stairs.

The darkness stopped and turned away from Dylan and faced the new sound. The water splashed. It was like something was walking through a large puddle. The water exploded outward as it shot for the stairs. The screaming inside the vault's interior went from unrecognizable to actual words as whatever was inside was encouraging the blackness to stop Dylan's two friends from escaping. Dylan heard the girl scream and the boy shout above him. Then he felt the impact as the girl was thrown from the staircase to the floor below. She hit with a loud splash of water and then the sounds of breaking of bones as her frightening scream was cut off like a shorted-out audio. Her broken and shattered tattooed arm slowly sank beneath the foot-deep water as the voice inside the vault became one of joy and satisfaction. As Dylan stood and started to turn, the light caught his friend in crime as he was lifted from the stairs and thrown across the basement to impact the cabinets where their riches had been stored. His body bent and broke as it struck so hard that his skin was pushed into the seams and vent openings on the old locker. His body popped free and joined his girlfriend in the waters of the basement.

The dark mass moved at lightning speed toward the remaining intruder and embraced him. The last thing Dylan could hear above the animallike derangement was his own spine being crushed by the enormous hand that stole the life from him.

The darkness roared with fury and anger, and then the basement became a blacker hole than it was before.

The joy from inside the vault settled to a cursory crying once more as if in remorse for the lives taken. Then the insanity started again as the last words broke free of the steel-reinforced vault.

"Find him!"

The blackness roared in delight as it was finally set free after half a century of being trapped like a wild animal. The darkness reached out and gently caressed the vault's door. The ice that accumulated from the touch flaked away as the dark hand moved lovingly over the surface. Once more, the anger subsided from inside, and the crying resumed, except for one last command repeated through the sobs of loneliness and terror.

"Find him and bring him home."

The blackness left Moreno and shot into the sky and smelled the day's cooling air. It turned and then vanished like a wisp of dark cloud to the east.

WASHINGTON, D.C.

He was known as the most ruthless person in the world—and this was still a planet inhabited by men like Vladimir Putin, Assad of Syria, and Kim Jong-un in North Korea. Per many news sources around the globe, these men were considered tame compared to the man who was giving up his power under extraordinary circumstances. The ruthless way in which he treated adversaries and friends alike had finally come full circle. He had abused the power of his office, and now the American electorate had concluded that the man had to go. So, in five days' time, the president of the United States was going to resign his office for health reasons halfway through his second term. The president wasn't a well-liked man.

The First Lady of the United States was thirty-five years younger than her husband. Dean Samuel Hadley would soon return to his billionaire lifestyle and live out the rest of his lonely life with wealth and power, still a lord over thousands if not millions of ordinary people and employees. The First Lady wanted to be sure by the time the next week rolled around he would be limited not only in the wealth department but in the power realm of his life as well. She stood in the doorway of the office of the president's chief of staff, Herbert Avery. He finally looked up as he carefully placed the legal documents into a secure file folder. He looked startled.

"It would be nice if you announced yourself. That would be the polite thing to do," he said as he stood and gestured for her to come in.

She stood momentarily in the doorway with her arms crossed over her ample chest—a chest she had to cover for six years because of her station as First Lady of the country.

"You should keep your door closed when you have that stuff out." The First Lady finally stepped into the office but was sure not to close the door behind her. Propriety still held sway over her actions. Right now, she was depicted as the wife of the insane man in the Oval Office, and that was where she wanted her persona to stay for the time being.

The chief of staff placed the file folder in his desk and then locked it. He smiled as she came in but noticed she did not sit.

"That 'stuff,' as you put it, is so complicated that even if someone saw them and studied them for a month, they wouldn't understand them. As far as anyone is concerned, they are nothing but financial statements from the president's holdings that will revert to his care after he leaves office, that's all," he said as he jauntily tossed his set of keys in the air and then pocketed them with a wink toward the stunning woman before him. "As far as his many faults as a husband and his proclivity toward extramarital affairs and proof of him having as many secretive women in his life as he does, well, that information is kept far from here, I assure you. I take it your meeting at the fund-raiser went well? I hope your skullduggery works." Avery looked the First Lady over and then smiled. "Nice outfit, by the way."

Catherine Emery Hadley ignored the compliment on her chosen attire. "So, after next week, we can move right in if your evidence of his adulterous leanings has been threatened? This new stuff that was uncovered by your friend in Virginia should strike a raw nerve, unhinging him even further. Then, when proof of adultery, attached to very strange behavior, is apparent to the courts, he will lose everything. The stockholders of his companies wish to end their relationship with him now at any rate."

"If you can get the president to voluntarily see things your way."

Catherine laughed as she moved toward the door. "When confronted with evidence of this last betrayal of the American people and his adoring, caring wife, his signing won't be a problem. If I must expose old family skeletons to do so, I am ready for the bones to fall from the closet. Any judge in this country is as fed up with him as I am. Our divorce will work out the way I have planned from the beginning. His infidelity, his tenure as president, and with the saddened and brokenhearted wife, the bastard deserves what he gets." Catherine looked Avery over and decided to ask even though it was upon her orders that the name and subject never be spoken aloud, especially inside the White House. "Did you place the pictures and the glasses where he will run across them?"

"Yes. I put some on his desk and another three in daily correspondence. The glasses are in plain sight under some files on his desk. I don't know what you plan to gain by dredging up childhood memories inside that head of his. I just don't see the point."

"You're not involved to 'see' the point, Herb. The things I had you plant where he could find them were done to assist the bastard in his legitimate jump toward insanity. If that file gets exposed by some gung-ho reporter, they'll see that insanity runs in the family. He is as insane as his old man was."

Avery smiled as he watched the mechanics of her devious mind playing across those beautiful eyes.

"Who is she?" Avery smiled as he asked the million-, or was it fifty-billion-, dollar question. "She the one from his childhood that got away?"

"Yes, Herb, she's the one woman my husband couldn't coax into bed."

"Must have been a while back, because those are the only pictures available of her. Black and white, ponytails, and bobby socks."

"You're thinking too much, Herbert. You need to stop that."

Avery looked up curiously as he watched her back. "Has he lost all interest in life? I just thought it was being president he was tired of. The way he's acting, it's like he just doesn't care about anything other than being the biggest prick in the free world."

"Give him a liquor bottle and women, and he'll live out the rest of his life alone and happy, just the way he wants. But if he has other ideas, the things you placed where he can accidentally find them will send him off in another direction in life, and that's into a mental hospital, where he truly belongs. All I have to do is show him what his precious daddy did in the war."

"Unbelievable. One of the richest men, not to mention the most powerful leader in the world, and he just wants to drop off the face of the earth. Amazing. It's almost as if he wanted everyone to hate him as much as he despised himself."

Catherine's eyes moved to an eight-by-ten glossy photograph of the president taken many years before, when he was only twenty years old. The bare-chested man staring at her from the photo wore nothing but a protective flak jacket and had a green beret tilted jauntily on his head. Of course, a smile was absent as they always were in pictures of his past. The framed picture was signed to Avery by her husband, and the sham way Avery had it displayed made the First Lady shiver. "By the way, when we leave here, I never want to see that thing again." She paused at the doorway and waited for Avery to respond.

Catherine was gently pulled back into the office, and Avery reached out and closed the door.

"I keep that here to remind myself of who it is I work for." He leaned farther toward her.

She laughed in his face as she turned to open the door. "His father has been dead since 1972. He's a prick because he chooses to be a prick," she said as she partially opened the door but was shocked when the door was closed from behind and hands gripped her shoulders. Avery didn't see the smile that raised the corners of her red lips.

The attempted kiss was sudden. Catherine placed her hands on his chest and gently pushed Avery.

"Not until this thing is completed. That's all I need is for another rumor to cloud the minds of those I need on my side when the time comes." She smiled for a moment. "Your richly deserved reward will come soon enough." She turned away and then stopped. His smile slowly came back until Avery realized this was nothing more than business and not a romantic pause. "Just make sure the deposition on his mental health is ready for all six boardrooms to see and sign." She opened the door but paused in the hallway. "And take down the goddamn picture; I never want to see *that* again."

Avery angrily shut his door.

The president stood behind his desk and watched the activity outside as protesters lined the street. They carried banners and placards stating that it was time for a change in Washington. His left brow rose, and he smiled as he was most assuredly in their corner. All interest in most things had waned in his life. He had billions waiting for him once he left office. He had a young wife who was currently trying to steal everything from him.

At seventy-two years of age, he was ready to call it quits on his personal life. Money didn't solve his nightmares and could not heal a past that was unsalvageable. Power was the same. None of it mattered, and he didn't know why. For the past two years, he had been feeling this way. He knew he had treated people badly for the better part of his life, and again he didn't know why. He had a mean streak in him, and there was no way to live with what his young wife called "the real people."

He turned away when several members of his staff came in through the door of the Oval Office. The vice president was with them. He frowned when he saw Catherine was the last to enter. He nodded, and the Secret Service agent closed the door as they settled into the two opposite-facing couches. He noticed the First Lady remained standing. He smiled as he moved to the front of the desk. As he sat on its edge, his hand struck a pile of opened correspondence, and the letters scattered across the desk. Catherine watched as the president stacked them back into a pile. His fingers hit on one of the envelopes, and he picked it up as all in the office waited for him to speak. He pulled out an old Polaroid picture. He raised the envelope and saw that it was addressed to the White House with his name on it but no postmark. He pulled out the old shot and saw the black-and-white image. It was her, and his face could not hide the anxiety the faded Polaroid picture instantly instilled. He swallowed, as this was the fifth time in as many days the picture or her name had appeared as if by magic. He looked for Avery, but Avery had not arrived for the meeting just yet. Herbert had to know, since it was he who was the last to see the day's mail before he placed it on his desk. He placed the photo back into the white envelope.

It was the vice president who cleared his throat to get Hadley's attention. The president looked up like he was awakening from a bad dream. He blinked and then smiled briefly.

"You dropped something, Mr. President," the thin man said and then stood from the couch and retrieved the item that had fallen to the floor. He stood and then handed the president the item. "Now those are dark sunglasses," the vice president said as he smiled and then sat back down.

The glasses were of tortoiseshell frames and were plain looking, except for the dark green lenses. He held them in his hands, and he felt his heart race. He rubbed his thumb over the cracked lenses. The hardened frames were damaged and had partially melted around the earpieces. He started to raise the dark glasses to see them better when he realized his guests were waiting. He swallowed and then placed the glasses on top of the photo.

"Sorry." He smiled but immediately lost it. His mind was racing in varying directions at one time. "Well, Jimmy, you ready to take over the reins?" he asked the vice president as his gray eyes kept flashing down to the desktop and the items there.

The nation's vice president, James Harwell, sat motionless as the president smiled down upon him from on high, a position of strength he knew the man loved for its effect on visitors.

"Yes, I believe I'm as ready as I'll ever be," he said as the other members of the closed circle of advisors didn't make eye contact with him. "But somehow I still think this is some cruel joke you're dealing me here."

"Ah, just because you wanted this job many years before me doesn't mean you would let me down. Our history says we'll never be close. Hell, we may never even speak after next week. Just be ready to fulfill the office. I honestly think it'll be in better hands with you than anyone." He smiled. "The country will agree with you. It's either this or be impeached. When all these so-called rumors are substantiated, believe me, you'll want distance between you and me, and this is the only way to get that distance."

"I don't know what to say," the vice president said as he turned his attention back to the silver-haired man behind the desk. "You've never even smiled at me before while you were in office. Now you just quit and give it all away. Excuse me, but I'm just astounded."

The president smiled as he looked the group over. His dark eyes settled on the First Lady. "Just be sure the new First Lady likes doing things other than photo ops and she'll be admired as most First Ladies usually are." The smile devolved into a cruel line across his lips. "Some First Ladies, at any rate." Again, the image of the young girl with a dark pair of sunglasses entered his mind. He grimaced and looked up and saw a hint of a smile on Catherine's face as she left the Oval Office.

The man, learning on his desk, waited for the door to be closed and looked at the others. His smile and friendliness was gone. The door was once again opened by one of his protection team, and Chief of Staff Avery was escorted inside. Everyone noticed the two Secret Service agents remained this time.

Avery knew immediately that his covert and very-much-behind-the-scenes manipulations had been found out. He swallowed as the president smiled. It was the cat staring at the canary.

"Mr. Avery, it's time we spoke candidly, and these gentlemen present are to witness your debrief. How exciting and unexpected. It seems you have been doing some digging in areas that have drawn the attention of some very smart people. Things about my finances. I think it's time you come to the side of the Lord, Herbert."

Avery felt his knees go weaker than a moment before as the president stood up and moved to the window just as the exterior lighting outside the office flared to life as the sun finally set.

"It has come to my attention that you and the First—"

The confused men in the room watching the man they all secretly despised became even more so when the president stopped speaking in mid-sentence. He stiffened, and then his eyes fluttered open, then closed, and then opened again.

"Mr. President, are you—"

Before the vice president could finish his own sentence, the lights inside the Oval Office went out. Emergency lighting immediately sprang to life, but they also dimmed and went dark. The two Secret Service men acted quickly by switching on the small flashlights they all carried. The beams illuminated the face of the president, and they moved aggressively as the man started shaking uncontrollably behind his desk. Then the president collapsed.

"He's having a heart attack!" the vice president called out as they all stood to assist.

As the two agents moved to help, they came to a sudden stop when the man before them rose off the carpeted floor of the office and was flipped backward into the desk, where he landed and then rolled free. The president tried to rise, getting to his knees.

"God!" someone shouted as more agents came into the office. The light from the reception area briefly illuminated the strange scene inside. Then those suddenly went out as well. As the first Secret Service agent reached the president and attempted to help ease him back down to the floor, he was thrown backward into the wall. The impact shattered the drywall and sent the agent sprawling. The second agent watched in shock as his partner was literally thrown across the room. The door opened, and more flashlights and agents streamed inside.

Chief of Staff Avery had gone from a man about to be outed as the man collecting evidence for court proceedings with the assistance of the First Lady of the United States to watching a magic show inside the most powerful political office in the world. He stood in shock as more agents reached the choking president, who could not catch a breath as he tried to sit up from the floor, the agents assisting him. Three of these agents were brutally lifted from their feet just as they reached the downed man. They too were thrown against the wall by an invisible force inside the White House. Finally, a fifth agent reached the president. He started to lift the leader of the free world up by his jacket lapels, but the room suddenly shook as if they had been hit by a six-point earthquake.

"*NO!*" came the echoing voice that shattered the bulletproof glass that faced Pennsylvania Avenue. The men inside ducked as if a bomb had exploded, which many would attribute the event to later. The president was again lifted into the air so drastically that they thought his back would break. President Dean Hadley was spun twice, and then the action slowed. Then his body crumpled in midair and thudded to the floor. The flashlights followed him all the way to the carpet while men, even the Secret Service agents, stood frozen inside the darkened office.

"My God!" the vice president shouted again as even more agents and uniformed White House guards came streaming through the door.

Then they felt the pressure wave as something seemed to get momentarily stronger. The smashing of drywall came to the ears of all present. It was a strange thing to hear, but it was like someone was intentionally punching a wall. Then they all felt that whatever it was had vanished as the pressure lessened and the air became quiet and still.

The lights came back on to everyone's shock. There were even a few yelps of fear as they did so.

The First Lady rushed in with several other armed men as the devastation inside the Oval Office was seen for the first time in the bright lights. The broken windows, the smashed walls, and the president who was now being attended to by three Secret Service agents.

"What happened?" the First Lady shouted, seeing for the first time the painted walls around the expensively furnished office.

As the president lay on the blue carpet while men tried to revive him, everyone in the room saw what had happened. The entire wall space had been damaged. As the First Lady moved her eyes from her hated husband, they fell on Avery, who had stepped up to the closest wall and saw what it really was.

"My God, what in the hell is going on here?" he said as the other shocked men saw what he was seeing.

Every inch of wall space was taken up. The pictures and portraits had been smashed and now lay on the floor. The badly damaged walls were totally covered, and they could not believe what had literally smashed into them. At least six hundred words were made apparent by the large holes that had been beaten into the walls. As the president lay comatose with medical staff finally taking charge, they all read the words that ran in a circular order on the light green paint and traveled from the trim of the ceiling to the mopboards.

Come home, and below that in six hundred words, repeated over and over again were physically annunciated through the holes that looked as if a large fist had punched them in that spelled out *Boo!*

PART I

THE SUPERNATURALS

Well, they've got a new dance and it goes like this . . .

—JOEY DEE AND THE STARLITERS,
"Peppermint Twist,"
Billboard Top 100, 1962

1

The buzz started once more when the man in the corduroy jacket, blue shirt, and tie walked into the courtroom. The presiding judge had ordered a three-hour lunch recess for more than just dietary reasons. The man was greeted immediately by his three attorneys, but they could see from his demeanor that he had not been swayed by the judge's earlier threats. As the bearded man with the wire-rimmed glasses took his seat at the counsel table, he locked eyes with the lead attorney across the way. His team of no less than five associates huddled around him, and they all seemed to be convinced the man they had on the hot seat was going to cave in to the court's demands. Professor Gabriel Kennedy smiled and winked, and the lead attorney immediately lost the confident smile he had shown for most of the morning.

"All rise," came the order from the large bailiff.

The judge rapped the gavel three times, and they all sat.

"Mr. Johnson, you had your recess. Did you consult with your client?"

"Your Honor, we still respectfully ask for at least a week of continuance before our client makes his decision, especially since that decision involves the personal lives of men and women outside of this trial."

The fifty-three-year-old judge pushed her glasses back up on her nose and then fixed her eyes not on the attorney but Kennedy himself.

"Counselor, is there a chance that your client's decision would be any different in a week's time than the three hours he has been afforded? He was warned last week that those names would be under subpoena."

The young attorney, the best that the UBC network could attain within the Los Angeles and Hollywood communities, looked from the bench to Kennedy. He took a deep breath as Gabriel sat stoically.

"Your Honor, we ask for this extended period for the reasons of convincing Professor Kennedy to think this over thoroughly. We—"

"Counselor, does your client have an answer to the question asked of him today, not next week or next year?"

"But if you will, Your Honor, we still—"

"Professor Kennedy," she interrupted, "will you comply with this court's order to produce the members of your scientific team for the purpose of placing their testimony into the official court record?"

Kennedy stood, buttoned the corduroy jacket, and then placed his right hand on the shoulder of his lawyer, who sat and took a deep breath.

"My answer is still the same as it was last month, last week, and today, Your Honor. I will not produce these people who have nothing to do with the conclusions of these cases that they were only assigned to by me. I am the person responsible for all conclusions on our cases. Not them. So, no, I will not produce my team." Kennedy nodded in deference to the judge. "With all due respect to the court," he finished and then sat. His lawyers all closed their eyes, waiting for the wrath of the judge to descend upon them. They didn't have to wait long.

In the courtroom, all the members of the press started talking at once, and a few even had to get up to leave to make calls, as they had expected the same thing as Kennedy's counsel. The man was going to go to jail. The judge pounded her gavel several times to get the gallery to settle.

"Before we continue with this, I'll ask for an opinion from the representatives of the aggrieved parties. Mr. Linden, do you or your clients have an opinion on Professor Kennedy's statement regarding the producing of his employees?"

The rotund man in the black suit who represented the most powerful producers in LA stood. His team at the table smiled, as they knew they had the ghost professor by the short and curlies on the point.

"Yes. The good professor's insistence that it was he and he alone who had the final say in the investigations, all seventy-seven of them discussed in these proceedings, is a whitewash of misinformation. I intend to show beyond any doubt that his team, jokingly called the Supernaturals"—here, he snorted, and Kennedy frowned, as he hated the nickname for his investigating team—"have come to many, many differing conclusions than the good professor on the authenticity of their investigations. Many of these team members will corroborate the testimony of the production companies we represent. He must allow us to depose these team members so we can start to get to the truth—the truth that they have conspired to say that there are no such things as hauntings, even though their very claim to fame is the result of the most notorious haunting in history that had been caught on tape—the incident at Summer Place over seven years ago."

"Your Honor, where in the record does it say that my client and his team of investigators have said unequivocally that there are no such things as real hauntings, or ghosts for that matter?"

The judge was about to speak when the opposing attorney stood, shooting to his feet.

"It doesn't have to be said in those exact words. Through seventy-seven investigations that were bought and paid for by many, many networks, this team has not found evidence of one haunting that actually took place. That means seventy-seven television broadcasts of reality programming were deemed hoaxes when there is actual proof on film that says Kennedy's team either ignored or overlooked evidence in the summation of their cases. They had an agenda of putting every one of these ghost-hunting shows out of business, regardless of their verifiable evidence."

"My client's organization was hired by these shows' own networks in the hopes that this famous scientific investigation team would verify outright lies and the gullibility of innocent viewers. In other words, the networks and their various heads of programming that hired Professor Kennedy fully expected a whitewash job on their behalf by those who they assumed would be team players in pulling the wool over viewers' eyes, or at the very least outright fabrications to justify their shows programming." Kennedy's attorney sat down and hoped he had swayed the judge as much as he could. He did not.

"Thank you." The judge nodded and looked at Kennedy instead of his attorneys. "Let's go through this one name at a time so I can count up the offenses, Professor." She raised a sheet of paper and then looked it over. "This George Cordero, are you aware of this man's whereabouts, Professor?"

Kennedy looked at his team of attorneys. Then with a sad nod, the lead counsel told Kennedy to answer.

"George has always been a little flighty. He could be anywhere from

Maine to Berlin. Mr. Cordero isn't well, and my knowledge of his where-abouts has always been limited."

"So, you deny knowing where we can find George Cordero?" the judge asked as she checked off the first name.

"Not a denial. I just don't know," Gabriel said.

"Mr. Leonard Sickles?"

"Leonard is the most brilliant software and practical application engi-neer in the country. I haven't a clue as to what he is doing." Kennedy smiled and looked over at the counsel for the networks. "The last time I spoke to him he mentioned going to the moon to think."

Again, the judge angrily banged her gavel down, silencing the crowded room of laughing reporters. Again, Kennedy's legal team all lowered their heads.

"So, you deny knowing where Mr. Sickles is at the current time?"

"Most definitely."

She checked off another name. "I understand that a deposition has been received from a member of your team, a Ms. Kelly Delaphoy."

"Which was nothing but lie upon lie, Your Honor." The counsel for the production companies stood angrily and faced Kennedy. "She was one of the main architects and field producer of the original Summer Place haunt-ing. Of course, she would tell the lies that the good professor here would ask her to tell. After all, it made her quite famous as a producer."

"Ms. Delaphoy *is* a rather famous producer. So famous, the woman can no longer find work in her chosen field in film and television production after the revelations at Summer Place. The events in Pennsylvania not only cost her a job, it cost her the future she had fought for. She gave her deposi-tion against my will, but Kelly told you the truth under oath. The people these gentlemen represent are thieves of not only money but of spirit and goodwill toward the home and business owners they were supposedly there to assist, and the viewers that watched them. In most cases, the pro-ducers of these so-called reality shows did what is known as 'tricking out' the houses and properties before shooting their footage. Hoaxes which my team exposed. We didn't start out to do this until we saw a pattern of de-ceit by the varying networks and their contracted producers."

"You make statements when I ask you to make statements, Professor. Now where are John Lonetree and Dr. Jennifer Tilden?"

Gabriel sat for the briefest of moments thinking about his best friend, John, a man he had gone to Harvard with and a person he would always protect. Lonetree, a former police chief of his reservation in Montana, was linked to Jenny in no uncertain terms, and Kennedy knew he would never interfere with either their personal or their professional lives ever again. Jenny Tilden, a doctor of paleontology, was also one he would never allow to sit in a court of law, explaining her unique abilities. She and John, and their special talents, had to be protected at all costs.

"I lost track of John and Jennifer after June of last year. They are on a sabbatical to Africa, if I'm not mistaken. May I suggest putting out feelers in Kenya or Somalia, perhaps?"

Again, that pen movement as the judge checked off two more names and ignored the small chuckles around the room.

"Can you tell us where Ms. Julie Reilly, former field reporter for the UBC network, is?"

"Ms. Reilly and I have not spoken since our last show airing two years ago."

Kennedy had just lied to the court for the first time. He knew exactly where Julie was. She was out with Jenny and John trying to find and warn Damian about what was happening in Los Angeles and the court case Gabriel was trying desperately to keep him out of. Another checkmark on the judge's sheet of paper.

"Now, former Pennsylvania State Police inspector Damian Jackson. Where is Mr. Jackson, Professor?"

"He's six foot four inches tall, and you can't find him?" Kennedy chuckled uncomfortably. "He's probably the only black man in the world who still wears a trench coat and fedora."

Again, the laughter erupted in the gallery, and again the gavel came down with an angry look from the judge.

"Well, here's something you also didn't know, Professor, and after your refusals to answer today, you will be seeing him very soon. We have former inspector Jackson in police custody for refusing to answer a court summons. Counsel found him last week, and he came up with the same excuse as you have. He refused to give a deposition, and now, sir, he is in contempt of this court."

Kennedy felt his heart skip a beat as he realized his weeks of planning at hiding everyone had failed and now poor Damian was paying for it.

"So, let's see here, Professor Kennedy. We have one, two, three, four, and now five. One last time. Do you know the whereabouts of these men and women?"

Kennedy stood, and for the first time, he allowed his anger to show as he removed his glasses. He looked at the offending team of lawyers from the combined networks first.

"I was never happy or proud to prove these reality shows as fakes or outright hoaxes, but I was protecting the innocent families who believe in a possible afterlife, and not to let them be used by men in powerful positions. They cared for no one or anything but their bottom line. The houses and properties we investigated showed zero signs of actual paranormal activity, and we refuse to lie to make money." He turned back to face the judge.

"Answer this court, Professor Kennedy, or you will be charged with contempt."

Kennedy smiled. "That falls far short of the contempt I have for the leeches these gentlemen represent"—he gestured to the table to his right—"and also the contempt I have for this court." He sat down as many in the gallery laughed and then applauded.

This time, the judge rapped the gavel so hard that Kennedy's lawyers thought it would snap in two.

"If that's the way you want to play this, Professor, that's fine by me. I hereby order the Los Angeles County Sheriff's Department to exercise the judgment of this court. You are to be immediately taken into custody for incarceration for contempt of my court. Thirty days in jail for each team member you have protected with your misguided thinking." The gavel came down again. "This proceeding is in recess until such a time as the good professor starts acting like a responsible citizen." *Whack, whack*, the gavel cried as the court was adjourned.

The jail was crowded and loud. The orange jumpsuit with the sandals made Kennedy feel guilty even though he was only in for contempt of court. The looks he received were frightening at best and murderous at worst. He waited at the large cell door for his restraints to be removed from himself and fifteen others as he held his bedsheet, pillow, and blanket closely to his chest.

Gabriel moved down the central aisle, the number of bunk-style beds stacked three high looked as if this place could hold three hundred. It was designed for only fifty-seven inmates. He noticed that most of these sleeping areas were already occupied. He walked down the central aisle until he spied a bed with no sheets or blanket near the far back wall.

"That's my space, tall and lanky," came the voice.

Gabriel looked up through his wire-rimmed glasses and saw the largest man he had ever seen in his life. The gentleman looked like the epitome of a biker. The large arms covered in tattoos that bulged from his orange jumpsuit explained to Kennedy in no uncertain terms that, indeed, this was the man's space.

"Sorry," he said as he gathered his folded bedding and stood as a few more of the inmates took notice. It was as if the men in the cell could smell blood in the air, and they wanted to witness where that blood was about to emerge from. Before Gabriel could stand up with his sheet, pillow, and blanket, the large hand came down on his shoulder and held him in place.

"That beard reminds me of that sweet spot between my old lady's legs," said the brute with the goatee and the piercings throughout his facial area. Gabriel knew he should have shaved his beard.

"Yeah, and if you ever want to see that old lady again, I suggest you start stepping, my fat, bearded, and very artfully colored friend."

The large man and his cronies turned, and Gabriel caught sight of the second-largest man he had seen that day. Former Pennsylvania police detective Damian Jackson stood looking at the assembled inmates, and Gabriel held his breath. As big as Jackson was, he was still graying in the hair area, and this was not one but many larger men confronting him.

"That right, Buckwheat?" the man said as he faced the smaller Jackson.

Damian looked down at Kennedy, and a smirk etched his lips. "Did you hear that? I believe that was a blatant black-a-phobia-style racist statement."

"Black-a-what?" the large biker said as even more interested parties joined the growing circle of fandom.

"Is this big, ugly pile of shit bothering you, Doc?"

"Uh, no, not really, at least not yet," Kennedy said as he studied his exit strategy. There was none.

"You're either awfully stupid or crazy. Can you count, Buckwheat?"

"Can you?" Damian countered.

The large men looked behind Jackson and saw at least five other black men and six angry-looking Mexicans. The man *could* count. With his three bikers in tow, they were quite outnumbered and in a bad spot for defensive purposes being in a corner. Gabriel hoped they went on the attack and didn't go to a fallback position, which of course would be right on top of him. The large biker examined the man confronting him and decided he spoke from the position of power. The eyes went from the missing fingers on Damian's left hand as it curled into a large fist and then to the fierceness in his brown eyes. The decision was quickly reached.

"We'll talk later, Buckwheat," he said as he sidestepped Jackson and his gang and moved off with his own group.

Damian looked back and then tossed the largest man of the black group behind him a wadded-up bill. Then he did the same with the leader of the Mexicans. Each unwadded the offering, and Gabriel saw the hundred-dollar bills Damian had just paid. He shook his head as the men moved off. Damian stood over Gabriel and then shook his head.

"Mind if I sit on your bed?" he asked as he sat anyway. "You owe me two hundred dollars."

"How in the hell did you get that money in here?" Kennedy asked as he slid over on the unmade bunk.

"You don't want to know, Doc."

"Oh."

"Not even five minutes and you almost get yourself raped and murdered by Los Angeles citizenry. Has to be some kinda record."

"And I thought you made a nice group of friends, winning them over with your sparkling personality."

Damian looked at Kennedy and smiled. "If someone in this joint finds out I was a state police officer, no amount of money in the world would get us out of that trouble. So, here we sit, the final act in your little morality play."

"I had no idea you were arrested before the judge told me this morning. You're the cop here," he said in a low tone. "I thought you could evade justice until this thing blew over."

"It was a private detective with the summons that got me. I was in a bar up in San Francisco."

"I can't believe you didn't smell a private detective, even in a bar."

"Yeah, well, you should have seen the legs on this detective."

"Oh."

"Yeah, someone did their homework. They knows my weakness, Master Gabriel. It's always the womenfolk that bring me down," he said mockingly in his slave impersonation. "So, what now? It's only a matter of time until the rest are rounded up." Damian looked away and then back at Kennedy. "Doc, you can't protect the group anymore. We're grown-ups. If they think that we defrauded the networks, they won't rest until they get us all. You throwing yourself on your sword isn't going to stop them. Although a noble act some of us would love to see, it's one that won't help in the end."

"I never thought we would get into trouble by telling people the truth.

It's my fault for outing those production companies the way I did. It was my morals and holier-than-thou attitude that got us here."

"Well, we all turned down the extra money in lieu of the truth, Doc, so we're all cursed with that particular and distasteful moral dilemma." Damian looked around him and then at his orange jumpsuit. He took a deep breath and then glanced at Gabriel. "I'll tell you, though, the money is looking pretty damn good right about now."

Kennedy sniffed, and then he got a crooked grin on his lips. "Yeah, orange isn't exactly your color, is it?"

Damian ignored the dig and stood and looked out over the vastness of the cell and its captured humanity. He turned and faced the professor.

"The others?"

"Kelly was caught in San Antonio at her cousin's house. The others, though, are still hiding."

"Would it be enough if we three took the blame? Would they let the others off?" Damian asked with hope.

"We pissed off some pretty powerful people in this city. And you know who runs this city, right?"

"Yeah, it's like going after Wall Street in New York—it just isn't going to happen."

"Exactly," Kennedy agreed.

"Well, I do know they'll have a hard time finding the rest. They're a little better at hiding than we are. The smartest man in the world with a computer? They'll never even get a whiff of that little gangster Sickles. He'll know before the arresting officers that they are coming. Unless he does something stupid," Jackson added.

They heard the cell doors open again, and several other inmates were herded inside. Gabriel sat silently as Damian glanced over at the new prisoners. His face fell as he saw the third man in line.

"I take that back. I guess he isn't as smart as I thought he was."

Gabriel looked up and then had to stand. His face, just as Damian's had, fell as he saw the small black man as his leg restraints were removed. They watched as he greeted several men he had known in his past life and had grown up with; they were all Crips from his old neighborhood. He saw Jackson and Kennedy staring at him, and he waved as if he were nothing but a visitor saying hi. Kennedy rolled his eyes and then sat hard onto the bunk.

"My brothers!" Leonard said as he slapped the palm of the large ex-cop. He held up his hand to Gabriel, but Kennedy didn't move an inch to greet him.

"Didn't I tell you to disappear?"

Leonard looked hurt and taken back. He adjusted the collar of his new orange jumpsuit and then gave Gabriel a tough look.

"I get arrested trying to get this big-ass motherfucker out of jail, and then here I am. How did I know they had tracers on their computer system?"

"Tracers?" Damian asked as he also sat on the bunk.

Leonard looked at the large man and then shook his head. "They set a trap for me is what they did. I never thought the LAPD and the sheriffs were that damn smart."

"It's because of punks like you that they had to get smart, dumbass."

"Oh, is that it?" Sickles said as he rolled his eyes at the former Pennsylvania detective.

"Wait . . . wait a minute." Gabriel stood and faced Leonard. "You're only here for contempt of court, right?"

Leonard saw the empty space on the bunk, tossed his own bedding down and then sat. He used Kennedy's pillow and placed it against the wall and then laid back with his tiny feet dangling from the bed. "Uh, yeah, man, contempt."

"Leonard?" Gabriel insisted far more angrily than he wanted. He felt responsible for the twenty-seven-year-old genius and knew he had gotten the boy into serious trouble.

Leonard sat up and then rubbed his hands over his face. "Okay, contempt and attempted break-in of a secured governmental computer system."

"What *are* the charges, Leonard?" Gabriel persisted.

"You tried to get us out by hacking the county court system, didn't you?" Damian asked, and not too kindly.

"Uh, no." Leonard stood and then faced both men. "I didn't try to get you out of here."

"Thank God," Damian said. "They'd throw away the key on that one."

"I hacked the judge and the law firm of the networks and the county sheriff's office. I was going to get all charges dropped for lack of evidence."

"So, you hacked them and got caught. That's not like you," Kennedy said as he faced the small black computer genius.

"I was stupid. I thought there was no one smarter than me and overlooked the obvious. They knew from my background that I would be coming."

Damian watched as Leonard hung his head and then placed one sandaled foot over the other and then shuffled again as he lay on the bed.

"Oh, shit, what else?" the large black man asked, looking down on the diminutive prodigy.

"Uh, I drained the bank accounts of the law firm the networks hired." He looked up and gave them both a false smile. "I thought it would be a kick, you know?"

"Shit, computer fraud, embezzlement, corruption of the county computer system for criminal gain, and harassment," Kennedy said.

"Don't forget contempt of court, which would have just cost you a few weeks. Now you're looking at least twenty-five years," Jackson said, slamming his hand down on his own thigh, making Leonard jump.

The three men were silent as they stood and sat around in the loud cell. Finally, Gabriel sat and then slapped Leonard on his leg as he sat next to him.

"I'm sorry, Dr. Gabe. I know I am a major screwup, but I thought I was helping." Sickles's pain was similar to Kennedy's when he was disappointed in the prodigy he'd saved from the very gangs that had taken the life of his brother and several cousins. If it weren't for Kennedy giving the young criminal psych evaluations when he was involved in the gangs while he was the chair of the Psych Department at USC, he would have gone down the same road and ended up like all other members of the gang—dead. He owed the man everything, and now he had disappointed him again.

"Well, Leonard, what did you do with the money you embezzled from the law firm?" Kennedy asked.

Sickles smiled and then sat up and leaned over to make sure they heard.

"You mean the six-point-seven-five million dollars I discovered in the Cayman Islands? That money that was illegally sent abroad for tax evasion purposes? That money?"

"Yes, that money," Gabriel said in exasperation.

"Let's just say the seventeen boys' clubs in the Los Angeles area and the thirty-five youth baseball leagues within the city limits won't be seeking donations for a while. And the great thing about all of it is the fact that I confessed to stealing only ten thousand dollars, which I promised to pay back, of course."

"And the crooked attorneys can't argue the amount, now can they?" Damian said with a growing smile.

"I wouldn't think so," Leonard answered with his own smile.

The three men drew looks from the ruffians in the large cell block when they all laughed as they sat on the bunk.

You found the strangest people in jail these days.

ATLANTIC CITY, NEW JERSEY

All six sets of eyes watched the dark-haired man who looked as if he had lost his razor along with the rest of his toiletries. The scrub of beard was sparse in places, and his odor was none too pleasing. The bloodred whites of his eyes told the watchers that this man had not slept in quite some time. He was small in stature and had a sadness to him that made his companions somewhat apprehensive. But now they were more interested in his prowess at cards—Texas Hold 'em in particular. The man had started out losing at least ten thousand, and now as his pile of chips was examined, they could see he had earned back five times that. The men exchanged looks of suspicion. When these men suspected they were being taken, someone was in trouble.

George Cordero looked at his two hole cards as his other senses became aware that his fellow poker players were starting to suspect they were being taken for a ride. Their thoughts came to him in jumbled waves of anger and frustration at not being able to find out how this small Mexican was taking them. He thought about turning over the seven and ten of spades and dropping out of the hand. He smiled inwardly and thought, *But what would the fun in that be?*

George looked at the four cards sitting on the table in front of the house-supplied dealer. He saw the seven of hearts and the two fours, one each of diamonds and clubs. So, he had two small pairs. But the rather large Italian gentleman across the way had looked to be leaning into a third four, or did he have a pair of aces? George smiled and hesitated when the other four players dropped out one by one when the Italian man's bet skyrocketed to $10,000.

"Let's see how brave you are now, my friend."

George smiled and looked closely at the rotund man in the nice suit. His eyes went to his own wrinkled and filthy white jacket and shirt. His eyes went to the man again, and he concentrated. He saw into his mind. He saw how his equally rotund wife spoke to the man when at home. She was a cowed and silent woman who feared her husband's wrath. His kids, three in all, despised their father. His feeling was that this man was not very well received as a father. George was getting ready to turn over his cards and cry uncle when another vision filled his mind—the man silently slipping into the room of his daughter. As he watched the man creep into the bedroom, he saw a door close, blocking his view. He could mentally get past this roadblock, but knew what he would see. Before the door closed on him, he heard the soft voice of the man's daughter as she whimpered and said, "No, Daddy."

George allowed his right hand to hover over his hole cards, and then the man across the way smirked as he saw hesitation in Cordero's actions. He exchanged looks with his fellow players who weren't very pleased with the smile that slowly crossed the Mexican's lips. The Italian gentleman lost his own smile when Cordero pulled his hand away from his cards and instead went to his pile of chips.

"How much do you have there?" he asked the fat man in the nice suit.

"Twenty-five thousand, give or take."

George counted his chips. With a smile, he pushed all his chips to the center of the table. He smiled broadly and looked to the man he now knew was a pedophile of his own twelve-year-old daughter. If this didn't meet the requirement for murder, or in his case, suicide by mobster, nothing would.

"I'm all in."

The fat man lost all semblance of composure at the brazen call. He reluctantly turned over his two hole cards, and George allowed the smile to grow as he turned his own over.

George then flipped his four cards over. "Fours and sevens." George, just to rub it in, looked pointedly at the man's cards. "And you have, oh, nothing."

"Another bluff call?" one of the men observing said loudly. "That's just a little too much."

"I would say that myself." The fat man stood so suddenly that the chair he was sitting in fell backward.

The other men slowly stood as George slid his winnings toward him. He stopped when he saw the angry looks surrounding him. He looked up and raised his brows. He was now expecting the bullet that would end his miserable life. Just in case it wasn't enough of a push, he decided to ask for that bullet.

"Oh," he said and then tossed a black $1,000 chip toward the fat man, who was busy glaring at him. "That's for the therapy you seriously need to get."

All six men plus the dealer stood and backed away from the table. They were confused as to just what in the hell that statement was supposed to mean.

George collected his chips and then slid them over to the dealer, who made no move to cash him out of the game. He suspected Cordero was about to be cashed out, but not in the way the winner was expecting. Cordero let out a breath and then sat as he realized these men were what he had suspected all along, very sore losers that would accomplish the thing he longed for—to kill him. His power of mind deduction had finally driven George Cordero to the edge. He didn't want to see the new day when the sun came up.

Again, the smile as he leaned back and relaxed. His next move was to force the fat, balding mobster into action. He had been searching for something to use all night against one of the ruthless punks he had chosen for his self-destruction.

"Yes, therapy," George said as he looked from man to man. "Did you know that this man sneaks into his twelve-year-old daughter's room several nights a week?"

The other men moved their eyes from George to the man who had suddenly gone white-faced.

"Now I know who you are!" a small, well-dressed man said as he took a step back as if George had the plague. "You're that psychic guy from that Halloween spook show a few years ago. I thought you looked familiar."

The other men saw that the large man regained his color as his anger replaced the shock.

"A known liar and cheat!" the man said overly loudly as the others were torn between their friend and Cordero, who sat with that creepy smile on his face. "Now we know how he cheated us at cards!"

"Fake, cheat, liar—I've been called all of those, but I have never once been labeled a pedophile, my friend."

"This man is nuts," the fat man said as his eyes finally left the psychic and went to those other now-accusing eyes staring at him. The fat man made a quick movement toward his chair, where he reached for something in the pocket of his coat, which was hanging on the chair's back. George closed his eyes and waited for the inevitable conclusion to his story of hating who and what he was. The gun was pulled.

The door to the private residence was bashed in, and a hail of shouts sounded as George opened his eyes. Police were everywhere. The men were being pushed and shoved against the walls of the living room, and the fat man with the gun was brutally subdued.

"Frankie DeLuca, you are under arrest!"

The fat man was thrown up against the wall with his associates, and his hate-filled eyes turned to a shocked George Cordero, who was also being handcuffed.

"I'll kill you!"

"You ain't killing anyone, fatty, at least not where you're going. You are all under arrest for trafficking in prostitution and money laundering," the man with the black suit said as he examined all the faces in the room.

"What about this fella?" a uniformed Atlantic City police officer asked as George was roughly turned around to face the detective in charge.

The man walked up to Cordero and then cocked his head in thought. "What's your name? You famous or something?"

"He's a fucking mind-readin' freak, man!" one of the handcuffed men said as he was led out of the house.

George remained silent as he was held by the arm. He looked away from the detective as much as he could until the man reached out and pulled his chin around. The smile came on slowly but surely. The cop reached into his jacket pocket and pulled out a notepad and flipped through the pages until he stopped and went back two, and then the smile grew.

"I saw that show you were on"—he looked at the notepad—"Mr. Cordero."

George felt as if he wanted to cry at his failure to dramatically end his own life.

"I'm a fan," the detective said as he slapped the notebook on his other hand and then slid it back into his coat. "But we do have an arrest warrant on you. I think a judge out west is waiting to discuss your exploits with the rest of . . . of . . . what is it they called your little spook-hunting group?" He turned away and then snapped his fingers. "That's right, the Supernaturals. As I said, I'm a huge fan."

SPOKANE, WASHINGTON

The twentieth day of October dawned cold and blustery in the small city east of Seattle. The day before, the weather had been as near perfect as anyone could remember for late September or October. Lights across the city started to come on and people prepared for their day. The occupants of one house in particular, a recent rental, had never turned off their lights from the night before, and neighbors had noticed only because the lights in the one-hundred-year-old house had not gone dark since the very strange people had moved in three weeks before.

The large man pulled the curtain back and spied the cold morning from the warmth of the immense living room. Nearly unrecognizable with his long black hair trimmed short, John Lonetree raised a brow as a milkman—yes, he was surprised that any major city still had milkmen—

watched the house as he made his local deliveries. Lonetree watched the
man in the blue uniform quickly move past the house.

"When did milkmen stop wearing white?" he asked, his words fogging the leaded glass window as the curtain fell back into place.

John didn't receive an answer, so he turned and looked and saw that
he was alone in the living room. He moved to the fireplace and stirred the
embers alight and then, frustrated, allowed the cast-iron poker to fall to the
bricks that made up the hearth. He slapped his large hand against the man-
tel and then angrily turned and left the room.

It didn't take long to find her. She sat at the kitchen table. She had both
her small hands wrapped firmly around a large mug of coffee. Her eyes
stared straight ahead, and she didn't react when John entered the kitchen.
He started to say something but stopped, as he didn't want his words to
come out as an angry rebuke. Instead he walked to the counter and poured
himself a cup of the overheated and old coffee and then turned and faced
the diminutive woman who sat with her sweater pulled tightly around her
chest.

Dr. Jennifer Tilden, renowned for her forensic anthropology work,
didn't raise her eyes as John pulled out an old yellow art deco chair that
had lost its argyle pattern right around the time that Ike was president, and
sat down. Jenny's eyes still didn't move. John reached out and forcibly removed her left hand from the mug and held it gently. She finally looked up
with the barest trace of a smile. He was about to speak when he heard a
loud crack as wood someplace in the old house separated from a nail. The
moans and groans of old houses never ceased.

"This place alone would have given all those ghost-hunting rags a
thrill of a lifetime."

Jenny looked as if she wanted to say something, but she lowered her
eyes instead. She never lost her smile, which to John was a reasonable start.
Ever since they had been on the run, only because Gabriel Kennedy wanted
them on the run, Jenny had been having bad dreams about Bobby Lee
McKinnon. The songwriter had been murdered by mobsters in the very
early sixties, and while investigating his death many years before, the ghost
of the musical composer was sewn to her soul like a patch on a ripped coat.
Bobby's ghost had come in handy in their efforts to stop the horrid haunting in Pennsylvania years before and had been blessedly absent for the
many years hence. Now it was apparent, with no real evidence other than
whispered thoughts and confusing dreams, that Bobby Lee McKinnon had
made a silent and hidden return.

"I'm going to ask you something, and I don't want that famous eye-rolling you do, okay?"

Jennifer rolled her eyes to make light of John's remark.

"Do you think your subconscious mind wants a return of Bobby Lee?" John swallowed and then plowed ahead. "Or maybe . . . maybe you miss him in some form or other?"

A shocked look came to Jenny's soft features. She was about to say something but stopped short. Instead of the angry rebuke she had primed and ready to fire, she deflated.

"Maybe. I just don't know. It's like he never left but has decided for courtesy's sake to leave me alone, at least in my waking hours." Catching John off guard, she smiled, and for the first time in months, he saw the real Dr. Jennifer Tilden inside those tired eyes.

He smiled back.

"Now are you, my Indian guide to the nether reaches, asking because you're worried about your insane girlfriend, or could it be that Mr. Wonderful Dreamwalker is jealous?"

John lost his smile and became falsely indignant. "Worried? Of course. Why, I—" Lonetree saw her smile grow larger, and he stopped. "Jealous, I guess."

Jenny pushed her now-cold coffee away and stood and went to Lonetree and then slid up onto his lap. She kissed him deeply and then ran her small hand through his now-short-cropped hair.

"You know, for a former chief of police and dreamwalker extraordinaire, you sure can be silly sometimes."

"Let's just say concerned, then, and keep it at that." This time, it was John who kissed her.

With a wink, he stood up and was about to offer to make breakfast when the front door opened. John instinctively reached for a sidearm that had not been on his hip for seven years. Jenny smiled and then stood from his lap and adjusted her green sweater. They heard the shrill greeting from the living room. Soon the image of former UBC field reporter Julie Reilly stood in the kitchen doorway.

"All they had was *The Seattle Times*; the Los Angeles papers hadn't arrived yet, and I waited so long it felt like everyone at the newsstand knew who I was, so retreat being the better part of valor, I came home. Is that coffee still hot?"

John watched as Jenny poured Julie a cup of the burned coffee and then relieved her of the newspaper.

"Call it paranoia, but it feels like everyone in town knows who we are."

"As long as we keep Sitting Bull here out of public view, we should be fine," Jenny said, patting John on the arm as he skimmed through the Seattle morning paper. His smile slowly left and Jenny removed her hand.

"Don't think for a moment that I didn't notice the anti-Indian sentiment in that remark." His face fell as he came to page 4. "Damn. They arrested Gabriel on contempt charges."

"Read on; they also have Damian and Leonard. Kelly was arrested in San Antonio."

Julie was about to say something when a knock sounded on the front door. At the same moment, they heard movement out on the old back porch as someone pulled open the raggedy screen door, challenging the old and rusty spring. John winced as he nodded at Julie and Jenny.

"Mr. John Lonetree, Ms. Julie Reilly, and Ms. Jennifer Tilden, this is the Spokane Police Department. We have warrants for your arrests."

"It's my fault for insisting we get some news. I must have been spotted. Someone had to have recognized me from my UBC reporting days," Julie said as she stood to open the back door, preparing to let Spokane's finest in. "We may as well get this over with."

Neighbors watched as the three were led out of the rented house in handcuffs. They saw the large Indian bringing up the rear with three of Spokane's finest watching the six-foot-five John Lonetree. Later Julie would be surprised to find out that it wasn't her life as a reporter that was their undoing but the mere fact that a little seventy-two-year-old neighbor lady had mistakenly thought the new out-of-place renters were at the very least the heads of Al Queda and ISIS, all living in Spokane and plotting evil deeds against the citizenry.

At seven thirty on the twentieth day of October, the scientific group known to the world as the Supernaturals were all taken into custody. A very sad ending to a group of men and women who had changed the face of parapsychology forever, an ending that opened a whole new world to come—a world where anything was again possible.

2

MORENO, CALIFORNIA

Anson Kilpatrick, a former Pomona, California, police lieutenant, looked down the empty street the locals called, rather euphemistically, Main Street and shook his head. He had never seen a town before that was so void of life. The empty shops, the civic center, the entire town was lifeless and barren. He knew he only had one more option in his search for Dylan Hanson and his two friends—the record store across the street. He spied the sign—K-Rave, as it was still apparent on the lifeless signage over the entrance to the old radio station—and he could see movement behind the filthy glass as someone watched him. He crossed the street without bothering to look, dodging, of all things, a lone tumbleweed as it rolled down the empty boulevard. He shook his head at the mall joke the town threw his way.

The detective had been looking high and low for the three missing high school kids for seven full days. Dylan Hanson's well-to-do father had guided him here but, thus far, he had found nothing.

As he faced the glass door and was about to reach for it, it opened, and a chubby, bearded man with an even heavier woman behind him greeted him with a smile.

"Didn't think you would ever come calling," the man with the ponytail said as he stepped aside to allow Kilpatrick entrance.

The detective looked around in what used to be the front lobby of the radio station. Racks and boxes of old vinyl records were everywhere. He saw the old triple-paned glass that used to house the disc jockey booth, and he could see the dangling wires and old empty-shelled broadcast equipment that used to send out fifteen thousand watts of rock-and-roll power to the Inland Empire.

"You're just in time! We just got a batch of brand-new titles in from Capitol Records," the woman proclaimed proudly. "We were the highest bidder when they cleaned out their warehouses."

The detective smiled as he took in the sad reminders of yesterday's technology all stacked and sorted.

"We have an original *Greatest Hits of Tommy James and the Shondells*, unopened and no damage to the cover. Still has the shrink-wrap on it."

"Tommy who?" the detective asked.

The man and the woman looked at each other as their hopes faded fast at a prospective customer gone awry.

"Anyway, have you seen this boy hanging out in the town?"

Both old hippies looked at the picture the detective produced of an unsmiling Dylan Hanson. His pockmarked face stared back at them, and they could see that he was a boy they would not have gotten along with as youths.

"Nah, we don't see many kids here, at least in the daylight hours. And those that come around here at night are troublemakers," the woman said.

"You?" the detective asked the woman's husband.

"Can't place him, man."

The detective took a deep breath and was about to place the photo back into his jacket when the man stayed his hand.

"Wait," he said as he examined the picture again. "You know, over a week ago, we were just closing up the store when I noticed movement where there should not have been. I think it was near, or even in, the old theater. Wouldn't swear on it."

"The old theater, you say?" the detective asked with hope. "That place looks like it was completely gutted by fire."

The man and woman moved away as soon as they both knew there would be no sale today, at least from this guy. The woman stopped short and turned as she moved a fresh box of old records out of her way.

"No, it's still mostly there. Only the old façade and main floor burned. Most of the interior, while not show ready, is still intact."

"Thanks," Kilpatrick said, turning to leave. He stopped when he saw that he needed to do something. He turned and faced the old hippie couple. "You wouldn't happen to have a copy of ZZ Top's *Tres Hombres*, would you?"

The woman's smile lit up the dingy old radio station, and her large bulk moved like an agile gazelle's as she made her way to the back. She was back momentarily and handed him an old album that had seen better days.

"Sorry about the jacket's condition, but the vinyl is just fine. Only one or maybe two scratches."

The detective looked at the album and then smiled. "I'll take it."

He didn't even own a phonograph any longer, but he felt obliged to give these people something in return for the little information they had given him.

"Nine dollars and fifty-five cents," the ponytailed man offered when the detective reached for his wallet.

He gave the man a twenty. "Keep the rest."

The man and the woman watched the well-dressed man leave the store, and they went to the window and watched as he turned right and then crossed the street once more.

"ZZ Top? Is he kidding?" the man asked.

"There's no accounting for taste, honey. Besides, there's one hell of a lot more than just a couple of scratches on that thing. I think I spilled a milk shake on it last year when I unpacked it."

"Serves him right," the man said as he watched their customer vanish down the street. "Rock and roll went downhill when Janis Joplin died." The man sniffed and turned as his wife handed him a lit joint. "Oh, Lord, won't you buy me a Mercedes-Benz—"

His wife joined in singing the old Joplin tune as they turned away from the window and continued their preservation of sensible music restoration and salvage.

Kilpatrick stood under the partially collapsed marquee of the Grenada Theater. He eased himself over and around some of the neon light tubes that had once made up the garish display that once upon a time illuminated the entirety of Main Street after dark. The theater was one of the old chain of movie palaces that crisscrossed the nation in the Hollywood heyday of yesteryear. He took a quick look inside the old pagoda-style box office that sat twenty feet into the courtyard leading to the main entrance, just as he had on his previous cursory search of the Grenada the week before. The old ticket dispenser was the only item recognizable inside the box office encased in fogged and broken glass. He turned to his right and left and saw the old spaces where posters advertising what films were coming to a theater near you were once displayed. The glass in the cases was long since gone and the lights that had occupied the same memory—gone. The tattered remains of the long strip of blue ribbon lay half-attached on the filthy tile. AIR-CONDITIONED FOR YOUR COMFORT, it said. The little penguin on each end of the banner proclaimed that at one time it was the only building in town that actually had real air-conditioning.

The intricately laid tile under his feet was covered in over fifty years' worth of grime and filth, to the point the yellow and gold tiles could no longer be discerned. Of the eight glass doors fronting the main lobby, only three were still hanging. The ticket-collecting podium was long since gone, and the carpeting, once a brilliant red color, was faded, scorched, and even missing in most places. As his feet slowly sank into the mushiness of the flooring, he saw the half-circular snack bar.

As the private detective looked around the shattered lobby area, he pulled out his flashlight and shined it around. The twin sets of stairs wound upward on either side of the large snack bar. He allowed the light to shine up those stairs, and a chill coursed through his body as he remembered the tales from that long-ago Halloween night. Because of what happened inside this theater, every police department in Southern California was trained on how to get patrons out of a burning movie house. He had to remind himself that six kids had been burned to death up in the balcony and five more crushed beneath it when it fell to the main floor after structural damage had weakened it.

Kilpatrick placed the album he had just bought, even though he wasn't really a ZZ Top fan, on the unbroken section of countertop and moved to the far right of the snack bar. His light fell on the manager's office he had searched the week prior, and then the light went to a spot in the darkened far corner. Just behind an old and tattered red curtain was a door. It was partially opened, and it was also a door he had not ventured through on his first trip. It was next to the manager's office, and he suspected that was the way to the basement. With a deep breath, he managed to sidestep debris that had fallen from the ceiling over fifty years earlier and made his way to the door. With the glass end of the flashlight he eased the door open and shined his light inside. The small platform vanished after only a few feet, and he thought that was where his investigation would end, as the light went away into nothingness. Then he saw there was a reason. The steps vanished down a very dark and very unstable-looking set of wooden stairs.

"Hello?" he called out. He felt stupid for doing so. The voice did not echo the way that he thought it would have. It was like his words went down and were captured and consumed by the darkness below. He stepped onto the landing and shined the light downward. He tested the first stair and then the second. They creaked and moved uncomfortably beneath his feet, and he stopped. The light illuminated the dust at his feet, and he saw the fresh footprints. He leaned over, careful to keep one hand on the railing, and examined them. It looked like three sets. One set was brave in nature as they traveled down the center of the stairs while the other two sets hugged closely to the railing on each side. He smiled as he suspected the brave one was the boy he was hired to find—Dylan Hanson. His father had detailed how the boy was brash and arrogant and was afraid of nothing.

He straightened as he knew his missing boy most likely had indeed come this way. The small set of prints had obviously been laid down by a girl. That also fit. He started down the stairs. Halfway down, he saw that the staircase took a sharp right and continued into oblivion. He made the junction, and as he did so, he felt the stairs shake under his loafers. He stopped. He shined the light around to make sure the whole thing wasn't coming down around him. There was nothing. No movement.

"Calm down," he muttered to himself. He shined the light downward as far as he could see, but the bottom stairs were still hidden from the weak light. He would have sworn the movement he felt was as if someone had stepped onto the stairs from below, ventured up a few steps, and then stopped. He swallowed as he felt like he were being watched—no, *examined* was more the word he was looking for.

"Dylan, are you down there?" he called out. The last two words faltered as he said them. He felt ridiculous for being so nervous. Still, what if it wasn't Dylan and his two companions? What if he had stumbled into a nest of homeless people who liked their privacy? Not uncommon in Southern California, as almost any abandoned building could be called home to many of the transients of the state. As the scurry of some sort of furred creature moved below through the water he was smelling, the detective leaned over and raised his right pant leg and brought up a lightly weighted .32-caliber pistol.

The stairs became oppressive. It was as if the oxygen were being usurped by an unseen force, and he was starting to feel dizzy for the lack of it. He steadied himself and was about to openly rebuke his faltering bravery of the dark when the stairs moved again. This time, the movement was accompanied by loud footfalls. The steps became heavier and more insistent.

He brought the pistol up and aimed into the darkness below what was still hidden by the turn of the stairs as they reached the bottom. He did not like his point of view and knew that whatever it was coming up those stairs would be hidden from him until it and he were nearly face-to-face. That wasn't a good proposition for the former police officer. He took a step backward and up, as he wanted to give himself time to react.

"Dylan, if that's you, you'd better let me know before you get a bullet in your face!" he said as his words once again faltered.

Two more pounding steps, and then they stopped. Kilpatrick backed up three steps and he also stopped, mimicking the action from below. His gun was still pointing down into the dark. Then the wooden steps started shaking and moving once more, this time more insistently. The detective swallowed, only this time, his throat movement stopped, as there was nothing but dryness there. He used the flashlight in his left hand to keep the beam pointed at the stairs in front and below him. The light showed nothing but the dust falling from the low ceiling as the heavy bass drumbeat of footfalls built to a booming crescendo. The movement below ceased.

As the detective let out his breath, the light bulb in the flashlight slowly dimmed. He banged on it with his pistol barrel, and the light flickered and then went out once more. He cursed and then banged the light again. This time, it came to life and remained that way. He smiled, relieved to be seeing again when he brought the light up. He saw what had come up the stairs to greet him—the entity stood right in front of him. The face was a mass of churning grays and blacks, looking as if it were nothing more than a swirling hive of insects. The darkness curled and swirled into itself as it stood over eight feet in height. As he looked into the blackness, he felt his extremities go numb. The gun slipped from his right hand, but the light remained frozen on the thing in front of him.

The detective's eyes widened when the blob of blackness moved closer. Another step up, and he knew he had disturbed something that was meant to be left alone. It was breathing. The entity moved slowly as it examined the man before it. Kilpatrick felt his bladder let go, and all thought of his duties as a detective fell away along with all the other accumulated knowledge of his life as the blackness slowly wrapped its mass around him.

Private Detective Kilpatrick was torn limb from limb just as the scream of rage and forlorn hatred shattered the stillness of the old theater.

As the door to the basement slowly closed up above, half of what troubled Moreno was now coming to full wakefulness and was gaining strength.

WASHINGTON, D.C.

The First Lady of the United Sates waited outside of the family quarters as the team of doctors finished with the president. She sat in a chair and read over the legalities of taking over the family investments, which had come as a surprise benefit of having an insane husband. If things continued as they were, she wouldn't need any signatures; there would be no court battles and no accusations from both parties of infidelity. She allowed a hint of a smile to cross her lips. It turned out that after the small fortune she had spent as seed money to Avery and his cronies in the intelligence field, all Dean had needed was a little shove from his past. If it weren't for the financial gain she would receive, she might actually have been interested in who this girl was who had haunted the man.

The news of the president's illness had made the papers and cable news shows. The White House damage control teams were kept busy by saying the president had a minor cold and that fever kept him isolated for the time being. It had been ten days since the events inside the Oval Office. Thus far, the secret that the president had been ready to resign from office had been kept strictly between those staff members and the vice president, who had also been there to witness the events.

The office area was still cordoned off as engineers and every intelligence agency in the nation went over the damage to the Oval Office inch by inch. It had been this way since the attack days before. Thus far, they could find no connection to an outside hostile source that could have caused the damage to the office and the assault on the president. Just in case, Herb Avery had managed to get the old photographs and the glasses out of the office immediately after the assault. Confusion had been his ally.

First Lady Catherine Hadley had not the faintest care how or why it happened; she was more concerned with the timing. Her placement of the items from his past had been a little too effective, if somehow it turned out that was the cause.

This may actually work against her. Had she pushed too hard on her husband? It cut short his fall from grace. It was now possible she would have to wait for him to get better before he could resign. Herb Avery said this could only go on for so long before the change at the top would be necessary. This was something unexpected in her plans. Instead of walking off with half the familial proceeds and fortunes through an uncontested divorce no one in the country could ever deny she had earned, she sat here with an uncertain diagnosis on a man who had clearly gone insane. The time was ripe for her views to be made public. Avery had been right on another, very unexpected point—this episode may just earn her 100 percent of Hadley Corporation, not a mere piece.

The team of United States Army and United States Navy doctors, everyone from psychologists to neurosurgeons, had gone in soon after the CIA and FBI made their official reports to the generally nonresponsive president. They had reported that they could find no external influences responsible for the attack in the Oval Office. The CIA suspected the Russians, while the FBI still hoped for an inside job. Both theories weren't holding much water since the wording left behind, smashed into the ornate walls of the office, were found not to have been accomplished by any action that required engineering. In layman's terms, the damage was not accomplished through any blunt-force delivery. The psychologists, on the other hand, suggested the episode had been caused by the president himself—his mind possibly doing the damage. This theory was scoffed at and disregarded by every physician outside the field of neurology. Even so, as a purely cautionary measure, the FBI had done background checks on any staff member within the White House that may or may not have issues in any form of mind control.

"Are the doctors still in there?"

Catherine looked up and saw the face of the man she could not wait to get rid of when all was said and done. The chief of staff for the sitting president slowly sat next to the First Lady without invitation.

"Look," she said as softly and silently as she could with a wary eye toward her Secret Service protection, "apparently, everyone in the Oval Office knew what that fool was going to do; you told me yourself. You were about to be roasted over a spit in there, and then we would have been exposed. Dean may be a very bad man and a womanizer, but he has never been anyone's fool, Herb."

"Look, I know I screwed this up. I just want you to know—"

"Although the doctors can't get much out of him because he comes in and out of consciousness, he ordered that his resignation from office be concluded."

"Excuse me?" Avery said, astounded that this had not been passed on to him.

"The vice president is being sworn in this afternoon. The chief justice of the Supreme Court arrives in four hours. Every news organization in the world will soon learn the truth. Not the real reasons, but they all know the Washington rumor mill and will be watching everything about me and you for the foreseeable future." She looked directly at Avery. "A future of mine that no longer includes you. That's the way it has to be."

The look on the chief of staff's face was priceless, and like her husband, she had a perverse fascination about making people hurt and could coldly rejoice at their failure. That failure was what she was seeing at the moment, and that made her mood a little better.

"But—"

"You'll still get what you want the most, Herbert. You'll have your money." She leaned even closer to the man. "But now you'll have to be patient, as the situation is too unstable, and too many people have hints as to why he was resigning. Some in that office know the truth about you and me, but decorum keeps them from saying anything since they all want to hop on the new ticket with the vice president. I have to wait to conclude our business with his companies and other assets." She smiled. "I hope you've been saving your money, because it may be a while."

The door opened to their private quarters, and the ten doctors stepped out to greet the First Lady. With one last look of disdain directed at Avery, she got up with a smile.

Avery winced as he stood to leave. It was all falling apart. He now knew he had been used to undermine the president for the gain of the First Lady. He now knew who the real rat in the White House was. The First Lady had played her cards, and him, very well.

Catherine Hadley joined the group of military doctors with the appropriate concerned face of a shocked and grieving wife. She made a show of twisting her handkerchief in her hands as she listened to the seven male and three female military officers. The group was joined by the vice president, who was now in silent if not total charge of the nation.

"First," said a tall, silver-haired commander who served as the chief resident of psychiatry at Walter Reed National Military Medical Center, "we have agreed that we need to bring in Dr. Haslam Assad from Johns Hopkins for a consult. He's the top man in the field of psychosis. The president only had very brief moments of clarity before he drifted off in what we think is a deep REM sleep, almost a memory state."

The lights in the room suddenly went out, and the emergency lighting came on. The two Secret Service agents flinched and then quickly relaxed when light filled the large room once more and then dimmed again.

"This is just like last week," the vice president said. He saw the faces of the doctors and the First Lady vanish as the light was sucked out. Only the weak light filtering in from the shaded windows made it into the room before even the sunlight slowly faded.

The scream startled all those present. The Secret Service agents moved to the bedroom shared by the president and the First Lady, and when the first man opened the door, he was thrown backward until his body smashed into the far wall, knocking free a painting of Ronald and Nancy Reagan. The doctors stood in shock, and the vice president's eyes widened as the last of the light vanished. It was as if the White House had been knocked into another world with no sun.

The second agent pulled a nine-millimeter handgun. He failed to see anything in the inky darkness, but his feet hit something wet and slippery. He fell to the floor, and his eyes saw the black-against-black movement near the far wall. He hesitated, aiming the gun from his back since he didn't know if his eyes were betraying him in the dark or if he was actually seeing movement. He couldn't afford to shoot for fear of hitting the president, whom he couldn't see lying in his bed with the now-powerless medical monitors around him. He stood and then finally found the bed by waving his free hand frantically. He threw himself on the prone body of the president.

The doctors decided they had to act, and with several Secret Service agents bursting through the door with flashlights waving, they also entered the bedroom. The lights picked out the bloodstained carpet and what looked like a small, thin arm that had been thrown halfway under the president's bed. Their eyes widened when they saw the Secret Service agent lying atop the leader of the free world with his gun out. And then the four flashlights died at the same time.

The First Lady backed toward the doorway without any chance at seeing into the room. The vice president stood next to her in the dark hallway. Before they could react to the darkness beyond the threshold of the open door, one of the four agents who had entered the bedroom came flying out, and his weight knocked both frightened observers from their feet. The First Lady hit with a crash, and the vice president fell atop her as the agent's momentum carried him to the far wall. All of this was happening in the dark.

The president's scream pierced the darkness, and all who had heard it felt their blood freeze. It was like he had seen the true presence of hell. Then three agents were thrown from the room, one right after the other, and then the door slammed closed and they were cut off and in the dark. A shattering boom sounded, and the house located at 1600 Pennsylvania Avenue jumped on its foundation as if an earthquake had lifted its old brick-and-mortar base. Alarms started sounding as far as the fire station a block away.

As soon as it had started, it ended. The lights flared to life, and the sun once more shined through the expensive drapes. Everyone was on the floor. Then they all looked up as the door to the family bedroom slowly opened on its own.

More Secret Service agents burst through the family quarters and then made for the bedroom. The first three inside vanished, but the fourth stopped and then, with a white face, turned and stumbled out of the doorway. The vice president saw this and then fought to get to his feet and then entered. He saw the three agents lifting the first responding agent off the president. The vice president's eyes widened when he saw that most of the agent's back was missing. It looked as if a giant spoon had simply scooped out his spine and ribs. The agents rolled the agent off until they could gently lay him on the floor. They then checked the president.

The vice president's eyes saw the carnage. The attending nurse that had been assigned to the president was lying in pieces on the carpeted floor of the bedroom, looking as if she had stepped on some antipersonnel mine in a forgotten field of war. Then his eyes fell on the far wall near the three windows of the east side. As more agents and the doctors entered the room, they all stopped suddenly as the written words once more greeted them. They were smashed into the wallpapered sides of the room and looked as if they had been written in perfect cursive with a gentle hand.

"My God," the vice president said as he took in the message.

The First Lady stepped inside the room and then quickly brought her hands to her mouth. The doctors even stopped taking the president's vital signs when they too saw the words that had been carved into the wall as if by giant clawed nails or talons.

You are cordially invited. The vice president read the top line nearest the ceiling. *Be there, don't be square.* Now everyone was reading the strange words. The wallpaper and the drywall was strewn across the bedroom and lay in a dusty white mess. *Bingo, bobbing for apples, and games to suit the average ghoul,* the vice president read as his eyes followed the strange script. *Spook show for the teens and treats for the kids. The whole town is talking. Celebrate the ending of the Cuban crisis and party with the ghosts! Start at the factory and work your way to town. A fun night for all!*

The vice president stopped reading as the doctors started administering to the president. When the First Lady started shaking and let out a miserable whine, all eyes went to what she was looking at. On the far wall was the conclusion. The same message as before. Only this time, it was a little more personal.

Come home, Dean, we're waiting for you. And again, the one word that made them all ask if they had lost their minds. *BOO!*

"My God!" the female lieutenant colonel said as she had unbuttoned the president's pajama top. They saw her jump back as the other doctors crowded around.

As every set of eyes in the room watched, the words were being carved into the president's chest. Something unseen scraped the skin and chest hair free as the words were brutally sliced through the layers of skin and blood flowed. The doctors at first stayed back until they saw how deep the cutting was. They moved to stem the flow as they applied pressure. One set of hands was violently slapped free of the injury, and the cutting continued. Doctors were slapped, hit, pulled, or pushed away from the bed by a force they couldn't see. The First Lady turned away and felt sick to her stomach as doctors fought to stop what was happening but were helpless to do so.

"Dear God," the colonel said as the carving finally stopped and three of them again hovered over the bed and applied the necessary pressure to get the wounds to stop their flow of blood. Even the Secret Service agents were frozen in place watching the strange events unfolding before their eyes. As blood again filled the deep cuts and then spilled over onto his open pajama top, they all saw what had been written.

Trick or Treat!

3

LOS ANGELES COUNTY JAIL

Even the gang members accumulated inside the jail moved out of the way of the new detainee. The large man looked straight ahead, and his eyes settled on the back of the overcrowded cell as he walked. The dark-skinned man was so intimidating even without the long, flowing black hair that even the gang members decided fairly quickly that this man was someone who would be left alone. Perhaps that was why the much smaller gentleman walking beside him had an air of invulnerability, at least as long as he stayed close to the large Indian.

The first man to greet John Lonetree and George Cordero was Gabriel. As the eyes of the crowded cell turned away, Gabriel shook hands with John and George. Greetings were shared by the small black man, Leonard Sickles, and then a handshake from Damian. The five men laughed as they all realized that their great plan for hiding out had failed beyond any measure.

"That was one hell of a plan you had there, Damian," John said as he was shown to their safe area in the back of the cell.

"Yeah, I guess I forgot to tell you not to attract attention to yourselves while you're on the lam. It took fifteen years to track down a goat herder in Pakistan named bin Laden, yet they caught you guys in less than a year."

George looked at the tight-fitting orange jumpsuit Jackson was wearing and smiled. "And just how did you get caught, Dillinger?"

"All right, we all should just admit we're not very good at hiding and running from the law. None of our past experiences prepared for us to be on the Most Wanted lists when we started this little foray into science, but here we are."

They watched Gabriel's tired features as he weakly smiled and then turned and sat down on the lower bunk. The others gathered around.

"What about Julie, Jennifer, and Kelly?" George asked. "Tell me at least the females were smart enough to escape the dragnet."

"Our legal team says they are over at the women's division, probably attired in the same type of clothing we find ourselves in," Gabriel answered with a sigh. He scratched at his beard and looked up at the men gathered around the bunk. "I got word to them that they will continue their silence the same as you. When I give the court my answers, and you are called upon to confirm my story, you will deny any involvement in the decision-making process. I, and I alone, am the responsible party, and it was I who stated that these shows were nothing more than hoaxes made up by producers and signed off on by their networks. As far as you are concerned, get this phrase memorized: 'I don't recall that.'"

John started to say something, but Gabe stopped him with a raised hand.

"I got you into this mess, and I have to get you all out."

"That won't happen, Prof," Leonard said. "We all signed off on those investigations, and I'll be damned if some producer and their legal mouthpieces will stop me from saying it." Leonard shot a dirty look at the others, who stood and watched. "And if you chumps choose to go Professor Gabe's route, well, you can also go and fuck yourselves. I won't do it."

John shook his head as he sat next to Gabriel on the bunk. He slapped his large hand on Kennedy's knee and nodded at Leonard.

"His articulate narrative notwithstanding, the little shit stated exactly what we all were going to say to you. If you expect us to allow you to get sued and embarrassed over the results of our investigations—investigations we all signed off on at their conclusions, just what would that make us? We're better than that. So, I agree with Leonard, but I will direct my response to you nonetheless. You really can go fuck yourself."

"Okay, that basically lays out our thoughts on the sacrificial lamb thing," Jackson said quickly, cutting off Kennedy's rebuke. "So, we all go in and tell the truth about ghosts. With the one exception of Summer Place and our shared experience there, we have no proof that hauntings have actually happened in those locations."

"We were all basically broke when all of this started before Summer Place, so we'll be broke again. So what?" Leonard said, looking for support.

John turned and saw the sad look on Gabriel's face.

"I don't think in the end we were all doing this for the money. After Summer Place, we actually thought we were on the verge of creating a new science that would not be scoffed at by the academics of the world. Well, we found out that actual hauntings are few and far between. That doesn't mean it's not a science. I am not going to stop looking for answers. I may be broke and shunned after this court thing, but I for one am not quitting," John said with conviction.

"Gabe, we're all going on the theory, after that night at Summer Place, that hauntings are not a natural occurrence in nature. That ghosts are created by the minds of men and women. Something so powerful that its entity— or essence, if you prefer—remains long after life has left its physical form and is able to affect the physical environment. That is why we were doing this. It's a sound theory and the only one that fits the scarcity of actual hauntings outside of what you experts call energy-driven apparitions, just photos captured in time. An imprint."

All eyes went to Damian, who frowned and looked away after his speech.

"If you can convince the most skeptical man on the planet of what your theory is, why not throw that same theory at the court and see if it sticks?" Leonard said, still looking at the former detective. "Just when did you become a believer, J. Edgar?"

"A smart man once said that if you rule out the possible and all that you are left with is the impossible, you have to go with the impossible, or something like that."

"That smart man was Sherlock Holmes, and the quote was actually—" George started to correct the big former Pennsylvania detective when Gabe stopped him.

"It doesn't matter. If you do as I say, maybe you can dig into the theory a little bit more."

"After *you* go to jail for fraud, *we* can continue is what you mean."

Kennedy looked up at John, and then fixed Gabriel with a glare that said he was tiring of the argument. "Yes, that is exactly what I mean."

The commotion at the front of the cell along with the whistling and shouts of approval stopped further discussion of the matter. With exchanged looks of confusion as to what had made the grouping of jail detainees shout with approving voices, the five men parted the gathered criminals and saw they were all watching the chained-down television set bolted to the wall. The news commentator was somberly describing the scene inside a most austere sitting.

"The new president of the United States was sworn in at three forty-five this afternoon, Washington time. The sudden and unexpected resignation of President Hadley has the world asking questions the new administration has yet to shine light upon. With a sketchy explanation as to the president's health condition that was confirmed through White House sources, the new president officially takes over the reins of a nation sorely divided over the powers of the presidency. We will continue to bring you news as to the reasoning behind the sudden resignation of President Hadley and will—"

"I hope the bastard dies," came the voice of a black man staring up at the television screen.

"'Bout damn time too," said another.

"Well, that was sudden," Damian said as they turned and headed back to their safe zone as the channel on the TV was switched. As the men walked away, they heard the familiar theme of one of the shows they had outed as hoax-filled garbage, Kelly's old reality program, *Hunters of the Paranormal*, which was still on the air with new producers and new hosts.

"We have bigger problems than that mean son of a bitch who is finally getting his just reward for being a dickhead," Leonard quipped as they left. "I say good riddance to President Hadley."

On the television, the theme song for *Hunters of the Paranormal* was turned up. The strains of Stevie Wonder's "Superstition" filled the large cell as criminal heads bobbed up and down with the beat of the popular old song. Little did they know the strange men in the back of the cell were the reason that particular show and song were still popular.

To the five very strange men, it was a song and television show they could all live without.

MORENO, CALIFORNIA

Bob and Linda Culbertson returned from grocery shopping in nearby Corona. The 1980 Plymouth Horizon had seen far better days, and both the Culbertsons could not wait until the jobs they had signed on for were complete. Their ten-year tenure in Moreno was all but up the weekend after Halloween. For a couple that had signed on as embedded security inside the old town, they soon found when looking into a mirror that they had actually grown old together.

Both Bob and Linda had filed for their well-deserved and earned retirements from Sacramento Security. It had been a ten-year job that would require only their eyes and ears, and also one that would net both security agents a nice retirement package that included $100,000 on completion of the assignment. That completion was now fast approaching.

It had been ten years of watching and waiting for the unusual—a happenstance that never occurred. The town was as dead as their employer had said it would be. Now they were getting word about the land asset being liquidated by ownership and they would not be replaced when their contract was up. As Bob removed the last bag of groceries from the small rust-covered Horizon, he looked up and down the dead length of Main Street. In a sad sort of way, he was going to miss the solitude of Moreno. The town was responsible for the wife he now had, and there was a sadness to leaving it.

Bob saw old man Leach open the double doors to Newberry's across the street and wave. Bob nodded in greeting, as his hands were full.

"You and Linda need the grill to stay open a little while longer?" the old man shouted as he allowed the doors to close behind him.

"We just bought stuff for chili," he said, and then he saw the brief look of sadness cross Harvey Leach's face even from that distance. Bob turned and saw Linda was still holding the Naugahyde-trimmed front doors open. The look was unmistakable. Bob stopped and then turned to face Leach, who was reentering the large department store. He exhaled. "We got plenty, Harve—you want to shit fire for a week and eat with us?"

"May as well. Haven't shit right since the Tet Offensive in '68. What's one more year?" He waved his hand and then turned.

"Seven thirty!" Bob shouted. He turned and gave Linda a dirty look.

"We've only got one more week until we say good-bye to all of this, so be nice." The doors swung closed.

"Oh, thanks. I'll get the door!"

As Bob struggled to shift one plastic bag from one hand to the other so he could grasp the door handle, he saw a brilliant flash of light from down the street. It was brief but unmistakable. He placed one of the bags down and then shaded his eyes and looked north along Main. As his eyes fell on the old and very damaged theater marquee lying partially on the sidewalk, he could have sworn he saw one of the old shattered neon tubes briefly alight and then just as quickly go out.

"Are you coming in or what?" Linda asked loudly from the doorway.

"Jesus!" he said when he turned. "You scared the shit out of me."

"What in the hell are you looking at?" she asked as she held the right-side door open with a beefy arm.

"Nothing. Must have been the sun shining off something." He finally looked away from the old Grenada Theater.

"Well, hurry up; you're the one that invited company tonight!" The door again closed on him.

"What? It was you—"

With a frustrated look from the closed door to the broken old theater, he shook his head.

"I guess ten years inside this menagerie is enough," he said as he struggled with the door and then entered.

Down the street, the marquee neon flashed brightly once and then went dark.

Bob and Linda watched as Harvey Leach crumbled another six saltine crackers into his bowl of chili—his third. For a man who cooked for a living, it seemed Harvey hadn't had a good bowl of chili in what seemed years. Bob smiled as he looked over at his rotund wife. He shook his head and then stood from the table and removed his and Linda's dishes and placed them in the sink. He then went to the old phonograph inside the remains of the booth and turned on an album on the turntable. Through the static of the needle making contact with the vinyl album, the soft refrains of the Mamas and the Papas echoed softly through the expanse of the old radio station. He started to turn away and rejoin his wife and his dinner guest when he thought he saw movement inside the booth. He cursed.

"Damn rats are getting out of control."

He angrily reached out and turned on the telescoping lamp that had been left over from the radio days and then swiveled it around so he could see into the back of the room where the old records used to be cataloged. Bob moved the lamp left and then right but saw no movement from the brazen rat. He saw nothing but empty space and the old abandoned restroom.

His gaze turned to the album now spinning away on the old felt-covered turntable. There were two of these with only one working. The strains of "California Dreamin'" came wafting through the old speakers. Satisfied it was a mere rat problem, he turned off the light and went to the reception area they used for dining.

"Harve," Bob said as he pulled out his chair and sat, "with us leaving

Moreno, that's going to cut the population around here to about half. Why don't you get the hell out and buy a condo in Riverside or someplace like that?"

Leach finished with the last of his chili and then wiped his mouth with a napkin and finished the last of his beer and then smacked his lips and winked at Linda in appreciation of the meal.

Bob stood and went to the small refrigerator and retrieved two more beers and twisted the cap off them and handed one to Harvey.

"Nah, I'm destined to die here. 'Bout the only time I spent away from here was when I left for the war in '67, and before that when I was born in Ontario. I think I'll just tough it out." He looked at both Bob and Linda seriously. "The real question is, what are you folks going to do? I mean"—here, Harvey smiled as if he had a deep and dark secret—"are you two staying together after your assignment is completed?"

Bob felt the mouthful of beer shoot from his mouth, as Harvey had shocked the hell out of him and Linda, who was openly staring at the old cook. The old man smiled and then used his napkin to dab at the wetness on the plastic tablecloth after the beer was deposited by Bob.

"Oh, don't be so shocked that an old man knows the deep and very dark secrets of the town he spent all his life in." Harvey stood and gestured for Linda not to get up and moved his empty chili bowl to the sink. He returned and sat. "If my memory hasn't completely abandoned this old brain of mine, I would think that you're the third . . . no, the fourth team of security folks that company has sent in here."

"You knew we were security plants the whole time?" Linda asked, her ample elbows planted on the plastic tablecloth.

"I knew that mean bastard would never take his eyes from this place. It began with the father and continued on through the years to the son." A far-off look came to Harvey's features as he absentmindedly took another pull from the beer. "It wasn't enough for the son of a bitch to kill the town; he has to know when the roofs cave in, walls fall down, and windows shatter through age. He has to know everything."

"Who, Sacramento Security?" Bob asked, exchanging looks with Linda.

Harvey laughed and then slid the now-empty bottle away from him and then stood.

"The folks you work for?" he smiled even wider but stopped the chuckle. It was a worrisome look to both Bob and Linda. "No, the real reason you're here is because of someone else. Your company is his eyes." Harvey nodded at Linda. "Thanks for the dinner, Linda. Excellent chili." He placed an old California Angels baseball cap on his head and then started for the front door as the Mamas and the Papas sang their signature song. "One thing, though. You are nice enough folks, so I'll tell you something." He stopped and faced both Bob and Linda. "It is indeed time to go. For me, I'll stay and see this thing through. But for you, I wouldn't even wait; go tonight. Things are different the past few weeks, and I don't know why. Folks comin' up missin' and all."

As the front doors to the station closed and Harvey left, the record stopped, and then Bob heard another start with an intro track. He turned and looked into the DJ's booth through the thick soundproof glass, as he knew they didn't have an autoloader for the turntable. His eyes widened when he saw the silvery visage of a man sitting behind that glass, wearing earphones. He had a finely trimmed jawline beard, and it was then that Bob heard Linda give out a frightened yelp as she saw the image also. They could see the man was speaking into a boom microphone that hadn't been inside the studio in more than fifty years. The music went from the Mamas and the Papas to the refrains of Dion and his hit "Runaround Sue." They watched as the DJ slid the mic away and then bobbed his head to the fast beat of Dion DiMucci.

The empty beer bottles slipped from Linda's fingers and crashed to the floor as her hands went to her mouth. This seemed to attract the attention of the bearded man behind the glass. His look was one of being startled. He waved his beefy hand at the glass, indicating that Bob and Linda should not be in there. Bob's eyes widened as the image slowly faded and then the music did also. The lights flickered, went out for the briefest of moments, and then brightened once again.

Bob quickly returned to the thick door of the studio and pushed it open. He looked around inside but saw nothing but the spinning vinyl disc on the DJ's podium. He reached out and flipped on the light switch, and the overhead fluorescents came to full life. The booth was empty. There was no boom microphone and no Dion and the Belmonts. After a quick search, he turned the light off and then closed the door to the booth. He faced Linda, who slowly lowered her hands from her mouth.

"What did Harvey mean when he said things around here are changing?" Linda asked as she finally broke through her paralysis and made her way over to the ponytailed Bob as he continued to look through the triple-paned glass of the DJ booth.

"I don't know and really don't care. But he is right; this place in the past four weeks or so is getting downright weird. November first cannot come fast enough for me."

For Bob and Linda, one week now seemed a year off, and Halloween was right around the corner.

4

In chairs behind the defense counsel table, Gabriel Kennedy, John Lonetree, Damian Jackson, George Cordero, and Leonard Sickles watched the proceedings and all felt their insides relax when they saw the three women escorted in from the Sybil Brand Institute, where they had been incarcerated for the past week. Gabriel nodded at each as they were escorted to the chairs where they would sit at the end of the long line of defendants. John leaned over and smiled at Jennifer.

The judge rapped her gavel, and the court became silent.

"Well, it looks as if the gang's finally all here." She moved some paperwork around on the stand and then fixed her stern gaze at the counsel for the plaintiff. "I believe we have a brief statement and evidence declaration from the plaintiff's counsel before we get into the much-anticipated deposing of witnesses. Mr. Giles, please."

Giles stood.

"Your Honor, it seems very clear through our conversations with the defendants' counsel that their attitude in not supplying truthful information to this court will continue, so at this time, I would like to introduce the words of one of them while giving evidentiary testimony to the FBI and the FCC immediately after the highly viewed incident at the vacation retreat known as Summer Place. This testimony was recovered just recently."

"Objection! Defense was not afforded a chance to review said evidence. This should be inadmissible, Your Honor."

Giles smiled.

"Since your clients refuse to make statements outside of the testimony already offered by Professor Kennedy, I have no choice but to use my discretion on what evidence to allow. You will have full cross-examination on any testimony given here today. I understand it is only a brief video clip of the questioning conducted by the FCC and the FBI."

"Video?" the defense counsel said as he stood once more from his chair. "Your Honor, I would find it very difficult indeed to depose a video on behalf of my clients. This is just too much."

The judge was opening her mouth to respond when her bailiff stepped to the bench and handed her a note. She read it as the courtroom went silent and the defense team was left standing after the interruption. They saw the judge look up, and Gabriel and the others saw the men standing in the back of the courtroom. Dressed in suits, they were accompanied by four sheriff's deputies.

The judge banged her gavel. "It seems the United States government has withdrawn its testimony regarding this case. The video of Ms. Delaphoy is hereby disallowed. This court will take a fifteen-minute recess." *Bang.* The gavel came down angrily as the judge quickly stood and left.

Everyone in the courtroom started talking at once. The sheriff allowed Gabriel to stand, and he briefly conferred with counsel and then turned away and faced his team as they tried in vain to console Kelly, who felt as if she had betrayed them all. Kennedy parted the ways and then took the small woman into his arms and hugged her.

"Don't worry about what we would have seen on that tape. We don't need to see a tape to know you told them nothing but the truth. I'm just glad those suits over there didn't get a chance to spin it in their direction."

The others nodded their agreement.

"All rise," came the booming voice of the large black bailiff.

"Will both counsels approach the bench, please."

Kennedy and the others sat down and saw the animated way the attorney for the networks waved his hands around in anger. Gabriel's lawyer had a shocked look on his face. Gabe turned in his seat when he was nudged by John Lonetree. He nodded to the back of the court. There were five men standing there they had not noticed during the break. Gabriel shrugged, not knowing anything more than John about the newcomers. The meeting at the bench finished, and the attorneys returned to their respective tables.

"This court is hereby in adjournment. Date to resume will be specified at a later time through respective counsel. I hereby order the defendants to be released immediately. This court is adjourned."

The judge angrily left the courtroom. The attention of the Supernaturals naturally went to the face of George Cordero. He shrugged, saying he had nothing to do with this sudden development.

"You'll be taken back to the jail and released after you are processed," the young attorney said. "The same for the women."

"I think we need to know what just happened."

The attorney turned and faced Gabriel. "For reasons beyond my understanding, I believe the networks and production companies are in the process of dropping all charges and complaints against you and your people."

"Why?"

The attorney turned away and finished placing his paperwork into his briefcase. "It seems you have very highly placed friends out there." He stopped and faced Kennedy. "Don't look a gift horse in the mouth, Professor; take it and run like hell." The attorney smiled and picked up his briefcase, and with a kind nod to the others of Gabriel's group, he left with his legal team.

"What in the hell just happened?" John asked as the others gathered around Kennedy as the sheriff's deputies approached to take them back to jail for their release.

"I don't know yet, but I think those salty-looking fellas back there do."

All heads turned and saw the five men in black suits with their sheriff's escort. They began filing from the courtroom as the crowd did, but then one of them stopped and nodded at Kennedy. Then he and his companions abruptly left.

George and John were getting a strange sensation that affected them simultaneously.

"What are you two picking up?" Gabe asked as he saw the looks on their faces as they spied the men in black suits.

George looked up at the much larger Lonetree and then both faced Gabriel.

"Fear."

MORENO, CALIFORNIA

The stretch limousine was accompanied by three San Bernardino County work trucks. As the grouping of four vehicles rounded the corner of Main Street across the cattle guard that stretched from one side of the road to the other, they made a sudden turn and went right before entering Moreno and climbed the hill that was once known to the locals as Drunk Monk's Hill. In actuality, it was Pleasant Street, and the only buildings on Pleasant Street were at the top of the climb—the mission and winery ruins. The caravan of vehicles stopped just short of the chain-link fence as one of the two security guards stepped to the sliding gate and unlocked it. The limo was the first through, followed by the orange work trucks. The gravel drive made a lot of dust and crunching noises as the vehicles pulled to a stop in front of the Santa Maria Delarosa mission.

"Well, does it look like a place vampires would hide out?" a man asked as he peered through the window.

"It does that," the slim woman next to him said as she jotted notes down on an electronic pad. Her attention went from the adobe mission ruins to turn and look down the hill to the town of Moreno. "What about the town? How much interference do we expect from the locals when and if we are allowed to shoot here?"

The chubby man in the thousand-dollar suit laughed as he lit a large cigar. He blew smoke and then faced the woman as the third man from the limo joined them. "Interference from Moreno?"

"Yes."

"Moreno has been dying for many years, darlin.' The damn place just isn't smart enough to lie down and die." The man puffed on his cigar and then shook his head. "Besides, if you have all the residents of that town coming to watch filming, you'll have about eight people to deal with." He faced the woman, who was feeling angry over the "darlin'" comment he made earlier. "Think the studio can handle that onrush of spectators?"

"Look, Mr. Freeman, I represent the studio's sizable investment here. If the county allows us to shoot here on location, they will want to make sure our liability is at minimum risk. This *is* a state-sponsored historical site."

"It's still just a bunch of mud bricks, if you ask me."

"Per my research, it was quite a bit more than that back in the day. Some historians still say if it weren't for the earthquake in 1821, this would have been one of the more important missions in California, and if you grew up here, you would know how important that is to a lot of people.

That's why we have county engineers here to protect the site and to ensure that we do no further damage. If this inspection reveals the areas we wish to shoot in are unstable, the county will rescind their support."

"Well, that's why we have these fine gentlemen," Freeman said as the film producer placed his arm around the smaller man and then brought him close. "Isn't that right, Mr. County Engineer?"

The man said nothing but waved the group of inspectors from the county trucks to commence with the flooring inspection.

"Mr. Freeman, this arrangement was made against my specific recommendation about molesting this site. The structures are just too unsafe. Why do you think we have security here?" He gestured around the one-hundred-acre site. "Why all the fencing? Why don't you see tourists here? Because this whole thing could collapse at any moment. And if you don't get those points, maybe you have heard about the instability of the ground in California? Well, they're called earthquakes, Mr. Freeman, and they tend to knock unstable structures down. Then we can go into the chemical spill in '62. Oh, there are dangers here, and if you don't heed warnings about how much danger, you can get people killed."

"Come on, Mr. Garvey. Your boss seemed very unconcerned. When it was explained to him through our artist's renderings of the shoot, he was more than satisfied we won't be molesting your historical site. Exterior shots of the mission, a few of the winery. The rest of the interiors will be shot in Burbank."

The county engineer exchanged wary looks with the studio executive in charge of finance and then waved his men forward. "Check out the old stone foundation and wooden flooring. Estimate its maximum weight allowance."

The group toured the winery. It was clean and still much intact. The county had kept the ruin clean over the years and the walls shored up. They stepped out into the sunshine of the dying day. The engineer conferred with his men and then joined the two people from Los Angeles.

"They are going to approve the weight standards at three and a half tons. That's your equipment weight limit."

"Should be plenty," Freeman mumbled. As he lit another cigar, his eyes were on the old winery a hundred feet away from the mission. He turned and faced Garvey.

"Man, those doors would make for a great shot." He smiled. "Just how unsafe is the winery?"

"Over half of the upper structure has collapsed into the basement and subbasement. No roof remains, everything inside is water damaged, and let's see, it's only two hundred and thirty-two years old," Garvey said, shaking his head and chuckling.

The cigar was removed. "Give us a look-see."

"Are you insane?" Garvey said, looking at the woman to see if Freeman was joking. She raised her brow, as confused as himself. He turned back to the film producer. "I said two-hundred-plus years old, collapsed, dangerous—you understand those words, Mr. Freeman?"

"You're the engineer; I trust your judgment. You know what's safe and what's not."

"You're right. I am the engineer, and I say you're insane. The only place that is even remotely safe where you get a sense of history is in the subbasement where the old wine casks used for long-term fermentation were stored. That's only because the area of the basement it's located in is the conjuncture of two walls. That's the only reason it survived the initial earthquake in the day and the factory explosion in '62."

"Then what are we waiting for?" Freeman stared at the man. "Come on. Any real danger and we'll forget about it."

The county crew waited nearby as the three talked. Garvey turned to his men. "We're all done here. You guys go ahead and take off; it's a long drive back."

The men were more than happy to oblige their boss.

Garvey turned back to Freeman and Ms. Deerling as the trucks left. "Don't make me regret this. As far as anyone is concerned, we never went in there."

Freeman crossed his heart with his cigar hand. "What winery?" he joked.

"We go through the double doors, and straight to your left is the basement stairs. It's the only egress point anywhere in the ruins." Garvey turned and waved the second security guard over. "Can I borrow that radio?" he asked.

The security guard handed him the radio. "It's set to the right channel. May I ask just what you are doing, sir?" the man asked with concern on his face. "No one ever goes in there." The tall and very thin black man looked around and then straight at the three people. "We call it the bad place." Again, the nervous look. "It's also getting dark."

"Well, then, we had better take this just in case," Freeman said as he reached out and unclipped the flashlight from the man's belt.

The doors were one foot thick and made of solid redwood. Garvey pushed open the left side and stepped in. The dying sunlight illuminated the complete and utter devastation of the ruin. The ceiling, gone for two hundred years, lay in heaps on the stone flooring. The old windows and their leaded glass had vanished right around the time of the War of 1812, and bushes and trees had started to take root and had grown as far as the absence of sunlight would allow. Grapevines coursed in and out of the old adobe walls like mythical snakes from a Greek tragedy.

"Maybe we ought to rethink this," Ms. Deerling said as Garvey moved to the far left of the main floor. There was a dark space there that gave both Freeman and Deerling cold chills as they gazed beyond into the blackness.

The two movie people became confused. Instead of turning on the powerful mag flashlight, Garvey shoved the long device into his coat pocket and then reached out and turned on a light. He gestured that his guests should join him.

"The winery actually has power to certain spots in the building. We never knew why, as it all took place before the tragedy of '62."

Freeman saw that Garvey was going down the stairs at a brisk pace. He tentatively placed a foot on the first riser and then gently placed his full weight down upon it. Garvey stopped and looked back.

"It's safe; these stairs are only about seventy years old."

"Why would the previous owner place new stairs in a building deemed unsafe?" the woman asked as she put her notepad closely to her chest and hung on for dear life to the steel railing lining the staircase.

"Possibly checking on the groundwater. The factory, at least before it blew itself sky-high, used to make gauges, meters, and triggering devices for the U.S. government. They used a lot of mercury in their designs, and the groundwater had to be checked on a constant basis for contaminants."

Their confidence in the reinforced stairs grew. They did notice that in the middle of each stair there was a major depression, as if a great weight had been placed upon each.

They came to a landing, but Garvey kept going down, making the woman more apprehensive about continuing the tour.

"That's the basement. Grape crushing, things like that. The subbasement is right down here."

As they continued, they noticed that this lighting was industrial in make and design. Each powerful bulb was encased in a steel mesh cocoon.

"Oh, we have to get a camera down here. This would be ideal for the vampire nesting place," Freeman said as he stepped into the subbasement.

The twenty-four wooden casks were huge. At one time, they each had the capacity to hold five hundred gallons of locally produced wine. Many of them were crushed and broken, but most were still intact and at least recognizable for what they were. The subbasement was in considerably better shape than even the mission above their heads. They could see steel reinforcement beams had been installed and a new floor put in. This one was smooth and shiny and made of hardened concrete. They saw old consoles and even older-looking electronic equipment. Wires and cables were strung throughout the basement.

"Doesn't look like the monks that made the wine here were that far behind us in technology," Freeman joked as he ran a finger through the dust that had accumulated over the years.

"We think this equipment may have been used to monitor earth movement. After all, an earthquake may have damaging consequences for any trapped heavy metals in the ground."

"Wow, look at this," Ms. Deerling said as she lifted the lid on a small box. Her smile grew as she looked the item over.

"What is that?" Freeman asked.

"It's an old battery-powered record player. And look at these." She held up two items with a paper sleeve covering them. "Old forty-five records too. Music's a little tame for me." She passed them over to Freeman, who gave them a cursory glance and then tossed the items back atop the portable record player.

"Tame? You mean *lame*, don't you? I think 'Johnny Angel' and this stuff came out twenty-five years before my mother met my father."

"This was the biggest mystery. It still is the talk of anyone who has ever seen it." Garvey turned on another bank of bright lighting as he vanished around the L-shaped turn in the basement. Freeman saw the large vaultlike box standing against the far wall. He saw Garvey run his hand over the still-shiny stainless steel under the bright fluorescent lighting.

"It's not a vault like we first thought. You can see vents, gauges, and dials. None of them mean much to any of us. Some of the older dials and gauges are written in German, the others in English. There are even viewing ports and an intercom system. We know the date of manufacture— 1940—and it was built in the old Yugoslavia and shipped out here after the war. For what purpose, we have never found out. After all these years, the mystery of this thing has died away some, but it's still a curiosity thing down at the offices."

"What do you think is in it?" Freeman asked.

"We don't know. Do you think the county would foot the bill for a safe company to come in here and open it? If you didn't notice, the damn door is welded shut."

Freeman had just noted that fact. His eyes went to a large sliding door that Garvey said was a vent. "What about that? Can you at least look inside?"

Music stopped Garvey from answering. Shelley Fabares was singing "Johnny Angel" as the old forty-five record spun on the player and the studio woman smiled.

Freeman was about to tell her that was enough when the vaultlike box shook. The movement was so fast and so furious that dirt and dust filtered down from the rafters and a crack formed in the floor. The metal and rubber lines running from the strange holding tanks atop the vault moved and swayed. Even Deerling stopped toe tapping and stared at the strange stainless steel box.

"What in the hell was that?" Freeman asked over Shelley Fabares. He walked over to the large vault door and looked it over. The handle that was used to open the thick steel door had long ago been welded to its frame. Freeman began reaching for it when the door was rammed from the opposite side with a force that moved the five-ton enclosure on its base. Freeman jumped back, and Garvey yelped. The movement caused so much vibration that the needle on the record player scraped straight across the record's surface where it came off and the music stopped.

"I thought you said this area was safe!" Freeman said.

"That isn't the structure—something moved in there!" Garvey said as he slowly backed away from the vault.

Ms. Deerling screamed as she felt something run up the inside of her pantsuit from the bottom. She jumped back and could have sworn she heard laughing. Then she screamed again when the arm on the player engaged and then lifted itself up and then over to the start of the grooves on the vinyl. "Johnny Angel" once more sprang forth from the small speaker on the side of the player.

Freeman looked from the record player to Garvey, who was still retreating toward the stairs. "Is this a joke? If it is, it's in bad taste, my friend. I'm sure you and your buddies will have a big laugh back at the office about how scared the movie people were."

The vault moved again. This time, it jumped and came down with a crushing sound of concrete being turned to powder beneath it. All three people stood frozen in shock.

Deep in the darkened bowels of the Grenada Theater in town, the vault there rocked on its frame. It started as a whisper that filtered through the old basement of the theater and then grew in power as if something inside became aware of the happening two miles away at the winery.

Freeman felt his bladder grow weak and useless as pee freely coursed down his leg and soaked through the expensive material of his suit. Garvey stumbled and fell to his back, and Ms. Deerling felt her vision tunnel as she came near to fainting. All thoughts of movie budgets and reality in general were not a part of her current repertoire. Then they all heard the booming voice from beyond reality as it smashed through the flooring above and burst into their ears seemingly from every direction.

"*Get them out!*"

They heard laughter, not from one but many, as they seemed to have been surrounded by energy. The vault shook and rumbled. Shelley Fabares's voice went from low volume to concert-grade decibels, causing all three to cover their ears as the pain shot through their brains.

Before anyone knew what was happening, they were all three being slapped, kicked, and had their hair pulled to the point it looked as if they were fighting off a flock of very angry invisible birds. Garvey tried to stand and was kicked so hard in the seat of his pants that he went headfirst into the concrete floor, breaking his nose. He went to his back pocket and brought out the radio. Just as he clicked the transmit switch, the radio was pulled from his hand. Then the voice became clear as it resonated with more power than the small radio could produce.

"*Get them out now!*"

The radio was thrown so hard against the floor that Garvey felt the plastic shrapnel cut into his ankle.

Deerling and Freeman forgot all about their great Hollywood production as they broke and ran for the L-shaped bend and then for the door.

Garvey was left standing aghast as they left him. He was slapped again and again. He remembered the heavy-duty flashlight and brought it from his coat pocket. He swung it like a small billy club at something he couldn't see. On his fourth swing, the flashlight connected solidly with something directly in front of him. The glass lens shattered, and Garvey could have sworn he heard a growl. The Maglite was wrenched from his grasp, and while he stared wide-eyed at the amazing scene of the light floating in midair, the steel housing of the expensive light was crushed by an unseen and very powerful hand. The damaged Maglite was tossed back to him, and he caught it in shock as the laughter filled the basement.

The two security guards waited patiently with the limo driver and smoked. They turned toward the old winery when the double doors burst open and the three visitors came running out. The woman was crying and scream-ing something they couldn't understand as she literally fell down the last four steps fronting the doors. As for the large man, he was vomiting as he ran. Garvey was the third out the doors, and he managed to jump from the topmost step to the ground and was soon passing both Deerling and Free-man as they cut a retreat for the limo.

The tall, thin black man tried to say something as the driver alertly got inside the stretch limo. As Garvey ran by, he tossed the crushed flash-light. It flew through the air, and the security man caught it. The three people didn't wait for anything as they brushed past the shocked twosome and entered the car. The limo screamed out of the parking area with the con-fused two-man security team standing in shock.

The limousine's harried driver fishtailed around the bend, and instead of turning left to get back to the freeway, he mistakenly turned right, head-ing in the opposite direction.

"You're going the wrong way!" Garvey said from his position half on and half off Ms. Deerling, who was trying desperately to remove the small man from her lap as the driver straightened the limo out and headed down Main Street past the derelict Texaco station, toward the town of Moreno.

"What happened back there?"

"Never you mind! Just get us the hell out of here and back to Ontario! The faster I get on that plane the better!" Freeman screamed.

The limo had already shot past the Texaco station and then past the half-burned feed store and the telephone exchange opposite it. They came to the dead cable-suspended traffic light and sped into the deserted town.

Bob Culbertson had just placed the Going Out of Business sign in the front of the radio station when he heard the scream of an overtaxed engine com-ing down the street. He was about to turn to see what the noise was all about when the dysfunctional neon sign that had hung in the window of the old K-Rave radio station, advertising fifteen thousand watts of listening power, sprang to life. It was bright enough that Bob stepped back from the window in shock and surprise as the sign illuminated the sidewalk and dispelled the dusk of the early evening. The sign hadn't worked for the entire ten-year commitment of their contract. As the black car neared, Linda stepped out of the record store and saw the look on Bob's face and then the scream of the limo coming down the street.

Across Main, Harvey Leach allowed Casper Worthington, a small-time walnut farmer, to step out of Newberry's as he said his good-byes after the chicken-fried steak dinner had been served. Harvey and Casper both heard the approaching car, and with curiosity ruling the boring evening, they stepped out toward the broken sidewalk. Harvey saw Bob and Linda across the way, and they were also staring out at the speeding car.

"What in the Sam Hill are they doin'?" Casper said aloud.

"Son of a bitch must be doing eighty!" Harvey said as he saw the limo hit the dip at the corners of Main and Jefferson Streets. Sparks flew as the long limo scraped bottom and flew into the air and then back down again.

As the limo approached, all four witnesses saw the old streetlights suddenly spring to life and glow brightly as the black limo sped past, only to dim again after the lights were in the black limo's rearview mirror.

"What the—" Harvey said but never got to finish.

After hitting the dip and slamming his passengers' heads into the roof, the driver managed to straighten the limo out as the old and mostly boarded-up buildings flew past their darkened windows.

"Stop trying to kill us and turn this damn thing around!" Freeman yelled mercilessly at the frantic driver.

Before the driver could turn around, the radio flared to full volume for no apparent reason. The voice that came through the surround speaker system was a professional-sounding blast from the past.

"This is Freekin' Rowdy Rhoads, and you're listening to K-Rave 106.5, Moreno. Here's something for the jelly bean crowd out there—the lovely Miss Shelley Fabares and 'Johnny Angel.'" The voice died away in time for the first words of the song to be heard. As the three people in the back seat were tossed mercilessly about, the surreal adventure was themed by "Johnny Angel."

The limo driver tried to shut off the satellite radio, but the illuminated lights refused to obey his orders. The music was deafening.

"Look out!" Garvey cried as the limousine came to the corner of Main and Park Streets directly across from the Moreno Baptist Church.

The streetlights flared brightly, and the driver looked up and saw the line of children and adults in the crosswalk, all within white lines that hadn't existed since the paint wore away fifty years before. Young and old faces alike looked up in terror as the car sped toward them. The limo was aimed directly at the center of the crosswalk, and there was little hope that the driver could miss killing them all. Men with fedoras were trying to pull women and children dressed in their Sunday best out of the way of death that was screaming toward them at eighty miles per hour.

The driver hit the brakes and then swerved to try to limit the death that was coming quickly to so many. The long limo spun and then hit a pothole in the road that had gone unattended for decades, and then the car flipped and spun in the air twice. The Cadillac hit roof down and then sped into the right side of the street. The driver was immediately killed as the windshield hit the disabled fire hydrant on the corner and disintegrated, removing the man's head completely. The limo careened onto the sidewalk, the hood hit the old pipe and tobacco shop, and then the gas tank ruptured.

Bob was the first one to the overturned and flaming limo. He tried to reach for the door but was pulled away by Harvey Leach and Casper Worthington.

"What are you trying to do, kill yourself?" Harvey said as the flames grew hotter and wilder. Casper helped in pulling Bob away and then started hitting him in the back of the head, and Bob recoiled.

"Your ponytail was afire there, son," the old man said as the smell of burning hair almost overpowered the smell of burning flesh inside the car.

Linda came running up and started slapping Bob with her free hand for taking a chance like he had.

"You stupid bastard! The sheriff and highway patrol are on the way with fire and rescue."

Bob completely smothered the smoldering hair and looked back at the overturned limo. "Tell them no hurry on the rescue part."

As the four people moved away from the conflagration, it was Harvey who saw the overhead streetlights slowly fade to darkness. He knew those lights had not had elements in them for years. The others noticed the same thing, and then they all backed away to the sidewalk as the sounds of sirens came to their ears all the way from the hidden interstate ten miles distant.

Down the street, the K-Rave sign did as the streetlamps had. The neon slowly faded to nothing.

The multigenerational family of rats that had occupied the Grenada Theater for the past fifty-five years scrambled up the rickety wooden staircase from the basement. They scurried past the dead snack bar and out into the night, never to return to their luxurious surroundings.

Singing could be heard inside the abandoned bank vault, and that was what had sent the family of rats to seek new accommodations.

Johnny Angel, how I love him . . . he's got something that I can't resist . . . but he doesn't even know that I . . . I . . . I exist.

The voice faded, and then the basement went quiet as four people burned to death only one hundred feet away. The thing inside its prison absorbed the power and then went to sleep, readying itself for the party yet to come.

5

Questions, there were many. Answers, there was none as Gabriel and the others waited in the uncomfortable plastic chairs at a private terminal. The men had been waiting for two hours before the three women had arrived. Thus far, the men and women watching them had no words to offer after their sudden freedom had started.

Through the darkness of the large window inside the terminal building, they saw a large Learjet as it taxied to their Jetway. They heard the twin engines slowly wind down as the white plane was quickly serviced by ground personnel. Gabriel watched one of the women wearing a black pantsuit with matching jacket open the Jetway's door.

"If you folks will step this way, please, the director is on board, and we'll take off very shortly."

Looks were exchanged, and it was Gabriel who stepped forward. "Can I assume you have a warrant for our arrest?"

The dark-haired woman tilted her head to the right and looked confused. Then understanding dawned on her official-looking features.

"Professor Kennedy, I apologize for our secrecy; you are not under arrest, nor is any member of your group." She reached into her small bag and produced a leather wallet and then opened it. "FBI, sir. Our director will explain the situation." The woman replaced her badge and wallet and then fixed Kennedy with a serious look. "We could not expose our interest in you to the press at the courtroom for reasons that will become obvious. That's why we used the sheriff's office."

Gabriel knew that was all they would get, and his team stepped past the agent and then onto the long Jetway.

Below, the jet belonging to the director of the FBI began spooling up her engines.

The pilots' cabin door was closed, and the aircraft's passenger compartment was empty. After standing for the briefest of moments, the eight confused men and women found seats. Gabriel and Julie sat next to each other, and John and Jennifer took the seat directly across. They faced one another as they fastened their seat belts.

The door to the cockpit opened just as the Learjet was being pushed back by the ground crew. A tall and very thin man stepped out and smiled after closing the door. He walked down the aisle and shook hands with everyone. As the government-operated plane began taxiing the one mile to the runway, the man remained standing as he shook the hand of the last person he came to.

"Professor Kennedy," the man in the white shirt and rolled-up sleeves said. He stood over the group and swayed back and forth as the jet moved. "I recognize you from television. My kids loved watching you and your team. It must be the natural policemen in them. They enjoyed your people exposing assholes to the world. They really got a kick out of it."

Gabriel remained silent as the man released his hand.

The man smiled as he spied an empty seat across from the group of four. The Learjet picked up speed and then lifted into the dark skies of Southern California.

The Learjet climbed to altitude as no further discussion was offered to them. Director Hartnett finally unfastened his seat belt and nodded at the female agent sitting in the back. She stood and vanished behind a small partition.

"It's against the law to have alcohol on board a federally operated plane, but I am the director of the FBI, so I can do what I want. For any of you that needs one, drinks are available." No one moved as they heard the tinkling of ice striking glass. "I think after our discussion, you'll find alcohol is a worthwhile escape measure."

The female agent reappeared and handed the director a glass of ice and amber liquid. She looked at the others, and they all shook their heads. She returned to the hidden bar. The director downed half the double shot of bourbon, then quickly the other half. He smacked his lips and then the smile was gone. He placed it on the fake mahogany table to his front. He looked at the others as they turned their chairs to face him.

"Okay, you've had your drink to buttress the fort now—can we know what we are being abducted for?" Leonard asked, not hesitating to make his opinion on law enforcement readily known.

"Agent Weatherby, you may start the in-flight entertainment."

As the confused eight members of the Supernaturals watched, a large television monitor lowered from the aisle's ceiling right in front of the cockpit. Gabriel turned to see Director Hartnett hold his empty glass out for Agent Weatherby to take.

For the next hour, the group watched silently as a grainy, FBI laboratory–enhanced video of the happenings they had been called in to comment on played, while the soft hum of the plane's twin engines became background noise. They watched the low-light photography of night vision in most cases. They saw the assaults as they took place. To the group, none of the surroundings looked familiar, but they knew they couldn't tell because of the low-light conditions.

The video finally came to an end, and Hartnett stood. He paced to the back and then returned with a fresh bottle of bourbon and glasses that he held between his chest and arm. He placed them on the small table.

"We don't know how the cameras still operated while the power to the rooms went out. Another unsolved mystery."

"Just who was being assaulted?" Julie asked as she accepted a glass from Gabriel. He also took one as did the others after viewing what had taken place. The video was so bad that faces remained unseen.

"The men and women being tossed about like they were toys were highly trained agents of the Treasury Department." Hartnett grew silent as he stared at the blank television screen. Agent Weatherby saw this and continued for him as he poured another drink for himself, refusing to say anything about who they were watching.

"The men in the video were a protection detail from Treasury. Secret Service. The man they were unsuccessfully protecting was the president of the United States."

It was Julie Reilly who stood and squeezed past Gabriel and retrieved the bottle of bourbon, but Damian got to it first. He caught himself and nodded as he refilled Julie's glass and then his own.

"Where is the president now?" Gabriel asked, placing a hand over his empty glass as Damian started to pour.

Jackson nodded as he recognized the way in which Gabriel asked the question—he was going into his parapsychology role. He saw a light in Kennedy's eyes he hadn't seen since Summer Place. Damian smiled and then went back to his seat, where Leonard and George struggled for the bottle of alcohol.

"Since his official resignation, he has been moved to a safe house in Virginia, deep in the countryside," Weatherby answered and then sat next to the director.

"Is this the reason behind his sudden departure from government service?" John asked.

"No, there had been other issues, but I think this one would suffice. The world thinks it was for health reasons or maybe his relationship with the First Lady. Who cares?" Hartnett said as he came out of his deep thoughts. He needed another drink but decided he had to give these—in his opinion, anyway—nutcases the best answers that he could.

"I assume you have investigated outside sources, maybe a foreign power?"

Director Hartnett looked over at Gabriel with what looked like renewed respect. "Thoroughly, Professor. The CIA and the bureau have concluded that technology of this nature just isn't the answer."

"As the historical record will substantiate through the CIA's own experimentation with extrasensory perception conducted throughout the fifties and sixties," Gabriel commented.

"Even those old files were investigated, much to the CIA's consternation," Weatherby said. "Even though that particular agency had some success in those early experiments, nothing, and I mean nothing, ever came this close to being a reality. No, we have ruled out foreign influence."

"What is the president's condition now?" Jennifer asked.

They could see by the look on her face and the way that she voiced the question that she felt just as the others about their former president—they despised the man as much as the rest of the country and world had.

"Comatose for the most part with moments of clarity that frankly scare the hell out of anyone who hears his words. He wakes up screaming. Something is eating away at him, and all the world's most accomplished doctors, neurosurgeons, brain specialists, and even psychoanalysts all agree it's memory based, whatever it is. It seems to manifest itself during REM sleep."

Kennedy's group became silent as they thought this over.

"If these descriptions of the event and the video evidence are to be believed, this is power even beyond what we faced at Summer Place," George said, quickly swallowing his fourth drink.

"So much so I think you're mistaken as to the perpetrators of this event." Kennedy stood and went toward the front of the aircraft. He started to pace and calculate, as was his habit when thinking. "This has to be an outside, human-inspired assault."

Hartnett didn't comment on Gabriel's protestations about their conclusions. He lowered his head in thought.

"The CIA and the NSA have their opinions, and they side with you. They think that an outside entity is behind this—either the Russians or the Chinese. Professor, we have exhausted all our resources. You're it," Weatherby said as she snapped the remote control and the television again came to life. "This was the last message received, two days ago, and it was decided to call in your group."

On the screen, they all watched as a shaky, handheld camera zoomed in on a damaged wall. The lens captured the words there, and they all froze.

Betrayal is the dark side of love. Come home, teen angel, we're going to rock around the clock.

The aircraft was silent as the television went dark once more. Everyone had sat when they had read the words. Gabriel finally took the drink that Julie offered and drank deeply. Then he placed the glass down and stood and faced Hartnett and Weatherby.

"We'll need one hell of a lot of equipment."

"Whatever you need will be provided," answered Weatherby. "Not that it will make a difference," he mumbled.

Outside the aircraft, the night just became a little bit darker for the Supernaturals.

VIRGINIA COUNTRYSIDE

The safe house was more of a mansion than just an ordinary farmhouse in the Virginia countryside. Since moving President Hadley from Washington, there had only been one brief instance of the strange occurrence that was currently plaguing the former commander in chief.

After three different checkpoints manned by menacing-looking military units, Avery finally parked his car and was approached by a plainclothes Secret Service agent. The agent took Avery's ID.

"The First Lady is expecting you, Mr. Avery. She is in the downstairs office with her secretary. Please, sir, remain on the first floor and attempt no movement upstairs."

He took his briefcase and made his way to the thick oaken doors of the house. It was opened just as he raised his hand to knock. A butler, which Avery knew not to be his real profession, allowed him in.

As Avery took off his overcoat, the First Lady gestured for the him to enter her office. Two agents dressed in black Nomex watched from the study directly across the way. As Avery nodded a greeting, the secretary stepped out.

"Thank you, Nancy. After I meet with Mr. Avery, we may have more for you to do. And thank you for staying up all hours to assist."

The secretary smiled and nodded, and as she stepped past Avery, she made a show of not greeting him.

"Either the help has picked up on the vibe that you and I are on the outs or they sense the smell of death about me. Which is it?" he asked as he stepped past Catherine and into the office.

She silently followed, closing the door behind her after a momentary look up the staircase and the bedrooms beyond.

The former First Lady was wearing a simple skirt of white and a black blouse that exposed more of her body than in the previous six years as First Lady. She crossed her legs one over the other and then raised the left brow in her "I'm waiting for good news" pose.

"The competency ruling came down this afternoon." Avery reached for his case and then opened it. He teasingly held out the file and then lowered it to his lap.

"Well, what did that blathering judge have to say?" she asked, noticing that Avery intentionally held back from giving her the report.

"Twenty-five percent."

Again, the raised eyebrow. She remained silent as she took in the small, arrogant man. Instead of giving her the file, he produced another flimsy piece of paper and instead slid that across the desk. She still didn't move.

"My official release from government service."

"Congratulations; you're a private citizen again."

Avery smirked at the First Lady. "That's my point of the twenty-five percent, Catherine. I am now an out-of-work, disgraced politician."

"And for that, you want twenty-five percent?"

Finally, Avery slid the file over. "All you have to do is sign where I have indicated, and then you will be solely responsible for a stock portfolio and corporate holdings statement that is currently in trust, worth more than fifty-six billion dollars . . . and change."

"Your valuable help in this matter is basically a finder's fee, Herbert. Ten percent."

"That was the going rate when other benefits used to be applicable," he said as he looked at her chest. She saw this but made no movement to button her blouse properly. "There were times when I truly believed you were interested. I thought we had a clear and precise understanding of one another."

"Oh, I understood you from the beginning, Herbert. And frankly our times together weren't worth twenty-five percent of fifty-six billion dollars."

"Once I leave here, I will be starting a new book. I have an advance offer from New York. Should I go into detail about what that book will cover during my White House years?"

"And you discussed those particulars with a publisher?"

"I didn't go into detail, but assured her that there would be plenty of dirt, sex, and intrigue to cover the gambit of information."

Catherine turned in her chair. "I see. Well, you have produced a better brief than you gave my husband over the years. Very convincing." She turned back to face the man who was now in the process of blackmailing her. "Deal, but only twenty percent, paid out yearly, not in advance."

"Acceptable. Just sign."

"And this book talk?" she asked.

"Why write a book for mere money when I will have enough to buy a publishing house of my own? No, your avaricious activities and sexual affairs will remain locked away."

"As I said, deal." She hurriedly signed the papers where he had indicated. Then Avery handed her the last—their private agreement of 20 percent. She looked it over and started to sign but stopped. The noise from outside of the office brought her to her feet. She went to the door and opened it and saw the hostage rescue team moving up the stairs.

"What is it?" she asked one of the running men with mock concern. She knew she didn't need the president alive any longer to get the trust that was started by the bastard's father in the late sixties. She now wanted the man to die and die quickly. So, with her heart racing, not for fear but for good tidings, she went up the stairs in a gait that said she still cared for Hadley. Avery, without comment, followed.

When Catherine gained the upstairs, she saw several of the hostage rescue team standing just outside of her husband's door. The lights in the long hallway dimmed and then brightened repeatedly.

"What's happening?" she asked as the agent in charge of the rescue unit stood and faced her.

"Nothing, ma'am. Just the electrical system acting up. He's safe for right now; we have three men inside with the duty doctor and the nurse."

Catherine showed relief and then, in an acting sequence that would have been guaranteed to win an Oscar, she started to faint. Avery shook his head.

Then the lights went out.

"Unit three, why isn't the emergency generator starting up?" the team leader asked into his radio as he went to the door with the suddenly unflustered First Lady.

"The generator is working; we just—" The radio also went silent.

The team leader hit the radio once, twice, and then a third time. Before he could curse about the instrument, two men in black Nomex clothing were thrown from the room to smash into the agent in charge, and then one rolled down the stairs and the other smashed into the wall. The wide-eyed team leader attempted to get into the room, but the door slammed closed hard enough to separate the man's gloved hand from his wrist. He screamed out in shock and pain as the door splintered at the frame from the force of the closing. They could hear screaming inside.

The former First Lady retreated to the far wall inside the hallway, and Avery joined her. They had both witnessed the attacks firsthand and were not thrilled about watching another. In the darkness, they could see the door open with a very dim view through the blackness, and then one of the hostage rescue team simply walked out of the bedroom. The dark form was featureless in the absence of light, but in the dim illumination filtering in from the security lighting outside, it was clear the man had no head. The legs buckled, and then an empty hand reached out, grabbing the stair railing but missing. The body fell over the landing to the floor far beneath as the screaming inside the bedroom continued.

As more of the hostage rescue team scrambled up the stairs in the dark, three gunshots sounded, and Catherine felt Avery's body next to her. The door to the bedroom was still open. She started forward just as the rescue team made it to the second-floor landing. She stumbled and Avery tried to stop her from approaching the blackness beyond the doorway.

"What are you doing?" Avery screamed.

"I want to see," she said as Avery pulled her arm.

"Don't be—"

Herbert Avery felt the resistance by the First Lady cease, and he felt her hands on his side and shoulder as she pushed him into the room just as two members of the hostage rescue team ran in. Catherine quickly reached out and pulled the door closed just as four more rescue team members burst from the stairs. Three more bounded up, with their own flashlights dying before they could see the satisfied smirk on the First Lady's face. The sounds coming from the bedroom were scaring the hell out of the men who battered the thick door to gain entrance. Catherine eased back to the far wall in total darkness as she realized that whatever was in there was not going to give an inch.

Herbert Avery couldn't see anything, but he heard plenty as men were torn to pieces. He flew to the carpeted floor and crawled away from the center of the room where he had been pushed, first by Catherine's shove and then by the two hostage rescue team members when they also became trapped. More gunfire. Avery felt the bullets fly by, and he could smell gunpowder as the bedroom illuminated with flame and light. His hands came in contact with hair, and in the next flash of gunfire, he saw the duty nurse's head on the rug in a large pool of blood. Then he saw that her body was in another part of the darkened bedroom. That was the push Avery needed as he gained his feet and ran headlong into a wall where he thought the door was. He bounced and then reached out in the dark as the gunfire ceased. He screamed as his hand encountered the metal doorknob. He turned it and felt the other agents on the opposite side of the door trying to break it in. He pulled, and the door surprisingly opened about a foot, and Avery and the agents tried in vain to get by—Avery out and the agents in.

Catherine couldn't see what was happening only feet in front of her. The lights from the outside caught brief glimpses in slow-motion–like reality as the door came partially open. Then she saw the backs of the hostage rescue team as they tried in vain to get past an obstacle.

"Get back!" one of the men yelled loudly, and Catherine heard a man on the other side pleading to be let out. Then in a brief flash of light from a flashlight that momentarily fought to come alive, she saw Herb Avery's head appear between the door and its frame. He was trying his best to get through the door that was being pushed in by the FBI agents. Avery's eyes were pleading as he struggled. Then it happened. The door closed with a force that none of them could have ever imagined. Avery's head was caught between it and the jamb, and then like an overripe grape, it came free of the body. The door completely closed, tossing the hostage rescue team members away like leaves on a fresh wind. The sounds from inside the bedroom suddenly ceased. The lights in the hallway flickered back to life along with the many discarded and useless flashlights. Catherine heard the many feet pounding up the stairs. Shouts and curses battered the upstairs as the door easily opened by its own volition. Slowly, easily, and even the small creaking was loud enough for all to hear.

Avery's headless body slid from the interior and then hit the carpeted floor runner like deadweight. Agents had to step over it. They ran into the room and saw what this new attack had wrought. Eight men and one woman were scattered throughout the large room. Medical monitoring equipment was overturned, and several were sparking on the carpet. Bullet holes were punched into the walls, and as the agents adjusted their eyesight to the brightness of the bedroom, they saw the president lying peacefully in his bed. One of the Nomex-clad agents reached out and pulled the naval doctor from the president's blanket-covered legs. The body hit the floor, and Catherine stepped to the doorway and then immediately turned and fled down the stairs. Her last vision as she looked back was that of the prone and very much dead Herbert Avery.

Two of the doctors that had been separated from their colleagues finally had their paralysis break, and they ran for the now-open door that was cracked straight down its middle. The room was brightly lit with most of the lamps on the floor and the emergency Klieg lighting smashed into the white-painted drywall of the room. Blood and bodies were everywhere. They jumped over the remains of Herb Avery and came to a stop. President Hadley had moved from his blood-soaked bed and was standing at the dressing table in front of a full-length mirror, and he was slipping on a white shirt over the blood-soaked pajama top. His pajama bottoms were at his ankles. He was slowly buttoning his shirt, and amid the blood and carnage around him, he was singing a soft tune that was barely audible.

He turned from the mirror with the white shirt that obviously belonged to someone else and slowly made his way to the closet. He opened the antique doors and started rummaging around inside.

The silver hair was askew, and the six-week-old growth of beard made Hadley look twenty years older than his seventy-two years.

The two doctors were quickly followed inside by three hostage rescue members, and they too were not only stunned by the carnage inside the room but also by the sight of the former president as his ass wiggled in front of the dressing closet. Even more upsetting was that he was singing. Most of the older men knew the song immediately, only instead of the fast pace the music called for, Hadley was singing in a slow, beautiful harmonic of the original. Neil Sedaka had one of his largest hits in 1962 with "Breaking Up Is Hard to Do," and Hadley was now doing a credible imitation. The voice seemed to come from the throat of someone else as he sang with ever-increasing power.

A doctor, a naval commander from Bethesda, took a step toward the president, and just as he reached his hand out to touch his back, Hadley suddenly turned and faced the shocked man. His eyes were frantic as the words to the song stopped.

"I can't find my letterman's jacket!"

The doctor flew backward and fell over one of the bodies that had been casually thrown to the floor. The other doctor and a hostage rescue team man tried to help him up, but Hadley was there first and stood over the fallen doctor.

"I can't be late!" Hadley screamed with spittle flying from his mouth. "I was late before and look what happened!"

"Jesus!" the other hostage rescue member said as he took a step away from the three men and the seemingly possessed man they faced.

"I can't be late; I can't let her down!"

The syringe caught Hadley in midsentence, and his mouth worked, but no more words came free of it.

A doctor from downstairs had finally arrived with a powerful sedative. He held Dean until he relaxed, and then the strength in Dean's legs gave out and he collapsed into the doctor's arms.

"God . . . please . . . please, she's out there, I . . . I . . . have to . . . go."

The words trailed away along with the consciousness of a very disturbed man.

As doctors and other staff ran up the stairs to face the aftermath of this new attack, Catherine Hadley fought to get down those same stairs. She finally hit the bottom step when she was almost knocked from her feet. Just as several nurses started forward to assist her, she quickly feigned illness and then just as quickly stumbled toward her office.

She paused at the door for effect and then waved the concerned medical people away as she opened the door and entered. As she closed it behind her, she had an inward smile. Her eyes immediately went to the last, unsigned legal document on the desk.

She shocked herself when a small, girlish giggle escaped her mouth.

"You did earn your percentage, didn't you, Herb?"

PART II

ATTENDANCE IS MANDATORY

So Mr. . . . Mr. DJ, keep those records playin',
'Cause I'm a-havin' such a good time dancin' with my
baby . . .

—SAM COOKE,
"Having a Party,"
#20 Billboard Top Hits, 1962

6

MORENO, CALIFORNIA

It was two thirty in the morning when the last of the California Highway Patrol, San Bernardino Sheriff's, and the Chino, Ontario, and Pomona fire departments and rescue services left the town of Moreno. Bob and Linda Culbertson stood watching as the last of the official vehicles left with all of them heading toward the interstate. Both private security people saw old man Leach watching from the third floor of Newberry's, where Harvey kept his private quarters.

Linda lowered her cell phone and shook her head. "Cell service is even worse than it was before. It took four hours, but I finally got through to the home office."

Bob's eyes lingered on Harvey across the street until he saw the light go out on the third floor. He finally turned and, with a yawn, waited for Linda to finish.

"Evidently, there are some sort of legal arguments going on about the ownership of the land that the town sits on. Something about a freeze on all properties pertaining to a certain real estate firm. They say to hang tight and they will be in touch."

"They didn't say anything about our request? It's only a few days we're talking about here. This place has stood for seventy years; a week or two won't make any difference."

"They said remain until the contract expires, or until the legal entanglements are finished. Either way, I think we're screwed."

Bob shook his head and turned back to the darkness beyond the window. "Something is going on here, babe, I feel it." He turned toward the cherub face of his wife. "You feel it too. So does Harvey." He looked toward the department store once more through the last light of the dying moon. "Missing teenagers. People dying on Main Street. Private investigator up and vanishing. We've been here for ten years, and in all that time, nothing like this has happened. And now we have three incidents in less than a week. And there's other things going on also."

Linda placed the cell phone down just as the bars indicating cell service availability went to zero. She shook her head and looked at Bob. "You saw it too, didn't you?" she asked.

"The lights of the theater marquee? Phones ringing in houses that haven't had power to them in over fifty years? Music playing where it shouldn't be playing? Hell, even the radio station is starting to give me the creeps. I even heard——"

"The DJ and music coming from the back?"

"You heard it too, then?" Bob said, finally turning away from the window. He felt the relief flood into his thoughts, knowing he hadn't started going insane—at least not alone.

"I hear things lately that are impossible. School bells ringing. Cars hot-rodding up and down the street when there isn't a vehicle anywhere near Moreno. I thought I was finally losing it being alone in this place. It used to be peaceful and tranquil in a cemetery sort of way, but now it has the opposite feel. It's turned oppressive and dark."

Bob saw the way Linda turned and stared off into the darkness beyond the glass and noticed that his wife, a woman not fearful of anything in the world outside of running low on coffee, was scared.

"The next incident that happens, they can take the last pay cycle and completion bonus and shove it up their asses. We'll take the loss as long as we get to someplace where there are people"—he gestured at the street beyond the protection of the glass—"not this powder keg."

"Powder keg?" Linda asked as she turned back to face Bob.

"Can't you feel it? It's like this place is building toward a detonation of . . . of . . . something, and I don't think I want to be here when it goes off. A week, and we're gone, no matter what."

"Deal."

As both Bob and Linda turned away from the window, they froze as the sound hit their ears. Through the coldness of the glass, the vibration had started. Then the music was as discernable as if it were coming through the speakers of their own stereo system. They both jumped when the old neon sign in the window flashed to blinking life as if a switch had been thrown. *K-Rave—Fifteen Thousand Watts of Music Power* came to its full bright red illumination with a humming that comes with neon lighting. And in the back of the radio station, through the triple-pane glass of the DJ booth, they heard the music and knew exactly what it was. Then the voice of the disc jockey came through the air, and it froze both security people in their tracks. The opening refrains of the instrumental intro were covered by the voice that sent chills down their spines.

"And now a slight blast from the past, from 1957, Mr. Buddy Holly and his gargantuan hit, 'Everyday' . . . bring it back home to Lubbock, Buddy."

Every day, it's a-getting closer, going faster than a roller coaster, love like yours will surely come my way . . . a-hey, a-hey, hey . . . hey . . .

The neon light blinked three times and then went dark once again as the music faded away to nothing. Of the gravelly voiced DJ, there was silence as the music, along with Buddy Holly, left the building.

Bob and Linda reached for the cell phone at the same time. They had to get someone to listen to their tale so they could leave this place. They soon gave up when they failed to adequately reach a distant cell tower. They even tried the landline from the wall-mounted pay phone, but it too was on the fritz—not an unusual circumstance, as the lines in and out of Moreno were seventy-year-old technology.

They didn't know it, but the fuse to that powder keg about which Bob was so worried had already had been lit . . . it had been burning since that night back in 1962, and that fuse was growing ever shorter.

It was five days until Halloween.

TEN MILES EAST OF QUANTICO, VIRGINIA

None of the eight frightened people had ever been in a military transport before. The UH-60 Black Hawk helicopter swept low over the Virginia countryside, and most of its passengers were happy that it was still pre-dawn so the imminently close ground wasn't visible. John, who was deathly afraid of heights and flying in general, held Jenny's hand as a reminder not to scream like a schoolgirl every time the Black Hawk dipped and rose over the trees. The U.S. Army crew chief watched the civilians with a smirk on his face, as they all looked as if they had boarded the world's riskiest roller coaster ride. The young specialist had seen these people on television and thought they lacked the necessary demeanor to be ghost hunters. The intrepid investigators were all frightened of a simple helicopter ride.

Gabriel saw the lights of the compound and its illuminated circular landing pad, and then he saw the cordon of U.S. military personnel waiting below.

The crew chief unplugged his helmet from the comm system and sprang for the door as it was slid open from the outside. He hopped out and assisted the three women first and then let the men stumble out for themselves. It was the first time the helicopter crew had provided transport to a shipload of nerds.

"Professor Kennedy?" a man said, the blades of the helicopter spoiling his finely coifed hair.

"I'm Kennedy."

"Sir, I'm Special Agent Jim Lipscomb, FBI. The director asked that I make sure you have everything you need."

Kennedy followed the agent and had to stop and turn when everyone else hesitated, and then they reluctantly fell in line. The group approached the large manor house that had been utilized by the FBI many times but never for anything remotely resembling what was happening now.

As the beating rotors of the Black Hawk helicopter became nothing more than background noise as it lifted back into the air, Gabriel managed to stop the agent before they reached the backyard and pool area of the house.

"Isn't the director going to join us?" he asked as the others caught up with them. The agent looked as if he were not going to answer at first. Then he leaned in closer to Gabriel.

"The director posted his resignation while in the air from California, sir."

"He quit?" Damian asked, worry crossing his features.

The agent said nothing, but turned and went into the house.

"I guess not having any answers drives some to the extreme," Gabriel said to no one. "Someone should have welcomed him to our world." He followed the agent inside.

The back entryway was filled with men and women. Some were dressed in black Nomex commando gear and others in dark suits. They all looked tired and haggard from whatever it was that was killing the former commander in chief. They were drinking coffee or standing in a small line in the kitchen with plates in their hands, getting ready to eat breakfast. They all eyed the motley group that came in the back way. The newcomers, in turn, studied a group of people that looked to be in a war zone—that forever tired and weary look a soldier gets after months of hard combat.

As the Supernaturals looked at the faces around them, there was one they all recognized. The First Lady—or former, if you like—stood in the kitchen doorway. She was looking straight at them. She also looked tired, but not like the others in the large space and in the kitchen. She was more focused on the group. Her eyes didn't hold hope; they looked as if they held contempt. With an upturn of her upper lip, one that could have been considered a sneer in most circles, she abruptly turned and left. Her assistant was right behind her.

"How is she taking all of this?" Jennifer asked as she watched the swinging door to the kitchen and pantry as it came to a stop after the departure of the First Lady.

"That's not my place to say, ma'am," the agent said. They could see in the way he spoke and the seriousness in his eyes that he had a very low opinion of the former First Lady. "We have the main library set up for your team, Professor. Every inch of video, disc, written eyewitness reports, and the sum of our investigations has been provided."

Gabriel looked from the agent to Leonard and nodded. The diminutive black man took the agent by the arm as Kennedy led the others out of the crowded room and to the large hallway.

"Look, I know that lady has a lot on her plate, but there are certain things I need from her."

"Such as?" the agent asked, not liking the fact that it involved Catherine Hadley.

"Such as family records—health, financial, legal, and other things that were placed into a blind trust when Hadley came into office."

"President Hadley."

"Excuse me?" Leonard said.

"He's still called the president."

Leonard smiled, and then he laughed and slapped the FBI agent on the shoulder as he started to follow Gabriel and the others. "Whatever you say, chief, but the man is an asshat that deserves everything he gets." Sickles stopped and momentarily lost his smirk. "Well, maybe not *everything*, but don't look to me to have respect for a man that ruined the economy, ruined the office, and is a cheating bastard. You worked for him; I did not. Now get with the queen and explain to her what I need. Provide it so I don't have to start digging into closets they don't want opened."

The special agent watched the black man vanish through the door and shook his head.

The library was large—enough so that George and Damian whistled simultaneously. Books from floor to ceiling lined the walls. Long tables had been set up with no fewer than ten computers. Printers, large-screen monitors, and phones were abundant.

Leonard entered the room and with Agent Lipscomb close behind. The agent closed the large sliding doors behind him as the noise and murmuring were cut off from the hallway and the rest of the house. Sickles didn't wait. He removed his jacket and tossed it on an antique couch and went directly to one of the four PCs. Leonard became angry but held that anger in check when he saw two of his personal laptops sitting in the table. He gave Kennedy an "I told you so" look but sat down nonetheless. He immediately started tapping commands on the keyboard. Gabriel nodded, as Leonard was now in his element—one of gigabytes and specialty programs of the criminal world. Yes, Leonard was at home.

"Professor, we have a team of researchers from Quantico standing by to assist you in—"

"I think for those of us not too tired from our travels and our prison breakout, we would like to see the president and his current condition."

The agent looked at Kennedy and nodded as he turned for the doors.

"We also need most of these people cleared out of the house. Send them outside or wherever, but get them out, all except for security for the president; I'll leave that up to you how many that is."

"If I had my way, it would be a battalion of marines." The agent finally nodded. "Hell, as nothing seems to be able to stop whatever it is, it really doesn't matter; most will be happy to get out."

Gabriel he reached for the aluminum case that had been delivered from Joint Base Andrews ahead of them. He opened it and then presented the agent with a stapled grouping of papers. "I also need the attorney general, the head of the FBI, and the Secret Service to sign these within the next hour, or I gather my people and we'll head back to face justice in Los Angeles."

"What are these?" Lipscomb asked as he looked at the differing pages.

"Release forms. They were drawn up while we were in the air and faxed to the plane. No matter the outcome of this investigation, we cannot be held responsible for any harm that may befall that man up there," Gabriel said as he pointed at the ceiling and the bedrooms. Kennedy produced one more set of papers and handed them to the agent. "This is for the general accounting office."

"And this is?"

"Our terms of service." Gabriel smiled at the others. "Since this is our final investigation as a team, we need to get paid."

"And rather handsomely too," Lipscomb said as his eyes found the numbers Kennedy was demanding. "One million apiece?"

"Nonnegotiable."

"That means you deal, or we walk," John Lonetree said as he stepped up to the agent.

"And if you just happen to prove this is a farce, that he is nothing more than insane and incompetent, you'll receive a one-million-dollar bonus per person. That's in addition to your fee."

They all turned to see that a back door had been opened and Catherine Hadley stood in the doorway with her arms crossed over her chest. She stepped into the room, closing the door on her female assistant before she could follow. She walked in and eyed the Supernaturals one at a time, and that look said she was not impressed. She paused in front of Kennedy. She did not offer her manicured hand for shaking.

"A farce?" Kennedy asked as he exchanged curious looks with Lonetree.

"You and the FBI are not the only ones capable of theorizing and doing research, Professor. My belief is that this is happening through Dean and Dean alone." She said this last with a look of disdain for the people she was meeting with. "It is highly possible he is doing this himself. Surely through your books and your reporting, you know it is far more likely that his brain is conjuring up all of this. You say it yourself, Professor—hauntings are mostly wishful thinking. This is nothing more than a child going through puberty, as your theory would suggest. Only instead of puberty, it's just plain old senility and brain trauma from his war years in Vietnam. He's insane. Nothing more. It's the president that is causing this, not ghosts."

"So, you don't believe the theory cast about by the authorities that this is an outside attack by a foreign power or source?" Damian asked for Gabriel, who was busy sizing up the woman almost as hated publicly as the president himself.

"Not at all. Why do this when he was on the way out anyway? As you know, he was going to be impeached eventually but had decided to resign before that. What would a foreign government hope to achieve?"

"A test, perhaps. Maybe they just tested this offensive strike before hitting a real target," the FBI agent infused into the conversation with one of the opinions forwarded by CIA and his own office, "like the sitting president or someone in intelligence."

"That theory is nothing but horseshit." Leonard continued to slash away at three out of the six keyboards in front of him.

"Excuse me, young man," the agent said. "I think we have a handle on this. Now it may not stand up to your higher scrutiny of how things work in the hood, but that's what most intelligence people think. This has to be outside influence."

John and Gabriel exchanged amused looks as Sickles stopped typing and turned to face the career FBI agent.

"The hood, huh?" Leonard said with a grin. "Let me explain something, my red-tape-bound friend. In the midsixties, a small group known as the Wheeler Team, a unit contracted by the CIA in July 1967, conducted unauthorized human testing on American military personnel in Germany—out of the way of nosy people, I guess. During those tests, they tried to project thought through space and time. They used drugs, hypnosis, and other nefarious ways to get substantially high ratings on telepathic ways and means. Never mind that the experiments cost no fewer than five soldiers their lives. For what? Nothing. Don't sit there and tell me something is viable when there is not one shred of evidence to support your theory outside of some whack-job doctors from the Middle Ages. No, this is not the work of some dark enemy in Moscow or Beijing. This is something that we've never come across before. Now say it with me . . . 'We just don't know.' It's not hard. 'We just don't know.'"

"And you seem to know a lot about classified data," the agent said, growing angry that he had been shown up.

"It's because all of us black folks in the hood are that way. We sit and sharpen our knives in our hangouts, and after we clean our AK-47s after our latest drive-by, we discuss all the new and unusual ways the enemy forces of the world can screw us up by gaining access to our minds. That's a high priority in the hood."

Gabriel smiled. "Okay, you made your point, Boy Wonder. Now get back to it."

"As distasteful as it is, I agree with this . . . gentleman," Catherine said, glancing toward Leonard. "I don't buy what the intel agencies suggest. It's psychosis, pure and simple."

"And he kills people in his sleep? That's taking Gabriel's theory to the extreme, don't you think?"

Catherine Hadley turned to face the smaller woman who had spoken. She smiled when she saw who it was. "Ah, the woman who was possessed. You tell me, Ms. . . . ?"

"Tilden, Professor Tilden," Jennifer said as she returned the smile even though the First Lady didn't mean it as a welcoming or friendly gesture in the slightest.

"As I was saying, Professor, the brain is a powerful thing; you of all people should know that. It can produce any number of physical and mental capabilities, and these are your own theories. So the faster you can declare the president mentally unstable, the sooner we can get him some real help."

Jenny was about to respond to the slight when she caught the look from Gabriel. She closed her mouth as John moved to her side.

"As I said, a one-million-dollar bonus to each of your team when you come to the obvious declaration of incompetence."

"And if our conclusions differ from the conclusion you have arrived at?" George asked, worrying about the wording of the offer.

Catherine smiled and then left the library.

"Leonard?" Gabriel turned for the double sliding doors.

"I'm on it," he said, never even looking up from the computer screens, which were all operating now.

"On what?" Julie Reilly and Kelly Delaphoy asked at the same moment.

"On just why our illustrious former First Lady wants her husband declared insane and thus incompetent to run his affairs. Just what does she have to gain besides the obvious divorce?"

"Motivation?" Damian asked as Gabriel pulled the doors open.

"Money, of course," Kennedy said as the others came toward the door. "Now shall we go see the president?"

Kennedy and the others went up the stairs, passing no fewer than twenty security men in their black Nomex fatigues and carrying M4 assault rifles. Julie held Kelly's hand as they stepped from one riser to the other.

The hallway was even more crowded than the stairs or even down in the kitchen. These men were a combination of very lethal-looking FBI hostage rescue team members, ten combat-ready marines, and no fewer than fifteen Secret Service agents. None of these groups looked like they wanted to be there. They saw Special Agent Lipscomb standing by the door of a bedroom. He was waiting for them.

"How many people are inside?" Gabriel asked as the other seven gathered around them.

"Two nurses, one doctor, and six security."

"With the exception of the security detail, we need to see the president in private."

Lipscomb nodded and then entered his security code into the doorway locking mechanism. The door opened, and Julie and Kelly smelled a familiar odor; it was like the subbasement of Summer Place. It was as if death were waiting for them right inside the brightly illuminated room. With a look at the others, Kennedy stepped inside.

The doctor and the nurses protested, but they eventually left with the promise that the door would remain unlocked for them to get back inside quickly if they were needed. Lipscomb then left the room, closing the door behind him. The six-man security team eyed the newcomers but kept their distance from the overly large bed and its occupant.

The president lay in bed with the blankets pulled up to his shoulders. His right arm was free of the covers and hooked up to an IV, which Jennifer went to and she eyed the two plastic bags full of doctor-ordered intravenous drip. She looked up at Gabriel.

"Saline to keep his veins open and a nutrient to keep him fed. No medicines or painkillers." She turned from the stand that held the IV bottles and faced the group. She reached for the chart at the foot of the bed and read. "Vitals are erratic at best. Yesterday he received an opiate for pain. How they came to the conclusion he was in pain is beyond me," she mumbled. "His temperature fluctuates in leaps and bounds. I'll have to compare these stats with video and see if these spikes in temperature coincide with the attacks. The damn doctors aren't noting the obvious here." Jenny went to John, and he handed her the black bag. She removed a stethoscope and went to the side of the bed and looked down on the former president.

John and the others joined her as she took Hadley's vitals. The man looked well beyond his seventy-two years. His brows were untrimmed, and that alone made him look insane. His pajama top was wet with perspiration.

"His temperature is up some from the last reading taken fifteen minutes ago," Jenny said as she released Hadley's wrist and then gently laid it aside. Gabriel saw something on the bedsheet and then pulled the covers back. He nodded at Jenny for her to continue her examination. She slowly unbuttoned the blue pajama top. When she finished, she took a deep breath and then raised the white T-shirt underneath.

Jenny slowly peeled away the gauze and the tape covering the recently received wounds. They all saw the healing scabs and stitches from the assault two weeks before. They saw the ugliness and how deep the cuts must have been. It looked as if he had been carved on. Even the security men in the room looked away from the sight.

" 'Trick or Treat,' " Damian said aloud. "Is it just me or is anyone else getting a little tired of these Halloween surprises?"

"Brutal," Julie said as she stepped closer to get a few pictures.

Jenny lowered the T-shirt and then buttoned Hadley's pajama top. She took a deep breath as she quickly examined the other injuries sustained by the assaults.

"You know, nothing we have seen goes against the First Lady's ideas on the brain," John said as he watched Jenny work.

"In my line of work, there has never been a case of this kind of aggression against a host," Kelly said as she finally broke away from the group and approached the bed to look at Hadley. Kennedy smiled when he saw her paralysis concerning her supposed betrayal was now gone, or at least closeted for the time being. "Outside of our own experience at Summer Place, there is not one documented case of physical harm coming from a haunting. The First Lady may be right in her assumptions that it's him doing this, not anything supernatural."

"George, do you want to take a crack and see if he's feeling anything?" Gabriel asked a staring Cordero, who didn't look too enthused about getting too close to Hadley.

George swallowed and nodded reluctantly. Jenny and the others made room as Cordero stepped to the bed, closed his eyes, and took the exposed wrist of the president. His eyes remained closed as he concentrated. He never, ever tried to see into someone's thoughts while they were asleep. When he had tried it in the past, he came away with a confused and jumbled look at a person's warped view of their lives through their dreams, and he didn't care for the secrets that most had; even if they were unconscious and unfettered thoughts, they still disturbed him to no end. He had learned that the base human thoughts when not controlled by wakefulness are those of violence and death.

He grimaced as a vision popped into his head. It was Jennifer. George tilted his head as if he were trying to understand something. He flinched and then released Hadley's wrist as he stepped back. He looked at Jenny.

"What is it?" John asked when he saw the worried face of Cordero.

"Hadley just named everyone in the room. It was like he was reading attendance for a class. After each name, he would say, 'Present.' He didn't mention Leonard, but he did mention someone else."

"Bobby Lee McKinnon," John said, not as a question but as a fact. Jenny looked from George to John.

"You knew?" she asked as the others looked on very surprised at the announcement.

"You talk in your sleep." Lonetree took Jenny's shoulder and squeezed. "I figure Bobby Lee came home to roost about two years ago, and he's once again gaining strength. Reapplying the hold he had on you."

They all knew that the ghost of the old rock-and-roll legend had been a part of Jennifer's soul for years. He had vanished when confronted by the evil inside Summer Place, and they thought Jenny's curse was finished for good. But it was now obvious that the ghost that attached itself to her during a routine investigation many years before had indeed returned. Bobby Lee McKinnon, while not evil, had almost cost Jenny her life through the use of her life force.

Kelly let out a yelp of surprise when President Hadley sat straight up in bed. He reached out and grabbed the hand of George Cordero and then with tremendous pressure squeezed it. George looked as if he had been hit by an electrical charge, hard enough that John reached out to steady him, but Kennedy stopped him.

"Let him communicate," Gabe said as he released John's hand.

"Sing it for me, sing it for . . . her."

They watched as the words spilled from the mouth of the clairvoyant. They were those of a much younger George, but they were clear and extremely intelligible. Cordero opened his eyes and looked straight at Jennifer.

"From the valley to the sea, from the Inland Empire to the streets of Tinseltown, here's Bobby Lee McKinnon and the Spotlights."

Before they could react, Jenny was pushed against the wall, where she crashed into one of the security men who reached out to help her, but again Kennedy stopped the man from assisting. "Leave her!" he said too loudly.

Somewhere . . . beyond the sea, somewhere waiting for me, my lover stands on golden sands . . .

They heard the male voice as it broke free from Jenny's mouth. In the corner, Julie Reilly went to her phone and started tapping out commands, as she too recognized the voice of Bobby Lee McKinnon and also the song. The voice died away, and the look on Jennifer's face was one of pain and shock as she just as suddenly snapped out of her trancelike state and slid down the wall. John rushed toward her and pushed the security man out of his way and assisted Jenny to her feet. She cried and leaned hard into Lonetree. Hadley slowly smiled and lay back onto the bed.

"Bobby Lee McKinnon will be live! Be there or be square!"

They watched as a peaceful look came into the president's face as he finally released George's hand from the viselike grip. Hadley's remote mouthpiece stumbled back and was caught by Gabriel.

The room came alive with motion as John moved Jenny away from the wall and George Cordero slumped into a nearby chair with the help of Kennedy. Gabriel then went immediately to check on Jenny and then stood and raced toward Julie. She held the phone out to him. She hit the right button, and the song started playing so all could hear it. The abbreviated verse stopped, and then Julie looked at Kennedy and then the others as she read from her phone.

"'Beyond the Sea,' recorded in 1959 by Bobby Darin." She hesitated as she looked from Gabriel to a frightened Jennifer. "Cowritten and scored by Bobby Lee McKinnon in New York. Bobby Lee wrote that song for Bobby Darin in the latter half of 1958."

"Oh, God, he is back," Jenny said as she buried her face into Lonetree's chest.

"And Bobby Lee's been invited to God knows what along with the rest of us."

All eyes once more went to Kennedy, but he wasn't done with his summation just yet as he walked over and looked down on President Hadley.

"I think we can rule out the Russians."

7

As dawn broke over the Inland Empire, there was more activity in Moreno, except for the bizarre traffic deaths the night before, than there had been since the first part of November 1962. Bob and Linda, with very little sleep under their belts from the night before, stood at what they now referred to as the haunted window at the front of the radio station / record store. They each had a large mug of coffee as they watched the activity outside. Every few seconds one or the other of them would allow their eyes to drift toward the broken neon sign in the window. Thus far, there had not been a flicker, and they were both silently happy for that. They saw Harvey Leach step through the glass doors of Newberry's. He still wore a bathrobe and pajama bottoms as he too sipped his coffee and watched the few remaining residents of Moreno leave for good.

The last four families, two of them with husbands and fathers that drove long-distance big rigs, had been up most of the night packing so they could get out in front of the traffic the next morning. The last of these families left as the sun crested the ruins of the Grenada Theater.

"This couldn't have been spurred on by the accident last night," Linda said as she finally turned away from the sad sight of the last of their friends and neighbors leaving them. "Do you think they have heard and seen the things that we have the past few weeks?" she asked as she refilled her coffee and started for the back rooms where she would get dressed.

With a deep breath, Bob turned from the window and faced his retreating wife's ample behind. "I wouldn't bet against it. Too much strange crap for just us and Harvey to have seen it. Half the families lived only a block or two from the church."

"Oh, you mean the church that was burned down and hasn't had a bell to ring in four decades, but it rings anyway for the past week—that church?" she said as she slammed the door to their modest bedroom.

"Yeah, that one," he mumbled to himself as he tasted the coffee, made a face, and then placed the mug on the counter as the first real rays of light burst through the glass. He watched Harvey across the street shake his head and then sadly turn for the doors of Newberry's. The last of his regular customers were skipping town.

It seemed Moreno was dying for the second time. This one was a slower coup de grâce compared to the sudden death in 1962.

Deep in the darkness of the basement of the Grenada, the filthy standing water began vibrating. The rats had long fled the basement for the upper reaches of their once richly appointed accommodations. The expended energy from the night before had sapped the power of the morning's awakening. It was learning fast what it needed to know from the nocturnal visits in the east. Now its strength was ebbing at low tide. It found new and entertaining information in that its enemy was gathering resources to help combat that which went unseen. This was a development that the entity had not foreseen. It was still weak and depended on the active vault inside the old winery for power.

Soon, together, both trapped entities would be powerful enough to break free of their confinement for good. The voice from the basement whispered its desire.

One mile away and up the hill unofficially known as Drunk Monk's Road, in the old winery ruins next to the Santa Maria Delarosa mission, the whispering of many could be heard in answer to the call from the theater not far away. There were no rats running in fear here, for they had abandoned the ruins more than fifty years before.

The ten-ton vault lurched in its floor mountings as the crescendo of voices spoke at once as the whispering from far below inside the town continued. The entity heard the young voice and heard her desires.

Then all at once, the movement and the whispering stopped as suddenly as it had started.

VIRGINIA COUNTRYSIDE

The house had become silent as the breakfast hour passed without further incident. The group of people that had arrived late the night before had remained in the bedroom after their unsettling incident in the early morning hours. The security personnel were already weary of the newcomers and stayed as far away from them as they could.

Gabriel looked at his watch and then the cold cup of coffee in his hand. He placed the cup down, stood, and stretched. He went over to the far corner, and after excusing himself to the black-clad FBI security man, he leaned over and tapped John on the shoulder. The large man looked up and then eased Jennifer's sleeping head from his shoulder and stood, softly placing her head on the arm of the small love seat where she had finally dozed off. As John moved away with Kennedy, they were joined by both Julie Reilly and Kelly Delaphoy. George had excused himself some time before eight that morning to see if he could find the liquor cabinet and, with a warning look from Gabe, went to find it.

"How is she doing?" Gabriel asked John as they stood by the bathroom door.

With a look at Julie, John nodded. The move was overexaggerated, and Kennedy noticed it.

"She's—"

"She's been exhibiting signs for months now," Julie said, cutting John's overly enthusiastic answer off at the knees.

"That right, John?" Gabriel asked.

He nodded silently as his eyes went over to a sleeping Jenny. "Yeah, she stares at herself in the mirror more than she should. She hums and sings songs when she doesn't even realize she's doing it."

"You have to have more than that," Kennedy said, growing frustrated at having to dig answers out of Lonetree.

"Hell, I don't think Bobby Lee ever left her. He's just been lying low, and the stress of being on the run has made it nearly impossible for her to hide the fact anymore."

"Is that what you think?" Gabe asked Julie, who nodded.

"She also talks in her sleep when she thinks John's out. I heard her more than once. It's nothing threatening. Bobby just comes out and talks. It seems like she enjoys it, if you ask me."

"Well, we differ on that point. I want the bastard out of her."

Kennedy walked over and looked down on Jenny as she slept. "Does she sleep well?" he asked.

"You mean does Bobby Lee drive her to insomnia?" John said, shaking his head. "No. It's not like before; he doesn't force her to sing or lie awake at night with his incessant complaining about how unfair his life and death had been."

Gabriel turned away and nodded at both John and Julie. "I'll talk to her later. The only reason I'm concerned is the fact she refused to tell me about the reoccurrence. And she obviously didn't feel confident enough to inform you of the truth."

"Maybe we should—" Julie began to say, but the deep male voice stopped her cold.

The voice was so different that the FBI hostage rescue team man took a sideways step when he realized the man's voice was once more springing from the small woman lying on the love seat.

"Maybe you should leave her the hell alone, Dr. Schweitzer," said the voice from the perfect face of Jenny, whose eyes were moving at a rapid rate underneath her eyelids.

Gabriel turned and went back to the love seat where Jennifer lay with her small feet and legs curled up like a sleeping child.

"Bobby Lee, I thought we had a deal," Gabriel said as he stood over the diminutive anthropologist.

"You had a deal, man, not me."

The four hostage rescue team men exchanged looks as the deep male voice came from the small woman lying there. The heavily armed men took another step away.

"Bobby Lee, we may be into something here that could cause Jenny trouble. We need her alert and awake."

"You have more of a problem than that daddy-oh on that bed. I think that nutjob has an enemy you don't want to meet, that's what I think. I think my Jenny girl will need me. No offense, Chief Red Cloud."

John angrily shook his head. He and the old rock-and-roller had more than just a casual dislike for each other; it was almost as if they were romantic rivals of a sort. Gabriel turned and shook his head at Lonetree, that now was not the time to get into an argument with a tormented spirit.

"Why do you say 'enemy'?"

"I'm sayin' enemy because that's what this dude is facing, whoever this nutjob is. And I'm not sayin' that this McCarthy-type asshole doesn't deserve it." On the love seat, Jenny's brow furrowed. It looked as if, at least to Gabriel, she was trying to follow along with what tormentor was saying. "I don't know who's the bad guy here, man. It's not like your last adventure in that house of horrors you sissies called Summer Place." Jenny's arm raised from her prone position and pointed, first at one of the Nomex-clad security men, who moved farther away, and then at the bed and its occupant. "I get the vibe that this bastard is worse than even the men that killed me. You want to talk about ghosts, that dude has ghosts." The arm flopped down until the movement made Jennifer's eyes flutter open. She quickly sat up and looked at President Hadley as his chest rose and fell in a calm sleep. She blinked and looked at the four people standing over her.

John went to her and sat down. "How you doing?" he asked, taking her much smaller hand in his own. She shook out of it and stood and went to the bed. The doctor and the two nurses came out of their stupors of the early morning and stood from their chairs as she approached. When they saw she wasn't a threat, they backed away.

Jennifer stared down at the president, and then she turned to face the others. "Bobby Lee doesn't like him very much."

"How long, Jenny?" Gabriel asked as he joined her bedside.

"He never left, Gabe. I didn't want to tell you, or you," she said as she faced Lonetree. "I wasn't sure at first, but then I knew, either in dreams or while doing research. He was always there. Hell," she said as she ran a hand through her short hair, "maybe I even wanted him there. When I thought he had left that night in Summer Place, I felt I would be fine with it. I felt I wasn't whole any longer."

John closed his eyes, and then Jenny saw it and went to him. He smiled, a false gesture.

"Easy, John. Bobby Lee has no romantic interest in this haunted vessel you call your girlfriend; he's always been interested in others," she said as she turned and faced both Julie Reilly and Kelly Delaphoy. They exchanged horrified looks.

"We need to know what drove this man to the point it opened him up to this attack," Gabriel said to change the sore subject, at least for John's sake. He couldn't help but give a teasing smile to both Kelly and Julie over Bobby Lee's choice of romantic possibilities.

"Leonard should have a starting point for us by now." Kennedy faced Jenny. "Is Bobby Lee going to be a hindrance, or is he going to help us?"

"Who in the hell knows? Remember the last time the little bastard skipped out right when the going got tough?" Lonetree said as he held Jenny's hand.

Jennifer's eyes flared bright momentarily, but then they settled as she squeezed his hand.

Kennedy gestured that they should leave.

As they started for the door, Gabriel noticed that Kelly Delaphoy stayed behind as she slipped on her sweater. He saw that it was intentional. She smiled, lost it, and then attempted it again.

"What is it?" he asked as he waited by the door.

With a wary glance at the others in the room, she took a step closer to Kennedy. "I'm so sorry for letting you down and getting the rest of them caught."

"You said it wasn't intentional; we can all live with that."

"Still, I wasn't as tough as I, or you, thought I was. I'm out of my league here. At least Julie has a track record of research and reporting. What am I? I'm a television producer who has screwed up everything I have ever touched in my life."

Kennedy understood that Kelly felt she wasn't much help to the team. He had found that her insight into how to sham a television audience had become invaluable in their work. Without her expertise, they would have been hard put to disprove any of the hauntings they had declared as hoaxes.

"You let me worry about who is valuable and who isn't. What do you want me to do, replace you with Bobby Lee McKinnon?"

Kelly smiled as she hugged Gabriel and then patted his belly. "You go ahead; I think I'll stay and keep an eye on our Mr. Wonderful for a while. One of us should be with him at all times."

Kennedy smiled and then adjusted his glasses. "Okay, I'll have someone relieve you in a while. I sent Damian on an errand, and he should be back by tomorrow morning. We'll have more eyes to help then."

Kelly watched as Gabe left, and then she looked over at the man in the bed. The hostage rescue team members were watching her as well as the two nurses and one doctor. She went over to the love seat that had been previously occupied by Jennifer and sat down. She again adjusted the sweater to the morning chill and then watched and listened to the heart monitor as it gave out its steady beeping.

Leonard wasn't tired. He went from one computer to the next and then read what was there. When he got what he needed, he would hit the Print button, and the copier set up in the corner would come to life. The computer genius was in his element, and he was determined to get as much information as he could. Kennedy always pushed him for more, and acting as though the request had always been too much, Leonard always smiled and dove into his work. If there were any people out there who thought they could hide information from him, they usually found out the hard way that they were wrong. He had only been disturbed once, and that was by Catherine Hadley as she stepped in to see what Leonard was up to. He eased the woman out of the study and then closed the door behind her. She was Gabe's problem and one he didn't have time for. He barely glanced up from his work when the others entered the room. George Cordero entered from the opposite door with a croissant in his hand as Gabriel pulled the sliding doors closed.

"Sorry, but I was starving. Did I miss anything?" he asked, finishing off the last of the croissant and then going to the coffeemaker in the far corner. John and Gabriel took a seat at the long table as Leonard continued to piece together his first report. "Do you know those people are eating steak and eggs out there? And you wonder why our budget deficit is so out of control."

"I'm sure that the supercarriers and out-of-control costs on fighter planes, coupled with overpaid members of Congress, have nothing to with it," Lonetree said as his animosity for federal spending came to the forefront.

"Reserve your opinion until you see the size of those steaks," George said as he too sat down with his coffee.

"Maybe with the situation you could say they are eating well for the simple reason it could be their last meal," Jennifer said not too jokingly as she and Julie Reilly sat down. "How many deaths are attributable to this event now—eight?"

George stared at the small woman and nodded to indicate that, indeed, he had not thought of that.

Finally, Leonard looked up and noticed everyone. He shook his head and then went to the coffee station and poured himself a cup. This was strange because the small computer man never drank anything but Mountain Dew. They saw three large binders sitting in front of Leonard as he sipped the bitter coffee. He made a face and then dumped at least half a dispenser of sugar into the black liquid.

"What do you want first—possible motive or the fact that everything we've been told about our illustrious leader is a lie? With the exception of his military and college records, everything has been falsified and done so in the most ingenious ways."

Leonard looked up and saw that his announcement was met with shock and a bit of skepticism. He picked up the first paper bundle that had been bound with plastic covers. He slid the report down to Gabriel, who made no move to open it. His eyes went instead to the rear doors of the study, and then he fixed Leonard with a look. He slid the first report back. Sickles caught his meaning with the look at the back doors of the room.

"Ah, our lovely Mrs. Hadley."

"Let's find out first if we have roadblocks to the truth before we delve into the whys, hows, and whats of it."

"Well, the president, as you know, has to place his personal holdings, which are vast, into a blind trust before he takes the oath of office. His net worth three years ago was staggering. Fifty-two point seven billion dollars."

"That's with a *B*?" John asked as he stole Jenny's cup of coffee and sipped, ignoring her glare at his blatant theft.

"From what sources do these riches come?" Gabriel asked.

"Inheritance, mostly. It seems Hadley's father was the real entrepreneur here, not the son." Leonard sipped the horrid coffee again and then made a face but continued. "Although a lot of the accumulation of wealth came after the sixties and early seventies, it was from a diversified and well-guarded portfolio of stocks, bonds, and real-time companies that are nearly impossible to trace back to the Hadley family. Look at the bottom line on some of these companies and you'll find names like Lockheed Martin, HP, and others just as impressive. Dig deeper underneath those bottom lines, you get the name *Hadley* buried deeper than any name. Hadley Sr.'s start was the manufacture of specialty gauges, meters, and temperature readers for the federal government, and it expanded from there into other areas of manufacturing."

"Did Dean have a direct working relationship with his father?" Julie asked, beginning her methodic note taking as was her habit.

"Not at all beyond cashing checks, at least until the old man passed away in 1978. Then he took a cursory interest in the company, but no more than that. He liked being the fat cat but didn't like working for it. After Vietnam, not many people who knew him would blame him for not caring."

"What do you mean?" George asked.

Leonard reached behind him and came away with a folder and opened it. He held it for a moment as if he were about to show them a surprise. "That man up there in that bed was a stone-cold killer." He opened the folder and slid an eight-by-ten glossy to the middle of the long table. Everyone stood to get a good look. It was Hadley in his far younger years. He stood with four other men who were similarly dressed in green battle fatigues. Hadley was shirtless, and though the other three men smiled somewhat, he did not. The green beret on his head was tilted at a jaunty angle as he stared into the camera's lens. It was a trick of shadow, of course, but the eyes on Hadley the younger looked blank, dark, and distant.

"Fifth Special Forces Group. He was on detached service in 1968 and 1969 to the Ninth Infantry Division."

"What was his duty?" Gabriel asked as he studied the young face in the photo.

Leonard opened another file and then read from his report. "The army is going to come knocking at any time, by the way"—he held up the flimsy sheet of papers—"because all of this was buried so deep in the St. Louis record archives division they thought it was safe."

"Classified, I take it." John said as a statement rather than a question.

"Labeled by the army and the Ninth Infantry Division's S-1, he had the highest clearance. It seems our boy was on detached service to the Ninth because of his specific set of skills. This cat was good at infiltration and killing people our government thought were unworthy to keep breathing—behind enemy lines and also on the friendly side south of the DMZ."

"An assassin?" Julie asked as her pen stopped moving on her notepad.

"Our boy was far more than that. His debrief in Washington and recovered hospital records both noted the fact that the man never even had a rise in heartbeat when he killed. In other words, he enjoyed it."

"How did all of this not come out when his party vetted him when he declared to run for office?" Lonetree asked.

"How could they know or find out? Along with his military duties, his records before college were all falsified."

"By who?" Gabe asked.

"As far as I can see, it started with the father, Robert Hadley, and the old man's influence was such that he had his golden boy's exploits in Vietnam hushed up."

"It sounds as if—" Julie began.

"His exploits would have been in the way of an eventual goal."

"Are you suggesting, Leonard, that his father was grooming him for his eventual higher office pursuit even at that age?"

"Suggest, no. Prove? Yes." Leonard opened the second folder. "Here is a list of high school classmates." He slid this over to Julie Reilly and Kelly Delaphoy, the team's best researchers outside of Leonard himself. He also slid a copy of a newspaper report over. "That is from the small newspaper in Ontario, California, the same town where Hadley went to high school. When Hadley began his bid for the California Senate seat that eventually led to the presidency, this newspaper could find no one in the Chaffey High

School graduating class of 1963 that could remember Hadley. You would think that someone with that much money and clout would have been remembered, but not one classmate does. For the times, it was one damn big high school, but come on, no one?"

"Yearbooks?" Jenny asked as she retook the coffee from John's hand.

"Got them all online. Every year from 1959 to 1963; it lists Dean Hadley as absent the day of class pictures. It says it in the captions of every yearbook. But get this—only online versions of the yearbooks; the actual hard copies have no mention of him at all, including being absent for picture day. No pictures of activities but lists everything he accomplished. Then I started checking area high schools, because you always choose somewhere close to where you really lived for ease of memory if asked. I went through all the local high schools. Claremont, Upland, Pomona, then I hit on Chino High School in Chino, California. I broke into the Chino Valley Unified School District records office, and guess what?"

"They have a full record of Hadley being in school during those years," Gabriel said for him.

"Bingo, Prof, bingo." Leonard looked pleased with himself. "The one mistake in the whole chain was the small high school who didn't get the cover-up memo."

"This couldn't be another case of a changeling, you know, like Summer Place?" George asked, not looking too comfortable about the current subject at all. "Maybe he's not really Dean Hadley."

"Possible, I guess. But his blood type and his DNA were matched to that of Robert Hadley. This was done by the FBI after the attacks started just to cover all bases. Now they could also have been falsified, but I doubt it," Sickles said as he opened another binder. "Now the fortune as it stands. I eased my way into the IRS database, which you'll also hear about, I'm sure. Since the family fortune was placed in a blind trust, only the trustee has access to the data and money. That trustee is dead. Died two years ago, and then it went to the next man in line at the law firm involved." Again, Leonard slid the paperwork down the table and Gabe picked it up.

"Barnes, Johnson, and Avery?"

"The law firm. The last name there ought to be cause for concern, one that every investigative pencil pusher in Washington missed."

"Avery?" Kennedy asked as he tilted his head in thought. He quickly shuffled through his own pockets and came up with a sheet of paper that was given to him on the plane on the most recent attack before the one that had occurred the night before. He quickly found the name. "Is this ac-curate?"

"Already confirmed it. Herbert Avery was the son of the trustee and holder of the Hadley family fortune."

"And now he's dead," Gabriel said more to himself than to anyone else.

"The president's chief of staff?" Lonetree asked.

"The one and only."

"Money is the motive?" Julie asked as her reporter's hackles rose. "If it is, I don't see how anything like this could be pulled off."

"That's why we'll play those cards close to the vest for the time being."

"It seems we need to know about his earlier years and why the need to cover up the fact of his military duties and high school location. Also, Julie and Jenny can maybe get some information from the White House staff if they ask nicely enough. They may be more forthcoming than they were with the FBI or the Secret Service about the goings-on in the White House. Particularly the behind-closed-doors kind."

"That's a big leap of faith to think there may have been hanky-panky going on in the Lincoln Bedroom," George said.

"It's no big secret that the president and the First Lady were not at all close. Every wagging tongue in that cesspool of a city knew that Hadley only married that woman for political gain—well, maybe her looks also, but mostly because it helped his career to be married and settled. And to suggest that there may have been a scandalous relationship between the president's chief of staff and his wife? I say we'd better be careful with that one," Jennifer said. John looked at her and smiled, as she seemed to be her old self again.

"As I said, we'll send our two intrepid sleuths to find out," Gabriel said. "In the meantime, stay clear of the First Lady; she may already sus-pect that we suspect. And to tell you the truth, that woman doesn't sit right with me," Kennedy said as he slapped Leonard on the back. "Now all you have to do is come up with the missing time from school to war and where our friend Dean Hadley was in those years."

"On it, Professor Gabe."

"Since—"

The large house shook on its foundation, enough so that Kennedy al-most lost his footing. The gunfire erupted upstairs but only lasted as long as it took for Gabriel and the others to reach the sliding doors to the study.

They, along with a second team of FBI hostage rescue team members, bounded up the stairs. They were held back as they saw men trying in vain to open the bedroom door. John Lonetree, the largest man on the second floor, pushed past several stunned Secret Service men and threw his weight behind the effort. The door, as it had the night before, opened and then suddenly closed as it was pulled away. They could hear bumping, screaming, and one or two more gunshots. None of them had noticed that there was no power to the entire house. The sunlight illuminated the battle for the bedroom door.

"God, Gabe, Kelly's in there!" shouted Jenny, who was twisting her shirt into a ball as she watched John and the others struggle with the door.

The hall lights came on, and the men at the door managed push it all the way open. Most of the men stood in shock at the scene. Gabriel angrily pushed by them and entered the room. His eyes went to Hadley, who lay in bed, peacefully sleeping. The lone doctor was nowhere to be seen. The two nurses were there. One was clearly dead, her neck twisted in a cruel and unforgiving angle. She lay at the foot of the bed. The four hostage rescue team men were there also. One was screaming in the corner as he grasped his shattered arm. The other three lay in disjointed positions on the floor. One of these men sat up and looked at his weapon, a smaller version of the Israeli assault weapon, the Uzi. It was twisted and bent to an extreme that a machine would have been hard put to produce. The other men lay dead beside him. The hostage rescue team man tossed the useless weapon aside as he rolled over. He was helped to his feet by Lonetree, who pushed him toward the open door of the bedroom. Gabriel was there looking for Kelly.

She was nowhere to be found. Kennedy looked through the broken panes of glass of the window. He saw the fourth member of the hostage rescue team on the grass far below. His neck was also twisted into a grotesquerie. Gabriel came back inside, and John held him. He shook him, and then his eyes went to the bed and the two small feet sticking out from under it. He saw the blood and felt his heart freeze. Others were trying to push their way inside the bedroom but were held back as John and Gabriel leaned down and, as gently as they could, pulled Kelly out from under the bed. Gabe felt his bile rise from his stomach. John had to look away. There was no need to check for a pulse. There would be none, they could clearly see. Gabriel placed his elbows on his knees as he took in Kelly Delaphoy. She lay faceup, and the teeth marks were plain to see. She was covered in hundreds of them—enough so that her sweater and blouse were punctured. Gabriel could see the small imprints.

Gabriel lowered his head. He had now lost the first member of his team since the original night inside Summer Place with the loss of Warren, his student who had been eaten by the summer retreat. He considered Kelly's lifeless blue eyes, and then he stood up and pulled the blanket off a slumbering Dean, not caring about the man in the least. He put the blanket over Kelly and then turned for the door to allow the doctors inside. He grabbed the first one he could catch.

"I need the autopsy as soon as possible. I want measurements taken of those bite marks. I want the number of them and the size of the person or persons making them. Got that?" he said angrily as the doctor pried Gabriel's hand off his white coat and collar.

"Come on, Gabe. Let them have this for now."

As he pushed Kennedy through the door, he turned and looked at a peaceful Hadley as he lay on the bed with just a sheet covering him.

"Why not you, you son of a bitch?"

As John left the room, he knew deep down inside what he had to do, and he didn't care for the thought one bit. It would mean he might have to get inside the head of the man in the bed, and that scared him to no end.

The Supernaturals, only a few hours after agreeing to help, had lost their first member to the unseen assault.

Four hours later, Gabriel stood before a door in the manor house and looked from person to person. His people were in shock at how suddenly events had turned. During their many excursions together after Summer Place, they had become complacent to the danger still prevalent with unknowns. In this case, they had become so emboldened by those many hoaxes they had uncovered, they—or at least Gabriel—had forgotten the consequences of a closed mind. That point had now been driven home by the loss of Kelly.

"Before we head down there, I know how you're feeling. Kelly's loss is a rough pill to swallow; she was good at what she did. I am to blame for allowing the failures of our group to color my judgment. Kelly should not have been left in that room without one of us being with her."

"I think you're being a little hard on yourself." John stepped up to Gabriel and faced the others. He looked from George to Leonard and then to Julie and Jennifer. Everyone had red and swollen eyes from shedding tears over Kelly. "We all became complacent. We began doubting the power these people were describing. This is no haunting. This is a possession. By what? We don't know. But whatever it is, it directed its attack against Kelly. The attack was on all of us."

"A warning?" Julie asked as she stood a little closer to Gabriel.

"Maybe not a warning, because I don't think this thing has any natural fear of us or anyone. It's playing with us. The writing on the wall, the scratches and cuts on the president. The music lyrics. It wants us to learn. It wants us to know why. Whatever that man up there did, this thing hates him for it. The deaths of Kelly and the others are just a way of informing us that nothing will be able to stop it."

"Why would it want us to know? Just to get our attention?" George asked.

"It surely got mine," Gabriel said as he finally turned around and opened the door. He stopped before stepping onto the steel stairs heading down in the cold confines of the manor house basement. He faced everyone one more time. "You don't have to do this. Leonard, you most of all."

"Kelly was a lot of things, at least at first, but she proved to be a good friend for the past seven years. I owe it to her to go."

One by one, they nodded in agreement. They went down into the makeshift morgue that had become crowded after the last few days.

They were met at the bottom of the stairs by two plainclothes security men who checked the IDs around their necks. They passed through a curtained-off area and found themselves in a small room with a large window facing a cement floor that had three tables on it. They could see the bodies underneath the sheets. Several men and women were in scrubs but wore no masks. The taller of the five people turned and faced the glass.

"Professor Kennedy, stop me if something isn't clear enough for you, and we'll try another tack."

Gabriel nodded as the pathologist and one female assistant pulled back the sheet on the first of the three bodies. It was the torn remains of one of the hostage rescue team men.

"We only have three to view since the others are so dismembered the explanation as to their trauma would be superficial at best." The pathologist nodded at a far corner and the bodies there on tables.

The door hissed open behind them, and they were all shocked to see Catherine Hadley standing behind them. She had her female assistant beside her, and they stood and watched. The former First Lady nodded at Gabriel and then approached.

"Professor, I understand one of your own people was hurt this morning. I am—"

"Yeah, she was kind of hurt to death!" Leonard said, forgetting who he was talking to. The Secret Service agents outside started to open the door, but the woman waved them away through the clear glass.

"I understand that, Mr. Sickles, and I am truly sorry. Now you see how serious this is." She turned to face Gabriel. "This is why you need to recommend an induced coma, for safety's sake, or this will happen again. I have twenty professionals from all walks of psychology ready to declare Dean dangerous to not only himself but to others. I believe I'm quoting your own work, Professor, about the power of the mind when you said that the human brain is more than equipped to manifest everything that has happened here. Am I correct on this?" Her right brow rose in challenge.

"I believe I said that, yes, but your quote is from a much larger statement about how the research has to be carried out until all avenues have been exhausted. This research, I assure you, ma'am, has yet to even start. I lost a close friend here this morning, and we will find out why." He leaned down a little closer to Catherine Hadley. "Trust me, we'll learn all there is to know about your husband."

The First Lady looked from the glass to her assistant, and then they left the room.

"I really don't care for that woman," Jenny said as she and Julie exchanged looks.

"She does have a particular charm about her," Gabriel said in agreement.

The lead pathologist said, "As you can see, the spine was severed through blunt-force trauma at the sixth vertebra. The skin covering the neck was stretched to its elastic limit, and the separation of tissue occurred here. Whatever force was applied to this man was enough to completely remove the head from the torso."

"Why doesn't he just say his head was ripped from his body and save us all a lot of time?"

They all turned and looked at Leonard. Only George was agreeing by nodding. Gabriel turned away after a warning shake of his head at his young computer whiz. The pathologist allowed two of his assistants to roll the second body forward.

"The second victim, a white male of thirty-one, had the exact same damage as the first. The same with the nurse, Beth Sauer. The only difference being that Ms. Sauer's head remained attached." Finally, the third body was rolled forward. "This is the casualty I believe you are most interested in, as were we because of the unique trauma it sustained."

"Her name was . . . is Kelly," Julie said.

"I am sorry. Kelly." He looked at a chart on the gurney and then looked up. "Ms. Delaphoy sustained massive blood loss. I am sorry to say that she has possibly suffered the most painful of all the deaths thus far." The tall pathologist pulled the sheet back. Kelly was there without any clothing or covering. Gabriel closed his eyes, and Leonard turned and left the small viewing room. Jenny squeezed John's arm until he flinched. Julie allowed herself to start crying again. George attempted to steady himself by leaning on a temporary wall that gave a little, but he didn't care. They all should have listened to Gabe and not ventured down to the basement.

"How many bite marks?" Gabriel asked, stopping the pathologist as he was describing her general health before the attack.

"Over three hundred. We have taken impressions of the wounds."

An assistant wheeled over a stainless steel table and removed a green surgical cloth.

"We called in a forensic maxillofacial surgeon, and these were the clearest sets of imprints and plates we could recover."

There were four sets of teeth, uppers and lowers. To the untrained eye, they all looked too small. Gabriel leaned in closer to the glass.

"Are those children's teeth?" he asked as loudly as he could through the separation of rooms.

"Yes, our surgeon suggests one is of a five-year-old, a six-year-old, and the other two in their teens, give or take a year on all. The others are not viable enough to get accurate age estimates."

"How many different marks, regardless of age?" Kennedy asked.

"Best guess, and that is all that we have at this point, is seventeen different bite patterns." The doctor placed rubber gloves on, and with the help of a female assistant, he turned Kelly's body onto her side so that her back could be seen. "The most unique pattern here was done by those smaller plates. We have never seen anything like this before. President Hadley had been raked by something sharp, possibly fingernails; we still haven't found out for sure. But these we know were made by teeth."

As hard as the group tried, they could not see what the doctor was describing.

"The bite marks are so plentiful and overlapping that we almost missed it until we took a skin scan of the traumatized areas." The doctor nodded, and to everyone's relief, Kelly was once more covered with a blue sheet. He then took the large x-ray folder and opened it. It was a black-and-white scan that showed the bite marks close up. He then produced a second scan. "We were clearly shocked when layer by layer we removed many of the superficial ones and then went with the deepest bite impressions. There was a section here that contained the older teeth marks, five differing sets."

He showed them the last scan. Julie gasped when she read the words that had been bitten deeply into Kelly's backside all the way down the back of her leg.

"My God, what in the hell are we dealing with here?" George said as he stepped forward to make sure he was reading the message right.

Regards from the Crypt Kicker Five.

Julie and Jennifer spent several minutes in the bathroom next to the study as the others gathered to discuss the autopsy of their friend. It sickened them that Kelly had been used as merely a message board by something that found this amusing. They all watched as the two women came back inside and looked far fresher than they had going into the bathroom. They sat and all were silent as they absorbed what they had seen.

"What in the hell did that mean?" Julie asked as she tried to focus on the faces around the table.

Except for Leonard tapping away at a computer keyboard, no one said anything. It was George who walked to the small wet bar and poured himself a stiff shot of bourbon before he spoke.

"We all know where we heard that before, so everyone just admit it. It's from that stupid song."

"I must have missed that one," Julie countered.

The others knew exactly what Cordero meant.

"'Monster Mash,' released in 1962," Leonard said as he continued tapping away. "The only hit for a singer called Bobby 'Boris' Pickett. The song premiered in time for Halloween in 1962 and was a huge hit with the bebop crowd."

Understanding finally dawned on Julie's face. "That silly Halloween song?" She stood and then paced to the window and the cloudy day outside. "Kelly once played that song for us when developing the Halloween special for Summer Place."

"Everything related to us through whatever this thing is stems from the early sixties," Gabriel said as he stood and went to the bar for a bottle of water. "Leonard, it's imperative that we delve deeper into Hadley's past. Why were his high school records forged? Why the blast-from-the-past music? And what could have turned this boy into a cold-blooded killer who has no remorse for the duty he performed? Most men of that ilk either commit suicide or—"

"Or run for president?" George said as a joke that fell completely flat. He quickly recovered from his failure. "This *thing* actually wants us to find out. So why doesn't this evil fuck just spell it out? Why screw around like this?"

"I don't know, George," Gabe said as he again sat down.

"I know a way we can cut down the research time on this," John said as he intentionally looked away from Jennifer.

"No. You promised—no more. Summer Place almost killed you," Jenny said as she tried to get Lonetree to look her way. He held steady.

"There I bucked up against the entity itself. Hadley here is the vessel, not the force behind all of this." He looked at Gabriel. "I think I can get in and back out again without the entity becoming aware that I am inside Hadley's head."

"No. Not yet anyway. We'll wait and see what Leonard comes up with."

"In the meantime, we lose more innocents? This thing isn't going to stop, Gabe. You know it and I know it. In some ways, this entity is more powerful than the evil spirit that haunted Summer Place. It's like this thing has been waiting and somehow it has awakened and it wants Hadley back. I can find out in a fraction of the time it would take Wonder Boy there to put a page of his research together," Lonetree said with a nod toward the computers.

"Wonder Boy? What the fuck?" Leonard protested.

"I'll think it over," Gabriel took a long pull of the water bottle. "If whatever this thing is finds out you're trespassing, I don't think it would be very forgiving."

"It's inviting us to come in. I want to accept the invitation. It just may let me find out what we need to do for it to get what it wants most—and that is the return of Hadley—to God knows where."

"George, do you think you can contact physically with our former First Lady and get a feeling for her motivation in all of this?"

"Just get me in the same room with her. Her mantra puts out enough vibe I could read her in ancient Chinese. Yeah, I can see what she's up to."

"And while he's doing that," Leonard said as he hit the Print key and the copier started up in the corner, "I do have a lead on a portfolio of investments that never went over to the family funds in general. It will take awhile, but I think I can get into their systems." He pulled a piece of paper from the printer, read it, and then handed it over to Gabriel.

"What is this?" he asked when he read the page.

"A list of former holdings by the Hadley Corporation. Sold off years ago."

"So?" Kennedy asked as he passed the page to John and the others.

"The properties were never relinquished. Hadley's father sold the assets to himself under an assumed name and corporation—three businesses that I have yet to track down. I have one, I think," Leonard said as he returned to his computer screen. He tapped the glass. "Right here. A small security company that is listed as privately owned, but if you read the small print"—he turned and smiled at the others around the table—"which I always do, you'll see a firm called Sacramento Security, and the name on the bottom line is that of D. Hadley. It's based in Pomona, California. I can start there and see if anything correlates with the Hadley Group of companies and why their sale was a farce."

Gabriel nodded, pleased that Leonard had given them a fighting chance without risking John's life in a dreamwalk with Hadley. He looked at his old college roommate.

"Sorry, John, but I'm not risking you just to get a lead. We'll go with Leonard for the time being."

Jennifer closed her eyes as she silently thanked Gabriel for deciding against John's idea.

That decision didn't sit well with Lonetree. John wanted to meet the true members of the Crypt Kicker Five.

8

VIRGINIA COUNTRYSIDE

As others took breaks and ate, Leonard kept at it. All his meals were wheeled in on a small cart and left the same way, usually without the food being touched. Gabriel was quickly becoming concerned at this different vibe coming from Leonard. As the others filed out of the study for dinner and a break, Leonard stayed behind, and this time, so did Gabriel. He pulled up a chair and sat next to Sickles, who had no less than five large-screen monitors in front of him. The technical group headed by the FBI computer crimes division was astonished at the setup and now cast a wary eye on Leonard, who demonstrated capabilities sometimes seen in cyber terror attacks against large corporations. Nothing was said, but many an agent left Leonard's company with a feeling this man needed watching when all of this was said and done.

"Pushing it a little hard, aren't you?" Kennedy asked as he leaned in close to get the man's attention.

Leonard looked startled at first, as he hadn't realized Gabriel had sat down. He looked around and saw that the room had emptied out. He rubbed his eyes and then fixed Kennedy with bloodshot whites. He seemed not to have heard him speak, and then he smiled. It was a sad-looking effort, and Gabriel allowed Leonard to talk it out his way.

"I always looked at this thing that we do as a challenge, a kick, not meaning much to the real world compared to what corporations want me to do. I took this ghost-hunting thing with a grain of salt, with the one notable exception of Summer Place." He sat back in his chair and then placed his small hands behind his head and closed his eyes. "But I learned this morning that this is some serious stuff we're playing with here." He opened his eyes and then glanced at the man who had saved him from a meaningless life of gang-related crime, and for that fact alone the psychiatrist had earned Leonard's lifelong loyalty. "I guess over six years of finding out just how devious people are when it comes to ghost hunting has colored me to a point to where I was becoming beyond merely skeptical of the science. Maybe I was phoning in my research after the fiftieth time we uncovered untruths of a reality show."

Gabriel was about to respond to Leonard's guilt complex when one of the monitors flashed.

"Ah," Leonard said, reading the incoming message. He once again hit the Print button, and the copier went into action. He stood and went to the copier and retrieved the printer page and then handed it to Gabriel.

"A start—not much, but a start."

"What is this?" Gabriel asked as he scanned the page.

"Account listings for Sacramento Security. Personnel records and complete client access."

"I don't get it. This is a small print investment by Hadley Corp and the only one thus far that you've been able to uncover. Why would they not have been able to hide this asset from their portfolio?"

Leonard smiled and then tapped the middle of the page. "Well, it was just a small company that had only one contract since 1973. But the kicker here is what I am interested in. Look at the outlay for Privileged Client Number 45624. That payroll outlay is for security at a site that is in operation 24-7. That's serious security for something not listed in the property protection contract. And twenty-four-hour-a-day security, seven days a week, means that they have an on-site security team in place at that location. Why?"

"Cut to the chase here, Leonard; you're losing this mere human being."

"It seems that the security company only handles three accounts. Well, only one now, because two of clients have canceled their contracts in the past year."

"So, the security company has how many clients?"

Leonard smiled. "One. At least that's all I can see. Now that kicker I said was coming. Two large properties the company had contracts for were canceled. The reason listed on the duplicate contracts stated they were taken over by a certain county I have yet to find. Just what the two properties were that were once guarded by the Hadley family, that were taken over by a local government, and who that local government is, I will discover soon. As I said, it's a starting point. I made a hole in the ground; now I can see if I can expand upon it."

Gabriel handed the sheet of paper to Leonard and slapped him on the back. He stood just as the door to the study opened and John was standing there.

"Gabe, you have to see this," he said and then vanished.

With a look at Sickles, Gabriel left the study and saw the activity on the stairs leading to the basement. He noticed the forensic doctors were there at the top of the stairs, and all of them looked as white as ghosts.

"What in the hell is this?" Kennedy asked as John held up a hand.

"Listen," he said as the room quieted from the thirty-five voices coming from scared government workers.

The voices were heard, but they were low and indistinct. Gabe tried his best to hear but couldn't. He looked from the open doorway to the chief pathologist. "What are you doing up here?"

"Because no one pays us enough to sit through that," he said, pointing down the stairs. "I've got two nurses that have fainted. Hell, even security doesn't want anything to do with this."

Gabriel looked at the pathologist as if he had lost his mind, and Gabe angrily pushed by him and headed down the stairs. Julie, John, George, and Jenny all followed. The other men and women looked uneasy as the strange group vanished down into darkness.

Gabe passed one of the Secret Service agents coming up the stairs and stopped him.

"I waited as long as I could, but I just can't stay down there anymore." The man pushed by Kennedy and the others like a salmon swimming upstream. Gabriel continued down.

He reached the bottom step and then reached for the light switch and hit it. There was nothing. A flashlight came on, dimmed, and then flashed on once more. John was there beside him, and Gabe was thankful for it. Then, just as Julie, Jenny, and George arrived, the flashlights died once more, leaving them in total darkness. George remedied the situation by pulling a lighter from his pocket and holding the flame up high as they saw the curtained-off morgue area. As the light flared to life beyond the glass, they could see nothing with the plastic curtain pulled over the viewing glass.

"Feel it?" George said as he stepped into the enclosed viewing area. He wanted to grab the curtain and sling it back but was terrified about what horror would be waiting for him. He swallowed and then stepped back as Gabriel relieved him of the lighter. John reached for the plastic curtain and, with one look at Kennedy, was ready to open the partition. The mumbling beyond stopped. John also swallowed his fear and then quickly pulled back the curtain.

They all jumped as one. The thing staring at them was right in front of the glass. There was no fogging of the window as the visage of Kelly stared at them through the viewing window. As the flame played light over the frightening image, they all saw the Y-shaped autopsy scar and noted that her hair was wet and clean after the pathologists were finished with her. Her mouth moved, but no words came out. Her eyes had turned a milky white, and her wounds were leaking clear and watery blood. Kelly tilted her damaged head first right and then left. The eyes fixed on Gabriel. The mouth tried to move again. Gabriel stepped closer to the glass.

Jennifer felt cold and had to turn away. Then an old and very familiar feeling came over her senses. It was dreamlike and frightening as she realized her conscious being was being pushed aside. Bobby Lee was in there, and he wanted to see and hear. She didn't fight it. This was where they would decide if the former songwriter would be a help on this case or if he would be his normal useless self. Gabe felt Jenny step up to the glass, and John reacted first by taking her by the arm.

"Unhand me, Chief!" came the male voice emanating from Jennifer's beautiful mouth.

Lonetree immediately let go with a look of distaste.

"Now that there is something I would find hard to get used to," George said as Jennifer placed her ear against the glass.

"No offense, Doc, but I have better hearing than you do," Jenny said. "I particularly didn't like that chick at first, but she grew on me, so let me meditate on this thing for a minute." Jenny looked up at Gabriel with an ugly expression as the professor stood there not knowing what to say to the ghost that had once tried to drive his friend insane. "Please."

Gabriel, with a look at the others, moved back to give Jennifer / Bobby Lee some room. Kelly stood there. Her mouth moved again, and this time, Jenny smiled and then stepped back and looked at the others.

"Nothing worse than talking to dead people. This baby girl is scared. Her soul is frightened. Just like I was when they offed me in New York. Angry, but mostly afraid."

None of them would ever be able to get used to Jenny talking with a male's voice.

Again, she leaned close to the glass as Kelly's hand came up and caressed the coldness there. They could see that her hand had been broken during the assault, and seeing the damage made Julie feel queasy. Bobby Lee / Jennifer lost the arrogant smile as he listened to words only he could understand.

"She says she has a message for Gabriel." Bobby Lee straightened and then stepped back. "She won't tell me, only you."

The lighter flamed out, and Kennedy cursed as he tried three times to get the flame to catch. It flared to life on the third try, and everyone, including John and the ghost of Bobby Lee McKinnon, screamed in abject fright as Kelly had somehow moved from behind the glass to the viewing area. She stood right in front of Gabriel, and he felt his knees go weak. Kelly reached out and took Kennedy's collar and pulled him close to her upturned face.

"They weren't supposed to do that," came the whisper through the fetid breath of the dead. "*He* is to be punished, not her or them." Kelly turned away, and the hand that was broken and twisted shot toward the glass and the corpses beyond. "They were not supposed to die. I want Dean. Give him to me or suffer the children as I did." Kelly turned to face Gabriel just as the lighter once more went out. Then they all jumped and yelped once more when the bright fluorescents of the basement sprang to full glory. They looked into the makeshift morgue and saw that Kelly's body was on its gurney where it had been before, and the sheet that had covered it was lying on the cold cement floor. Everything was as it should have been with the exception of the sheet coiled at the foot of the gurney.

"Did that just happen?" Jennifer said as she felt herself once more after the very brief invasion by Bobby Lee.

"Feel it?" George asked as he looked around.

"What?" Gabriel asked. He knew George was more in tune with the other side than they were.

"Remorse. I get the feeling of remorse here. It's like—"

"Like whatever we're facing has a specific target in mind, and Kelly and all the others were accidents in the attempt to get at Hadley. So, the real question here is, why doesn't it just kill Hadley? If it hates the man so much, why not do it and get it over with?" Jenny said.

"Exactly," George said as he peered into Jennifer's face to see if it were truly her or not.

"Jenny, what are you coming away with? What does Bobby Lee say or even feel?"

Jennifer smiled up at John. "Feelings. Hard feelings, and they are memories, I'm sure of that. Bobby Lee knows the anger, but this is far beyond even what he felt about his death."

"What are his feelings?" Gabe persisted.

"That whatever this thing is, Bobby Lee thinks it was another woman overlaying those words Kelly spoke. He thinks it's another woman speaking through Kelly and that Dean Hadley murdered her."

The room became silent as they realized that their suspicions on the sanity of Hadley may have just been confirmed.

"My God," Gabriel said. "His wife may be right. Guilt may have sent Hadley over the edge." He faced his people. "We may have to consider *it is* his mind doing all of this. He's trying to get forgiveness for what he's done, and that may be driving him into a psychosis of massive proportions."

"We have to look deeper, Gabe. I don't trust that woman as far as I can throw her," Jennifer said as she took John by the arm. "This is too convenient a diagnosis for our friend Catherine Hadley."

"We can't hide what could be the truth. Maybe Hadley *will* have to be placed into an induced coma to stop this killing. We just may be out of options at this point. Kelly's death changed the equation for a lot of us."

"What about the warning that Hadley is wanted by this . . . this . . . thing?" George asked, his fear clearly showing on his dark features.

"One way we can confirm it," Gabriel said as he looked at his watch and moved toward the stairs. "We check the EKG upstairs. If it spiked during this or any of the other attacks, we can assume it may be Hadley himself doing this."

The Supernaturals were frightened that the man they were there to help was nothing more than a killer who sought forgiveness at the end of his life. There was more than one documented case of the mind's ability to produce supernatural phenomena through sheer willpower. If that was the case, Catherine Hadley would get her way and the former president of the United States would basically be put down like a rabid dog. He would be put to sleep for the remainder of his days in an induced coma just to stop the killing.

They hoped it wasn't him.

MORENO, CALIFORNIA

Bob and Linda sat at the old stools of the lunch counter. Most of those stools refused to function as designed and didn't spin. They studied the old fifties-style architecture of the fountain counter and were amazed that Harvey had kept it up as well as he had. But they knew that his time, as well as their own, was coming to an end in Moreno. They had watched the last of Moreno's residents leave that morning. Harvey was so saddened by this fact that he offered dinner, and they had accepted. They turned and saw that another had joined the last supper for Moreno. Casper Worthington had finished with the mechanical shaking and the collecting of walnuts from his stubborn grove, and that would be the last of his business in the dead town. He had decided that walnuts were not the way to earn the last of his fortune. He was going to sell the small farm and buy a condo in Ontario.

The department store was far different at night than in the day. The cordoned-off shopping areas of the main floor were far more haunted than even the rest of the town. At one time, everyone in town frequented Newberry's Department Store. The old echoes of shoppers past seemed to stain the store, and Bob and Linda didn't know how Harvey had handled it all these years. They smiled as they watched him in the large square of empty space as he cooked over the grill. Casper sat silently as he took in the old lunch counter.

"You know, in 1960, before that malt shop on the corner of Main and Santiago—Peppermint Lounge, I think it was called—us kids used to take up all the counter space here after school." He shook his head at the memory. "I was just a younker at the time, but we made this place a pretty penny, I can tell you. We would order food by the pound. Newberry's had the best damn french fries in the valley, let me tell ya."

"The secret is my dad gave orders to never change the oil in the deep fryer. He said it added extra flavor to his fries."

Bob and Linda made a face as Harvey placed three plates of food in front of them and then turned to the service window and gathered his own dinner. He stood behind the counter and would eat that way.

"In honor of a heyday Moreno never really had, I give you the Big Bopper Burger and Idaho Jim's home fries," he said with a crooked grin. "I thought of that myself back in, oh, I guess it was 1961. It went over well. My dad said I was a natural restaurateur." He raised his glass of fountain soda and tipped it toward his guests. They did the same. Toasting the official death of Moreno was sad to them in a way, at least for Casper and Harvey, who had been there all their lives.

Bob bit into his cheeseburger and smiled. He chewed and rolled his eyes. "Man, I can see why that really took off."

Linda smiled. She liked hearing the old stories. She took a sip through her straw of the most wonderful soda fountain Cherry Coke she had ever had. Harvey saw her appreciation.

"It's the amount of syrup. I cheated at the recipe and always had. Dad never could figure out where the shortage in yield sprang from."

"Is that how you seduced the local girls?" Linda asked.

"Nah." A far-off look came into Harvey's eyes as he wiped his mouth with a napkin. "But there was one who I loved from the first moment I laid eyes on her."

"Tell us," Linda said as she felt a cold draft at her back and shivered. Bob and Casper smiled, as they too wanted to hear of the crush Harvey had on a girl long ago gone from this place.

"Ah, she was out of my league. She was the daughter of one of the town's founders. I was also, but this girl commanded attention. Not in a mean way, but because she actually cared for people. Even though she was a blind girl, everyone loved her."

"What happened to her?" Bob asked as he finished his burger and fries. It was Casper who answered for Harve.

"The fire department never found her body in the Grenada Theater after the fire."

"Oh, I'm sorry," Linda said.

"We all felt we let her down. We knew who she was with that night, and we all knew no good would come of it. Everyone tried to warn her, but she knew better. She knew he was a creep, but she felt there was more to him than being a bully and the son of the richest man in town. There was no stoppin' that girl once she set her mind to something." Harvey stopped talking and then attempted to eat his burger but instead placed it on his blue dinner plate and then pushed it away.

"So many people died that night, but it's her image that haunts this place more than the empty buildings and businesses," Casper added. "Why, I bet—"

The light in the middle of the cordoned-off section of Newberry's came on. The overheads had not been functional since 1967.

"What in the Sam Hill?" Harvey moved from behind the chipped counter and looked into the vastness of the store. He produced his set of keys and made his way to the center of Newberry's to the large chain-link fencing separating the lunch counter and booths from the store proper. He found the right key and opened the large lock. He swung the gate open and was startled when his three guests joined him. Casper was still eating his burger as he looked past the stacked shelving and the boxes of old hangers and dress stands. He chewed as his eyes went toward the bright lights.

They went inside, and as Harvey moved old boxes out of the way, Linda was the first to see the display. It was done up like a cornfield, complete with fake scarecrow. There were racks and racks of packaged and cheesy Halloween costumes and plastic pumpkins kids could use instead of the old grocery bags for gathering candy.

"What the fuck is this?" Casper said as his appetite suddenly vanished.

Bob recognized some of the display costumes arranged for maximum effect to entice children to harangue their parents for such a Halloween getup. There was Sylvester the Cat, Tweety in all his yellow glory, and Superman masks, most likely made of the most toxic plastic available in the early sixties.

The sudden blast of the speaker system startled them all. *Attention, Newberry's shoppers! Today we are offering 50 percent off on all Halloween apparel and candy. Don't let your trick-or-treaters down! We have the best selection of candy in the Inland Empire. Happy Halloween from your extended family at Newberry's!*

Harvey felt his legs go weak, and he had to grab Bob by the shoulder to keep from falling as the announcement faded and echoed inside the mostly empty department store.

"Hey, you okay?" Bob asked as he helped Harvey straighten.

"I haven't heard his voice since the day he died in 1973."

"Whose?" Linda asked, not liking where this conversation was heading.

"That was my father." Harvey looked upward toward the second floor. The escalator had not been functional since the store closed its doors officially in 1965. He leaned over to see if he could view anything, but there was nothing but darkness.

"Someone is messing with us, Harvey," Bob said as he looked around for any form of explanation.

The music made them all jump, and Casper let out a scream as the remains of his cheeseburger slipped from his fingers. The entire intercom system sprang to life with music on all four floors echoing throughout Newberry's.

I was working in the lab late one night . . . when my eyes beheld an eerie sight . . . For my monster from his slab began to rise, and suddenly to my surprise . . . he did the mash . . . he did the Monster Mash . . .

The song was old, and it was loud enough that Linda placed her hands over her ears and cringed.

"What is going on?" Harvey shouted.

Bob's and Linda's occasionally operational cell phones went off at the same time the old escalator to the second and third floors began creaking and moving in a jolting, halting motion.

The overhead fluorescent lights went out, and the music was silenced. Then slim light returned as the illumination from the lunch counter finally pushed the darkness away.

All eyes searched faces hoping for a logical explanation, but all they saw in each other was the impossibility of what had just happened. They each turned slowly toward the area where the ghostly Halloween display had been and saw nothing but empty racks and old boxes. The area had not been used since 1965.

"Well," Bob said, taking Linda's shaking hand in his own, "thanks for the burger and the floor show, but I think it's time we start packing our things."

"Yeah, things are getting a bit spooky around here," Casper said, echoing Bob's unease.

On that night, they never realized that Newberry's had remained dormant until a certain topic of conversation had been brought up. It was like a knee-jerk reaction the town had for bringing up bad memories.

Now the small town of Moreno was physically starting to react as the anniversary of that long-ago Halloween night drew near.

Inside the old ruins of the winery, the vault shook on its cement foundation, and dirt and dust showered down from the weakened and age-worn rafters.

In the basement of the Grenada Theater, there was not one sound other than the humming of an old song about someone needing to worry, because her man was coming back home. *My boyfriend's back, and you're gonna be in trouble.*

The entity was spiking in power, and it had just drawn more strength from the display it had just put on at Newberry's and the witnessed reaction to it. It fed off the fear and lack of understanding of those who felt the town escalate in its waking. The energy Bob, Linda, Casper, and Harvey had just spent being frightened made the things in both vaults stronger.

Fear was the fuel it fed upon.

9

VIRGINIA COUNTRYSIDE

The United States marshal served the papers after the quiet night in Virginia. Gabriel and the others, including Leonard, finally got seven good hours of sleep. The evening and then into the late night, there had been no activity with President Hadley, who was still in and out of consciousness. Unable to speak or to even move, he was still being fed intravenously. It was past eight in the morning when a light knock sounded on Gabriel's third-floor bedroom door, and Kennedy answered with a towel in his hands.

"Madam First Lady," he said as he turned and tossed the towel, where it snagged on the corner bedpost.

"Mrs. Hadley will do; the title always made me feel old for some reason."

Gabriel poked his head out of the door and looked left and then right, and then his thoughts turned to devilry. He must have been hanging out with Damian a little too much. "I would ask you in, but that may start rumors we would just as soon avoid." He smiled and waited for her to state her business and see if she had a reaction to his probing wit.

"I understand your reference to the rumors in Washington, Professor; you shouldn't watch so much of that reality television you're so fond of berating. Now if you will follow me, we have some business to discuss before your team meets this morning. I believe this may have some bearing on how you proceed."

Kennedy reached for his coat and then followed Catherine Hadley down the stairs. On the second-floor landing, he looked down the hallway, and everything seemed quiet. He saw Julie Reilly dozing in a chair next to three standing hostage rescue team agents and smiled. He told everyone they didn't have to keep watch, that the FBI could handle it for a night, but Julie insisted that they be close for observation. No better eyes than their own, she said. But after Kelly's death, Gabe had a hard time leaving anyone remotely close to that bedroom.

When he reached the bottom of the stairs, he saw the First Lady's assistant standing in the foyer talking with a bear of a man in a brown uniform shirt and faded Levi's. He held a white cowboy hat in his right hand, and with his left, he battled with a too-small china teacup. The assistant saw Catherine Hadley and then quickly excused herself after relieving the man of his troubling cup. Gabriel stepped up to both as he cleaned his glasses.

"Ben Hyatt, United States marshal, Professor Gabriel Kennedy," Catherine said as she smiled and stepped back.

"Professor, I am officially serving you this warrant. You are to cease and desist all your study of the president. He is to be transferred to Ring-wald Clinic in New Hampshire by three o'clock today." The burly man handed him the folded document. "Have a good day, sir."

The United States marshal turned and left with a dip of his head at the former First Lady. Gabriel unfolded the warrant and scanned it. He took a deep breath and then faced the woman who intimidated all she ran across, much like her husband had. She learned well.

"You people were the ones who requested we take part in this. Why didn't you just order us out?"

Catherine smiled and then went to the credenza and straightened out a vase of freshly cut roses. She acted as if she were fussing with them.

The front door opened, and Damian entered. He had been gone since the afternoon before when Kennedy had sent him out to dig up some information. Gabriel had surmised that Catherine could keep a lot to herself, but she had one requirement that any wife has—she had to obey the law. Damian went to find out what she had waving in the wind, legally speaking.

"I see that the marshal was just here," he said as he removed his ever-present raincoat and then the fedora and tossed them on an expensive Hamilton chair next to the credenza. "I imagine you were surprised when he served you with papers?"

"Quite surprised," Gabe said as he absentmindedly handed Damian the order to release Hadley to the New Hampshire hospital.

Damian smiled as he read the warrant. The large black man then lowered the paperwork. "You know this hospital in New Hampshire?"

"Yes, it's well known. A place for the rich and famous to go and die quietly so as not to embarrass the other rich and famous. It's a vegetable-monitoring station." Gabriel turned and watched Catherine and her roses and then stepped up to her. "You know your husband is still functioning rather well upstairs, right?"

"Is that what you call it?" she said as she straightened and turned. The smile was no longer there.

"Why?" Kennedy asked.

Leonard and Jennifer stepped off the last stair and saw John Lonetree exit the pantry with a cup of coffee. They remained silent as they watched the drama they had stumbled onto play out. They knew when not to talk.

"She had to prove to the world that she was actually making an attempt to help her ailing husband. Otherwise, what would people in polite society think of our poor First Lady?" Damian said as he turned and went toward John and relieved him of his coffee. It looked like the former state police officer hadn't slept in three days, which was completely accurate. He sipped and then winked at the even larger Lonetree. He turned back to Gabriel and Catherine, who stood amused. "In the time we have been here, Mrs. Hadley has been using *her* time well. At least her lawyers have. She got the injunction late last night after a conference call with a superior court judge, Lyle Buellton, a friend from many years ago. Thus, your service of writ this morning, Gabe." Damian drank again and then smiled up at Catherine.

"So, we're fired?" Leonard asked as he rubbed his eyes after joining the group. Even a few of the doctors and nurses were gathering to see the outcome. At this point, Gabriel could see that Catherine was becoming uncomfortable with so many people hearing their speculation on her motives.

"Your services, though appreciated deeply by me and my husband, are no longer necessary." She turned to leave.

Leonard got Gabriel's attention and waved a large file and then raised his brows.

"May we conclude our exit exam?" Gabriel asked, acting as if he had acquiesced to her decision. "Just to close out our files." He smiled. "Legalities, you know how they are. Five hours alone, and then you can whisk him away."

"Four hours, Professor. The helicopter arrives this afternoon to transport him to New Hampshire." She nodded and then left them all to stand there feeling used and very much the underdog in this fight.

Kennedy immediately went to Leonard, who turned and went back inside the study. The others followed.

"That was my coffee, you know," John said as he beat Damian to the twin doors of the study.

"Next time, less sugar." Damian smiled as he paused at the doorway. "I'm sweet enough."

Lonetree gave him a dirty look as Jenny patted him on the back as she too went inside.

Damian went to Gabriel before Leonard got to him. "That phone call last night"—he shook his head—"what in the hell happened?"

"I'll have Julie catch you up. We informed Kelly's father in Brooklyn. It wasn't easy to tell a man that he lost his daughter and that we don't know exactly how it happened."

Damian placed a beefy hand on Gabe's shoulder. They were joined by John as the others sat at the long table. Jackson looked at Kennedy and then John in turn.

"I haven't said this in many years, at least since that night in the Poconos, but by God, Gabe, this is enough. We have no real idea what we are doing here. Kelly's death proves we don't know enough about reality, much less the supernatural. We're babes in the woods, and now someone has paid the price for it. Let's shut this down and get the hell out of here." The words were whispered, but they carried well to the others. "Sorry, but I liked that girl, even though I didn't show it a lot. She had guts, and that's something I appreciate. Do right by her, Gabe."

"That's what this is for," Leonard said as he finally got Gabriel's attention and slapped the file into his chest. "This came through last night."

"What is it?" Kennedy asked as he watched Damian finally moving off to the table.

"Gabriel—"

Kennedy ignored John; he knew what he was going to say, and he didn't even want to go there. He gestured for John to sit down.

When he opened the file, his eyes widened. "Leonard, this would have been good if we were after the First Lady, but this doesn't do anything to stop Hadley from being transferred."

"What is it?" Julie asked as she stood and started pouring coffee for everyone. Jennifer assisted just to do something.

"It seems the former chief of staff, the now deceased Herbert Avery, assisted Mrs. Hadley in acquiring a little bit of clout. Avery was about to try three months ago before the president began showing signs of insanity,

giving her full power of attorney. All his holdings in the Hadley Corporation, according to Mr. Sickles here." Gabriel tossed the file on the table and
looked at Leonard. "We'll turn this over to the FBI for a possible criminal
case, but it doesn't help us"—he looked up toward the ceiling and the bedrooms there—"or him. Besides, as I said, she no longer needs power of
attorney; she'll get everything anyway."

Leonard became frustrated and then snatched the discarded file from
the tabletop. He opened it and then slammed his palm down upon it.

"As I mentioned yesterday, Sacramento Security has only three holdings. One now, after the state took over two of those properties. There is
only one property requiring security, and they require security, as I said,
24-7. I found the payroll outlay for two employees on a long-term contract.
I even found their marriage license in the State of California records. The
security team actually married."

"Well, being cooped up together twenty-four hours a day will do that
to people," Damian said as he sipped coffee.

"Leonard, what are you saying?" Gabriel asked.

"It's the lead we needed."

"Why?" Julie asked as she finally placed a cup of coffee in front of
Gabriel and then sat down.

"It's what they had been contracted to secure."

"Come on, Sickles. Stop playing this out," Damian said, trying to get
the frustrating kid to get on with it.

"Who hires people to watch an entire town?" Leonard said with an
impish grin.

"Town?" Kennedy asked, confused but now more interested.

"Yep. It's called Moreno, and let me tell you, this place has a history.
And guess what?"

They all stared at Sickles, not saying anything and surely not rising to
his climatic bait.

"The town was incorporated after World War II—1947, to be exact,
when the first real business went in. Moreno, California, was the first investment of one Robert Hadley, the father of the president."

Gabriel smiled. He finally sat down. "Go on."

"I figured the key here may not be Dean Hadley but his father. His
past isn't that well covered, except for a few specific areas in his wartime
service. Can't get much out of the system because those war years are so
highly classified that even I couldn't get into the army's file at the main database in St. Louis. But I did get into a system that stores payroll information

for an agency that didn't think past payroll was a high priority for security. Robert Hadley was a spook during the war."

"A spook?" Jenny asked.

"A spy, worked for the old OSS, and served his last few months in Europe in Czechoslovakia and Yugoslavia. What he was doing there, no one says on paper. But guess who came home from the war a rich man?"

"Robert Hadley," Gabriel said as his smile grew. He wanted to stand up and give the small black man a kiss.

"Exactly. His newfound wealth started the Hadley Corp Gauge and Meter Company of Moreno, California, in the summer of 1948. It employed over three hundred workers, who were set up nicely in Hadley housing and basic services. The man basically owned these people and housed them too."

Leonard turned and paced as he left the file on the table. "Now we know his son was born before the war ended. Now we know he went to Chino High School and not Chaffey, as his official record states, but why there? Well, Moreno was large enough for kindergarten through eighth grades, but there weren't enough older students to justify a high school class, so they were bused to Chino, eighteen miles away. We now know it was all a lie. Real records show he went to Chino High School and graduated in 1963. Now let's assume that Chino is somehow relatable to Moreno." Leonard turned one of the computer monitors around and then pointed at a Google map. "Here's Chino, Ontario, Pomona, Corona, and here is"—he tapped the screen hard—"Moreno. Eighteen miles away in the hills surrounding the valley."

"I'll be damned; it was right there," Julie said, admiring Leonard.

"What happened to the town?" Gabriel asked as he examined the screen.

"Industrial explosion. The equipment they made used mercury, the deadliest heavy metal. The building exploded one night and killed thirty-six factory workers. The fire rained down on the town below, where many more were burned and killed. The town was officially declared dead in 1965 because of groundwater contamination from mercury poisoning. The security is there to supposedly keep the town off limits to squatters."

"When did all of this happen?" Jennifer asked as she reached out and took John's hand. She didn't like the way he was listening to Leonard's report.

"That is the real capper here. The plant exploded on one of the busiest nights of the year. Halloween 1962. It seems the town had a kids' holiday and the adults had another."

"What do you mean?" Gabe asked.

"The Cuban Missile Crisis had just ended. For weeks, the population thought they had seen the last days, but instead, at the last minute, reprieve from Armageddon." Sickles finally sat down. "Everyone was happy. The kids, the mothers, the fathers. Then it suddenly turned into a town of death. One night wiped out a whole community, and the world never even noticed."

"Hadley had that much clout?" Damian asked, incredulous at the idea.

"No, he didn't. But the people who owned the old winery and mission in town did. Those were the two properties that the State of California took over in the seventies. The Santa Maria Delarosa mission, and the winery occupying the same property, were owned by none other than the United States government at the time, and then Moreno later, at least until the State of California sued Hadley Corp and wrested the property from them for historical sake."

"When did the U.S. government go into the historical preservation business?" John asked, with his hackles rising.

"They didn't." Leonard pulled out a sheet of paper from the file and slid it down the table to Kennedy. "As far as I can see, the government was working with Hadley Sr. on something, and whatever that was revolved around this property. That something was important enough that he was well compensated for his trouble. Compensated well enough that he became one of the richest men in the world through that initial seed money from Uncle Sam."

"Anything else?" Gabriel teased.

The computer whiz looked taken aback and then caught on and smiled. "Remember, this is mostly speculation."

"Your speculation is better than hard evidence sometimes, kid," Damian said as he fixed Leonard with his police officer's eternal stare.

"As a matter of fact, a little article online caught my attention. It seems our Hadley Sr. influenced his son from the start for a career in politics. That's from Hadley's own mouth, and the interviewer at the time felt the future president was not all that pleased about being pushed in that direction. I guess he had changed after that night long ago—if he was even there, of course, which we cannot prove at this time. That's all I have, and I don't think the feds will give us any more. Everyone here knows what eventually became of the old OSS, right?"

"The Office of Strategic Services?" Julie said with a quizzical look on her face.

"The CIA." Damian helped her place the history. "And I don't think our little criminal friend can get into their system all that easily."

Sickles gave Damian a dirty look. "Give me time and that would change, copper."

The room became silent as Leonard finished.

"You know and I know how we can fill in the blanks," Lonetree said as he angrily slid the coffee cup toward Gabriel. "And we only have four hours to stop that transfer from taking place."

Gabriel Kennedy looked around the table until he finally settled on Jennifer. He raised his right brow above the rim of his glasses as he asked the silent question. She closed her eyes and nodded. Kennedy angrily slid the folder away from him and then stood.

"Okay," Gabriel said with a resigned sigh. "Get the prep work started, and I'll clear out the bedroom of the security detail. I'll get some alone time with the president. I think it's dangerous, as this thing is more powerful than any one of us could have imagined. Since this is likely to kill not only John but Hadley also, I should have no trouble in getting the First Lady to agree. Let's move. Leonard, get a computer upstairs in case John relays something we need you for. Damian, you'll act as security."

"Yeah, since all these heavily armed men has helped thus far, I'm thrilled."

Gabe smiled as did the others, and they prepared for one of the more dangerous scientific experiments ever conducted.

It was time for John Lonetree to dreamwalk with an insane man.

10

VIRGINIA COUNTRYSIDE

It took John and Jennifer thirty minutes to prepare. Lonetree had been given a depressant by Gabriel that would allow the large Blackfoot Indian to set his mind free. The task would take complete silence with only the team in the bedroom as witnesses. The hostage rescue team members, the Secret Service, and the medical staff complained bitterly about being excluded from the room during the experiment but eventually complied, with official protests being lodged to their superiors. Catherine Hadley had come to their rescue, not for humanitarian reasons but for the mere fact that the team would be expelled from the property soon after that.

The last of the tinfoil went on the windows, and Julie pronounced the room as ready. Towels had been stuffed under doorframes and windowsills to absorb sound. Any external interference from either noise or light could bring John out of the dream state he needed to achieve. Gabriel checked Lonetree's pulse and, upon removing the stethoscope, pronounced him as ready as he would ever be.

Leonard had his setup in the far corner of the room, and the others would be placed in chairs around the bed. They would try to protect Hadley the best they could. Damian chose to stand by the door.

Two candles were brought in, and the door was locked and sealed by Damian. Jennifer lit the candles and placed them on either side of the bed. Gabriel would be nearest John's left and Jennifer his right, as his chair would face Hadley and be the closest to the patient. The team was as ready as they would ever be.

"George, do you have any feelings coming from Hadley?" Kennedy asked as he took a chair to the left side of the president. He wanted to be in position to view both him and Lonetree.

"Nothing but ease coming off him in waves. I think he knows we're here. As for whatever threat there may be, I get nothing." George swallowed as he closed his eyes one last time to make sure he didn't miss a feeling he should have seen.

Gabriel was tapped on the shoulder, and Leonard informed him the video system was recording and that a live feed was being sent to the security team in the hallway, where it looked like a platoon of fully armed combat troops waited.

The room went silent as John closed his eyes and then touched Jennifer's hand for a moment. He opened his eyes and then gave her a quick wink. "Tell Bobby Lee to watch himself while I'm gone, or I'll excise *his* ass."

"You got it." She kissed his hand as he once more closed his eyes.

As everyone watched, John said a prayer in his native tongue, asking for guidance into the dark world. His last dreamwalk was in Summer Place, where he had connected with an inanimate object, the house itself. Here he would match brains and souls with a human being, which meant that, at least for a while, Hadley's insanity just may well be his own.

"Okay, John, watch your ass in there," Gabriel said as he watched Lonetree drift off. The lights went out, and the candles cast an eerie sort of shadow play on the bed and the man lying there.

Leonard threw a small blanket over the video monitor to cut down on the light in the bedroom.

For the briefest of moments, as Lonetree went into a deeper sleep, everyone in the room felt John pass through their minds. It was like his thoughts reached out to connect with all. Then they felt the sensation pass, and they saw Hadley jerk in his slumber. The IV line went taut, and Jennifer started to rise to keep the line securely attached to the president, but Gabe held up a hand as Hadley settled. Lonetree tensed in muscle and facial expression, and in the candles' weak light, they saw his eyes working under the lids. He was now entering REM sleep.

John saw blackness, and then he saw a bright flash of red and then white and then blackness again. The light was blurry, and John felt a powerful wind and a cold chill as his body sped through the dreamworld his mind was creating with the help of Dean Hadley. He was now mentally connected and there in Hadley's time and space of the past.

The speeding car passed a school bus, and John heard the blare of the driver's horn and then the laughter of the boy sitting next to him. Lonetree looked over and saw the letterman-jacketed teen with the wavy blond hair. The speeding Corvette screeched to the right and into a large parking area. The car's engine was shut off with a powerful roar as the kid hit the accelerator one last time. This was the time in every dreamwalk where John was more confused than he was aware.

Lonetree watched Dean pause as he stepped from the Corvette, and his eyes went to a dark-haired girl who stepped easily from the bus he had just sped past. The girl then unfolded a walking cane. John saw that her eyes were hidden by dark sunglasses as she was greeted by several of the local high school girls. The group moved away with the rest of the bused students from other areas. Lonetree watched Dean move off arrogantly to class.

John suddenly found himself inside and sitting atop a vacant desk at the back of a large classroom. He looked around and momentarily felt dizzy because of the time jump. Not that he wasn't grateful for not having to run to class like he had in his own past. Hadley was seated in the back and from the looks of it had very little interest in world history.

"Hey, look," came a whispered command.

Dean took some gum out of his mouth and firmly planted it under his desk. "What?" he growled at a boy with a bad case of acne, seated across from him.

"Look at Gloria's blouse; you can see her bra through the material," the boy said and then giggled as his pimples turned a brighter shade of red.

Dean looked up and saw the back of the same girl who had exited the bus. She sat at her desk, listening to the old female teacher who was busy pointing at a map of the Ottoman Empire. Dean made a face and then turned on his friend.

"Knock it off, you backward-thinking Alley Oop. Gloria's blind," he snarled.

John watched as the girl named Gloria turned, and though he couldn't see her eyes, he knew Dean had drawn her attention. Along with another.

"Is there a problem, Mr. Hadley?"

"No, Miss Kramer; do you have one?" Dean replied.

The class nervously chuckled.

John raised his brows at the arrogance of the boy.

"Young man, you are on thin ice with me. One more trip down to the counselor's office and you'll have some explaining to do to your father. That wouldn't be conducive to an active weekend of fun, would it?"

Dean took a breath as the class erupted in laughter at his embarrassment. Even Lonetree smiled at his predicament.

"No, ma'am." He saw Gloria as she listened. Although she was blind, John felt as if she were aware of her surroundings just as much as the kids with sight. She smiled at the uncomfortable silence from the back of the room.

"And, Mr. Weller, I think we have heard quite enough on the accessories of women's clothing from you. Is that clear?"

"But I—"

"'But I' nothing. Now use that book for something besides a prop, please."

"Yes, ma'am."

John looked up, and then he saw that the girl was no longer smiling. It was quite evident that she had heard the remark about her bra also but was willing to let it go until the teacher called Jimmy Weller out on it. The blind stare was not at the boy with the serious cratering problem on his facial skin; it was directed at Hadley. Gloria's unseeing glare was so intense that Dean looked away. John felt the girl intimidated the boy for some reason. Maybe it was the fact that she had the ability to stare without the use of her eyes.

"Thanks a lot, asshole!" Dean hissed as he finally picked up his own volume of world history and opened it to cover his talking.

"You know you like what you see. She must be lonely, right? How many dates could a blind girl have? And you've been through most of the bitchin' babes in this school, so why not go for the trifecta?"

"Gloria is the daughter of one of my dad's partners. Leave her alone."

"Oh, the man's in love."

"I'm going to kick your ass, you little—"

"Mr. Hadley!" the voice was much louder than the first assault. The smallish woman took her pointer and stormed down the row, slapping the four-foot-long wooden stick on the students' desks as she moved. Dean closed his book, and his eyes widened. "I guess we have to speak with your father. That won't do much for your weekend. Nor the new car I understand he bought you . . . on the condition of good grades, I believe he said at our last parent-teacher meeting." The small, short-haired woman, who John suspected had been teaching at Chino High School since the days of Prohibition, slapped the wooden pointer on the desk in front of Dean. To give the boy credit, he didn't jump or even flinch. But he did not answer back.

Lonetree smiled, not believing this session of dreamwalk would bear any fruit, when he saw the teacher turn and start back to the front of the class. Then she stopped and turned with a smile.

"But we don't need to do that, do we, Mr. Hadley?"

Dean didn't comment, as he suspected a far worse punishment was on its way.

"I think an extra credit assignment is in order. I believe that will take care of that weekend I just spoke of. I have assigned Miss Perry to do a special report for the class in honor of Halloween next Wednesday. It is to cover historical haunted properties. I suspect she may need some help doing her research. Isn't that right, Miss Perry?"

The dark-haired girl stood so suddenly that her braille copy of world history fell to the floor.

"I don't think that I need any help. Especially from him. He would only be in the way. I'll need this grade for my scholarship if and when I get one."

Again, the classroom erupted in laughter at someone saying that Dean Hadley, the handsomest boy in school, would be in the blind girl's way.

"No, I think he needs to adjust his busy weekend schedule to accommodate a straight-A student. Don't you, Mr. Hadley?" The teacher again turned as Gloria faced Dean and flipped him the finger, causing his friend Jimmy Weller to laugh uncontrollably.

John was about to stop the dreamwalk when the bell rang, and he stopped from waking himself up as Gloria slowly approached Dean. She was facing him as though she could see the kid's gray eyes. She leaned over the desk.

"Listen, Daddy's boy, this report is very important to me. The place is important; it may mean a scholarship, which I know you don't understand, so you'd better not screw this up. Do you hear?" Then she turned and faced the boy with the acne.

"And while you think commenting on my bra or clothing is funny, you ought to stop and smell yourself, you little bastard. It smells like you have shit your pants." She wiggled her nose. "Just one of the many curses of being blind is that you are cursed in your other senses!"

"Oh!" Dean said mockingly as he laughed, and then he stood while his friend tried his best to vanish into the scarred-up desktop.

Dean approached Gloria as she gathered her books and walking cane. She turned on him when her excellent hearing told her he was right behind her.

"Look, no pleasantries, all right? I'll say you helped. Miss Kramer will never know; she lives in Montclair, not Moreno."

"Look, I never said a word about you, so don't go tellin' your dad that I did. He'll only get into it with my father, and that won't do either one of us any good."

Gloria glanced around as if she were hearing a little voice. "Is that groveling I hear?"

"Good for you," John said, watching the little drama play out.

Strangely, the girl turned her head in John's direction as if she had heard him. Then she returned her attention to Hadley. Lonetree didn't think much of it; after all, the girl could hear other things, so it didn't have to be his voice that caught her momentary attention.

"Why do you hate me so much?" Dean asked as he angrily placed his schoolbooks under his arm, slipping on his jacket one arm at a time while juggling his things.

"Hate you?" Gloria stopped gathering her things and turned to face the cocky and brash kid. "We've been growing up in the same town for four years, and you have said less than three words to me. Even when our fathers were close, you treated me like blindness was a communicable disease."

"Comm—what?" he asked, not understanding the word *communicable*.

"A sickness that spreads. But you caught something else, didn't you, Dean? You caught the arrogant bug. God, you're such an asshole."

John could see the wince of the rebuke on Dean's face. The comment actually hurt the big man on campus. He saw Dean take a deep breath, and then he tapped Gloria on the shoulder.

"Okay, what is this big report you have to do that now seems to be in my immediate future?"

"God, you just don't know when to cease and desist, do you?"

"Why do you try to use words you know I have to look up to find out what they mean?" he protested. "You say I'm a snob—do you think I like it when you try to embarrass me? Maybe that's why I avoid you at home. You've always been that way."

Gloria seemed like the air had been taken out of her, and her shoulders slumped. She slowly turned and then with her dark glasses slipping down her nose, she adjusted them and shook her head.

"If I did that, I didn't mean to. But you know you think you're better than the rest of us in that town. Going to school here has even made you more arrogant. But as I said, if I did embarrass you, I'm sorry." She again took her books and turned toward the door as the second bell sounded.

"So, tell me about this Halloween report."

She turned and frowned. "You're just not going to stop, are you? Why would you want to spend your weekend with a blind chick? There are plenty of girls that would appreciate your company far more."

"Come on!"

Gloria stopped and in resignation said, "Okay, it's a report on some of the strange things in Moreno."

"Like?"

John's ears perked up, and he stepped closer to the two kids.

"Like the old ruins, for one."

"You know my dad and yours keep everyone out of there."

"Ah, I see. Afraid of Daddy again, are we?" she said as she turned and walked away. She called out over her shoulder as she tapped the chosen path with her cane, "Pick me up at nine tomorrow. We have to sneak in just before the guard change. But if I were you, I would just sleep in until the maid wakes you up, and then you can go and drink beer with the rest of your mutant friends out at Hog Road. I am capable of doing this on my own. Frankly, you would be in the way. But if you insist, I'll see you tomorrow morning."

Dean watched Gloria go and wondered just how bad this idea was. He saw her exit the class, and then he slowly left. John felt as well as knew the boy's thoughts and knew he was truly puzzled by the girl's passion when it came to her project, which interested Lonetree to no end.

John thought about Gloria's project and thought they may be onto something. In his dream state, they were mere days away from the disaster that would eventually destroy the town of Moreno, and he was short of time.

He felt the weariness grow inside him and knew he was close to waking. He started to leave the class when suddenly he was no longer inside. His breath came in short gasps, as he was now standing in a cold wind as he looked at the ruins. He could see one was an old mission from the aerial photos of Moreno that Leonard had shown them. The other, a run-down shamble of old adobe bricks. It looked abandoned, but John knew better. He tilted his head, as he thought he heard something. The chain-link fencing surrounding the property allowed the wind through, and it made a sad whistling sound as it passed. His eyes moved first toward the ancient mission. Then he turned to his right and spied the ruins of a building which, for a reason he couldn't understand, made him feel vulnerable and alone. The wind came on stronger, and he knew they had stumbled on a hot spot in the small town of Moreno. He immediately started drifting toward wakefulness as the words echoed in his dream.

Přived' ho domů.

John had never heard the language before in his life, but for a reason he couldn't fathom, knew the meaning of it. He didn't know how he knew, but it translated in his mind as if he was being spoken to. The strange words in the foreign language were being said right into his ears as the wind had faded and the dream came to an end. He would wake up with Jennifer and the others hearing those repeated words that had been brought in on that cold breeze.

Bring him home.

Julie was furiously writing down John's every word. Leonard had already seized on the last three words to come from the dreamwalk and was running the phonetic trace to translate the strange language. Jennifer was lightly rubbing John's hand and wrist to get him to come completely back to a wakeful state. Gabriel watched with the syringe with 10 cc of Adrenalin in case John had trouble waking. Kennedy relaxed when he saw Lonetree's eyes flutter and then come back. The action had taken far less time than Kennedy had hoped for.

"Look," George and Damian said at the same moment Dean started to move. John straightened in his chair and stretched his arms just as Hadley sat up straight with his gray eyes wide.

"Jenny, move John away from the bed," Gabe said as Hadley turned his head first right and then left, as he searched for something he could not see. As John stumbled from the chair, still groggy after viewing a brief moment in Hadley's life, Damian and George moved quickly to assist Jennifer in getting him clear of Hadley. Kennedy had explained once that when John dreamwalked while connected to a human host and not an object like Summer Place, the recipient of his strange talent usually awoke with resentment at the fact their most inner thoughts and dreams had been compromised. Even those who had requested John's intervention woke with a sense of being violated. Damian moved to turn the lights on after he had secured John and Jenny in the far corner next to Leonard's station.

"No, Damian, leave the lights off," Gabriel said, replacing his medical aids in the small black bag and standing to monitor Hadley's heart rate. It had skyrocketed. He was in danger of a stroke if they couldn't get him to calm.

"Where is she? What have you done?" Hadley said as he continued to move his head as if searching for someone or something.

In the corner, John came fully awake and then stood on shaky legs. He quickly gestured for Leonard to give him a writing pad. Sickles, wide-eyed, handed him a yellow legal pad, as John was still asleep. Jennifer was also confused, and she stopped Lonetree and mouthed, *Are you awake?*

John ignored her and wrote something on the pad and then pushed it hard into Jenny's hand. The anthropologist read the few words there and then started to hand the pad over to Gabriel, who became aware of the activity behind him and turned as Jenny pointed to the pad and started to give it to him. John vigorously shook his head and tapped Jennifer hard on the shoulder and pointed. He tried to speak, but it was like his mouth was full of cotton. He finally managed to get his point across. "You read it to Hadley," he said and then accepted the water bottle from Leonard, who was still scared and confused.

Kennedy nodded when Jennifer showed him the question. Jenny cleared her throat and approached the bed where Dean was still searching the darkened room for someone he knew to be lost.

"Dean?" Jenny said in a soft, motherly voice. Hadley stopped his search of the bedroom and then fixed his tired eyes on Jenny. She felt he wasn't seeing her but knew where to look. She definitely had his attention.

"Why are the ruins in Moreno so important?" she finished the question.

"That's private property, you know," he mumbled, and then his brow furrowed. "What do you mean you've been going down there since you were twelve?"

The others exchanged looks as Hadley slowly replayed something in his memory.

Suddenly, Hadley broke out into a laugh. It was an unnatural sound, it was forced like a soldier joking during a fierce firefight, it was for bravery's sake alone.

"Hey, don't touch that; that's mercury. This stuff shouldn't be here. Look, it's all over the damn thing. My dad will have a conniption fit if he discovers someone stole mercury from the plant; this stuff could contaminate the entire town, if not the valley if it got into the groundwater."

Hadley stayed in the sitting position, and then he slowly fell back onto the pillow. His eyes remained open, and they all could see the tears welling there. They watched as those tears slowly rolled down his cheek to soak into the white pillowcase.

"Meet . . . me . . . at . . . the . . . Grenada . . . we . . . can . . . kill . . . it . . . there . . . we . . . can . . . kill . . . it . . . there . . . we . . . can . . . kill . . . it . . . there . . ."

Gabriel watched as Hadley closed his eyes. And then in a soft voice, Hadley murmured, "Take me home."

The president had gone. He drifted away like an outgoing tide, and they watched the lined face relax. Kennedy nodded, and in the flickering candlelight, Damian flipped on the lights. Both bedside lamps flared, and they all blinked at the brightness.

Jennifer took Hadley's vital signs. Gabriel stood and went to the door after blowing out the two candles and then opened it and gestured for the doctors and nurses to enter. They were soon followed by the security detail. Leonard shut down his system after securing it and then transferred the data he had recovered over to his smaller laptop. He nodded and then followed the others out of the room.

The study was silent as they all recovered from the tense session with John. Jennifer gave Lonetree three aspirin, and he dry swallowed them as he stared at the table's shiny top. He rubbed his eyes and looked up at Kennedy.

"Those ruins are the key, I believe. When I looked at them, I knew there was something bad connected to them—maybe not the mission so much as the building next to it."

"The winery," Leonard said as he passed around a set of pictures he had downloaded and shown previously.

They all perused the photos once more, this time with far more interest.

"He kept talking about mercury. Why?" Jennifer asked John, who shook his head.

"Outside of the fact that the factory employed most of the town and used mercury in all their products"—Leonard passed another set of printed photos out—"it is the excuse used for the town's eventual death rattle. Other than that, I have no idea. But Hadley seemed to worry about it quite a bit."

John rubbed his eyes again and then opened them. "I got the feeling from the kid that it wasn't his knowledge that he passed on but his father's dire warnings about the effects of mercury on the human system. He was basically ignorant. A kid's warning to another kid. I don't know. I have to sort out my own feelings."

"What did you think of the girl?" Gabriel asked.

John smiled and felt as if his headache were easing up. "Gloria? I got the intense feeling that all of this, everything, revolved around her in some way."

"The report? Halloween?" Julie asked as she reread her notes from the dream session.

"I have to go back in. And this time, I need to have you tank me, Gabe. There's a lot more there. It's like something wants the story told, and I feel it's coming from the girl."

Gabriel looked back at Leonard, who sadly nodded and then leaned over from his chair and slipped him a sheet of paper. Kennedy read it and then closed his eyes. He finally opened them and then saw John was anxiously waiting for the bad news.

"Gloria Perry, seventeen years, two months, missing, presumed dead in the Grenada Theater fire. Her body and that of four others were never recovered."

John felt immense sadness at hearing that. The room was silent as Lonetree absorbed Leonard's research.

Julie cleared her throat, ever the reporter. "Her family?"

"Father only," Leonard said as he read from the computer screen. "Mother died while her father served overseas during the war, basically the same as our friend Dean Hadley. Raised by an aunt until her father returned." Leonard raised his brow when he noted an interesting fact. "The father, Franklyn Perry, was an intelligence officer. A captain. Guess who he served with and who his commanding officer in S-2 was?"

"Robert Hadley Sr.," John said through pursed lips.

"Franklyn Perry operated a bar and grill in Moreno and received profits from joint ventures with Hadley. The bar and grill business afforded him the time he needed to assist in his daughter's infirmity," Leonard said.

"She was blind, not infirm. I got the distinct impression that if that girl had not died before her time, we would have heard amazing things about her. No, Leonard, no infirmities."

"Bad choice of words."

"Hey, do I have competition for your affections?" Jenny joked, and John smiled.

"Can we agree that it all revolves around that small town in California?" Gabe said as he stood and paced. They all nodded.

"A disaster this size, why isn't this incident that well known? The deaths of that many should have been an historical black eye," Julie said as she again went into her conspiracy mode. This time, Gabriel didn't think she was wrong.

"Cover up," Leonard said. "Who were these men really working for? The United States Army or the OSS, or was it someone even more nefarious?"

"During the war years, the lines were a little blurred," Damian said. "I was approached by the CIA after my tours in Iraq. It's not all that uncommon."

"Leonard, is there any possibility you can find out what duties they had during their service time?" Gabe asked.

"None. No files exist that can be . . . well . . . stolen. Whatever they did was blocked from their 201 files. I do have a clue here. The words *Přived' ho domů*—and I hope I spelled that right—is Czech and also basically the same meaning in the Yugoslavian dialect. It means, 'Bring him home.' I can start there. Maybe their service careers had something to do with the Eastern European liberation by Allied forces."

"We may not have the time to wait for what you may come up with." All eyes again went to John. "I have to go back in, and this time, Gabe, you have to give me a kicker. Tank me until I am deep."

"I disagree, John. A kicker will send you down too deep; even with stimulants, we may not be able to wake you. Your heart may seize."

"I'm willing to take that chance."

"Well, I'm not!" Jenny said. "You think you can solve something that happened decades ago by tapping into a man who more than likely has murder on his résumé? You heard the tapes of your own voice describing Hadley as an arrogant little prick who has love for only himself."

"I always toss initial impressions, you know that. I get a feeling that the kid wasn't as bad as everyone believed. Why the cover up of the factory explosion? It was widely reported, but there was not one investigation outside of the local authorities. Look, this company made their bones on government funding. Are you telling me that the feds wouldn't have been all over this? And why didn't the State of California sue the crap out of Washington over the supposed groundwater contamination that the very same disaster brought on? And most importantly, why would Hadley Corp continue securing a place that was dead and buried in 1962?"

"Geronimo is right; there's too much bullshit here to not believe that something happened in Moreno that no one, and I do mean no one, wants out."

Everyone looked at Leonard. John was staring a hole in him.

"Sorry for the Geronimo thing."

"I think this stuff has been buried so long that everyone has forgotten where the bodies are, so to speak." Damian stood and went to the coffee maker. He saw and smelled the old coffee and decided that water would do. "No, as much as I do not appreciate the science as much as you do, I think we stand our best shot with Lonetree." Damian looked up and shook his head in acknowledging Jennifer and her own dilemma about the dangers posed by John reentering Hadley's memories.

Lonetree bit his lip. He didn't want to say anything about the troubling fact that he suspected Gloria Perry had heard him when he inadvertently laughed during the dreamwalk. That information, as troubling as it was, would be a death knell for going back in. Gabriel would never allow it if there was a hint of interaction between himself and the occupants of Hadley's dreamworld.

"Halloween."

Everyone turned to see Gabriel as he continued to pace. He stopped and saw that he had inadvertently spoken aloud.

"That's the deadline. It's gearing up for that point in time. Why now, after all these years? We may never know, but I suspect that all the clues point to Halloween and a supposed homecoming party for our Mr. Hadley."

"And everything revolves around that night?" Julie asked.

"It's been staring us in the face the whole time. Leonard, what is the current population of Moreno?"

Sickles looked at his notes. "Sixteen—mostly migrant families that have squatted there illegally, and several hangers-on, not counting the two security plants. There are four operating business, but the rumors of contamination have been successful in keeping most sane individuals out of there. Moreno is like the strange brother that California has hidden and chained in the attic."

"We have to get out to California and see what's up out there firsthand. We need to speak with survivors and the people who work there." Kennedy picked up his own notepad and looked it over until he found the section he wanted. "I especially want to interview this Bob and Linda Culbertson, the security team."

"Gabe, we don't have the time." John stood up, angry that he was being thwarted by his best friend. "That woman is relieving us in"—John consulted the grandfather clock and its swinging pendulum—"two hours."

Leonard stood and passed Gabriel the same folder he had produced earlier. "I think you need to start playing by the old rules, Professor Gabe. If this bitch wants to play hardball, play that way."

Kennedy slapped his hand down on the folder, and a smile slowly crossed his lips.

"I have a feeling we may find our asses right back in jail. Anytime we start taking advice from Mr. Spock here, we get into trouble," Damian said, referencing Leonard.

"Why, I'm just turning in a report the First Lady may or may not appreciate."

Damian shook his head at Gabriel and decided that it was close enough to noon, so he went to the bar. "God help us, blackmailing the First Lady of a grieving nation. We are truly wonderful people."

A knock sounded on the door, and the First Lady's assistant popped her head in.

"The White House Press Corp is out in front. The First Lady has called a news conference to inform the nation of the medical decision to move the president to hospital care in New Hampshire. She expects you to be available in case anyone has questions about your participation. It starts in fifteen." The sliding door closed.

The second battle for the soul of Moreno would start then.

11

MORENO, CALIFORNIA

Bob Culbertson hung up the phone. They had had to go to the old landline inside the radio station to get a clear message out. Their cell service, spotty at the best of times, was completely out. Bob picked up the heavy plastic handset and slammed it down again, feeling his first gesture of frustration was not good enough. For emphasis, he did it one last time as Linda watched from the record stacks that she was inventorying.

"I take it the office didn't give you good news," she asked as she moved her bulk from the stacks and made her way to the front of the radio station.

Bob angrily stalked to the window and looked out upon the overcast day. The entire valley had been covered in a fine mist most of the last two days, which didn't improve anyone's mood.

"There has been some sort of financial takeover of the company." He turned and faced his wife. "They say we may not have replacements, that we may be the last security detail assigned to Moreno."

"What does that have to do with us? Our contract is up as of November 1. Fuck them."

"I would normally agree, but I was informed to take a gander at section five, paragraph two of that contract. We are obligated to remain on station until we are officially relieved by the new security team. They are holding us to that clause until they find out what new ownership wants to do with the town."

Linda turned away and in an almost panic looked around the radio station that was disguised as a used record store. She shook her head. "This place is like sour milk; it's getting worse, not better." She turned back to face her husband. "You feel it as well as I do, Bob. We have to get the hell out of here," she said with finality.

"Well lose that ten-thousand-dollar bonus if we do," Bob said as he watched Linda blatantly light up a joint. Lately, she had become far more than an actress playing a part; she was starting to live the alias. He decided to join her.

Bob had just taken a hit and was coughing when he heard the music and the voice. He dropped the joint on the tattered rug between the record aisles as he looked up and back at the glass partition of the old DJ booth. It was completely dark inside.

"A friendly reminder from your favorite radio station, a day of freedom this Thursday, the day after Halloween! No school, no work. We are officially off so we can party hearty the night before. So, tune in for the announcements of the fright fest planned for Moreno. We are gonna party all night as the anniversary of the birth of Moreno happens right here, covered live, Halloween night on K-Rave. A special hello from the grateful town of Moreno to the president of the United States, John F. Kennedy, who faced the Russians down, and I mean faced them *down*, and sent them back to Russia with a swift kick in the derrière! What a country, what a town! And now to serve that very point on this cloudy October day, here is the Everly Brothers, and 'Crying in the Rain,' this is Freekin' Rowdy Rhoads at K-Rave!"

As they listened to the speakers overhead, the old song by the Everly Brothers started, and they jumped when they heard the tapping on the glass. Their mouths fell open when they saw the light in the booth was on. They could see the telescoping microphone, and most disconcerting, there was that same beatnik bearded man with the headphones on his ears tapping the glass just as he had three days before. Bob and Linda stared wide-eyed.

"Hey, I told you kids before you can't be in here!" he said through a static-filled intercom. "Roberta, what in the hell is going on out there? Do I have to run the reception area too?"

Bob finally looked at Linda, who was frozen to the spot as she watched the angry DJ pound on the glass hard enough that it shook. Both startled people turned around to see if someone was behind them, but they soon saw that the DJ was speaking only to them. They turned back and faced the angry man. Freekin' Rowdy Rhoads threw off the headset and stormed toward the soundproof door. Bob's eyes widened, and Linda took a step back as the door flew open and then—nothing. The light in the booth vanished as fast as Freekin' Rowdy Rhoads had as he exited the booth. The door creaked closed on its ancient hinges and then closed completely as the Everly Brothers's melodic voices faded to nothing.

Security for the town of Moreno stood rooted to the spot for at least a full minute as they stared into the darkness of the DJ booth. None of the equipment inside was seen, because it had been removed in the decades prior to Bob and Linda taking the job. Bob took a very long and deep breath as he finally turned to Linda, who was shaking from her massive thighs to her feet.

"I feel like lunch," he said, shaking and nodded toward the doors of the radio station. "You feel like lunch?"

Linda turned without a word and headed for the double glass doors of the station. As Bob opened it for her, there was one last insult to their sanity.

"And get a haircut, you damn beatnik!"

The casual stroll from the record store as if nothing had happened only moments before turned into free flight.

VIRGINIA COUNTRYSIDE

The gaggle of reporters pushed and shoved as all the decorum they had shown during press conferences at the White House was a thing of the past. They all needed closing chapters written about the last days of the American Caesar, Dean Hadley.

The president's press secretary was still on the job, working for the new administration and was not available. Instead, the First Lady had representation consisting of her personal assistant and the lead medical doctor. Catherine stood by with a neutral expression, nodding and looking sad at the appropriate moments. She turned her head slightly as Julie, followed by Gabriel, stepped out onto the front steps underneath the large portico. Kennedy held the report that was supplied by Leonard. The rest of the Supernaturals remained inside.

Gabriel took a sly step toward the First Lady, and she dipped her head for the benefit of the gathered reporters. As the lead physician gave his report on the president's condition, Kennedy discreetly handed Catherine the large folder.

She smiled and leaned into Kennedy. "And what is this?"

"The opening page will give you the gist," Gabriel said as she placed her hands over his and the file and then smiled as if greeting a friend for the benefit of the reporters.

Catherine, still smiling, opened the folder and read. She looked up, never missing a beat with the offending smile. "Speculation that would be torn apart in a court of law."

Kennedy smiled. "But not the important court—the court of public opinion." He smiled and nodded as if he and the First Lady were having a nice and friendly conversation. "This could dog you for quite some time. As a matter of fact, the assets may have to remain in trust for years until this is figured out. It's an awful lot of wealth. You would have gotten away with it if you had Avery stick with the insanity thing."

Catherine closed the file folder and nodded, again playing her role as professionally as possible.

"Do you think you have that much credibility with the public?"

Kennedy smiled, and this time, it was no act. "I direct the same question to you, Madam First Lady. Do you have the credibility to fend off the innuendos printed there?" He eased closer. "Your Mr. Avery left tracks in the snow, so to speak. This report will attract attention. With as many enemies as you and the president have collected over the years—him through actions, you through rumor—I think CNN would have a field day investigating this little gem."

Showing her teeth but smiling nonetheless, Catherine handed the folder back to Gabriel.

"What do you want, Professor?"

"Time. Not much to ask considering what you stand to gain." He smiled and then faced her fully. "You give us until November 1, and you can have that file and the two copies we made. It will be our little secret. On the condition, of course, that we don't find any evidence of your collusion in the president's predicament. That's three days and a flight to California. Also, if we find the need, we want to take the president back home."

"To Moreno? You've got to be kidding."

Kennedy tried to hide his astonishment, realizing Catherine knew exactly where Hadley was from—not the purified, made-up story everyone else knew but the truth.

The First Lady saw the shock on Gabe's face. "Oh, don't look so shocked; there's nothing Hitchcockian about it. Dean always talked in his sleep, the poor tormented bastard. And I know about that little blind slut he cries over too. As I said, the insane son of a bitch talks in his sleep—some things even his maniac father and his cronies in D.C. couldn't cover up."

Kennedy remained silent as Catherine made her point. He slapped the file on his thigh as he awaited her answer.

"So, to explain things more on the personal side, I give you the First Lady of the United States, Catherine Hadley."

She heard the announcement from her assistant, and then without missing a beat, she half turned back, still smiling, and nodded at Gabriel.

"November 1, Professor—not a day later."

Kennedy took a breath and then turned away as the press corps was fed a line of crap from the First Lady about how a mistake on dates had been made, much to the doctor's standing alongside of her confusion about the timetable to move Hadley to a hospital for special care. He failed to hear the rest of her presentation as he entered the house.

"Well?" Julie asked as she and the others joined them.

"We'll be heading to California tonight. We have our two days."

Sickles's plan of blackmail had worked, at least for the time being. How long it would last until the First Lady gathered her senses and courage, no one was sure. It would be at least until Catherine got real legal advice from the five-million-dollar-a-case law firm representing her. They could only hope their delay reached the thirty-first of this month—in three days.

"Well, let's see if we can save this man's life and find out just what in the hell Hadley's father brought to the small town of Moreno that killed it in 1962."

The Supernaturals were again going into the field, all with memories of Summer Place and the horrors discovered there still as fresh in their minds as if it happened yesterday.

VIRGINIA COUNTRYSIDE

After the White House Press Corps returned to Washington, things at the country house settled down. The bedroom upstairs had been quiet after it was decided to monitor the president's condition remotely. The deaths surrounding Hadley's illness were garnering attention, and the new administration was finding it exceedingly difficult to keep the details from public view.

It was after ten at night when Gabriel could get everyone together in the study. The arrangements had been made by the Secret Service and the FBI to fly the team to Moreno. They would arrive in Ontario a little after five in the morning and be inside the town no later than seven.

"Before we get started, I think I'm needed out there with you guys. I'm the detective here. You need me," Damian said, looking far fresher than he had that afternoon after getting a good five hours of sleep. Damian had been informed earlier that he and Leonard would remain behind for security reasons to keep the team informed directly of any change in Hadley's condition.

"I need you here with Hadley. More to keep an eye on"—he hesitated as he looked toward the back door Catherine Hadley had a habit of popping out of—"certain family members."

"Babysitter," Jackson corrected angrily.

"Yes, a babysitter with a gun and legal knowledge. I need you to make sure that woman sticks with our agreement. We all may dislike that man up there in bed just as much as the country—and the world, for that matter—but we need to know what is happening to him. We can all agree we have never seen anything this intense before that is being done remotely."

Damian shrugged but finally nodded.

"Leonard was able to dig up a little more."

Leonard Sickles turned away from the two PCs and three laptops he had up and running. He stood and went to the conference table and sat with an armful of papers. He dropped a few, and John Lonetree picked them up. Before he handed them back to Leonard, he saw the agency logo at the top of the page. Leonard smiled when he saw John take notice of the header. He winked at Lonetree, who pursed his lips and whistled softly.

"We have rumor, innuendo, and speculation, but nothing really solid about Hadley Sr. and his wartime activities. For a man with a college degree and no money before the war, he seemed to come out of it in pretty good shape."

"Did you find out where his windfall came into play?" Gabriel asked as he lowered his glasses and looked over the rims at the computer whiz.

"Again, speculation only. We have a how, but not a why." Leonard pulled a sheet of paper out and passed it down the line. "Moreno sits on land once owned by the federal government, even before the State of California got involved over the local historical aspects of the area, meaning the old mission and winery. The government had owned it since late 1928."

"Why would the feds be interested in old ruins?" Jennifer asked as she received the old papers that Leonard had dug up from the National Archives.

"It wasn't the ruins; it was the small deposits of a mineral found in the hills surrounding the future town. This source of mercury occurs in deposits throughout the world, mostly as the mineral cinnabar, or mercuric sulfide. The red pigment vermilion is obtained by grinding natural cinnabar or synthetic mercuric sulfide into a thick paste. The government needed all the mercury it could find for the war effort in the forties. Thus, the small work camp known as the Alfred Moreno mining concern was started. It was named after some local Mexican cowboy from the western days."

"The work camp that eventually became the town of Moreno, I take it?" George Cordero asked, not too enthused about his impending trip to the town.

"That clairvoyance never fails you, does it, George?" Leonard joked, and George shot him the finger. "Anyway, I suspect that was the initial basis for Hadley Sr.'s interest in the area. It's the mercury he needed for his high-tech gauges and meters—not too mention mercury for lighting and temperature variance applications."

"Was Hadley's father a chemical engineer?" Julie asked, smelling something fishy in the story.

"No. As a matter of fact, he didn't even run the day-to-day operations of the company; he was too busy investing elsewhere. And get this— investing before the gauge and meter company even started to turn a profit, meaning—"

"He had a lot of money before he should have," Gabriel said, heading Leonard off at the pass.

Sickles cleared his throat. "Yeah, that's right. Where did all of this come from?"

"Obviously, the feds, right?" John asked as he to finally read the investment report.

"Again, speculation only. It's hard to follow a paper trail when that paper is just money. There is nothing other than a bill of sale in the national accounting office."

"What did Hadley pay for the land?" Julie asked.

"One dollar in 1946."

The others looked at each other when they heard that Hadley Sr. had gotten something free from a federal government that was flat broke at the time after the long and costly war.

"I hit dead end after dead end in my search for the hows and whys of this thing, until I thought that if Hadley Sr. had no chemistry background, someone sure as hell had to. Mining cinnabar, or mercuric sulfides, is a

process with tremendous dangers and even more state and federal government oversight. They had to have a top man in the field, so I went into the
Internal Revenue database."

Again, the smiles came at the mention of Leonard's special skills at
backdooring computer systems.

"It was reported that the highest-paid person at the Hadley Corp Gauge
and Meter Company was an engineer by the name of Alfred McDonald.
And guess what? He was also in Hadley Sr.'s intelligence team during the
war. I guess he had a lot of partners after the fighting stopped. It was like
splitting up the spoils."

"Spoils of what?" Jennifer asked.

"Spoils of whatever it was they found during the fighting." Leonard
shuffled through his papers and handed George the sheet, who passed it
down the line. "One interesting point. A consultant was also on payroll
with a salary and a material outlay paid for by Hadley." Leonard smiled.
"It seems this consultant, a Dr. Jürgen Fromm, was paid an annual salary
of over three hundred thousand dollars and had a business expense account averaging over two million dollars a year."

"That would raise eyebrows even in today's dollars, much less the
forties," Damian said. That was a lot of money being thrown around by
former soldiers in the field and possibly their federal backers.

"Background on this doctor?" Gabriel asked, and Leonard smiled.

"I don't know, but I did hit on an interesting cross-reference when
checking the military database. It seems before 1945, a Dr. Jürgen Fromm
was listed as a war criminal by the Allied commission on crimes against
humanity. After the war, he was taken off that particular list. Why? I don't
know. It was buried so deep I could find nothing."

"Hadley and his friends had some very interesting acquaintances,"
Lonetree said, beginning to see a pattern of bad behavior going far beyond
than just the younger Hadley.

"Very," Gabe said, pushing his glasses back up his nose. "What was
this German doctor's specialty?"

"Don't know, but I do know where his funding was coming from, no
matter what he did for it. The good doctor was paid by the Luftwaffe."

"Where?" Gabriel asked, knowing beforehand where the doctor
practiced.

"Czechoslovakia and Yugoslavia."

"Interesting coincidence, isn't it?" Julie asked with a smirk. Her
reporter's hackles had gone into full-drive mode.

"So, to summarize, our Robert Hadley, a full-bird colonel in army intelligence who also worked for the OSS, hired and paid for a war criminal that the government was hiding here in America."

"I don't know any other way to interpret this," Lonetree said. "George, do you have any feelings hearing this news?"

"No, other than the fact that Leonard's telling the truth. If I could be around Hadley when asked about it, I could get a better feel for it."

"You may get that chance in a few short hours." Gabriel looked around the table. "Anything else, Leonard?"

"Just this," he said as he gave them another paper to look at. "Found it in the National Archives database."

"What is Operation Caged?" Gabriel asked, his brow furrowed.

"Don't know," Leonard said, giving them the last paper. "Operation Caged was a code name for some army OSS black mission at the end of the war. I came up with it when I cross-referenced Hadley, Fromm, and S-2 OSS. This is what the operation was about."

The paper was passed from confused person to confused person. It was headed by the operational order number, and then every single word, line, and signature was blacked out.

"Not very forthcoming, were they?" Gabriel said when he saw the censorship of the operational order and its results.

"Not much to get from the Freedom of Information Act. This was what met the War Crimes Commission when they requested info on the missing Fromm." Leonard finally sat down and looked around. That was all he could dig up about Hadley's past. "I am still digging into this Nazi doctor's specialty. I'll have something in a few days, as I am still trying to see what the German database has to say."

"Good. Stay on it."

A knock sounded on the door, and Julie opened it. A member of the doctor's staff was there, and she looked quite nervous.

"The president is awake, well, sort of semiconscious. He wants to see someone he called the Indian."

"We happen to have one of those," Julie said as she tried but failed to hide her surprise that Hadley was awake and somewhat coherent.

Gabriel stood and gestured for them to follow. Now was the time to get some answers while they had the chance.

The hostage rescue team commandos allowed the group to enter as the last of the doctors left the president's side. They gave the team dirty looks as they were shuffled aside for whatever voodoo these people performed. None of the medical staff wanted them there. This was a problem with the mind, and they didn't need amateurs mucking up their efforts.

Gabriel was the first to see the president, who was sitting up in bed and staring straight ahead at a damaged wall. The group filed in, and John stepped to the forefront.

"Mr. President, do you know or have you ever met anyone in this room?" Gabriel asked as he pulled a chair close and then sat as the others formed a circle around the bed. It looked like they were viewing some form of rare animal in a zoo. Hadley noticed.

"It's been that bad, huh?" he asked as his eyes moved from damaged wall to damaged wall.

"Let's just say you've made things interesting, sir."

Hadley finally turned his head and found the man speaking to him. His gray hair was a tangle, and his beard was getting rather long. His eyes were bloodred, and he had a hard time focusing on Gabriel's face. Then his eyes went to the others, passing each with no knowledge of who they were. His eyes did linger on the last man in line, John Lonetree.

"Don't know any of you—except for him," he said, nodding toward John. "It seems I've seen you before recently." He coughed, and Gabriel handed him a glass of water. The president drank deeply and choked, alarming those watching him. He settled and handed the glass back to Gabe. "Or maybe I don't know you. It's confusing. A long-ago memory, or recent—I just don't know." Hadley closed his eyes. "I'm tired." He looked at Lonetree. "You saw her, didn't you?"

John knew exactly who Hadley was referencing. He eyed Gabriel, who lightly shook his head, and John understood. "Who, sir?"

Hadley looked more intently at Lonetree. "I'm too old a dog to play that game, my good man. Now quit being the mysterious Indian you like to personify and tell me if you saw her."

John nodded. "Yes, I saw her."

Hadley actually smiled. "It was you in class, wasn't it?"

John looked shocked at first, and then Gabriel encouraged him when he nodded to answer. Jennifer wasn't so sure.

"Yes, I was there. World history with Miss Kramer."

"You weren't a student; I would have known. I knew everyone who went to high school in Chino, and my friend, you are not from Chino."

"Not Moreno either," Gabriel said for John.

Hadley looked from Lonetree to Kennedy.

"And who are you?" Hadley's brow furrowed. "You look familiar, to say the least."

"A doctor of sorts."

"What kind of answer is that? You sound like my wife, always hiding something."

"You hid quite a bit yourself over the years," Damian said as he made his large presence known.

"Okay, so you know about Moreno. I'm not concerned with that. I need to ask this gentleman some questions. Can you step closer to the bed?"

John looked at Jennifer and then Gabriel as he did as requested.

Only George saw the change in Hadley's eyes. From one moment to the next, his demeanor changed from a friendly one to one of malice. His fears grew for no other reason than the vibes he was getting. The room changed as Lonetree stepped up to see Hadley closer. The light dimmed, and George had to say what he was feeling.

"No, it's a trap; that's not Hadley!"

The lights went out as the president's hand grabbed Lonetree's wrist. Jennifer and Gabriel stood at George's warning shout, but it was too late. John's eyes rolled back into his head as he collapsed onto the bed. The others felt the warmth sapped from the bedroom, and they all heard the locking mechanism on the door engage. They could hear pounding from out in the hallway as the power went out throughout the house. Then the electric shock coursed through their bodies, and each person in the room followed Lonetree's example as they too collapsed. Damian hit his head hard against the wall, and George fell onto the silk-and-wood dressing screen, knocking it over. Julie fell from her chair, as did Jennifer. Gabriel felt his eyes tunnel vision for the briefest of moments, and before his conscious mind let go, he felt the time frame he was in change. The sense of speed hit him, and he briefly remembered the description John had given him once for the initial stages of a dreamwalk. This was what he was feeling, as he too fell back into the chair he was sitting in just as Hadley, or the thing inside Hadley, laughed, and the sound echoed throughout the enormous house, shaking the wooden frame and foundation.

The entity in Moreno was now in control.

12

Julie hit her head. "Ow!" It was an automatic reaction to looking up at the sky and the feeling of falling and then the expectation of the impact. It never happened that way. In the sense of a dream, Julie landed without pain.

Leonard fell on his tailbone, and he lost the ability to breathe as the pain struck with a vengeance. And that was exactly what his mind told him to think.

John and Jennifer bumped heads as they fell to a cold sidewalk, and Damian and George awoke sitting down on a tiled surface with people walking around them and through them. George panicked and crawled away, as did Damian. Men and women simply moved through them as if they weren't there. Damian crawled until the flood of feet and ankles vanished and he found himself on the sidewalk next to Leonard, who was still trying to catch his breath. Before Damian knew what was happening, hands were grabbing at him as someone helped to get him standing again. He tried to focus as he saw Leonard and George helped to their feet. He saw Lonetree, Julie, Jennifer, and Gabriel as they stood there with the same look on their faces.

"I think I'm going to be sick," Julie said as she braced herself for the embarrassment that comes from vomiting in front of your friends.

"It will pass in a second. I always feel the same way." John tried in vain to orient himself. He would later admit the truth to all—he had never experienced a dreamwalk in quite this way. He was not in control, and he didn't know if the sensation of movement through time was a real one. His head was spinning.

"The same way as what?" Leonard asked, realizing that he was rubbing his ass for no apparent reason.

"I suspect when he dreamwalks," Gabriel said, trying to focus on where he was. His eyes widened when he saw where Damian was standing. He reached out to pull him back, but knew he was too late. The red Corvette convertible swung toward him, and the hip-high hood passed right through him as the car swerved to the curb and then stopped.

They all saw what had just happened and stood with mouths agape. He swallowed and then stepped quickly out of the street.

The blond driver sat for a moment and then turned the sports car off and athletically jumped out without opening his door. The radio playing Buddy Holly stopped, and the world became silent as each of them looked around.

"Is this—" Leonard began.

"Moreno," John said as he watched the men, women, and children stroll along the sidewalks. He turned and saw the blond kid walk into a darkened doorway and vanish.

"What?" Damian asked as the others turned to face John as if it was his fault they found themselves here.

"We're in Moreno," he said as he faced Gabriel with a questioning look. "Hadley?"

"I don't think so," Kennedy said as he too took in the town around them. The passing cars that sprang from another era. The storefronts from out of a back-lot movie studio. The dress of the men, the hats they wore. The children with their Saturday clothes on. The rolled-up cuffs of jeans, the crew cuts on the teenagers.

"It wasn't Hadley; that was something else in that bedroom inside the bastard. I thought he was too nice and agreeable at seeing us," Jennifer said just as George nodded in agreement.

"I saw the change in Hadley right before this shit happened. The vibes coming off him were not just a single mind but many. We were ambushed," Cordero said as he saw the strange dress of the people coming in and out of varying shops and stores. He turned and saw the neon sign in the darkened window that announced that they were standing in front of the Bottom

Dollar Bar and Grill. "That was something else in that bedroom. I don't suppose you can get us the hell out of here."

"I don't even know how we got here." Gabriel looked down at Cordero, and it was plain to see he was confused. "Can you give us the time to work this out, or do you have something you have to do?"

Cordero frowned. "Look, we are not you. I happen to be scared to death."

Gabriel stepped up and took George's shoulder and squeezed. He didn't feel the material of the coat under his fingers. He also couldn't feel the pressure he was exerting on George either. This was a definite dream state—or a nightmare, depending on the person. George's stance was clear on the subject.

"Take it easy. We got in; we'll get out somehow."

"I guess we can start by seeing what the kid is doing here," John said as Jenny took his arm and closed her eyes, not believing where they found themselves.

"What kid?"

"That blond kid who would have run down Damian if we were solid and not just a temporary fixture here."

"Hadley?" Damian asked. "Damn, he was a spoiled kid, wasn't he?" Damian looked at the shiny Corvette as Gabriel turned and reached for the wooden door handle of the Bottom Dollar. His hand went right through it, and Lonetree laughed.

"That's not the way things work here." John stepped past Kennedy with Jenny, and they walked right through the door.

Gabriel smiled. He felt a little nauseated, and then he and Julie went next.

"Hey, hey, can we figure out first how we got here and if we can get back?" Leonard said, eyeing an old lady walking by him and then another as she walked through him. He shivered and then smelled an old woman's perfume. It was a fragrance his grandmother used to put on, and it curdled the dinner he had in his stomach. Lavender. The old ladies walked into a shoe store with a giant red goose in the store's window.

"Red Goose Shoes," Damian read aloud just as a child inside the store went to the felt-covered goose inside the display window. They watched as one of the store's employees allowed the boy of about ten years old to pull down on the goose's neck. The long neck and the golden bill bent, and then much to the delight of the laughing and happy child, a golden egg rolled out of the goose's backside and slid down a winding track and then settled into a nest of the fake bright green grass used in Easter baskets. The employee gave the egg to the boy, and he opened it until candy fell free, much to his delight. Damian smiled.

"My ma"—he choked up a little at the memory—"told me about this place when she was a kid. Used to be a national chain of shoe stores. Went out of business in the late sixties or seventies, I think."

"Well, I guess that goes a long way to proving we're not in Kansas anymore, Toto," Leonard said as he watched the red goose in the window as they finally followed Gabriel and the others into the darkened bar. "Is it me, or was bending the goose's neck like that a little creepy?"

"Man, I don't like this," George said, standing close to Damian as they literally walked through the door to follow the others. This fact scared the hell out of all of them. They found the others standing in the dimly lit bar.

"I don't know about you guys, but I'm shaking, I'm so freaked out right now," George said. "I am getting no thoughts from these people at all. It's almost like . . . like—"

"Window dressing for the mind?" John said, wanting to get George back to study and not fear.

Gabriel, John, Jenny, Julie, George, Damian, and Leonard all stood just inside the door as they took in the bar and its patrons. Of course, they couldn't see the newcomers to town. There were several men and a few women at the bar and even more at the small round tables arranged in the dance area. The smell of old grease and hamburgers, along with stale beer and a smell none of them could place, wafted through the Bottom Dollar Bar and Grill. As Kennedy looked around, John tapped his shoulder and pointed at the bar where the kid was leaning up against it. A smaller man delivered a glass of something dark and placed it in front of their ghostly host—or was he the culprit?

They saw Dean's face not only in the bar's back mirror with its myriad of bottled libation but also from the many neon beer advertisements hanging on the walls. Pabst Blue Ribbon, Coors, the Banquet Beer, and Budweiser, the King.

"I'm with George; I'm just about ready to scream. This is too much," Leonard said, swallowing as he stepped closer to Hadley. He leaned in to study the boy's face more clearly. Only inches from his left cheek, Dean felt nothing of the intrusion.

"One Coke, no ice," the bartender said as he placed the coaster and the glass down in front of Dean. "That'll be two bits, kid."

Dean looked at the man and smiled. "My good name doesn't allow for a Coke on the house?" he asked while his smile grew.

John looked at the others and then shook his head. "Told you, a real asshole."

Dean momentarily looked their way, and Kennedy and Lonetree exchanged looks of interest.

"Your good name stops at the front of my door, boy. As Charlie said, two bits," said a good-looking man walking in from the back as he wiped his hands on a dirty towel. He tossed it over his shoulder to hang as Dean produced the quarter for his drink and plopped the coin on the bar. "Now, what are you doing in here? I don't like kids hanging out. Looks bad, and we both know your father would crap his pants if he caught you in here."

Dean smiled before he sipped his Coke.

"I told him to pick me up here, and you know that," came the sweet voice of a girl as she came through the same door as her father had a moment before. She smiled at the older man as she eased her way around and felt for her father. She found his back, turned him away from his little confrontation, and then went to her tiptoes to kiss him on the cheek. "You know that because I told you yesterday I was going to be stuck with him for a school assignment. I don't like it either, believe me."

"Gloria?" Kennedy asked John.

The girl kissed her dad and slipped her dark glasses on, shutting out the view of her magnificent blue eyes. Dean swallowed more of his Coke and then turned white when the man came directly to him.

"Where are you going?" he asked Dean, who looked to them like he wanted to leave in the worst way.

"All these years that you've been my father's limited partner, and you don't even trust his son? What is the world coming to? President Kennedy and old Nikita learned to work things out. Why can't you and my father?" Dean said as he placed his Coke down on the bar. They all noticed the boy really did expect, or at least hope, for an answer, but Gloria's father stood silently in front of him. They could also see that the father had little love for the boy or the father Gloria's dad had served with.

Gloria stepped closer to Dean and leaned across the bar. Her head tilted as she smiled. "It's too late tonight to go where it is we need to go," she whispered. "No one goes there after dark. Tomorrow morning will do. In daylight," she said with an aura of mystery lacing her words. "Now go away, Richie Rich; you can hang out with the common folk someplace else."

Dean looked embarrassed and remained silent as Gloria left the bar and then went into the tavern proper. He watched as she walked about the barroom, talking with the patrons sitting at small, round tables.

"She is something, isn't she? Confident for her condition," Jenny said as she watched the girl move from table to table, removing empties and speaking with each of her father's customers.

"Told you," John said.

Kennedy stepped closer to the bar so he could see the exchange between Gloria's father and the boy.

"Look, boy, the situation between me and your father is better left alone. As for you, I know how you drive and how you treat people. Do I have to tell you what I would do to you if something happened to my little girl?"

The look from the teenager actually moved the emotions of those watching him. They saw real hurt in Dean's eyes that made this scene very interesting.

"I would never allow anything to happen to Gloria."

They could see he was serious.

"I hear how you and the others at school talk about those kids that are different. I hear you're the biggest mouth there is." The man leaned in closer to Dean. "That's what I hear."

"Dad, stop it," Gloria said as she stepped to the bar and placed empties there with no difficulty. "I'll be a minute, and then we can talk about what we have to do tomorrow. Right now, Charlie wants to play something for me," she said while facing the bar. "Tomorrow we can go exploring if you have the courage."

"And just where is that?" her father asked as he poured a beer from the tap and handed it to the man sitting next to Dean.

"Can we drink while in this state?" George asked, wanting a shot of bourbon so badly he could feel the jitters in his body. *If I had a body*, he thought.

"How about we find out how this *thing* has so much power behind it that it can pull us, at least temporarily, into its world? Or a mirror image of its world," John said as he turned and joined Jenny at the piano, where Gloria waited.

"She wants to take me to the place she's writing about for her Halloween story. No big deal."

Her father raised a brow and then fixed Dean with a look. "Everything concerning my daughter is a big deal."

They could see that Dean wanted to say something, but he held off as he too turned to watch Gloria.

Charlie, the man that was just relieved at the bar by Gloria's father, came in and then handed the young blind girl a sheet of paper. "Freekin' Rowdy Rhoads said it came in yesterday," he said as he pulled out the piano stool and sat.

Gloria smiled as she ran her hand over the sheet music. "Can you play it?"

"It's not that complicated," Charlie said as he took the sheet music from her small hands. "You sure you know the words?"

"Are you kidding?" Gloria said as she stepped around the piano.

The men and women in the bar became aware that Frank Perry's little girl was about to sing.

To the ghostly visitors to the Moreno of the past, it looked that this was a regular event at the Bottom Dollar. They could see by the smile that finally etched its way across Frank's gruff and tanned face that he encouraged her to do so, even in a shady bar with people twice her age. Even Dean forgot about his interrogation and stepped to a nearby table and sat down, interested in what Gloria was up to. He didn't know this side of the girl he always knew but rarely spoke to. He looked from the anticipatory smiles of the customers to the girl. She seemed to be entering into a world Dean never knew existed for her.

"Just play it at the right speed: slow. I don't have Neil Sedaka's voice and pacing."

"You would embarrass Sedaka," Charlie said as he raised the keyboard cover and started jingling the ivories.

To Jennifer, all of this seemed so familiar with her haunting memories of Bobby Lee McKinnon still fresh in her mind. Even John saw the connection and held her that much tighter as a familiar refrain from an old song started to be hashed out by the burly bartender. Far slower than the original, it had everyone's attention—especially Dean, who didn't even know Gloria could sing.

The song was slow and her voice was full of real talent as she opened with the haunting words from decades before their time. The Supernaturals knew them well.

Don't take your love . . . away from me . . . don't you leave my heart in misery . . .

Everyone, real or dream, could not believe their ears at the soft, melodic voice. It carried well across the small barroom. Even Dean turned and looked at her adoring father as words and song came from her mouth. John nudged Jenny, and they both saw the smile form on the spoiled kid's face as he realized how talented this girl was. Gabriel smiled. Leonard and Damian did the same, as did Julie and George. They were enraptured by Gloria as she sang sitting next to Charlie, who was grinning from ear to ear as he played.

If you go, then I'll be blue . . .'cause breaking up is hard to do . . .

Dean was staring at Gloria as her father stepped from behind the bar, listening to his little girl. The customers weren't just being polite because it was the owner's daughter; they had never heard a voice like Gloria's before.

The song slowly dwindled, and the barroom was completely silent. They saw the girl become uncomfortable, and they called out to her and clapped their hands together as she stood up and then leaned down and kissed Charlie's cheek. She gave them all a fancy curtsy, her knees bending until the hem of her skirt touched the top of her black-and-white saddle shoes with her plaid shoestrings. Embarrassed, she walked back to the bar, feeling her way carefully to where her father greeted her with a bear hug, lifting her from the floor. Dean stood and looked absolutely miserable at the way her father adored his daughter. The group could see the interest in Dean's eyes.

"Man, that girl can sing!"

Everyone, with the exception of the materially real people, turned and looked at Jenny when the male voice exited her mouth. It was Bobby Lee commenting.

"Sorry," Jenny said in her real voice as she placed a small hand over her mouth. "That was like a burp I couldn't hold back. I guess the young lady's song met with Bobby Lee's approval, and he never, ever gave anyone credit for anything if he had nothing to with writing it or singing it."

Gabriel smiled as he realized that Bobby Lee was with them and that the ghost might come in handy, especially the period they found themselves lost and scared to death in.

"For now, I'm just going to explain my assignment to Howard Hughes Jr. here. I'll have him drop me off at home." She kissed her father, who was busy glaring at Dean.

"Think we ought to follow?" George asked. "Watch that damn kid," he said direly, and both teens left the bar. The others followed them out. They watched Gloria chuck off Dean's hand when he tried to assist her to the car.

They heard the Corvette rev to full life, but they noticed the sound faded before the car pulled away. It was like the sounds were now coming from a great distance. John felt his legs go weak, as did the others. Leonard fell to the cracked sidewalk and then saw the light fade from the sky and just as quickly return.

"What's happening?" Damian asked as he tried to lean against a parking meter and then shocked when his hand passed right through and he fell into the gutter.

"It's weak," John said, shaking his head. He felt his eyes growing heavy. "It has expended a lot of its power in getting us here."

Gabriel and Julie tried to remain standing, but Julie fell first at Kennedy's feet. As he felt his legs start to go, a man wearing a brown fedora stepped up to him. The hands reached out and steadied his shaking frame. Gabe felt the pressure of the man's hands on his chest, and he looked up as he steadied. The man's eyes were dark, and he smiled, showing gold caps and filings. The wire-rimmed glasses reflected Gabe's image, which was shocking, since he knew he shouldn't be able to see himself inside the dream. The man had stained teeth but was well dressed in a gray jacket and white shirt buttoned all the way to the collar.

"Yes, it fades. Your time here is at an end."

Gabriel tried to focus. He half turned and saw John and the others staring up from where their legs had given out. He saw that they were just as startled as he was.

"Powerful, are they not?" the man said in an accent Kennedy knew well. The man was German. The words were thick with disdain for Gabriel and his people. "I thought I had caged them, but I was fooling myself." The man moved his hands from Gabe's chest to grab his collar and shake him until his drooping eyes fluttered back open. "They toy with your mind. They are powerful, just as my work said they were. Now I am believed." The man laughed and then let go of Gabriel, who fell backward toward the sidewalk. "Let the boy go; they always win in the end, and the girl cannot assist you. She is blind in many more ways than just the loss of sight." Again, the laughter, but this time, Kennedy heard it as his own lights faded and he once again fell through time and space. "She's the cause of it all. The little bitch ruined my work and killed us all!" The last words echoed in Gabe's brain as he vanished into nothingness.

The first person in the room Gabriel checked on was the president. After such an active awakening, Hadley lay with eyes closed. Two went to the president's bedside, and the others assisted the members of the Supernaturals to their feet and into chairs or sitting positions on the floor.

"Amazing brain activity for thirty-two seconds," one of the military doctors said as he read the EKG readout.

Gabriel heard the fact repeated three or four times before it registered in his mind. John Lonetree, with Jennifer leaning heavily against him, wandered over. They both looked to Kennedy like they had been through hell's e-ticket vision of dreaming.

"Thirty-two seconds?" Gabe asked as he removed the EKG tape from the doctor's hand and scanned it for the obvious mistake.

"Yes, that was the duration of the event."

"Thirty-two seconds?" Leonard moved his small frame from the floor to a chair. He now had a headache that pounded the space between his eyes and the back of his head.

"You mean while Hadley was dreaming, we were only gone thirty-two seconds?" Jenny asked incredulously.

"Wait, my watch says we were in here for twenty-five minutes, at the very least," Julie said as she helped the much larger Damian to sit in a chair, where he rubbed his temples.

"Mine says the same thing," the former state policemen said as he finally chanced a look up into the bright lights of the room.

"We know through clinical testing that dreams are naturally short in duration. This proves we were not actually in Moreno," Gabriel said, leaning over and raising Hadley's eyelids to check for dilation. "The human brain dreams it, compacts it, and displays the dream, all to keep it short in duration, or the human mind could never totally be at rest. It's a defense mechanism against the dream running in real time. It would exhaust the mind even in sleep."

"That's yet to be proven," one of the younger doctors said from the president's side.

George Cordero tapped the doctor on the shoulder as he came close to the president to see if he could get a feel for the man's current state of mind. "You see the professor there?" he asked as he too leaned over Hadley. "He says it's true, so it is. He has many more years of study about the human mind than all of you put together." George felt Hadley's wrist and then closed his eyes. He opened them and looked at Gabe, shaking his head. "I get nothing, not even a sparkle of thought. He's deep again."

Kennedy shook his head, deep in thought, as the doctors looked at him strangely.

"How could this have happened, John?" Julie asked as she handed Damian a glass of water.

"This wasn't me. Something knew what I can do and expanded on that. It took us; I had nothing to with it." He stepped aside and forced Gabriel toward a more reclusive corner of the room. "Gabe, this thing, whatever it is, is far more powerful than we first thought. I felt more than one presence. It was like they want to relive this thing all over again."

"The man at the end of the dream?"

"What man?" John asked, because he hadn't the foggiest notion of what Kennedy was talking about.

"He means the German guy with the bad teeth," Damian said, raising the glass of water and sipping the coldness. He lowered the glass and faced the two men as the others gathered around them. "I saw him before I started to go bonkers. How did that fella see you, Gabriel?"

Kennedy looked to John. "Have you ever made contact like that before?"

"I have never interacted. I am dealing with human thought when I dreamwalk. I have little or no control where the subjects take me. Hell, they have little control themselves. But remember, this was not a dream. I suspect we were seeing a real memory."

"Whose memory?" Jenny asked. "It had to have been the younger Hadley; he was there."

"We just don't know enough." Gabriel turned and looked at the doctors as they gave Hadley an exam. He turned back and faced his very scared people. "We need to delay our trip west. At least until John is capable of finding out more."

"Oh, no, not another attempt at dreamwalking. We don't even know if John's really in control on this one. I say no; it's too risky. Whatever kidnapped us was not doing it to show us a good time. It did it because it could. A sort of nice way of warning us that we can't control it."

John kissed the top of Jennifer's head and looked at Kennedy. "I think it used a lot of power to do what it did. I felt it toward the end of our journey. It was weakened by the act of taking us mentally to Moreno. Now is the time to act when it can't get in the way. Only this time, I have to find a way to get to Gloria. I have a deep suspicion that all of this revolves around her, not just because of a teenage infatuation but because her part in the dream was the key point. I think it was Gloria's memory that we shared, not Dean's."

"Too much guesswork. If I were still a cop, I would have to say no, there's not enough evidence to support your conclusions and that we need to delve deeper."

They turned and saw that Damian had regained his strength. The man never had been through anything like that with the exception of the events at Summer Place. They could all see the adventure did not sit well with the former Pennsylvania detective.

"And a little futile," Jennifer said, angry at the chances John was willing to take for the unconscionable bastard lying in the bed. "You need to link with your subject, but unfortunately there is no subject in which to accomplish that. From what Leonard said, Gloria Perry was on the casualty list from Halloween night in 1962, so that makes your point moot."

"She's right," John said, giving Jenny a sour look for dashing their hopes so quickly. "I have nothing to connect with in regard to Gloria."

"I do."

They all turned and saw Catherine Hadley standing in the open doorway with a cordon of hostage rescue team men around her. Hadley's personal assistant was there also, and she handed the First Lady a small black box as she stepped in and politely closed the door.

"And suddenly you know far more things about your husband's past than you let on," Damian said, smelling a rat.

Catherine looked at Damian and shook her head. "Just what was I supposed to do, Mr. Jackson? Cry out that my husband, the most powerful man in the world, was so obsessed with a teenage crush that it drove him insane? That he risked everything this country had because of a guilt complex he has about killing that very girl? I don't think so," she said as she handed Kennedy the small black box and then turned but hesitated for a moment. "That was in a safe-deposit box in New York. I didn't find it until an asset check by my legal team. Evidently, Dean kept them all these years. You wanted a physical and material connection to that child from his past? You now have it." She started for the door. "I have informed the medical staff of your wish to continue."

"Does this mean you're giving us more time?" Kennedy asked as he held the small box.

"More time?" she had a smile on her face as she turned back to face the team. "Yes, as a matter of fact, we're going to grant Dean's wish, and yours. I have arranged for you and your patient to go to the one place in the world where you can figure this out. I monitored your last foray into the past with my husband. I heard him speak and also heard his request. I agree. He wants to go home."

"Moreno," George said.

"That is not what we are doing," Gabriel said as he watched her. "He could never survive the trip. He's exhausted."

"Nonetheless, my husband is being granted his dying wish. If you accompany him, that's fine; if not, my people will give you a ride to the airport."

To the surprise of all, it was George who confronted the powerful woman. "You'll be going also?" George winked in a show of confidence he hadn't shown in years. "With your love for your husband, you do want to find out what's causing this breakdown, right?"

Catherine smiled and then left the bedroom.

"I get the distinct feeling that she's trying to speed along the president's death." John looked from the closed door to Gabriel as he stated what the others also knew.

"And guess who is going to be there when he dies?"

"We were set up from the start. I would bet my life who recommended we be brought in on this. The natural fall guys, the nuts," Gabriel said, examining the black box he twirled lightly in his hand. He suddenly opened it as if it were a jack-in-the-box, expecting a demented clown to pop free. His eyes widened when he saw the box's contents. He pulled them out and showed the others. They recognized it because they had just seen them in the dream. Gloria Perry's green-tinted glasses were wire-rimmed and made for the blind.

The room was silent as they all saw Gloria's glasses. The lenses were cracked and the earpieces bent and out of shape. Gabriel swallowed as if he were holding an ancient artifact of tremendous importance.

George stepped up to Gabriel and eased the glasses out of his hand. "Do you mind?" he asked as he took the item. He held them in his hands and then wrapped his small fingers over the frames. He closed his eyes and then just as suddenly he allowed the glasses to fall from his grasp where they hit the carpet. He backed away a few steps and then he looked from person to person.

"What?" Leonard said as he stood from his chair at the sudden change that had come over his friend.

"Fire, water, quicksilver. It was everywhere. Betrayal. How could he?"

George said and then went silent. He blinked several times and took another step back from the glasses at his feet.

"Fire, water, quicksilver—what did you mean by it was everywhere, and betrayal?" Kennedy asked Cordero.

"It just came into my head." George never allowed his eyes to stray from the glasses as Kennedy retrieved them from the floor and looked at Lonetree.

"Watch out what you ask for, John. It seemed mighty convenient for the First Lady to give us this as a gift."

"I still want to do it," John said, turning to face Hadley and then looking at Jenny. "I don't know if it's to help him"—he turned to the door—"or to stop her. I just know I have to see things from the girl's side."

Jennifer nodded. "How deep will you have to go?" she asked.

John looked at Gabriel and raised his eyebrows.

"I suspect pretty damn deep if you want to really connect. All other times you had a living person to link with; even at Summer Place, you had the house itself and the personal memories it held. But now you'll be trying to connect to a dead girl."

"Are you saying you're going to do that kicker thing you talked about?" Damian asked.

Julie shook her head. "Put me on the record of saying that is the worst idea that I have ever heard."

"George, what do you think?" Gabe asked.

"Whatever and wherever the enemy is, it's not here right now. I believe John's right about it being taxed by the power it had shown us earlier. It won't remain weak for very long. I got the feeling of immense strength that hasn't been fully realized yet. I think if you're going to try something this stupid, now is the time."

"Gentlemen, can we have the room, please?" Kennedy said to a shocked team of physicians. They protested, but Gabriel's look said they must vacate. They filed out, again under protest.

"Like Julie, for the record, I'm against this," Damian said, angrily pouring more water from the carafe next to his chair.

"Let's get John ready." Gabriel looked at his old friend. "You're sure you are strong enough?"

"No, not at all," John said as he removed his blue shirt to expose a white T-shirt underneath. "But look at it this way—I get one of your famous downer cocktails to go on. That's one hell of a kicker."

Jenny didn't like the joking, but she knew when John and Gabriel were afraid, they joked, a tendency she never acquired after Bobby Lee McKinnon's haunting of her soul.

"Okay, let's try to get Gloria Perry's attention, shall we?"

13

It was after midnight when Leonard and Jennifer connected the last of the leads that would monitor John's health as he walked among the thoughts of a dead girl. John sat in a high-backed chair as he watched Jenny sticking the last lead to his chest. He smiled, but she didn't return it. She slapped his muscled arm.

"If you think you're going to get stuck in there"—she tapped his temple hard enough to make the big man flinch—"you'd better find a way to come back and get me. I would rather live in the days of Old Yeller and Khrushchev than here without you."

"Hell, Jen, if he gets stuck there, he'd damn well better find a way to make money off fifty-plus years of Super Bowls and World Series winners," Leonard joked as he finished hooking Lonetree up to the monitors. "If you're going to be stuck in pre–civil rights America, it's better to do it with money, right, Chief?" he said as he too slapped the large Indian on the bare shoulder and then wiggled the pain from his fingers.

"He'll be back, or I send Bobby Lee McKinnon after him," Jenny said, finally smiling and then quickly kissing the top of John's head as Gabriel eased her aside and looked at his friend. He held up the syringe.

"Ready for Professor Gabe's Magic Carpet Ride?" he asked.

"Dream between the sound machine? You bet," he said with a nervous smile as George Cordero placed the glasses into his hand.

"Good luck in there, my friend," he said and then left the bedside.

With a look at Hadley, George shook his head. "Risking too damn much for this guy, that's for damn sure." He looked at Kennedy as he wiped an alcohol pad across John's skin. "You know this man was responsible for killing that little girl, don't you? Just because I can't read this guy's thoughts doesn't mean that mean bitch downstairs doesn't know the truth. It just turns out this guy is worse than even she is. A match made in hell."

Kennedy nodded that Cordero had a point as he eased the needle into John's arm and swabbed it again, covering it with a small Band-Aid. Gabriel patted Lonetree's leg and nodded.

"Watch your ass in there. You are definitely the visiting team, and I don't think this thing will be too welcoming if it knew you were again coming unannounced into its backyard. I forget who said nothing is darker than a dream of love and life," Gabriel said. "Oh, wait, that was me."

"Boy, you guys should write Hallmark greeting cards—real sentimental stuff," Lonetree said. He felt the first heaviness start to creep into his eyes, and the sounds of voices had an echo-type quality to them. His eyes closed as he gripped the broken pair of dark glasses.

The Supernaturals watched as Lonetree drifted away on a tide of Demerol and the other special mixers Gabe had made for him. Kennedy looked at Leonard, who was going to be monitoring Lonetree's vitals. He nodded that everything was up and running. Gabriel made sure the syringe was close by in case he needed to be brought out of his state if needed. The Adrenalin was placed in two locations for quick access. He looked at everyone and nodded at Damian, who used the bedroom's rheostat to lower the brightness of the lamps. Kennedy went to the far corner and looked up into the camera. He gave the doctors out in the hallway a thumbs-up and returned to John's side. Jenny finally released his hand as Lonetree had told her to do. He must not have any physical contact with anyone during the walk.

John's eyes started playing under the lids, and Gabe got a knot in his stomach as Lonetree returned to the world they had just come from. He just hoped this worked.

"We're going to be late! Let's get a move on, girl!"

The voice was not John's. Jenny's eyes widened when the familiar snarl escaped his lips. She looked at the others around the room and could see that they had also recognized the voice. It was Gloria's father, Franklin Perry, the very man that they had seen only an hour and a half before. Then John was gone. The eyelids still showed movement with the REM sleep he had achieved.

Lonetree was now a part of America's past—a past they hoped he could return from.

The music was the first thing John recognized. The song seemed distant at first as he tried to open his eyes but failed as it always did. His vision and clarity would come; he just had to be patient.

Many a tear has to fall . . . but it's all, in the game . . .

John smiled, or at least he thought he did in his dream, as he recognized the old song from the late fifties. Tommy Edwards, if he remembered correctly from when his grandmother hummed the tune while she cleaned houses for a living when he was a kid on the reservation.

All in the wonderful game, that we know as love . . .

"We're going to be late! Let's get a move on, girl!"

John's eyes opened wide and he immediately jumped back as he saw his own reflection in the full-length mirror. He stumbled but steadied himself, realizing he had been frightened by his own image. For the first time in a dreamwalk, he found his own face. He shook his head as the man left the door without opening it and went about his business in another area of the house.

Somewhere, a radio was turned down, and then he heard her voice. It wasn't what it should have been. It was like that of a younger child. He turned and saw the bathroom door open, stumbling as the young girl suddenly appeared with a blue below-the-knee-length skirt with a small dog or something on its hem. She was only wearing a bra. He turned his head as she lowered the antenna on a small radio and placed it down on the bed. She then slipped into a white blouse. Lonetree assumed this because he was too embarrassed to actually turn and see. The girl, maybe twelve years old at the most, had dark hair and blue eyes. Once she was covered, John braved a look at the girl as she finished dressing. The way she fumbled with the blouse and the way she tilted her head told John he was looking at a younger version of Gloria Perry. Confused, Lonetree stood next to her as she reached for the mirror and removed a pink scarf from its frame. She fluffed her hair as she pulled it back and fashioned a ponytail with the use of the silky scarf.

"I'm ready!' she called out.

The bedroom door opened after a brief but firm knock. Frank Perry, Gloria's father and onetime officer assigned to Robert Hadley's OSS unit, was smiling, not irritated as the voice had been a moment before. He saw his daughter and shook his head. She sensed his good humor, which had been short lately.

"What's so amusing?" she asked as she turned around, placing the dark glasses on her nose.

John smiled as he saw the young woman she would become in a few years. Why he was at this point in her life, he didn't know.

"Not used to seeing you in those clothes."

"I know you would be just as happy with me never taking off that Catholic plaid skirt you like so much, but I like this." She twirled until the skirt unfurled as she spun. She stopped and felt her way to the door. She found her father leaning against the doorjamb and hugged him. "Thank you for giving in."

"I didn't have a choice, did I?"

"Never did," Gloria said as she released her father's neck and turned and grabbed her new school supplies from her dresser.

"Well, I guess it's time to see if you can handle public school. Can't hang on to you forever, can I? Next thing you know, you're off to Washington to help Ike settle things there."

She pursed her lips and made a kissing action as she moved past her father at the door. "Eisenhower doesn't need my help. After all, didn't you and Ike win the war all on your own?"

"Funny girl," he said, reaching for an item on her bed. "Hey, are you forgetting something?"

Gloria stopped and then held out a slim-fingered hand as her dad gave her the telescopic walking stick. She took a deep breath, and John could see that she hated her predicament of blindness. Lonetree followed them out of the house.

The day was warm, and he sensed it was September. Gloria and her father went to an old 1952 Dodge pickup truck. John turned to see the small house that was well maintained. The yard was green and freshly cut, and the house looked to be painted just the year before. He could almost smell the newness as the sun warmed the exterior. He shook his head, and before he knew it, he was sitting between Frank and Gloria as they drove away from their cozy house.

The truck took the back way, or so Lonetree was thinking, because they skirted the town of Moreno as the pickup truck climbed a hill. The manual transmission of the Dodge was kept in low gear as it strained at the uphill fight on the old dirt road that no one ever used. John sensed that the kids out to neck after the movies avoided the place they were going. He knew in advance through his inner sight that they were heading to that place.

"This won't take long, will it? I don't want to be late on my first day of real school."

Frank looked at his daughter right through John's head as he sat there feeling uncomfortable in his spying.

"Real school?" he asked.

Gloria smiled as she turned her head to face her father. "Real as in real teachers, real students, and not nuns running the dog and pony show."

"You're getting as saucy as your mother used to be."

"Yes, I am. You bet she would have never have been as paranoid as you about public schools."

"Paranoid?" Frank Perry shook his head as he turned onto another dirt road even steeper than the first. John turned and saw the town of Moreno sitting below them, confirming where they were going. "Where are you learning words like that?"

"*The Twilight Zone.*"

"Damn, isn't this world strange enough without adding that crap to it?"

Gloria turned and gave her father a condescending look.

"Good writing is good writing, and Rod Serling is the best. And that's what I'm going to be. The best damn writer in the world." She huffed and then moved her head as if she were looking away.

Her father smiled as he pulled up to a fenced off area and stopped the truck.

"Rod Serling, huh?"

"Yeah, and it wouldn't hurt you any, sir, to get a little imaginative in your television watching. There's more to life than *Wagon Train*, *Dragnet*, or *Wanted: Dead or Alive*. I can't even see, and I know those shows are a little bit formulaic."

"Where in the hell are you learning these words?" he asked as the pickup was approached by a man in a uniform. John could see the MP armband and knew that he had struck pay dirt. He watched the army cop tap on Frank's window and gestured for him to roll it down. "Never mind, *The Twilight Zone* again, right?"

"You got it, daddy-oh."

"Smart-ass," he said as he rolled down the window with the use of the crank and then held out his ID to the sergeant. The man checked it and then looked inside.

"Your daughter will remain within the confines of the vehicle, Captain

Perry?" the military police officer asked as he handed back the identification.

"I'm not a captain anymore, Sergeant, and yes, she knows not to leave the truck."

"Fascist," Gloria mumbled loud enough for all to hear.

John cringed as the gruff-looking sergeant leaned in to look Gloria over.

"Excuse me?" he asked.

"I said Fabian; you look like Fabian."

"Uh-huh." The sergeant stood back and opened the gate. "The colonel is inside the security office, Captain."

Frank hit the accelerator, and as he passed the uniformed guard, he said, "*Mr. Perry*, not *Captain*."

He rolled up the window and looked at Gloria. "*Fascist* is not a word you toss around lightly these days, young lady."

The truck bypassed the security hut and a 1956 Cadillac parked next to the two army jeeps used by military police.

"Sorry. I just don't like the men here. They're mean and always seem to be on edge. You know that one of them actually pulled a pistol on Ronnie Granger last summer?"

"And what was Ronnie Granger doing to get a gun pulled on him?" Frank asked as he shut off the motor. John sensed Frank had business to perform—unpleasant, more than likely—so he parked far enough away to protect her from hearing too much.

"He was just trying to get his dog that had wandered off. He was looking around . . . on the other side of the fence."

Perry opened the door but hesitated. "I'm sorry about that. But you know as well as I that this place is dangerous. These ruins could collapse at any time." He looked at the winery and then over toward the ruins of the Santa Maria Delarosa mission. "Ronnie Granger got off lucky. This is no place to get caught wandering around."

"Yes, sir."

"Oh, don't give me the poor blind girl routine; it only works on special occasions. Now stay in the truck; this won't take long. Then we can get you to that real school you're so anxious to get to."

Gloria smiled and nodded as she opened one of her braille books and ran her fingertips over the special characters.

Frank smiled, shaking his head and closing the door, only to turn and see a man in a ragged white coat exit the old winery. He gave Frank a look that said he was not pleased to see him, and then with a huff, he moved off toward the mission. Perry joined him, and together they walked the hundred yards toward the mission and the meeting that would end their commitment.

John found himself outside the truck, watching the two men as they moved off. He was convinced the man in the long white coat was the very same man who had accosted Gabriel in the earlier dream of Moreno. The man wearing the glasses was most assuredly the German.

He turned away from the two men and saw Gloria as she read and hummed the same tune she had been listening to earlier in her room. Lonetree could hear the squeaky preteen voice as the beautiful one it would eventually become in just a few short years. Then he saw her stop reading, and her humming trailed away as she looked up and tilted her head to the left and then slowly to the right. Lonetree thought she was frozen, because she sat so still with the exception of her head movements as she seemed to be listening for something. Another tilt of her head in the opposite direction, and then just as quickly back again. She closed the book and then rolled down her window. John heard her start humming again. A few bars and then she would stop and listen. Again, she hummed "It's All in the Game" by Tommy Edwards and then stopped once more. This time, her head bobbed up and down as she heard what she was listening for.

John's eyes widened when Gloria opened the door. He turned to see if her father had noticed but instead saw him vanish into the oddly overly large aluminum guard shack on the far side of the mission. He wanted to stop her but was powerless to do so as he realized her father was right: the winery did look like it would fall at any moment. Lonetree even said, "Hey, do what your father said," but Gloria of course couldn't hear him. She used her white cane to ease forward across the gravel lot toward the thirteen steps leading to California's oldest documented winery. Lonetree fell in beside her with unease clouding his thoughts.

Gloria stopped and listened only thirty feet from the crumbling steps of the winery. Again, that tilt of head told Lonetree she had heard something. After a moment, John heard it also. It was at least two men laughing. The sound had an echo to it, and he could hear that it was coming from the large double doors of the ruin. Gloria deftly hurried to the side of the south adobe wall, rapidly swishing her cane side to side, scanning for obstacles. John was surprised just how confident the girl was without sight. John caught up to her and saw that she was leaning against the wall, listening intently. He stayed where he was on the gravel lot.

The left side of the partially restored oaken doorway opened, and two men exited the ruin. They were both army MPs and were armed with M1 carbines slung on their shoulders. One of the men turned and started fumbling for his keys.

"No need," the second man, a PFC, said as the first looked up at him. "This screwed-up assignment will be officially over in"—the second man looked at his wristwatch and then over toward the guard shack—"hell, it's probably over with already."

The first man stopped looking in his pockets and then shrugged. "Can't say as I feel sorry for that bastard. I hope they deport his sorry ass."

The two men turned away from the doors and started down the steps.

"Hell, scuttlebutt says the son of a bitch may be tried for war crimes if he gives the bigwigs any grief when they shut him down."

"Nah, they can't do that without explaining why he was here under our protection. No, the Nazi bastard will just slip away like all of them generals and such after the war, head to Argentina or someplace like that. That's where *True Detective* says they run to."

"Yeah," the second said as they slowly moved off. "Bullshit science anyway. The guy was just milkin' the gov'ment tit."

Lonetree watched the two men avoid the security shack and move off toward the back of the property and then to the front gate to have a smoke with the guys there. John smiled when he saw how fast Gloria left her hiding spot behind and started tapping her cane along the damaged wall of the winery. She carefully moved up the steps, only stumbling once, and even then Lonetree saw himself trying to help her. She finally made it to the partially collapsed overhang at the top of the thirteen steps, with John eyeing the crumbling structure they now stood under. She stopped before reaching the door and again cocked her head to the left and then right. She turned until she faced the mission and the guard shack, then back again at the ruin. She placed her palm on the left side of the large, sturdy door.

With a deep breath, she depressed the old wooden handle on the door and pulled it open slowly and carefully. She stopped when the dangling lock banged and swayed in its hasp. Lonetree also took a deep breath as she stopped at the threshold and listened. He thought she was going to satisfy some curiosity and then leave the ruin, but his hopes were dashed when she entered the winery. John stepped in before the door closed as if the heavy oak would have crushed him if he didn't hurry. The dreamwalk was confusing at most, silly in the least. Sometimes, no matter how hard he concentrated, he did things that didn't make sense. He could not get used to being in someone else's mind.

The interior of the winery was far worse than the exterior. Fourteen-inch-wide beams of nearly petrified wood had collapsed into the immediate space upon entering. Gloria navigated these beautifully, easing around the fallen roof and its support like a champ.

John took this opportunity to look around the interior. For something so important that it needed U.S. Army personnel to safeguard it, this place was a mess. One item left over from the original winery was a small alcove, in the wall, and inside was the Virgin Mary. The small statue captivated Lonetree, and the image, headless and with only one arm, gave him the creeps. He was glad deep inside his soul that Gloria didn't have to see it. He didn't know why that image found purchase in his fears. Gloria was brave, but that one sight alone would chill anyone. The damaged statue symbolized a place that had gone bad, and as John looked around, he knew this was indeed a bad place.

Many a tear has to fall . . . but it's all in the game, Gloria sang soft and low. After the first verse, she paused and listened. Lonetree saw the smile slowly come to her lips as she tilted her head to the right and listened, gently swaying to a sound only she could hear.

"Damn, this is not good." John took a few steps closer to Gloria and almost stumbled as he backed away when she suddenly moved as if she had working eyes. She quickly tapped across the old mud floor and suddenly stopped and listened again. John saw that she was nearing the far wall of falling adobe mud and near a door that looked very much out of place.

All in the wonderful game . . . that we know . . . as love.

Lonetree watched as the second verse was sung by one of the more sensitive and beautiful voices he had ever heard outside of his own Jennifer back when Bobby Lee McKinnon would perform through her.

The girl listened intently as her smile grew. She had the look of a child on Christmas morning. She tapped her way toward a steel door which, as John noted a moment before, looked very much out of place. She leaned forward and hit the steel twice with her cane's tip. The hollow clicking sound returned. Her smile faltered.

"Damn it," she grumbled as she straightened. "Stairs!"

Lonetree was amazed that she could tell that the door was hiding stairs behind it. He guessed that she could hear a return echo of space that he couldn't.

Lonetree cursed when Gloria reached out with her hand and took hold of the latch-style handle and pushed down. It opened with ease. She stepped through the threshold until a chill from far below stopped her.

"Thank God, you're coming to your senses," he said, trying to be loud.

Once in a while he won't call . . . but it's all . . . in the game, she sang, somewhat louder than before. It was loud enough that John flinched, thinking that had to have been heard all the way into Moreno.

"I know I left the chorus out, but I forgot where I was," she called down the darkened stairs.

John saw the light switches on the wall just inside the door but was again helpless to turn them on, and Gloria, bless her, didn't need them. He also saw that the electrical lines were relatively new. The high-wattage bulbs were encased in that cagelike shell that most government buildings are equipped with for outdoor use, which the old winery most definitely came close to being with all the damage done throughout the nearly two centuries since it had been built.

Gloria was humming the tune as she listened to something only she could hear and understand.

"If you would all sing together, it would be a lot better," she called down the stairs. To Lonetree's horror, she actually took a step down, then another, and he again tried to reach out and grab her arm, but his fingers caressed nothing but damp air.

"Damn!" he said loudly, hoping that she would at least get a sense that he did not want her to go down that stairwell. She did just that. She moved fast for someone with no eyesight. John hurriedly followed as he too knew he would not fall, or if he did, he would just open his eyes and he would be safe at the bottom—dreams, he thought, not bad at times.

Gloria reached the bottom of the stairwell and faced another door. This was also new and made of steel. John saw light coming from under the door. The girl tilted her head and was listening to someone, or something, through the door.

"No, I'm alone," she said, leaning close to the door. She suddenly turned, and John thought for sure she was looking right him. Even in the darkness he could see a slight reflection of himself in her dark glasses, though it could have been just his imagination. Gloria returned her attention to the door once more, and her hand went slowly to the same type of latch as upstairs. John froze. She listened once again. She huffed and then lightly slapped the door with her hand. "I said there is no one with me; I'm all alone. If you would talk one at a time, I could understand you far better."

Again, she listened. She cursed something John couldn't hear and then turned the latch and opened the door.

The world once more had light, and Lonetree was never so grateful for it. He never liked the absence of light, but he lived with it because of the line of work he was in. He hated the dark more than anything.

The basement was not the basement that had been dug out by Mexican labor almost two centuries before. Instead of the earthen walls used for ancient wine-making and storage, these were concrete and very much new. John was amazed as he looked around the large room. There were even three or four of the old three-hundred-gallon wine casks used for fermenting purposes in the day. Two of these had collapsed since the days of the monks, but one was still showing an old wooden spigot at its base.

The room was L-shaped, and Gloria started walking toward the bend. Lonetree saw equipment that was old to him but would be considered new to someone in this time period. Large boxlike machines were wired up, and others that looked as if they came from the set of a Universal monster movie from the thirties. All of this sat upon a rubberized flooring used to disburse electricity and provide grounding. Lonetree didn't like the way this was shaping up at all. Gloria looked as if she knew exactly where she was going, like she had been here before.

Stainless steel tables lined walls that had been reinforced by not only wooden beams but steel. A fire-suppression system had been installed, and there were places where the ceiling had come under intense renovation. John wondered why the federal government would set up shop in this manner.

"I think I've known for some time that you were down here," Gloria said.

She felt her way past four massive steel tanks with warning signs stenciled front and back. These tanks fed into the farthest area of the basement. Gloria seemed to follow these pipelines without even knowing it. John ran his fingers along one of these steel-jacketed lines, and he could see the frozen condensation adhered to the metal. They were carrying something akin to nitrogen or some other mysterious chemical Lonetree didn't understand. As he moved past the large tanks, he saw the manufacturer's plate. He pursed his lips as a connection was made.

"R. D. Hadley Container Company—Los Angeles, California. Manufactured 11/19/1948." John saw the welded-on plate and raised his brows. "More than likely a division of Hadley Corp Gauge and Meter Company of Moreno, California." John knew the links in the chain were coming together, and he wondered what affairs of business Hadley Sr. had with the federal government that had to be guarded by armed military personnel. He was startled out of his thoughts when the girl spoke once more, seemingly to no one—no one he could hear, at any rate.

"Was it you singing in the night?" she asked as she rounded the corner and stopped, her hand with the cane tapping out a spot that seemed to be clear. "They were wonderful! I couldn't understand them, but they used to lull me to sleep most every night. I thought it was my inner voice singing. You harmonize better with your songs. More so than mine, I guess, because you don't know them as well."

John eased around the bend in the L-shaped room and found Gloria standing in front of a large steel boxlike structure that dwarfed her. Spotlights shone on its shiny surface and reflected back on Gloria's upturned face. It reminded him of a neighborhood bank vault; there were vents and sliding portals for viewing inside the box. It stood at over fourteen feet in height and at least twelve in width. Electric motors were installed every few feet around its bottom and circulating fans at its top. The strange lines from the tanks ended atop and looked to feed two large steel tanks there. It looked as if they left those tanks and then lines spiderwebbed across its top, bottom, and sides. The lines appeared welded to its frame. He leaned in and read, LINES UNDER PRESSURE.

"What in the hell is this?" John asked himself as he stepped past Gloria and placed a hand over the cold exterior. At least he was assuming it was cold because of the dripping of melted ice from the lines that were fed by the mysterious tanks. More feed lines running through from the tanks were directed right down into the top of the enclosure. He could make out the words EMERGENCY VENT LINE—DANGER stenciled on the tanks.

"My father says that I hear things that others can't," Gloria said as if she were answering an unheard question from someone. Without knowing it, she had heard John. Her own words were directed at the large vaultlike containment box. "I guess because I'm blind, my other senses are more acute than others with sight. I learned that in health class at school."

Lonetree tilted his head like Gloria did when she was straining to hear something. It was a habit he hadn't known he picked up by watching her.

"Yes, school. Did you go to school?"

John froze at sounds seemingly coming from the interior of the steel vault. He couldn't place the words, but he could hear something for the first time. For a reason he couldn't understand, the sound was filled with a kind of sorrow that he hadn't heard since he was a child, when he used to listen to the old folks on the reservation talk of better days from their pasts. This was like that. The sounds were almost foreign in nature, but Gloria seemed to have no trouble hearing or understanding them.

"That's so sad," she said as she stepped closer to the giant vault. "All of you?"

For a dream, John realized he had never once been this apprehensive. Even while in the mind of a killer and reliving a murder, no matter how gruesome, in the old days of law enforcement, he had never felt he was in danger. While inside a basement of an old ruin, he found that he was terrified of what was with Gloria, even while behind at least four inches of solid steel.

"Why would someone do that to you?"

Lonetree stepped back as the vault shook on its concrete block foundation. Dust filtered in from the newly installed rafters over their heads, and for a moment Lonetree thought the entire winery would come down around their ears.

"I am so sorry for you." Gloria moved to the vault's front by tapping her way past steel tables and machines John couldn't recognize. "Can you get out of there? Do you need help? Maybe I can tell my father and he can help get you out. He's a good—"

This time, the response was unmistakable. The vault's door actually pushed outward. It popped three small steel rivets, and then the room became silent as the steel relaxed. A small warning bell dinged from somewhere, and Lonetree froze as he heard those very same lines he had been examining vibrate as they were filled with a chemical. The lines had been flushed and charged, and two little red lights came on at the topmost tanks that fed directly into the vault from above. All of this seemed to be an automated reaction to the assault on the vault's door. John stepped back.

"What in the hell did you people bring back?" he asked himself.

"I said no one was with me. Why do you keep asking that?" Gloria said as she placed a hand on the cold steel of the door and pressed. Then she turned, and again her dark glasses settled right on the spot where John stood staring at her. "No, no one." She gently and lovingly moved her small hand over the steel. "Yes, I can come back. For a blind girl, I can get around better than people think, but that's our secret. I can tell you like secrets." A sad look came to the girl's face as she lowered her hand. "Sometimes, secrets are all that I have, besides my daddy."

Again, there was a loud thump of what could only be described as anger from inside the vault. Gloria placed her hand on the door and pressed once more, and the vibe inside the basement changed as whatever was trapped in the steel cage calmed.

"I'll bring books to read to you," she said, and then her face was a mask of excitement. "I can also bring you music. I got a battery-powered record player for Christmas last year. I have all the best records. The guys down at K-Rave give me all their duplicates." Again, she tilted her head as she listened. "K-Rave is a radio station. They play all the cool stuff. Bobby Vee, Roy Orbison. They are even starting to play some of the new beach stuff. Freekin' Rowdy Rhoads is even beginning to like the new music. He'll never admit he's still in mourning for Buddy Holly."

John smiled as Gloria made promises to whatever was inside that she would come back.

"I have a hundred books in braille." She listened. "They are books for the blind," she said, answering the unheard question. "I can't read regular books." She stopped and listened with a small smile coming to her lips. "I can come on Sunday mornings, I promise. Since my mother died, Daddy doesn't make us go to church anymore. He said I should, but he lets me skip it while he sleeps in because he works late on Saturday nights. That's when I can come and visit. And maybe someday we can get you out of there."

The lights dimmed momentarily, and John felt that Gloria's new friend was pleased at her prospect of return to the outside world, or just excited for the chance at escape. The thing in the vault sought to get out. He looked around and realized that this structure was made to keep something inside.

"What are you doing in here?" came the loud voice that startled Gloria and Lonetree.

John turned to see the very same man who had left the ruin only fifteen minutes before with the two guards. Still wearing his white coat, he slammed a set of files down on one of the stainless steel tables. His glasses were askew, and he looked like he was fit to be tied. His graying beard was a mess as he came at Gloria.

"Was there a reaction from the containment area?" he asked as he angrily stepped past Gloria and eyed the vault.

"I . . . I . . . don't know—" The man took Gloria by the shoulders and shook her. John became angry when he saw her glasses fly from her head.

"Who were you speaking with? Was there activity inside?" The man shook her again, this time even harder.

"Let go of her, you son of a bitch!" Lonetree shouted, and he was shocked when Gloria acted as if she had heard him.

This time, the vault shook as his words escaped his mouth. Then it quickly settled.

Suddenly, large hands grabbed the madman from behind. He was thrown to the floor where he sprawled. He grabbed a steel table leg and started to pull himself up, but a foot came down on his back with enough force to send him back down.

"If you even look at my daughter again, I'll do to you what we should have done in Yugoslavia, you murdering son of a bitch!"

John saw Frank as he moved away from the German and then took his daughter into his arms. He bent down and picked up her glasses and wiped them on his blue chambray work shirt. He eased them onto her nose and pulled her close once more.

"What are you doing in here? I told you never to leave the truck."

"She was interacting with the elements!" the smaller man said as he started to rise. Frank left Gloria's side and then lashed out with his boot once more, sending the man back to the cold floor.

Lonetree smiled, thinking the man was getting off lightly.

"That young lady has my proof that they are still viable," the man said as he felt at his chest where Perry's boot had connected. "The orders from your government must be rescinded."

"As far as I'm concerned, we can send your ass to Israel. Try explaining yourself to a tribunal there, you sick bastard. I think they may have a few tough questions about your life's work."

"That is one can of worms we and our associates would rather not have made public."

Lonetree saw a man standing just at the bend of the room, and he had the MPs with him. The two enlisted army men moved to assist the German scientist to his feet.

"Colonel, that girl was interacting with the experiment. They must have been communicating!"

The well-dressed man stepped forward, and John recognized him immediately—Robert Hadley. He was tall, and his hair was silver, just like his son would be in the future. He wore an expensive suit and had the distinguished look of a man that had life by the short and curlies. Hadley stepped by the man that all of this was built for and handed him a handkerchief as he did so.

"Wipe your mouth, Doctor; you're drooling all over your lab coat."

Lonetree watched as Robert stepped up to Gloria as she hugged her father. Frank pulled her back as her father's hand came up to her chin. The rich man raised his brows, and Perry relented. He touched her cheek, and she reflexively flinched as his fingers made contact.

"Don't let this man frighten you, Gloria; his bark is far worse than his bite. He's used to pushing around smaller people."

John looked to his left and saw the German doctor was fuming. His hatred was directed at Hadley and no one else.

"Now, were you speaking with someone down here?" he asked.

Gloria shook her head and remained silent.

"Really? I know my own boy would lie to keep the truth from me, but you? No, I have watched you for a long time and find you far more intelligent and factful than Dean. Now were you speaking with someone down here?"

"No, I was just curious, and then I got lost," she said as she buried her face in her father's chest once more. Hadley looked at Perry. Frank shook his head in warning that Hadley had gone far enough, and it looked as if Gloria was one subject he would not push with his wartime buddy.

"Good enough for me." Hadley turned to face the doctor. "Gloria, this is Dr. Jürgen Fromm; he works for me as a chemical engineer. He handles our most dangerous chemicals; that's why we keep him ensconced in a secure place where his chemicals can cause no one in Moreno harm. He keeps monitoring our mercury containment, you know, to protect us all." His head turned as he moved his eyes away from the angry Fromm.

By the look on Frank's face, Lonetree could see that Hadley was lying. That was not this man's job. He was here for a whole other purpose, and it surely wasn't to protect the citizenry of Moreno.

"But his job here is at an end."

"It is too soon! This girl can prove it!" Fromm cried from the arms of the two MPs.

Hadley turned back to face the German. "And this little blind girl did in moments what you could not do since 1952? An amazing feat."

"Perhaps it has something to do with her handicap. I must be allowed to speak with this child and then study what happened here today. You must allow me to carry on my work!" Spittle again flew from the man's bearded face.

"All those files are empty observations, Doctor. The government is pulling you off the federal tit, so to speak." Hadley turned and faced Perry and his daughter. "And you, young lady, my guess is that you have learned your lesson as far as wandering into dangerous places?"

Gloria merely nodded and kept her face hidden.

"You don't have to have guarantees from my daughter, Robert." Perry hugged her even closer. "If she says she was lost, she was lost. She's not like all the other kids; she tells the truth."

"You mean like my boy?" Hadley asked with a smug smirk even though he had just offered the same observation on Dean Hadley himself.

"I mean kids in general, Colonel, and you know that."

Hadley smiled for real this time and then faced the two MPs. "Allow the good doctor to collect his personal belongings from the lab. Nothing of company property is to leave here with him. Certain people will arrive soon to take custody of Dr. Fromm and escort him to another location, where he will be debriefed. Until said time, the man is to be under constant surveillance. Keep him in his motel room. Is that clear?"

"Yes, sir."

"Gloria, please excuse this man for his bad behavior. He's upset, but he should have known better than to harm a child." He turned and looked at Fromm. "Any child."

"You cannot do this. My work is too important."

Hadley smiled as he started for the door and the long climb up into the real world.

"Doctor, I assure you, I can. And if you keep talking about wild things in front of strangers, you'll find I can do far more. With President Eisenhower wrestling with the Reds in Europe and Berlin about to burn once again, the time for subterfuge with former enemies must come to an end. There are other, more important concerns. The United States Air Force may have saved your ass after the war, but your rhetoric about power from the mind has scared even them off. They will use the benefits of your altitude experiments, but your other theories, well, they are a little farfetched, and your own failed experiments prove it."

"Robert, that's enough," Frank said, nodding at Gloria, who was still holding onto him.

Hadley knew he was saying too much in front of Gloria, so he nodded.

"We're finished here, Professor. Good day, sir. Captain Perry, will you and your daughter join me upstairs, please?" Hadley said and then vanished around the bend in the room.

"My name is Frank," Perry called out to remind the man that he was no longer his subordinate. He was a partner, and he now wanted that partnership dissolved just as they had dissolved their connection with Fromm.

Franklin smiled down at Gloria, who had remained silent throughout the confrontation with Fromm. Fromm was being led away by the military police, still with a look of fury and hatred directed at Gloria.

"Come on. Let's get the hell out of here and get you to that new school."

Gloria nodded, and with a last look back at the enormous vault, they left.

John had learned a lot on this trip. He was starting to feel the fatigue that came with dreamwalking and knew he was close to waking. He started to follow the two toward the door when he felt the cold fingers around the back of his neck. He was lifted from his feet and turned in midair. He was facing the vault with his feet dangling four feet off the floor. He fought the grip that held him with frantic movement. He shouldn't have been able to be physically touched by anything or anyone inside a dream, but here he was being treated like a rag doll in the grip of some horror he could not begin to fathom. Then he knew that the questions Gloria had been answering made sense to him. The thing inside knew John was there and didn't like it.

The coldness of the hand, something he shouldn't be able to feel, chilled his blood. He was shaken once, twice, and felt his neck being strained beyond endurance. Then, before Lonetree knew what was happening, he was flying through the dank air of the winery's basement.

Everyone in the bedroom saw John's body lifted out of the chair and watched as his large hands went to his throat as he was lifted free of the chair and the floor. He was shaken until they heard his joints pop, and then his six-foot-five-inch body was flying across the room until it hit the drywall at the opposite side, his limp frame sliding to the floor. Jennifer was the only one to scream as the others stared wide-eyed.

Gabriel sat at the long table inside their assigned meeting area. He was drinking whiskey and trying to decide how best to tell the team that they were now finished with this case. He took a long swallow of the burning liquid and stood to get a refill. Leonard, Julie, and Damian watched from their seats and exchanged looks of worry. As Gabriel poured his fourth drink, the study door opened, and Jennifer stepped inside.

"He's awake and he's fine. A little sore he said, but he'll live. He's changing clothes and will be here soon to present his report. George is drinking pretty heavily with some of the nurses in the kitchen. I think he's more scared than even John."

Gabriel turned as he capped the crystal decanter of bourbon. He nodded at Jennifer and then gestured for her to sit, draining the glass as he returned to his own seat. He placed the empty on the table and sat down.

Most of the group had only seen Kennedy drink on very special occasions, maybe a holiday or two. But this was different, and they saw it in his eyes.

"I want all of you to put your observations down on paper. Anything that you think is relevant. I'm putting an end to this. I have a feeling it's too much for us. Hell, maybe it's too much for any defense. Whatever this thing is, it wants confrontation. I'm not losing John or anyone else. Kelly was too much."

The room was silent.

"John took a risk, and that is enough. I don't care what he learned on the dreamwalk. Something threw him out of that dream with enough force to kill him. That's enough. If we go into this without any advantage as to what we are dealing with, we could all end up like that torn soul upstairs."

They had never heard Kennedy speak like this before. His guilt over Kelly's death was evident, but he was showing fear where there had never been any before. It was the fear of the unknown power at work here. Nothing they had experienced in the past two days fell into any category of haunting ever documented.

Damian pulled a cigar out of his coat pocket and lit it.

"I thought you quit those disgusting things," Leonard said, waving away the smoke cloud that gathered around him and Jackson.

"And so did I until I saw a man that weighs two hundred and fifty pounds and stands six foot five fly through the air like fucking Peter Pan." He puffed until the cigar flared to full life and then gave Leonard a dirty look. His fixed Kennedy with his dark and intense eyes as he puffed away on the smelly cigar. "I say we finish this thing. Then, if you want to quit, we'll quit this bullshit altogether. But I say we see this thing through."

"No. It's too damn expensive," Gabriel said as he looked around the table. "And that man upstairs is not likable enough to risk the people I love and respect."

"Professor Gabe, I'm sure we are on the right track with this thing. We need to know how this entity works in our world. To have the power to cross over decades to affect the time frames of two completely different worlds and eras? Man, oh, man, we can't ignore and just walk away from that. The boy in me tells me to run like hell, that the beast inside the closet is real and coming for my ass, but the analyst in me says to stay and finish this. I agree with Sergeant Friday here; let's do what we do."

"This isn't up for voting. Once we complete some semblance of a report and hand it to the First Lady and the Secret Service, we leave."

"And let that dragon lady claim her spoils? I dislike her as much as the rest of the world hates Hadley," Julie said. "Vote nothing; it's what we do, Gabe. We can't run from that after we claimed that hauntings are so rare that they are practically nonexistent. Kelly would hate us for quitting over her death. She was a lot of things, but a quitter she wasn't."

Jennifer remained silent, listening. She knew that if she threw her weight behind leaving, there would be no talking Gabriel out of walking out on Hadley. She would remain noncommittal until she had John's feelings on the situation.

Kennedy was about to speak again when the door opened and George came barging in. Breathing heavily, he closed the door like he was holding back Frankenstein's monster. It was so startling that Damian rose from his chair and, with cigar clamped in his mouth, reached for his gun in its shoulder holster.

"With as much crap as we've seen around here, it's not wise to scare the already scared!" Damian said angrily, sitting back down.

George tried to get his actions and breathing under control.

"They're getting ready to move the president," he said as he finally removed his weight from the door and John Lonetree pushed his way inside.

"Hey, they're moving Hadley to another location," Lonetree said as he closed the door and then assisted a still heavily breathing Cordero to a chair. Lonetree looked none the worse for wear after his flight through the bedroom. He was dressed in a white shirt and black slacks, and his shortened black hair was still wet from the hot shower he had taken.

"I was having a drink with the nurses in the kitchen when they were called upstairs to prepare the president for travel," George said as Leonard slid a drink down to him.

"That is no longer Gabe's concern," Jennifer said as she placed a hand over Lonetree's when he sat down next to her. "He said the investigation is over."

"The hell you say," John said as Jenny stopped him from rising from his chair. "You decide this before I file my report on the dreamwalk? Being dictatorial is not your strong suit, Gabriel."

"Am I supposed to allow another friend—or *friends*," he said, looking around the table, "to die for this?"

"After almost seven years of nothing, we come on a case that exhibits actions that have never once been documented in a haunting, and we just quit?" Julie Reilly said, reaching out and removing the drink from George's hand and downing it in one gulp before slamming the empty back into his suspended hand. "I say bullshit," she said, hissing out her breath as the burning liquid slid down her throat.

"Wasn't Kelly enough?" Kennedy asked. "People dying for a science that is only good for entertainment? The world doesn't want to know the truth; it would shatter too much delusional thinking about the afterlife. Why do you think we were being sued? It wasn't because we outed the television networks about the hoaxes they perpetrated on the public. It was for shattering people's belief in what-if and pointing to the other person and saying, 'I'm glad that's not me,' while not thinking about the real problems of the world, and that's just the way the controllers of this country want it." Gabriel lowered his head. "The chance John took was the line we won't cross again. I cannot handle the thought of losing another friend for a science that will never be proven, just speculated upon at cocktail parties and in spook novels."

"Perhaps we should hear from John about the chance he took."

All eyes went to Jennifer, who was looking at Lonetree. She smiled. "Is Gloria as much of a charmer as you thought?" she asked, squeezing his hand.

Lonetree surprised them all by smiling, but he also rubbed at the sore spot on his neck that was bruised and discolored. "Charmed? You bet," he said as he fixed Gabriel with his brown eyes. "Hell, she even charmed the thing that used me as a lawn dart. Yes, we made a connection." John released Jennifer's hand and then leaned forward in his chair until he knew he had Kennedy's attention. "She needs our help, Gabe; we have to help her and that town if we can. Kelly would agree. We all agree; we need to see this thing through. I know now that this thing is not just about Dean Hadley."

For the longest time, Kennedy remained silent, even when Jennifer got up and went to the bar and poured a drink and then returned with the glass and placed it in front of John.

"Explain why we have to help, John," she said as she kissed the top of his head and sat back down. "Take us on a journey to Moreno."

Lonetree looked at Gabriel, who pursed his lips and nodded.

"My firm belief is," John said, stopping long enough to drain his glass, "that Moreno was never a town in a real sense. I believe it was like a movie set and the people on that set didn't know they were even in a movie. It was window dressing. It was real, but all of it was a cover up, and when I say that, I mean a cover up that makes others seem feeble by comparison."

An hour, one full decanter of whiskey, and another of vodka later, John had completed his tale of time travel to a place they all now feared even more than the haunting at Summer Place. It wasn't until the knock on the door that Gabe's mind was made up.

Julie Reilly, feeling a little tipsy, walked to the door and opened it. Catherine Hadley was standing there as if she were posing for a photo op inside the White House. One of her delicate hands was placed in the other at her waist, and she was smiling. Her hair and makeup were perfect for that time of night.

"A chartered 737 will be waiting at Andrews in three hours." She stepped aside just as the gurney carrying President Hadley made it to the bottom of the stairs. "My husband, if he is to die, will die in what he considers his home. I am taking him there."

"You know that will kill him?" Gabriel said as he remained seated as a point to his denial to continue the investigation.

"That is the opinion of many, but not my husband. He wants to go home." She smiled again and then started to turn away, and then stopped, with the smile still in place. "There is a rumor about that you and your team are discontinuing your investigation. Even after so much work toward your blackmailing of me. What a shame. Good luck, Professor. I'm sorry you fell short in . . . well . . . everything."

Gabriel Kennedy stood and walked calmly to the door. After John's take about his visit with the young Gloria, he had decided to take this thing to its inevitable conclusion with the help of the arrogant woman who had just left.

"Madam First Lady?" Gabriel called out as he poured another drink.

They could see through the open door that Catherine had stopped but not turned. "Yes?" she said.

"What terminal at Andrews?"

"Very good, Professor, very good. Private concourse thirteen." She moved off, Gabriel watching her back as she followed her husband and doctors from the house.

"The bitch needs her scapegoats along for the ride," Julie said as she watched Gabriel from behind.

"Terminal thirteen. Lucky number," Leonard said with an uncomfortable chuckle.

Kennedy finished his drink and then shook his head in wonder at the woman who wanted to control everything. This time, they could all see it was his turn to smile.

"Little does she know that it's not scapegoats traveling to Moreno. Just us."

Damian raised his glass and surprised everyone with his belated enthusiasm.

"Just us! The goddamn getting-drunk-on-their-asses-and-on-their-way-to-California Supernaturals!"

Two thousand, five hundred and thirty-five miles away, laughter sounded from two different locations within the city limits of a small town that officially died fifty-five years before.

The Supernaturals would make a stand at Moreno.

PART III

HOMECOMING

I'd like to thank the guy who wrote the song . . . that made
my baby fall in love with me . . . yeah . . .

—BARRY MANN,
"Who Put the Bomp (in the Bomp, Bomp, Bomp),"
Billboard Top 100, 1961

14

The mudslide began at 3:20 a.m. and coursed down a small dry-wash area high above the Santa Maria Delarosa mission and winery. The slide was caused by rain that refused to soak in, in certain hardpan areas, and in combination with the softer dried dirt of the region, the wall of mud turned itself into a living thing. It picked up boulders that had been buried in the hillside for a millennium, and that was enough force to speed up the wall of mud and water as it cascaded down the small hills surrounding Moreno.

The crest of liquefied earth slammed into the north wall of ancient adobe and disintegrated it as the wave moved on. The small walnut grove beside the old mission was inundated and swallowed. Then the mud slammed into the rear wall of the mission and the winery. Since the state had reinforced the walls of the mission with the takeover of the property, the slide was pretty much contained. It was in the winery where the world came crashing in. The slide hit the north wall, collapsing it under the on-slaught. The wave continued until the old flooring couldn't withstand the tremendous weight any longer. The ancient wood gave way, and it and the boulder-filled mud slammed into the basement, the rafters of steel and aluminum coming down atop the remains of a laboratory that was never supposed to be.

The old and rusted tanks atop the vault ruptured and spilled out their last remaining fluid. Then the crack in the steel made in Yugoslavia almost eighty years before split and collapsed in on itself. The gases and a thousand pounds of mercury were free to soak into the wet earth of the slide.

Darkness was content to stay isolated while the world outside exploded in thunder and lightning. They knew they were free and would once more have designs on the invasion of Moreno, California. This time, they would remain free by killing anything that threatened them. Even with requests for calm emanating from the bowels of the old Grenada Theater and the vault there, the entity ignored it, grew in power, and waited.

Bob had been up all night, obsessed with the old DJ's booth. He had pulled his favorite TV-watching chair over toward the middle of the room, moving several of the half-empty record racks out of the way, and sat, waiting. He was placed in the approximate position the receptionist had occupied many years before. He had a blanket pulled up to his chin as the drumming of the rain on the roof of K-Rave lulled him to only half-wakefulness. The company-issued .38-caliber Smith & Wesson revolver was tucked firmly between his left leg and the seat cushion. His eyes were fixed on the triple-paned glass of the booth.

Linda shuffled by, lacking for sleep as much as her husband. She had spent the night huddled in the old cast-iron tub in her bathroom, and her mood was witness to the fact it had not been a very comfortable night.

"I'll ask again, Bob—what are you going to do if it does show up again? Shoot it?" She laughed, but it was without mirth. She slapped the back of the chair but leaned over and kissed his cheek anyway. "We have never once in the years that we have been here had cause to even get those damn guns out of the boxes they were issued in." She patted the top of his head and then moved to the front window. "Eleven in the morning and it looks like near dark out there."

It had been raining steadily since the night before. The television reports were saying that the Inland Empire and most of San Bernardino County were under flash flood watch. It was a warning that anyone near the hills had to take most seriously. There had already been reports of massive mudslides near Big Bear and flooding in Los Angeles.

"I'm just hopin' old Drunk Monk's Road doesn't come sliding down in our laps, which it will if the damn rain doesn't stop." Linda spied Harvey Leach across the street as he poked his head out of the double glass doors of Newberry's. He was undoubtedly checking to see if the rainwater was ready to breach the sidewalk and come into the alcove of the old department store. Linda didn't want to see that happen because they would more than likely be called upon to assist in sandbagging the doors and alcove. Linda waved, and Harvey shook his head and then went back inside. She suspected she, Bob, and Harvey were the last people in Moreno, an unsettling predicament to dwell on. All that was left outside of the townies, as they were now calling themselves, was Casper Worthington.

"Do you want some lunch?" she asked as she finally turned away from the dismal morning. She strolled into the kitchen. She cracked two eggs and put them in the butter she had melted. She again looked up, but Bob still sat motionless.

The sound of movement stopped her speculation. She leaned over the small counter and looked into the reception area. She saw Bob's head. His hair was splayed out on the top of the easy chair and was undone from its usual ponytail. She then looked toward the booth, and her heart skipped at least five beats that were, at that moment, badly needed.

The light was dim but very visible through the triple-paned glass. She saw the microphone stand that she knew wasn't there. She saw the rows upon rows of 45 records stacked into wooden shelves behind the console with its two turntables. One was spinning, its arm and needle scratching through the small black disc. Linda swallowed.

"Bob?" she said, but her voice had failed somewhere around the back of her teeth. Then another six or seven heartbeats came up missing when she heard a toilet flush from a small bathroom at the very back of the DJ's booth that hadn't been in operable condition since Nixon first took office. "Bob?" she said once more. This time, she could almost see the words exit her mouth. Then she realized that there had been a reason for that. The weather wasn't that uncomfortably cold for this time of year in Southern California, just a chill that came with bad weather. Today had been no different, but now she saw her breath as she said that one word. She tested it again by blowing through her mouth, and her suspicion was confirmed. The temperature had dropped by at least thirty degrees in the last minute inside the K-Rave radio station.

Linda tried to move her feet but found that her muscles had become frozen. She even smelled burning eggs and butter but still couldn't move. Her mind was protecting her from a stupid action. Then her face flushed free of blood as she saw the door to the old bathroom open and the same man from the night before came out drying his hands on a paper towel that he then tossed into a wire basket. The light from the small bathroom lit up the booth, and she saw all the detail in horrid clarity. The stacks of records. The turntables and the mic stand. The rolling chair the DJ used, and

the mug of coffee that was now steaming on the console. Then she heard
the music playing. It was an old rock and country crossover song she remembered from her very early childhood. She couldn't remember the artist. She knew the song—"Sea of Heartbreak." It was an Elvis-style song
that became very popular. As she watched, the bearded man looked through
the glass. Linda thought for sure he would react to Bob's presence in the
chair only feet away from the glass, but he acted as though there was nothing there. The man reached out and hit a switch.

"Roberta, you out there?" he asked, and Linda heard it through an intercom system that had never worked in her entire tenure in Moreno. She
looked around just as the DJ was doing for this Roberta. Whoever she was,
she was nowhere in sight. Linda turned back in time to see the man reach
for something out of view, and then the bottle of J&B whiskey appeared.
He poured the amber liquor into his coffee mug. He again looked through
the window as if afraid of being observed and then smiled as he sat down
in his chair and placed a set of headphones on. The music coming from
speakers inside the old reception area was scratching out the song and was
winding down.

"That was Don Gibson, 'Sea of Heartbreak.' The time here in Moreno
is eleven o'clock. You're listening to Freekin' Rowdy Rhoads here at K-Rave
on this dark and stormy Halloween Wednesday, an appropriate setting for
tonight's festivities planned by the good folks at Hadley Corp Gauge and
Meter Company. Remember, if it's raining, Newberry's has plenty for the
kids to do, so parents, don't go throwing yourselves into Lytle Creek—
there's still hope! So, drop off the teens at the Monster Mash Bash at the
Grenada Theater for a night full of frights, and then mosey over to Newberry's. I'll be there live and in all my remote glory, so come by and see old
Freekin' Rowdy on this most ghoulish of nights. Now here's Pat Boone and
'Moody River.'"

Linda could not move, even as the eggs in the frying pan began smoking. She watched as the DJ swirled in his chair and then downed a good
portion of the coffee-and-whiskey mixture. She was terrified thinking that
the motionless Bob must have had a heart attack or a stroke at the very
least. She saw the man lower the cup and a look of exasperation came over
his features. He put the mug down and then hit his intercom switch, auto-
matically lowering the volume of Pat Boone. She even heard the feedback
from the interruption.

"Damn persistent, aren't you?" he said as he leaned forward with his
hands on the console. His eyes moved from the spot she knew Bob was sit-

ting at and then over to her. She froze solid. He hit the switch again, obviously frustrated because he wasn't being answered. "Look, she wasn't pissed when I tried to warn you before, but there has been a lot of interference from others since then. She won't be too forgiving after this. You need to leave this place." He hit the intercom switch again, and the music turned up. He was still taking turns looking from Bob to Linda, who shook her head, still unable to call out Bob's name. Again, the frustration showed as he hit his infernal switch. "Damn, would it help you if I said the *Others* are out, and *they* won't allow her to have any mercy? Are you two beatniks braindead or something? What will it take to get you to beat feet?"

Linda had hope when the DJ looked down at the soon-to-end Pat Boone hit, when again he looked up angrily.

"I died trying to save those kids in the theater. That's why I am still here. The Others keep me imprisoned simply because I interfered, as did others. Now get out of here before all hell breaks loose!" Rowdy Rhoads leaned toward the glass, and his appearance changed in seconds.

He burst into bright flames, and his skin crisped and peeled away. His head was smashed in on the left side and looked as if his brains were leaking out of the other. He took a stance as if he were about to hurl himself out of the booth and into Bob's lap, who still hadn't moved an inch in the easy chair.

Linda finally managed a horror-movie-type scream as the immolated and partially crushed man launched himself at the glass.

The gunshots echoed in the confines of the radio station. Four shots shattered the triple panes of glass just as Freekin' Rowdy became airborne. The glass blew inward as Linda's scream overshadowed even the gunfire.

Then there was nothing. Bob was standing up with the blanket at his feet and the smoking Smith & Wesson pointed at the empty space where the glass had been. The booth was empty and dark. None of the things she had seen earlier were there. No records, no turntables, and most assuredly no Freekin' Rowdy Rhoads.

"Why didn't you answer me, you son of a bitch?" she screamed as the eggs in the frying pan burst into flames. The smell immediately got her attention, and she retrieved the flaming pan and then slammed it into the small sink, running water on it.

Bob started shaking, and Linda felt horrible. He had been there, watching everything all along, and she supposed with both of them looking like deer caught in the headlights of a car, it pissed Freekin' Rowdy off enough for him to show his true form.

Linda ran from the kitchen area and then slowed as she approached her husband. She saw him shaking. The gun hadn't moved from his aiming spot right behind the glass. She easily removed the .38 from his trembling hand, and then his paralysis vanished. He looked at her and shook his head.

"Forget the clothes and other things. Get your purse. We are so outta here!" Bob said as he turned and they both made for the door, he in his pajamas and her in a robe and slippers.

They ran into the pouring rain and started for their beat-up Plymouth Horizon that sat hubcap deep in the rushing water.

"What's the company going to say?" Linda asked as they neared the car and safety.

"I don't give a good goddamn what they say. It would take an army to keep me here!"

At precisely that moment, a caravan of black Chevy SUVs with blue flashing lights in their grilles turned the corner from Jefferson onto Main Street. Bob stopped, and the keys to the car fell into the rain-swollen gutter. Linda placed a hand over her mouth as fifteen vehicles and one very large motor home came at them. Several of the black Blazers went down the street, and the others started pulling to the curb. Three of these even blocked the street at Jefferson and Wilks Avenues, placing their vehicles sideways in the road. They watched as men dressed in raincoats and black windbreakers took up station on the sidewalk on both sides of the street while the expensive motor home pulled into a vacant lot near the old Texaco station. That then was surrounded by four California Highway Patrol cars. Men piled out of all the vehicles, and they all were armed. The final blow was the black step van that pulled to the front of Newberry's, and fifteen FBI hostage rescue team members hopped out and took up station near the flooding sidewalk. Their eyes were roving everywhere and even took in Bob and Linda.

"I think that army you mentioned has just arrived," Linda said hopelessly.

After Bob and Linda had been questioned, they were escorted to the radio station, where three FBI agents checked the inside for anyone else. Bob even saw several of them go into Newberry's to question Harvey. Then they saw a black sedan pull up and two men escorted the very angry walnut farmer, Casper Worthington, and his Yorkie named Peckerwood inside Newberry's.

Bob was handed back his driver's license and his contract for Sacra-

mento Security Systems. The agent seemed amused at the state of the
so-called security for the town but was polite enough not to say anything
to the very harried-looking hippie couple. Overall, the federal authorities
found the state of security in the town laughable.

"Now can you tell us what in the hell is going on?" Linda asked as she
came from the bedroom with fresh clothes on. She found her bravery again
with so many men and women around, but she still sent a nervous glance
toward the DJ booth and its windowless frame.

"Someone will be in to explain shortly. There are some people who
wish to interview you both." The agent smiled. "Do you have firearms on
the premises?"

"We wouldn't be very good security if all we could do is throw foul
language at trespassers, would we?"

"Gun," the other agent said as he picked up the Smith & Wesson that
had entwined itself in a blanket on the floor. The agent picked it up by the
trigger guard and then smelled the barrel. "Recently fired."

The FBI agent talking to Bob smiled as he nodded at his partner. It was
then that he noticed the DJ booth and the shattered window. He faced the
smaller man again as Bob pulled his hair back and then applied a rubber
band to it and formed a ponytail, much to the agent's amusement.

"Perhaps you'd better stick to foul language, Mr. Culbertson."

"Accidental discharge." Bob eyed his wife, who nodded at the small
lie. "Now, why are you here?"

The door opened, and several people that were dressed differently
came in shaking rainwater from their clothing and hair. The tall man in
the front shook his raincoat and then looked up with an apologetic smile.

"Sorry. I think we're making a mess here."

"Don't worry about it," Linda said as she moved toward the front door
with a mop. She didn't greet the newcomers as she started swabbing the
water from the old linoleum flooring.

"We'll just hang onto this, sir," the first agent said as he held the gun
up to show the tall man.

"Thank you," the man with the well-trimmed beard said, looking at
the agents. "We just have a few questions for Mr. and Mrs. Culbertson."

The two agents left the station with a warning look at Bob about firearm safety.

"Wow, this is a blast from the past," a small black man said as he
looked the K-Rave station over.

"Can you please tell me why we are being held here?" Bob asked as he eyed the seven people standing near the door. The two women looked uncomfortable.

"Yes, sir. My name is Professor Gabriel Kennedy. These are my associates, Mr. John Lonetree, Dr. Jennifer Tilden, Mr. Leonard Sickles." He stepped forward and clicked his heels together. "Mr. George Cordero, Ms. Julie Reilly, and the surly-looking fellow there is Damian Jackson. We're—"

"The Supernaturals," Linda said as her mop moved back and forth across the faded flooring. She never looked up from her task. "Knew it as soon as I seen ya." She looked up and fixed them all with her tired eyes. "I must say, your recent troubles about hoaxes and people faking their experiences fails to hold water, in my humble opinion." She bent to her mopping. "As a matter of fact, I think your theories on the subject are bullshit," she said more quietly.

"There's nothing to do but watch television here. We didn't have much of a choice; this town has never had cable. We were kind of stuck with what programming we could get out of LA over the air." Bob looked from person to person and then shook his head.

"Can we have a seat, Mr. Culbertson?" Gabriel asked with a smile after such a good review of their television work.

"You can have this whole fucking town if you want, man."

Linda appeared with two chairs and placed them in the reception area, pushing a wooden record box out of the way before returning to get more chairs. With everyone seated, Linda brought in coffee after opening a window to get the smell of burned eggs out of the studio. The place was silent, with the exception of the rain falling on the old and battered roof. Everyone waited for Gabriel to speak. Before he did, he pulled out a sheaf of papers.

"This contract says you have a few days to go before your obligation here is fulfilled." Gabriel looked at the pages and then placed them back into his coat pocket.

"I don't give a flying f—"

"Whoa," Linda said as she poured Gabriel's coffee. "A little early to be rude. After this morning, I think we can dispense with that crap."

"We have fulfilled the contract. The town is still standing, and it looks as if our relief has arrived. And to be perfectly frank here, you didn't bring enough men."

Gabe looked at John, and they both knew something was showing itself in Moreno. The room went silent as George stood up from his chair with coffee cup in hand. He walked straight to the DJ's booth window as they all watched. Bob looked nervous as George ran his fingers over the empty frame. He closed his eyes. He opened them once again and turned and looked at Bob.

"Bullets can't harm them, you know."

Bob swallowed and then turned in his chair and faced Gabriel and John.

"Let's just say it made me feel a lot better."

"I know how you feel." Damian sipped his coffee.

"That's right, I think I remember you unloading an entire clip of nine-millimeter rounds at something that just laughed at you and kept coming," Julie said as he smiled at Jackson over her memories of Summer Place.

Damian lowered the coffee cup and smirked. "As Mr. Culbertson said, it made me feel better."

Gabriel saw the ease in which Damian and Julie disarmed the man sitting with them. Even his wife snickered at the small tale of terror.

"Freekin' Rowdy Rhoads." Cordero raised his cup and drank coffee. Kennedy could see that he was also doing his part in making the couple feel less like fools. He knew his team was very capable of making people relax in their presence.

"That's the name he said on the radio this morning. Harvey over at Newberry's says Rhoads used to be a DJ here until his death," Linda said, amazed with George.

"Died, October 31, 1962," George said, turning to see if he were right.

"Old man Leach said the same. We don't know the particulars, but he did mention that fact," Bob said, looking at the two men seated right in front of him.

"This morning?" Gabe asked.

"I knew that cat!"

The voice and its tenor made everyone turn and look at Jennifer, who was seated next to Julie.

"Oh, shit." Leonard partially stood from his chair in fear of Jenny, but Damian made him sit with a warning look. Leonard was never fond of Jennifer's reaction to an invasion of her mind by one Bobby Lee McKinnon.

Linda, however, stood up and with wide eyes quickly moved away from Jennifer, who had her eyes closed and her head tilted back. John made to move to her side, but Gabriel held him in check. He then turned and held a finger to his lips telling Bob not to speak.

"Met him in LA one summer—1957, I think." Jenny's mouth moved, but the voice was that of a man. "Damn talking head. One of those old Payola boys from Chicago. He was drummed out of the big markets along with Alan Freed for taking payoffs for record pushing," Bobby Lee said.

Most knew that Bobby Lee was referring to the scandal-plagued days of music payola, where money was paid to stations to play certain songs and to push them onto the public. The practice had cost many a station manager and DJ their careers, including the famous Alan Freed, the same man who had coined the phrase *rock and roll* in Cleveland in the fifties.

"Freekin' Rowdy was a war vet, and he obviously got a break coming here. Check my Nubian friend on the little TV thing you have."

Jennifer stopped talking as everyone turned to face Leonard, who was still thinking about the term used to describe him. He had never been called a *Nubian* before. He finally caught on and then placed the laptop on his thighs after handing a smiling Damian his coffee cup. He typed in his command and then gave the slumbering Jenny a dirty look. "Asshole, Bobby Lee, why don't you just call me a *Negro*, like the old days?"

They waited as George continued looking through the empty window space at the interior of the booth.

"Here it is—from the St. Louis army records center. James M. Rhoads, sergeant first class, discharged September 1945." Leonard looked up with a smile. "He was S-2 for the Fourth Infantry Division, assigned to a special unit of the OSS. Commander was one Colonel Robert Hadley."

"Small world," Damian said.

"Crazy as a shit house rat. He said he had seen things that drove him to drinking during his time over there," Bobby Lee said through Jennifer, who immediately sat up straight in her chair and swiped at her mouth as if she had been caught sleeping and was drooling. "What?" she said as she looked from person to person as they all stared at her. "Was I snoring or something?"

"Or something," Leonard said with a sideways look at her.

"Man, I don't know which is worse—this place or you guys," Bob said, casting a wary eye at his startled wife as she moved back to her chair.

"We grow on you," Julie said with a concerned smile as she patted Jennifer on the leg.

The door opened, and two agents stepped inside, shaking water from their coats and eliciting a scornful look from Linda. The first man spied Gabriel and came forward.

"This was just faxed in from our field team in Washington. It's the debrief you requested on men who served with Second Lieutenant Dean Hadley in Vietnam." The agent looked concerned. "The fax transmission from Washington was spotty, and now we are having trouble with cell service. We still have reliable satellite phones, but everything else is headed south because of this storm."

"The cell service is always spotty. The hills." Bob waved his hand in the air.

Kennedy took the offered papers from the agent and then excused the men. He perused them, and then his brows rose.

"What did they dig up?" John asked as he turned and winked at Jennifer, who looked lost after her brief possession from her old friend Bobby Lee McKinnon.

"He served his country with distinction. Not one bad mark in his 201 file." He moved papers around, and then he settled on the ones he was looking for. "However, his commander, upon interview from an old folks' home, remembered a different soldier from the one described in his official file. He said, and I quote, 'The lieutenant was disturbed. A loner. A man who slept very little and disdained the men he served with. He was a frequent volunteer for work outside of his Special Forces regiment. Thirty-six confirmed kills. All in black operations against the North Vietnamese. In 1967, he became unhinged after a visit from a civilian, his father. After that, he was arrested twice by the army's Criminal Investigation Division for the illegal killing of North Vietnamese nationals.'" Gabriel read ahead. "He was found not guilty in a general court-martial that isn't mentioned in his file. Although innocent of the charges, which he never denied, our boy was discharged. Honorably." Gabriel held the papers up a moment and then shook his head.

"May I ask, why are you people in Moreno, and who is that you are talking about?" Bob asked as lightning flashed through the plate glass window.

"Mr. Culbertson, will you and your wife join us for lunch? I assume the food at Newberry's is passable as such?"

"Harvey's a good cook, but maybe not too happy to do so today. Now who was that you were talking about, and is this nut on the loose here or what?"

"That nut is here, Mr. Culbertson, but he's not on the loose. He's in a motor home being attended to by his physicians." Gabriel was helped into his raincoat by Julie, who had brought it to him.

"Who?"

"The man who grew up here," Gabe said, looking at both Bob and Linda. "And that is one thing that I bet old Harvey Leach didn't tell you."

"Tell us what?" asked Linda. She was handed her own coat by Damian, who then helped her into it.

"That the president of the United States grew up here and is now back home in Moreno for the first time since 1962."

Bob looked at Linda as the team of Supernaturals held the door for them.

"I'm asking that lying damn company for that goddamn bonus, damn lying bastards," Bob said as he and Linda moved out of the station and into the rain.

None of them saw the flicker of light from the heavily damaged marquee or heard the teenage screams of horror coming from the old collapsed façade of the Grenada Theater.

She knew that the full cast of Moreno's passion play were present, and the show was about to commence.

15

Harvey had to open more space up inside Newberry's. With the assistance of several FBI and Secret Service agents, the chain-link fencing was moved back and the old clutter of boxes and old hangers pushed elsewhere as men brought more chairs and tables up from the basement. Harvey had coerced Casper Worthington into performing prep-cook duties in the kitchen. More frozen burger patties and fries were also brought from the freezer in the basement, and they had hooked the old soda lines that had been serviced last in 2005. The federal employees could hear Casper cussing up a firestorm about being drafted just like he had been back in 1968. His dog, Peckerwood, remained by his side just beneath the prep table, where the Yorkie could hear most of the more colorful swear words escaping Casper's mouth.

"President, my ass," Harvey said as the last of the old rounded tables were placed in the general area where there used to be ornate booths. "I suspect that you fellas are just looking for free stuff and shoot any name straight out of your asses to do it. President, my ass," he repeated.

The two Secret Service agents helping Harvey smiled and nodded at the old man and then excused themselves. Harvey finished wiping down the years of dust that had adhered to the old Formica that made up the tabletops.

The door opened, and seven strangers came in followed by Bob and Linda Culbertson, both looking uncomfortable in their new company. They all shed their coats, and Harvey knew he was going to be spending the better part of the day mopping up wet spots from the flooding outside. He stopped swiping with the rag when he focused his attention on the new arrivals.

"I see the damn feds have kidnapped you two also," he said as he saw an ashen-faced Bob shrug out of his coat. Linda kept her sweater on. The other seven people again shook the water from their extremities just like Peckerwood had done earlier. "They give you the same bullshit line as they gave me and Casper?"

Bob didn't reply. He and Linda moved to a small table away from the window and then sat. They were silent and clearly as confused as the two old men. The largest of the men stepped up to Harvey, who had to look up until he winced and grabbed his neck in pain.

"Don't remember putting no tree here," he said as he eyed John Lonetree. Harvey immediately regretted his choice of words when John introduced himself. He moved off some feet away before he regained his bravado. "And along with the president, I suppose this fella is in charge of Injun Affairs?"

Jennifer flinched at the insult, but as she looked at Lonetree, she saw him smile and then sit down at a table. She joined him.

"Mr. Harvey Leach, we need a few words, if you don't mind?"

"And you are? The vice president?" Harvey joked, but no one laughed, with the exception of Casper in the kitchen, who cackled away with Peckerwood barking along.

"Name is Kennedy, Mr. Leach." Gabriel moved toward the man and extended his hand. Harvey looked at it and then with the filthy rag still in his hand reached for Gabriel's and shook. Gabe smiled and then wiped his hand on his trouser leg. "I understand your consternation, but we believe you have information that no one else may have."

"I don't know about constipation, but I do know I don't have any information about diddly squat." He moved away a few steps and then stopped and turned. "Who's gonna pay for all of this? Me and Casper have far better things to do around here than wait tables for a bunch of gov'ment thieves."

"I'll issue you a ten-thousand-dollar deposit check for your services, and then we will settle up before we leave."

Everyone in the Newberry's old forlorn lunch counter and tables turned and saw several men with a woman at the center standing just inside the double doorway. At the curb with water running above the bottom of its tires was a brand-new Cadillac extended limousine. The woman was removing a set of expensive leather gloves as she looked the department store over. She removed a large hat, and Harvey's face went white. The First Lady of the United States, Catherine Hadley, had that effect on most males. Harvey and a wide-eyed Casper, who was staring at the group through the kitchen counter space, were aghast.

"Not much of a going concern, is it?" Catherine spied Kennedy and moved toward him and Harvey, who stood motionless as the beautiful woman excused herself as she stepped by him. She stopped and turned to face Newberry's ownership. "I take it the women's department is up the escalator?" She smiled and looked at the partially collapsed moving stairs. "Maybe not."

"Mr. Leach, this is—" Gabriel began.

"I know who it is, you damn fool, I'm not blind and stupid both. Well, maybe stupid at times," he said as a partial way of apologizing for not believing anyone this afternoon about the president being in town. He gestured for Catherine to have a seat, and she obliged by taking one at the table Gabriel was standing nearest. He made no move to stand up, and Harvey yelped in terror as the First Lady started to pull her own chair out. Harvey ran the few steps and then quickly pulled out the old cane chair.

She nodded her thanks. "Chivalry isn't all dead, is it?"

"Not around here, ma'am," Leach said as he nodded and then hurriedly left, forcing Casper to stop his gawking and get back to cutting up tomatoes.

"Well, here we are," she said as she demurely smiled at Kennedy, placing her leather gloves in her hat and then resting them on the table. The other members of his team took seats around them. Damian and George Cordero sat at the extensive counter and looked at menus. "To let you know, the security element and medical staff will remain in place as long as my husband is here. I, on the other hand, will be staying at the Radisson in Ontario." She looked around the small luncheonette. "I believe they have a better buffet," she said, leaning forward as if not to hurt Harvey's feelings, but Gabriel knew differently. She was as mean-spirited as her husband and liked to show it.

Harvey arrived with two glasses of water. "I don't normally wait on tables, but seeing as you're the First Lady and all."

"There are usually no customers; that's why you don't normally wait on tables!" Casper spouted from the kitchen.

Harvey smiled as his eyes went wide and then quickly excused himself to hurriedly beat Casper Worthington to death.

"Colorful cast of characters you're gathering, Professor." She spun the glass of water around with her manicured nails.

"Did you know about your husband's affinity for killing during the Vietnam War?" Gabriel asked as they were finally joined by John, who sat down and smiled at the First Lady.

Catherine slid the water glass around the table and smiled in return. "I believe I told you before, Professor, my husband talked in his sleep—not just about lost loves but also the things he did to people. Not because it was his job but because he was angry at himself and others."

Gabriel could see that although he suspected Catherine Hadley hated her husband, she was mad because she couldn't sway him to love her. It was a need that Gabriel had seen many times before in patients.

"Explain 'angry at himself and others'?" John asked, picking up on the same conclusion as Kennedy's.

"Gentlemen, may I suggest you dedicate what time you have left to help the president and not try to analyze me? I could never begin to explain a man that is quite unexplainable." She stood and retrieved her hat and gloves from the table. "Mr. Leach, I'll have that check brought over to you immediately." Catherine started for the door as men moved to assist her with her coat.

"Nah, that won't be——" Harvey began.

"If I were you, I would get cash," George said, stopping Harvey cold.

"Good luck with your experiment, gentlemen."

They watched her leave with her security detail.

"What now?" John said.

"I think we need a tour of the town. We've seen some of it in its heyday, but perhaps we should get familiar with Moreno's current state," Gabriel said as he stood up. "Mr. and Mrs. Culbertson, I ask that you be patient with us. We're just getting up to speed here. However, I would prefer if no one wanders around town alone for the time being."

"I'm beginning to think that anywhere you go inside Moreno, you're not alone."

Kennedy nodded in understanding as the others smiled, knowing exactly where Bob was coming from.

"Mr. Leach, can you spare yourself for the next half an hour or so? I expect the lunchtime rush won't start until the chef returns. We would like to know more about where the president grew up."

Harvey appeared from the swinging doors of the kitchen, wiping his hands on a towel. "I'm just surprised you all quit lying about him growing up in Ontario and going to Chaffey High School and finally admitted that he was here in Moreno for the better part of his childhood. Lucky there were no more people in Moreno to make a fuss about where he hung his hat as a kid and then at the White House."

"I imagine it cost his father plenty to keep that information in the closet," John said as he stood and put on his coat. "Gabe, I'm going to skip the tour. I think Jenny, Damian, and I will take a ride up the hill and take a look-see at the ruins up there. The factory also. Get a lay of the land."

"You be careful."

"Security won't let you get too far."

They looked at Harvey, who was cursing as he slipped into a tattered coat. "Those boys are the only ones who get paid what they're worth, because they work for the state and county."

"We can arrange for all of you to be moved to a hotel in Chino or Ontario," Kennedy said as he moved toward the double front doors. Several of the security detail stepped inside. "After we get a feel for the town, I can see no reason to keep you here if you wish to leave."

"Casper, you have customers out here. You have to pull double duty until I get back," Harvey said, looking at Gabriel and John, "*if* I get back."

The sky at that time exploded with lightning, and the world shook with the power of the thunder that quickly followed.

George and Julie got up to follow Gabriel, and Damian went with John and Jennifer. Leonard put a menu down and then placed his hands in front of him. He would stay and set up shop in Newberry's.

"Hey, Casper, I'll have BLT and fries."

"I can get the fries, but we're plumb out of bacon," Casper said as he leaned into the opening. "I can get you a burger. You want a burger?"

Leonard turned in his stool and saw Gabriel. "I'll just be here having—" He gestured at a leering Casper, still looking through the space between the counter and the soda station.

"A burger," Casper finished for him. Peckerwood barked in agreement somewhere in the kitchen.

"A burger," he repeated. "I think we're going to have a lot of burgers here."

Damian, John, and Jennifer had the FBI give them a lift up Drunk Monk's Road, the dirt track that led to the ruins, while the others—with Harvey Leach in tow—started their tour of the ghost town.

"So, Mr. Leach, you've been in Moreno most of your life," Gabe said as they fought the umbrellas that the wind pushed around handily.

"Before you get too far, Professor, yes, my daddy served with old man Hadley." He looked up from trying to keep dry under the umbrella, "I mean, the colonel." He laughed. "Ain't no big deal; anyone who owned a business in town served with him during the war. The loans from the colonel were cheap, and his men were beholden to him. Even Hadley's main partner in all of this"—he waved his hand around Moreno—"Mr. Perry, paid the colonel due respect. Even after their falling out."

"When was that?" George asked, getting the vibe that Leach was telling the truth about everything thus far.

"Oh, right before that night, I suppose. Maybe a year or two, I don't know. You get to be my age and things tend to blur together." He was silent as they walked through the ankle-high water cresting the edge of the sidewalk. He stopped at an alcove and stepped under it. The rain still came down through large holes in the wooden awning. Gabe saw the display windows on both sides, but the entire front of the store was missing. "Take this place—it was once a shoe store owned by Staff Sergeant Jerry Jenks."

"Red Goose Shoes," George said as he and Julie stared into an empty display window lining the outside entrance. "There used to be a big plastic goose, and kids would pull down on its neck until an egg rolled out. It was full of penny candy."

Harvey looked flabbergasted. "Now how in the hell did you know that?" He looked at Cordero more closely as lightning flashed across the dark skies.

"He's a good guesser," Julie said.

With a lingering look at the small Mexican man, a distrustful Harvey continued. "Anyway, as I was saying, if you served with the colonel, you had more breaks come your way than problems than you would normally. Hadley even owned the bank. Bought out the old Moreno Savings and Loan and opened the brand-new Moreno First National Bank right across the street there." He pointed across the river that was Main Street at an abandoned building that had some fire damage. "Hell, I even remember the day they moved the old bank vault from the Savings and Loan to the basement of the theater when they installed the new one at the First National. In those days, anything that shut down traffic like that was an event, let me tell you. Big to-do with a giant crane moving that damn heavy vault."

"Mr. Leach—"

"Look, stop calling me that. Every time you do, I look around for my old man."

"Harvey, did you know President Hadley back then?" Gabriel asked as the wind blew in rain from the street.

"Well, who in the hell didn't know him? If you didn't know he was the richest kid in town, give him enough of your time, he would explain it to you. In action or in words. He was arrogant either way. But yeah, we hung out together, mostly through circumstance. You see, Moreno wasn't big enough to have a high school, so us older kids were bused into Chino."

"Yes, I think we were told that. How was Dean there?" Julie asked as she stepped up to Harvey.

"You wouldn't have to ask if you knew how bad Chino's football team was. You see, Hadley was a star. Chino protected its only star. So yes, young lady, the bastard was in total control there too."

"He had to have some redeeming qualities," George stated, remaining fixed on the display window and the dreamwalk he had shared with the others. It seemed he was totally intrigued by that damn red goose that previously called the display window home.

Harvey thought a long time. "Yeah, toward the end. Maybe the last week or so before the fire. Yeah, I would say so. That was when he had dealings with—"

"Gloria Perry?" Gabriel asked, surprising Leach with his knowledge.

"Yeah, Gloria. Little blind girl that did something to Dean that no one had ever done before. Hell, it was all over town those last few days."

"What did she do?" Julie asked.

Harvey smiled at the memory. "Bewitched the son of a bitch, that's what." Leach shook his head. "It was a sight to see. That boy fell in love so hard, so fast, that we didn't recognize him in the last few days. Why, do you know he fought three of his best friends that morning over her? They said the wrong thing at the wrong time. It was bad enough that Chief Thomas tried to throw his ass in jail for two hours until his daddy would be able to come to get him."

"What did his father say?" Gabriel asked.

"Didn't say anything. The arrogant bastard broke out of jail before he could get there." Harvey shook his head as he remembered the last days.

"That boy was transformed by Gloria. And if you knew Dean Hadley, you wouldn't have thought it possible. With the way he ran around that night trying his best to save people. Then when he heard . . . he heard that he had lost Gloria at the Grenada when the fire broke out and the balcony collapsed, he just went crazy. We never saw much of him after that. Heard a few things here and there, but until he became the president, we lost contact. When I was overseas, I heard rumors about Dean, but they were so outrageous, I didn't believe them."

George turned away from the display window and nodded at Gabe when he knew Leach was telling the truth.

"His father?" Julie continued as Harvey stepped away and into the driving rain.

Leach turned back as the others brought their umbrellas up and followed him.

"The colonel was as persona non grata as his boy after 1962. We heard he took over several large firms with insurance money from the factory, but other than that, we didn't hear anything until we saw the news reports that he had died in '78. As much as most of us owed Hadley for the lives we had in Moreno, not many people shed a tear that day. A lot of good folks around here blamed the tragedy of that night on those two men."

"Two?" Gabe said.

"Sure. As much as everyone liked Frank Perry, he was also responsible for things. It didn't matter if the colonel and the captain were no longer partners, he was still blamed, just not to the point of Hadley. Even my old man, a part of the original investors and a member of Hadley's unit, was ridiculed. Ah, hell, it didn't matter anyway. Frank killed himself after learning about Gloria's death." Lightning flashed over their heads, and thunder shook the world. "Blew his brains out right up there in the old ruins. Just sat down in the basement and put a gun to his temple and blew his brains out."

"Damn, this town has a short but violent history," Julie commented as they turned into a wreck of a building.

"Some idiots say it was a penance for what our fathers did during the war. My daddy never said a thing, but he would wake up nights in a cold sweat. He didn't think me and Mom knew, but he did it most nights. He would cry too. Scared the hell out of me and Mom."

Gabe reached out and stopped Julie from tangling her feet in a large pile of debris near the sidewalk. "Be careful; it looks like something fell down."

"Yeah, it was so fire damaged that night that it finally gave way to weather and the other elements," Harvey said as Julie leaped over the pile of glass and plastic. "The damn thing finally gave up the ghost, so to speak, about this time fifteen years ago, when a Santa Ana wind blew through."

The group of four started walking again, avoiding the larger lakes that had formed in the damaged sidewalk as best as they could. As lightning flashed and thunder clapped its mighty hands together, the hidden sun began to sink into the western sky.

They were slowly approaching October 31 . . . Halloween night and the anniversary of the murder of Moreno.

The Chevy Blazer powered its way up the dirt road toward the mission and winery. The rain was so dense that the wipers on high speed couldn't push the water away fast enough. The FBI driver had to slow to fifteen miles per hour. Finally, they crested the hill and there it was. John swallowed when he recognized the Santa Maria Delarosa mission. He adjusted his line of sight as they passed the last small curve and then he saw the winery.

"Hey, you hanging in there, big guy?" Jennifer asked, squeezing Lonetree's hand.

Damian saw the unease that made John clench and unclench his jaw. Even the driver risked a look in his mirror.

"Something's not right," he said as the guard shack stood before them and the vehicle slowed.

"Where are those county boys?" the agent in the passenger's seat asked, his eyes narrowing as he peered through the windshield. The steady thump of the wipers was unnerving. It reminded Damian of that old Hitchcock film *Psycho* with Janet Leigh. The view through the slashing windshield wipers was not that different from the terrifying sight of the Bates Motel.

The gate was standing open, and they could see a San Bernardino County truck in the parking area by the security shack. The two guards were nowhere to be seen. The agent driving eased up to the building with a wary eye on the monstrosity of the ruins before them.

"If those guys make us go searching for them in this rain, they'd better expect to hear an ass chewing from yours truly." The FBI field agent opened the door, and without an umbrella, he sprinted for the guard shack. He opened the door, and bright light escaped into the mounting darkness of the late afternoon. He reappeared a moment later, sliding the nine-millimeter handgun back into its holster. He shook his head toward the car and pointed at the mission only a few yards away. The driver nodded as the man held his coat up over his head to act as a shield and then ran toward the large mission and its stone steps.

"Damn amateurs, if you ask me," the second agent said.

"Something is wrong," John repeated, his gaze fixed on the winery. It was hard to see through the downpour, but he could tell that the front doors were both open. Lonetree opened the car door, and without regard to getting wet, he ran across the gravel drive until he was under the partially collapsed portico. He shook the water from his soaked head and then examined the place he had only seen in a dream. It was hard to say for sure, but if he remembered right, there hadn't been this much damage to the structure back when he ventured inside the dream state with Gloria. He anxiously watched the open doors and the blackness beyond.

"Don't do that again," warned Damian, replacing his own pistol in its shoulder holster as he too gained the near safety of the overhang.

"I agree," said Jennifer, making her way to the relative dryness of the winery.

As Lonetree stood considering the open doorway, the song that Gloria was singing in the pickup truck that morning started running through his head. Tommy Edwards singing "It's All in the Game" was loud enough in his memory that he closed his eyes. Then he again surprised everyone by hurriedly entering the winery.

"Damn it!" Jackson said as he and Jenny followed. They saw the agile Lonetree as he dodged the fallen beams and adobe brick that had fallen inside and the swimming pool–sized lakes of water, eventually vanishing beyond their line of sight.

"John!" Jenny called out as lightning illuminated the inside of the winery. She saw him tugging at a doorway against the far back corner of the main floor, and she bumped her knees and shins repeatedly as she made her way to him. Damian was having the same trouble in the near-dark conditions and swore that someone was going to get shot if he fell through the rotting floor to his death.

As the two caught up, John finally managed to pull the old and rusty steel door open, which then fell immediately to the floor with a crash. Lonetree dodged it and looked back at his friends.

"Whatever was in there before is gone," he said as he produced a flashlight and headed down rusty steel steps. Damian shook his head.

"I don't suppose I can convince you not to go down there?"

Jenny didn't answer as she started down. Damian, cursing both of them, also descended into darkness.

Jennifer stumbled into John's backside when she hit the bottom step. Lonetree was just staring at the wall of mud that greeted him. The steel door leading to the strange laboratory-type basement was gone, buried by the torrent of mud and debris that had smashed into the old winery the night before. John reached out and took a handful of mud and saw that it was relatively fresh. He tossed it away and then shook his head.

"You two maniacs had better start looking before you leap!" Damian said as he made it to the bottom in one piece, bringing with him the benefit of light. "Did you guys see the condition of those damn stairs?" He moved the light toward the steel steps, and Jenny felt her blood go colder than it already was.

"They're gone," John said as he turned away from the slide that blocked their path. Then he saw what Damian was pointing out on the stairs.

"Yeah, and I think they went thataway," Damian said, inching the flashlight beam up one step at a time.

"Oh, shit," Jennifer said in her mousy and very scared voice.

Each of the steel grated steps was bent in the middle and looked as if someone weighing at least several tons had used them last. John and Jennifer could not believe they made it down without breaking their legs or worse. As the light moved up, so did their anxiety.

"How big did you say that steel box was?" Damian asked as he again withdrew his pistol.

"Big."

"Like, King Kong big?"

The question was not meant as a joke as the light beam played over the damage. Rust had broken free of the steel underneath, and they could see fresh, unprotected metal. The steps that had bent the stairs had been made recently.

"You know, I really don't relish the thought of meeting up with something that big and heavy with a flashlight and what amounts to a peashooter. I think we should get back to the car." Damian turned to look at John and Jennifer. "I have always said ever since I joined this fucked-up group, never leave the car when it's a dark and stormy situation. Never."

John nodded and pushed Jenny before him as they started climbing the heavily damaged steps. With agonizing slowness, they finally made it to the top without a misstep. They moved outside and saw that the two agents had decided that the three of them could check the winery for the missing guards as well as they could. They were in the Blazer waiting for them with the vehicles headlights pointed at the doorway. The agent behind the wheel waved.

"You think the past few weeks are starting to get to some of our brave boys in government service?" Damian asked as they ran for the car with the uneasy feeling that something very large was lurking nearby.

"You said it yourself," Jenny said as she opened the back door, "never leave the car."

"Amen," John said.

The last of the agents had rotated into Newberry's for a hot meal served by a surly Harvey Leach and an exhausted Casper Worthington. Even Peckerwood was tired and sleeping underneath the front counter.

The lead field agent for the FBI explained to Gabriel and the others as they ate that the Secret Service would handle securing the president's mobile hospital unit and expensive motor home built to specifications from the Treasury Department and constructed by Pace Arrow. The San Bernardino Sheriff's Department would patrol from the interstate to the border of Moreno, keeping any prying eyes away from the town, and the California Highway Patrol had all the streets coming in and out of Moreno blocked. The hardest thing would be to forestall the press if they ever got wind of what was happening in the small Southern California ghost town. The FBI agents and the hostage rescue team unit out of Quantico would handle all the security inside the town, with regular patrols of the residential neighborhoods and the town itself.

John and the others were convinced that something had escaped from that basement facility, and Gabe wasn't taking that conclusion lightly. Damian was the main contributor to that conclusion for the simple fact Kennedy knew that the former police inspector didn't scare easily.

"Our recommendation is, with this storm not due to let up until tomorrow night, we have to be prepared to get everyone out quickly. The local boys say they have seen this before; these hills could roll down at us like a wave and bury us all here without warning. We have a medical evacuation helicopter on standby at Chino Airport just in case we must evac the president fast. Other than that, I would advise you keep your team together and to not wander the town alone without armed escort."

Gabriel stood and shook the field agent's hand and thanked him for the update. He sat down alone at the table. The front doors opened before the lead agent got to it, and he stepped aside as a hurried Bob, Linda, and two agents came through, shaking water from their clothing. The agents gave them their garbage bags with the few clothes they had gathered from the radio station, and the couple thanked them for accompanying them.

John came over with a pot of coffee and two cups. He put one before Gabriel and poured. He repeated the same for himself and then sat down across from him. Lonetree took a deep breath and then played with his coffee until Gabe looked up.

"You sure you want to do this?" he asked.

"Do we have a choice? If we had other witnesses to get the story from, I would be more than happy to do it the old-fashioned way by interviewing them. Julie can get anything out of a witness, you know that, but she has limitations when it comes to getting memories from people that have forgotten the smaller details we need." John turned his head and smiled at the rest of the team who had placed three of the round tables together to eat. Then he moved his brown eyes to Casper and Harvey, who were finishing up in the kitchen, putting away the restaurant supplies brought in by the federal men three hours earlier. Most of the items had not been on Newberry's lunch counter menu for decades, and Harvey seemed to be pleased with the abundance of food choices. Casper, on the other hand, was not that thrilled and kept complaining that they had no right to keep him and Peckerwood away from their farm. Lonetree jabbed a thumb toward the kitchen. "I'll do the simple stuff; it's you that has to convince Laurel and Hardy in there to cooperate. Is Leonard ready?"

"He and George said all is ready to go. You'll be recorded, and George will be linked to you through touch, so no matter what you are seeing and feeling, he will relay everything to us."

"I imagine he didn't take to the idea too well."

"No, he did not," Gabriel said as he sipped his hot coffee. "Well, this isn't getting the job done, is it?" Gabriel said as Harvey walked by and removed the coffeepot on the table. He stood and then followed Harvey toward the kitchen. John smiled as he fantasized about the colorful language about to be spewed from the kitchen when Kennedy made his request. The larger table was also interested, and Damian and Leonard were actually betting on the outcome. They didn't have to wait long.

"Are you out of your ever-lovin' mind?" came the shout from the kitchen where the view of the engagement was obscured. They all heard Casper Worthington laughing and Peckerwood barking. "You tell Injun Joe out there he's not crawlin' into my head like some alien bug!"

John smiled when he saw Leonard handing over a twenty-dollar bill to Damian, who sat with hand out, smiling. Obviously, Sickles had expected a different outcome.

Pots and pans were jostled and Peckerwood kept barking, and Casper slowly wound down his laughter at his friend's predicament. It was twenty minutes later that Gabriel exited the kitchen, eating a grilled cheese sandwich. The others watched on with curiosity masking their anxiety. Gabe stood in front of the group and chewed. Then he finished and used a napkin to wipe his mouth. Kennedy looked pleased with himself.

"He'll do it."

"And how was this miracle performed?" Julie Reilly asked, knowing the type of person Harvey Leach was. He wanted to be left alone, and his memories of his past, what he could remember of them, were his and his alone.

"You complimented his food," George said with a large smile on his bearded face after reading the feelings coming from Kennedy.

"I complimented his food," Gabe acknowledged.

16

An hour later, the team was as ready as they ever would be. They were on the second floor of Newberry's, where Leonard had set up all their equipment. No fewer than four video cameras would record the session, and audio inputs were in place to take in even the smallest nuances of memory from Harvey Leach. The man himself sat against the wall wide-eyed and looked terrified. Kennedy watched Damian hand the man a small shot glass of whiskey on Gabriel's orders, to still Harvey's nerves. The rest of the team was spread out in a wide circle to make sure nothing was missed. The store was locked up and secured, and the feds were warned that for the time being, Newberry's was under quarantine. They would guard outside and warn them of any activity through their radios, which Leonard would also be monitoring. Bob, Linda, Casper, and Peckerwood would sit this one out downstairs near the lunch counter. Casper was the only one disappointed he wouldn't see his friend go through the ordeal.

Gabriel mixed the two cocktails of Demerol and other special ingredients and placed the three syringes on the table in front of him. Jennifer was assisting with the emergency equipment. She had the defibrillator and the syringes of Adrenalin and atropine, a drug used to kick-start a heart. The danger was spelled out for Harvey, and though he said he wasn't afraid, they all noticed how his faded blue eyes jumped to the two women in the room, Julie and Jenny, when he said it. The better part of his machismo had not been lost to the old-timer. In any case, Gabriel was aware that the dreamwalk, no matter how short in duration, was extremely dangerous for a man of Leach's age.

Gabriel rubbed his eyes, and Jennifer leaned over and asked if he was all right.

"John is right; this needs to be done to get the feel of the town that day, but he's taxing his physical makeup by doing the dreamwalk too many times with such a short recovery window."

Jenny smiled. "He knows I would run off with Bobby Lee if he kicked the bucket on us, so he promised he wouldn't. Don't worry, at least on this one. I don't think Harvey Leach is hiding anything in that brain of his that could be considered dangerous." She then lost her smile. "Unless he's behind this whole thing, an evil plan to wrest Newberry's from his father's control."

"Smart-ass," Gabe said, kissing the top of Jenny's head and then turning to face a brave-looking but totally frightened Harvey Leach, who sat on the edge of his chair, waiting.

John was sitting on the bed across from him with a casual look on his brown features. He winked at Leach, who flinched in return. Gabe approached with his best disarming smile. He placed his hands on his knees and leaned over to have direct eye contact with the old man.

"Harvey, we're going to give you something that will send you into a light sleep. It will open your mind up, and that in turn will relax your entire body. All you have to do is sleep, and we'll guide you to the places that we know you will be capable of going. We can't ask you about anything you didn't actually witness. You may be able to relay secondhand information to us, but John won't be able to envision it, because your eyes didn't witness it yourself, so the brain subconsciously denies John the ability to see. Clear so far?"

"Not a goddamn word of it."

Gabriel and the others smiled. "Good," he said, patting Harvey on the knee as he straightened. He turned back and looked at Leonard, who nodded that he was ready.

The last thing was for Jenny to kiss John, and then her small hand held his face for the briefest of moment.

"Be careful in there." She looked at Harvey and smiled and then leaned in to whisper to Lonetree, "California authorities never caught the Zodiac killer." Her eyes flicked over toward Leach, who tilted his head after hearing the strange comment.

"Did I ever relay the fact to you that you can be a b—"

"Good luck," she said, and then she allowed Gabriel in to administer his injections.

"I always hated those days at school when they gave those gov'ment-funded inoculations. They hurt like hell," he said as Gabriel frowned at him, holding the empty needle. "Oh, you done it already," he said with a macho smile. "That wasn't so bad." Then he saw Julie roll over the defibrillator. "What's that?" he asked with his eyes a tad wider than a moment before.

"Oh, it's nothing; it's for John. Sometimes he needs a pick-me-up after he does this," she lied, and she also patted Harvey on the leg. "Good luck, champ."

"You know, with all these good-luck wishes, it feels like the day I shipped off to Vietnam. You people do not inspire confidence."

Harvey looked from person to person as his eyelids grew heavy. Lonetree, sitting directly to his front, was already drifting, but his own excitement delayed the reaction to his Demerol enough so that the world became an echoing mockery of its real self. Then he was gone. His eyes closed and his body relaxed. Gabriel and Jennifer both checked his vital signs and were satisfied that Harvey was sound asleep. Gabriel sat down.

"John, can you hear me?" Gabe asked with a soft and gentle voice in the chair next to Lonetree. He watched as John's eyes moved rapidly under the lids.

"EKG jump," Leonard said from his darkened corner with only the light from his many monitors illuminating his face. "He heard you."

"Harvey Leach, can you hear me?"

Nothing. Gabriel looked back in the darkness, and Leonard shook his head.

Gabriel checked the leads on Harvey's chest, and they were attached correctly. He then looked at George, who was holding Harvey's hand and then released it after getting the feel for the man's brain activity. He also shook his head. Gabriel sat back and thought a moment. Harvey may have a hard time relaying his memories because he was a nonbeliever in John's abilities. He had to make Harvey think while he dreamed. What could he say to get the man's attention?

Julie cleared her throat from her chair in the circle. She pointed at the far wall as lightning flashed through the windows. Gabe didn't see what she was suggesting until she mouthed the word. Then he saw the painted logo on the wall that said *Newberry's, the Family Department Store!* Gabriel smiled understanding.

"Harvey! You clocked in late again!" Gabe said loudly, making Harvey jump in his sleep. George smiled and nodded. Leonard in the far corner gave a thumbs-up as he watched the brain activity on his monitor increase.

The idea was to get Harvey's attention, and Gabe's voice was falling short of the mark. So, at Julie's suggestion, he had used the two things that terrified Harvey more than anything, and these were things he had mentioned in passing throughout the day as they spoke with him—the department store as an attention getter and his father's commanding voice as the root of his base fear.

"Harvey, are you there?" Kennedy asked in a more forceful voice. "I need more soft-drink syrup brought up from the basement! Harvey, are you hearing me?"

"Yes, goddamn it, I hear you!" George said, repeating what he heard from the feelings of Harvey Leach.

John was actually viewing the boy wherever he was in his memory.

"Harvey, your father says never mind about the syrup; the cans they already have behind the counter will be enough." Gabe waited.

"Of course they are; you're so damn cheap with the syrup, we never run out! Always complaining about the yield!"

George finished explaining what Harvey was saying in his mind.

"John, where are you?" Gabriel asked.

"I'm in the basement of Newberry's, I think. Oh, come on!"

"What is it, John?" Gabe asked, becoming concerned.

"In a slow walk-through," John answered. His voice was low, conspiratorial as he watched the scene as played out in Harvey's memory.

"This guy has the largest collection of girlie magazines I have ever seen. He has them stashed in an old boiler."

Julie and Jennifer stifled a laugh.

"Harvey, do you recall the day of the thirty-first—I believe it was Halloween 1962—and the whole town was excited. The Cuban Missile Crisis was finally put to bed by President Kennedy, and everyone was happy. Do you remember? You must go all the way back to when you were sixteen. Halloween 1962. Do you recall that day?"

"We were thinking that most of the things planned for that night were going to be rained out. I was sure I was going to have to work the lunch counter that night. My dad always pushed me into working when the store was busy."

"How did your day start?" Gabe asked.

"School that day was canceled because of the rain. Didn't break our hearts. We hung out the bus stop for a while before we were told that there was no school. All hell broke loose over some stupid crap started by Jimmy Weller. He and his two buddies, Sam Manachi and Steve Cole. They usually hung out with Dean, but he was late picking them up that morning, and they were pissed off at the prospect of having to ride the lame school bus. No, not a good way to start out that day."

George reached over and raised a glass of water to his lips and drank after speaking for Harvey. He nodded that Harvey was totally under and in the past, and Leonard had to agree. Harvey was in a deep REM sleep, just the place they needed him.

John's eyes moved under the lids, and Gabriel knew the big man was watching the life and times of Harvey and his memories of that morning. George started talking, but his words were becoming slurred as the dream was now running far faster in Harvey's mind than Cordero could keep up with. Now it would be up to John to remember all that happened after that.

Gabriel sat back, and the others watched as John Lonetree connected with the past of Moreno to get just a little more of the tale.

The twelve kids tried their best to stay dry as the rain pummeled the world around them. The Texaco station, and that asshole Dave Deinks, the station's owner, wouldn't even allow them to wait inside the garage to keep from getting soaked. Instead, they were all huddled against the wall of Dr. Lawrence Lillywhite's office. The eave edging of the roof was just enough to keep most of the rain off them, but every time the wind picked up, so would their discomfort at getting soaked. Harvey was by himself as he waited at the end of the line of teenagers and their despair at the prospect of school. Harvey reached into his coat pocket and brought out a Phillips transistor radio, extended the ridiculously long aerial, and tuned it in. He caught the tail end of a country and western hit that made the kids waiting moan and groan and threaten Harvey's life if he didn't find decent music.

"And that was Patsy Cline, and this is KWOW, fifty thousand watts of power in Pomona. The time is seven fifteen on this rainy Halloween morning. Now here's—"

The threats as to the manner of Harvey's imminent murder drowned out the DJ, and he quickly spun the small knob on the Phillips. He breathed a sigh of relief when K-Rave came across loud and clear. The strains of Dee Clark calmed those teens listening, and they settled back trying to avoid the downpour.

There must be a cloud in my hea-ea-ea-ead, rain keeps falling from my eye, eyes . . . oh no they can't be teardrops . . . for a man ain't supposed to cry . . .

The Dodge pickup pulled to the curb, sending a wave of rainwater crashing over the sidewalk and onto the shoes of those waiting. They all tried to jump at the same time as the wave, but most failed, and that earned many shouts and curses—until, that is, they saw the man driving. It was Frank, and as of late, most kids stayed out of his way. He had been in a terrible frame of mind for the past five years after losing his wife. The only time old man Perry was decent to anyone was when his daughter was around. Luckily, she was this morning. The truck's door opened, and Harvey saw Gloria step out and then lean back inside while her father gave her a light kiss on the cheek.

"Sorry I can't take you all the way into school again, baby."

"I'll survive, Daddy," she said as she turned and opened an umbrella. It seems the blind girl was the only one smart enough to bring one. Harvey pursed his lips as he thought about how far ahead in life this girl was than they. Lonetree watched as Harvey admired the girl, as most did without her knowing it.

"You still meeting that little—"

"Daddy, stop it. He was assigned to me, and that's that. After he missed the last five days, he'd better make it today."

Frank looked upset but nodded anyway. "The little creep was probably out drinking with his friends, and that was why he stood you up. If he tries anything with you, you tell me."

Gloria took her schoolbooks and cane from the front seat and then pushed her dark glasses back onto her nose. "I am capable of handling Dean Hadley. Stop worrying." She pursed her lips and then closed the door as she moved away. Her father lingered for the briefest of moments and then gunned the Dodge forward, sending another wave of water hurtling toward the teens lined up like a firing squad against the wall. Harvey was amazed as Gloria, the one who didn't have the use of her eyes, blithely jumped up as the wave reached her. The others who saw it coming fell short, and more curses sprang from their mouths. The girl took a spot near Harvey at the end of the long line as she too waited for the bus.

"I love Dee Clark's voice," Gloria said as she held her books in one hand and the umbrella in the other. "Is that you, Harvey Leach?" she asked, tilting her head.

"How do you know who's standing next to you without seeing them?" Harvey asked with a dumbfounded look on his acne-covered face.

"It's no big mystery, Harvey; you always smell like french fries."

Leach got a hurt look on his face but raised his arm nonetheless and smelled his armpit. "Really?"

Gloria smiled politely. "Really." She leaned over and Harvey got the brief benefit of her umbrella and the soap that she used. Gloria always treated him nice, unlike the others. "A secret, Harvey," she said with conspiracy lacing her voice. "There are far worse smells coming from others right now. More of a wet doggy smell." She smiled at him.

Harvey laughed.

"Why listen to that Black Sambo music all the time?" came a sour voice from the front of the line. "Sam Cooke, Chuck Berry, all them jiggaboos are ruining music."

Harvey sighed, but Gloria's left brow rose so high that it eclipsed her dark glasses.

"Uh-oh," Harvey said as he tried to blend into the brick wall they were leaning against.

"That is something I would expect a dumbass like you to say, Jimmy Weller," Gloria said loudly enough to be heard over the cascading rainfall. "If it weren't for the Negro sound of Chicago and Detroit, the rock and roll you listen to today wouldn't be anything special, but a backward asshole like you would never understand that."

Harvey Leach found that the brick wall wasn't as pliable as he had hoped. He saw all three boys—Jimmy Weller, Sam Manachi, and the skinny Steve Cole—lean forward from their space under the eave. Leach knew it was trouble, because the guys were averse to water in any shape or form, and now they were getting soaked in their interest of Gloria's insult.

"Yeah, Sambos are about as worthless as that coward in the White House," Jimmy said with a smirk.

Harvey rolled his eyes, knowing that the forbidden door had been opened.

"Yeah, chickenshit if you ask me. Letting the Reds push us around like that in Cuba. My dad says Kennedy needs to be shot for treason," Sam Manachi added as he braved the rain to make his point.

As the radio played Bobby Darin's "Beyond the Sea," Gloria handed Harvey her books with a look that told him that hell was about to be set loose right there at the medical plaza in the middle of a rainstorm.

"Oh, don't," Harvey said as he fumbled with Gloria's books.

"Something I have to do, Harvey."

Gloria turned and strolled over with the use of her white cane to the front of the line and faced the tallest of the three boys, Jimmy Weller. He was smiling as she did so.

"Ooooh," both Steve Cole and Sam Manachi mocked terror as she faced the much larger boy.

Harvey Leach had no choice. His dad would kill him if he got wind that he stood by and had the daughter of one of his partners accosted right there on Main Street without him lifting a finger to stop it. It was better to have punches to his face by these assholes than that of a full-blown assault by his dad. He and John Lonetree in his dream state followed Gloria. Harvey fumbled his books, her books, and the radio as he attempted to assuage the bully of the town.

Steve Cole saw Harvey and grabbed him by his coat collar. Leach's eyes went wide, realizing it had taken all of three seconds to get killed. He was thinking that he should have taken his chances with his father.

Gloria opened her mouth to speak but was drowned out by a car's engine as it raced down the street. The red Corvette pulled into the vacant lot and stopped, spewing gravel and mud in all directions. The driver everyone knew. He leaned over and rolled down the passenger window.

"Hey, you dumbasses, school's been canceled!" Dean shouted out the good news. "They're afraid half the old lady teachers will melt away with water hitting them."

The kids all laughed at his reference to *The Wizard of Oz*. Even Harvey gave a nervous twitter, and Steve Cole laughed, still holding him by his collar. Now he was just waiting for Gloria to get them both killed.

"Yeah!" Jimmy said, pushing by a fuming Gloria. He ran to the car and started to pull the door open, but Dean held it closed.

"What are you doing?" he asked Jimmy, who stood aghast.

"Going with you. No school, Halloween . . . let's do something."

"Have plans. Sorry, dude." Dean looked up past Jimmy and saw Gloria and the situation that little Harvey Leach was in. "What's going on here?" he asked.

Jimmy swiped water from his crew cut and then turned. He laughed. "I'm about to teach that blind bitch a lesson on how to talk to her betters, and that little creepy burger flipper, Leach, is about to meet the end he so richly deserves."

Dean took a deep breath and then shut of the car's powerful engine.

He stepped out of the car with his letterman's jacket on and open to reveal a white T-shirt as he went around the Corvette and then to the wall with Jimmy laughing and following, thinking that Hadley was taking up the cause.

Gloria heard Dean's approach and then turned on him. Her attack had changed direction faster than Harvey could ever have imagined.

"You didn't show up Saturday or Sunday, and you missed school Monday and Tuesday. I thought we had a deal, Mr. Ass Wipe."

"Oh!" Sam and Steve voiced at one time with smiles.

Dean ignored Gloria for the moment as he stood in the rain. His attention went to Steve, who was holding a completely frozen Harvey Leach.

"Let him go," he said calmly.

Steve lost his smile as he looked away from the much larger Hadley to Jimmy, whose eyes went narrow as he saw his friend turn on them. Finally, Steve released Harvey, who dropped most of the books just as the song "I Can't Stop Loving You" by Ray Charles started playing on K-Rave.

"We can do that thing today if you still want," Dean said to Gloria, but his eyes never left Sam's or Steve's. Jimmy took up station behind Dean.

Gloria, instead of answering Hadley, turned until she could smell Jimmy's aftershave, a sickly blend of Old Spice and the purloined morning cigarettes he and his two cronies had smoked earlier.

"If you ever say anything about Negro entertainers or President Kennedy again, I'll gouge your eyes out, you little prick," she said so calmly that everyone listening had no doubt that little blind Gloria would do just that.

"Gloria, go wait in the car. Harvey, give her a hand, will ya?"

Gloria huffed but started moving away with Harvey assisting her in the right direction.

"Thank you, Harvey, for backing me up," Gloria said through clenched teeth as she moved away with her cane swishing through the air ahead of her steps.

"You're—" The word came out as a squeak, so he tried again. "You're welcome."

As Jimmy Weller watched Gloria leave, he turned and stepped in front of Dean. John Lonetree, instead of following Gloria and Harvey, was waiting to see what happened next. Dean looked at the three boys who stood defiantly, even ignoring the rain that was pummeling them.

"Lucky you came when you did. I was about to fuck that b—"

The punch in the face stilled Jimmy's mouth. Dean's strike was so hard that it slammed Jimmy against the wall before he could stop from falling. Sam was the first to react as he reached out and took Dean by the jacket and raised his fist to strike, but Dean brought his forehead forward first, connecting directly with Manachi's wide nose. The boy screamed as blood shot from his nose and he went backward into Steve, who was in shock at how fast the day had deteriorated. Jimmy recovered faster than anyone would have thought possible. He had always respected Dean, but the straight-D-minus student had never feared him. He was up and had Dean around the neck, and then they fell into the mud and the gravel of the vacant lot.

"What are they doing?" Gloria asked a wide-eyed Harvey as he stood next to the passenger door.

"Dean's, uh, saying good-bye, I think."

Freekin' Rowdy Rhoads stood at the bay window of K-Rave with the receptionist, Roberta, watching the teenage brawl across and slightly down the street as it escalated. The whole thing was being staged with "I Can't Stop Loving You" as accompaniment. Freekin' Rowdy turned to Roberta.

"If this is any indication how this day and night are going to go, I expect great things," he said as he sipped his coffee with the whiskey chaser and watched.

Dean thought the gravel was going to rub his face off, but he managed to throw his head back as Jimmy was on his knees, hitting him from behind. The back of Dean's head caught the boy square in the nose, and he flew from Hadley's back. A bleeding Sam and a shocked Steve took over in a tag team.

The next thing anyone knew, Gloria had joined the fray. She quickly lashed out after she smelled Jimmy start to rise from where he hit the wall. Her saddle shoe caught him right on the side of the face—a glancing blow, to be sure, but well enough struck that Jimmy went back down. Gloria was thrown off balance, and she fell backward and into a mud puddle.

Two on one was never a good place to be. Dean thought his anger at the three boys would carry him through, but the sight of Gloria getting knocked down sent him into a rage where his motor functions were all but failing him. He thought he had had it until some of the weight was off him. Harvey had slammed his transistor radio into the side of Steve Cole's head, sending him to the muck and quickly silencing Ray Charles in the process as the remains of his transistor radio fell to pieces in his clenched fist. That gave Dean an opening. He lashed out, catching Sam in the jaw and sending him sprawling next to Jimmy and Steve. He got up, dazed but alive. He grabbed Gloria, who surprisingly didn't fight him, and they both ran for the car.

Harvey started to pick up the remains of his radio but instead kicked Jimmy in the jaw with his black Converse tennis shoe, which sent him for the last time back against the wall. He slid down into the mud and gravel for the second time, and this elicited a loud moan and *oohs* and *aahs* from the other eight witnesses at the bus stop. The legend of the great Halloween fight was born that day.

Harvey looked around in near panic and quickly decided that it was a good day to help his dad at Newberry's. With one last look back and seeing Gloria and Dean spinning out as they left the vacant lot, Harvey ran all the way home.

Gabriel saw Harvey Leach's relaxed face as the memory of that morning fifty-five years before started to fade back into his personal closet. He examined George, and George nodded that he was all right. They didn't catch much of his interpretation of the events, but he was also a witness, like John, to what had happened to start that last day in Moreno.

"Amazing," Damian said as he took a seat again after the exciting exchange. He was amazed that a prick like Dean had come to Gloria's defense. He had to at least reevaluate his opinion of the earlier version of the president.

With the small dose of Adrenalin administered to Harvey, the old man started to come out of it. He opened his eyes and then stared straight at Kennedy.

"Didn't work, did it? I told you hypnotism was for the weak-minded."

Gabe slapped Harvey on the leg, a new appreciation for him after his semi-heroic acts on that morning. "You were right, Harvey; your brain is too active to be hypnotized."

"See!" Harvey said, looking around at those in the darkened room.

"Gabe," Jennifer said softly, "John's still dreaming." She looked at Kennedy with worried eyes. "He's still there."

"How can that be?" Julie said as she joined Leonard at the medical station to check Lonetree's vital signs. She shook her head when she saw he was still deep in REM sleep. "Gabriel, this thing isn't over. John's going deeper on his own. He's made a connection here—with what or whom, I'm not sure—but he's still walking inside someone."

"Heart rate is dropping," Leonard confirmed, becoming concerned. "Blood pressure is also on the skids."

Gabriel had expected John to come out of it on his own, but instead, he found himself reaching for the second syringe of Adrenalin. He had just uncapped the needle when Jennifer reached out and touched his hand, staying him. She shook her head.

"Are you sure?"

"I think he can come out if he wants, but he's reacting to something. Whatever he is connected into wants him there."

"The way things have been going, I don't think that's a good thing."

Jenny still held John's hand, and her eyes never wavered.

Gabe placed the syringe down and nodded. He was tapped on the shoulder. He turned and Damian was there with a radio in his hand. His face was grave. "It's the mobile med unit. They report the president's blood pressure has dropped severely. They say any lower and they'll have to call in the helicopter and evacuate him."

"Coincidence?" Julie asked, joining them. Even Harvey was awake and listening from his chair. He was rubbing his arm from the shots he had taken, but he was now worried about the big Indian.

"We learned the hard way there's no such thing," Gabe said. He came to the decision Jenny hoped for. "Let John go."

"I think I'll step over here with the little black guy," Harvey said as he bobbed to his feet like a prizefighter getting off the mat. Julie helped him to a chair so he wouldn't trip in the dark.

"George, are you picking up anything?" Gabriel asked as he and Jenny took their seats.

"I know that John's out there. I feel he's a little scared, but not in the way we're used to. It's like roller-coaster scared, if you know what I mean."

John could swear he felt his stomach being left behind in the road somewhere as he was somehow squeezed in between Gloria and her driver, Dean. An impossibility, he knew, but here he was sandwiched center line between the two, and every time Hadley shifted gears, John braced for the inevitable pain of his nuts being crushed. But the proper gear was hit without any pain. He would have to force himself to stop flinching.

"If you don't slow down, you're going to kill us. You may not feel it, but my ass does. Every time you take a corner, you almost lose it. It's wet!"

Even John, who wasn't really there, breathed a sigh of relief when Dean finally down shifted and the powerful sports car slowed.

"I'm sorry you got into a fight with your friends, but I didn't ask you to help!"

"They're not my friends, and you're welcome. You know, you may think you're so smart, but you're really not," Dean said as he slowed to take a corner and then immediately sped up. "You think that every action can be explained with logic and reason, but it can't."

"What does that mean?" she asked, finally turning his way as the Corvette moved down the road.

"It means that old saying that he would never hit a girl that you were hoping would save you in the end. Well, it wouldn't have. I know that creep Jimmy Weller; he would have hit you and not thought twice about what would happen to him," Dean said as he brushed his wet hair back.

Lonetree raised his eyebrows. Gloria opened her mouth to say something and then suddenly closed it. She opened it again and then closed it just as fast.

"I guess the words *thank you* are stuck in there, huh? The way you keep opening that mouth and closing it."

Again, she turned her head and faced him. "Thank you."

"I hope poor Harvey got away." Dean laughed. "I forgot all about him."

Gloria turned away, wishing for the five millionth time she could see the rain. She smelled it. It was to her a wondrous thing to smell rain, and she could only imagine seeing it.

Lonetree smiled as he picked up on her thought. Not exactly the way she thought them, but close enough that John knew that she was happy for this brief moment.

"Did you bring that key?" Dean asked, drawing John's close attention.

"Yeah, my dad's in El Monte setting up some entertainment for the bar for the end of November. He left the keys on a hook. He would never suspect that his own little girl is a klepto." Gloria got a concerned expression on her face and faced him angrily. "Why are we up here?" she asked. "I smell eucalyptus trees, and they only grow in one place. So, I'll ask again, why are we here at your home? It's the only eight-bedroom house surrounded by eucalyptus trees, so tell me why!"

Dean pulled the car over to the curb and put the emergency brake on. He faced her. "Look, I have to get some clothes. I'm wet and I'm muddy, and I think I have gravel in my underwear. But the real reason we're here is because when you told me about what your story is about and where, I thought taking a peek at what that spooky-ass, Peter Lorre–looking Kraut doctor was up to for all those years while our fathers and the U.S.

government were paying him large sums of money. My dad has something in his office, I just know it. I'm going to get whatever there is. I've seen these old-looking journals once or twice that I catch him looking through. I can tell they are important to him. They look really old. That may be what we need to shed some light on this wacko Nazi doctor."

"You be careful and don't get caught."

"Hey, it's me!" he said and then quickly opened his door and was gone.

John felt as trapped as Gloria. She sat and listened, and with every car that approached, she cringed, thinking it would surely be Dean's father returning home and catching him in his office. John had tried to join Hadley inside, but he was attached to Gloria and couldn't leave her presence. To John and Gloria, it seemed Dean was in the house for an hour, when it was actually only fifteen minutes.

The driver's-side door suddenly opened, and Dean jumped in with an excited whoop.

"Got one of them. It was inside his locked drawer. Here, check this out." Dean handed Gloria what looked like a leather-bound journal.

"What's embossed here?" Gloria asked as her delicate fingers ran over the fine lettering of the imprint.

"*Journal*. Then below that, *1941–1943*. Then at the bottom, *Dr. Jürgen Fromm*."

"I don't like that thing," she said as she hurriedly handed the journal back to Dean.

"I know. Creepy." Dean took the book and opened it. "It's daily entries in German." He looked up with hope. "Do you *Sprechen sie Deutsch*?" he asked, saying one of his favorite war movie lines.

"I got stuck with Mrs. McCauley's French class," Gloria answered with a grin.

"I got Spanish; I guess they thought I was language challenged." As he closed the journal and started the Corvette, a bundle of paper fell free of the journal's binding. "Look at this," Dean said.

Gloria sat there and then slowly turned her head in exasperation. "Hello? Blind. Can't see."

Dean closed his eyes and silently cursed his stupidity. "Sorry." He picked up the official-looking documents. "This is a daily report written in English. Look, it—" He caught himself again just as Gloria raised her right brow in exasperation. "Sorry, it has a Department of the Air Force header and logo. Looks like a report of some kind."

"What does it say?" she asked.

" 'Report filed June 17, 1947, 0340 hours,' " he said as he caught the next line, " 'in the Moreno Complex.' Let's see. 'Professor Fromm has misled the field reporting officers on his repeated attempts to re-create high-altitude experiment 3419—451 C. It is stated in his report and journal that he used the exact same parameters as his process did in 1941. The experiments are documented by film made by the doctor during the dates stated in last report. He insists that the experiment will continue to fail unless the direct specifications of his original discovery be followed to the letter, which this officer has stated on many occasions is an impossible request. Addendum—Colonel Robert Hadley (Ret.) has been informed of the continuing failure of Dr. Fromm.' "

Gloria heard the thunder and shivered as Dean read to her.

"January 1957." Dean shuffled through the papers and then frowned. "None of these are in order. A lot of years missing here. He must have tossed the rest."

"Maybe these three were the only ones your father was interested in keeping," Gloria countered.

"This has my father's company letterhead. Hadley Corp Gauge and Meter Company. It's a request for more funding. 'As of this date, transport vault #11251-A has shown no activity since arrival date of 12/15/1947. All activity inside ceased upon transport to this country. The primary cost of containment and disposal of wastewater and mercury contaminate has become a serious threat to the security of this project. Moreno is now a high priority for inspection certificates from state and local authorities. In short, gentlemen, because of the lack of internal activity from the containment vessel, it is my humble opinion and that of my partners that Operation Necromancer be canceled immediately and Dr. Jürgen Fromm be debriefed and deported to his native country. Signed, R. D. Hadley, Colonel, United States Army (Ret.)' "

"Anything else?" Gloria asked, becoming even more afraid of the growing thunderstorm.

" 'Checked final preparation for shutting down Operation Necromancer at Moreno Complex.' " Dean looked closer at the report—and then even closer. "This isn't my father's handwriting," he said, and then his eyes went to the bottom of the report. "This was signed by your father, Captain F. Perry."

"My dad?" she asked, not feeling so good about her father's involvement with this.

"What is a necromancer?" Dean asked without shame of not knowing.

Gloria was still deep in thought. It seemed she never even knew her dad went to the old winery. With the exception of one or two times.

"Hey, what's a necromancer?" he asked again.

"A magician, a trickster. Magic," she said.

Dean read again.

" 'Broke viewing port on containment vessel this date. Opportunity for viewing and documenting original subjects in high-altitude experiment and the former Operation Necromancer. The interior had been unchanged since the original experiment date in 1941, inside the borders of Axis-controlled Yugoslavia. Compartment was separated into two sections—side A and side B. Observed the remains of eighteen adults in section A and twenty-eight juveniles ranging in age from six months through pubescent stages. All subjects were deceased. Project observers suspect original example of activity inside vault B conducted in March 1945 for the benefit of operational forces of the Office of Strategic Services were completely and utterly false in nature. Suspect the high-altitude experiment was a total failure and its aftereffect a hoax perpetrated by Jürgen Fromm. Included in this final report are all graphs, medical feeds, film, written documentation, and specs on containment vessels. Request massive chemical cleanup of support structure (i.e., the town of Moreno and surrounding area). Responsibility for original report falls to the field team involved (i.e., Team Five, Colonel Hadley, who refused to cosign final report).' "

"If it was a project commanded by your father, why was it my dad who signed the papers, basically stopping whatever this Operation Necromancer was?" Gloria bit her lip as she thought how to press Dean about what his father was up to. "My father killed this thing over your dad's objections."

"Looks that way," Dean said, feeling guilty for no apparent reason except for knowing for sure that his own father was in the wrong. "I guess maybe that explains the falling-out they had a few years ago."

"I think I was there the day it happened. I never put two and two together."

"That's it," Dean said, placing the papers back inside the journal as he started the engine. "I think I'll hang on to the journal and see if maybe we can get Casper Worthington's ma to read it. She's German, you know?"

Gloria smiled. "No, I didn't know that. You surprise me, Dean Hadley."

"Why's that?"

"You just do. Let's just leave it at that."

They heard a car approaching over the falling rain.

"Damn, it's my father!" he snarled. "I forgot he was coming home early to get ready for the Halloween stuff tonight."

John watched with Dean and Gloria as the Cadillac moved slowly down the opposite side of the street toward the house Dean had just left. Dean instinctively ducked low and with his right hand he reached out and lowered Gloria's profile. John wanted to also hide but then caught himself. He felt the guilt of the boy and girl as Robert parked his car in the drive-way and entered the house. Without hesitation, Dean placed the car in gear and slowly moved off. John once more tried to leave Gloria and Dean, and this time, he felt his body leave their presence and enter the house Dean shared with his father. John was now witness to history written by another outside of the two teenagers.

Robert went to the closet and hung up his coat and slid down the knot in his tie. He was still whistling as he went through the mail he had retrieved from his mailbox. He tossed the letters on his desk and then the whistling stopped. His eyes went to the desktop. Then they fell in a puddle of water. His smile vanished and his demeanor changed. John stood watching from the entrance hall and felt the chill as Robert moved down the long hall-way toward a set of doors, opened them, and passed through.

John Lonetree followed after seeing Dean's wet footprints on the ex-pensive floor tile. John wished he could tell the kid he wasn't as good a burglar as he thought.

Hadley produced his set of keys and then opened the desk drawers. He examined their contents and then looked up in anger. He knew his son had developed a curiosity that had to be reined in. He picked up the phone.

Suddenly, John was whisked from the house and was again sitting on the center console of the Corvette as it sped away toward the town of Moreno. The sun was getting lower in the afternoon skies as the thunder-heads built over the Southland.

Halloween night was arriving on schedule.

17

John was still deep in REM sleep. George was watching him closely and keeping his right hand on Lonetree's left. Gabriel would carefully raise John's right eyelid to check for any pupil dilation that would indicate that the Demerol used was possibly interfering, a problem he and Lonetree had many years before during a session in college. John had became incoherent in his deep thoughts during the dreamwalk and nearly flatlined. The drug wasn't enough to overdose him but had been enough to confuse his dreaming mind. The body usually did what the brain ordered, and that was the danger they had watched for. He nodded when he was finished, and Jennifer took a breath of relief.

"I'm picking up a rise in anxiety," George said. "Not much, but John is experiencing possibly fright or mild excitement."

"Your visions are as clear and precise as usual," Damian muttered, and George shot him a dirty look. Jackson looked at his watch. "He's been under for thirty-five minutes."

Gabriel watched John's serene face with worry. The longest he had ever been under was twenty-two minutes. In that instance, John found himself unable to concentrate for days afterward.

George let go of Lonetree's hand and then fixed Gabriel with a worried look. He shook his head at Gabe's reluctance to end the session. He was under the illusion that his friend was in control, but he was thinking something entirely different. This wasn't a normal dreamwalk. He was getting the vibe that John was being led down a trail by poisonous bread crumbs.

"That thing, whatever it is, is using John and doesn't really give a damn if it kills him. It's having fun reliving this through him." George pointed at John's sleeping form. "Bring him out, Gabe; we can get to the bottom of this by allowing this thing to play out real time."

"We would be sacrificing the president," Jennifer said. "You know John would never protect himself if there is the slightest chance he can help in *his* way."

Gabriel looked at George for the longest time and then reached behind him for the syringe of Adrenalin from the small table. He looked at Jennifer.

"Another person lost on this team is not going to solve anything," George said, sitting back in his chair with his eyes on Lonetree.

"Trading one life for another—is that what we do now, Gabriel?" Jennifer asked in protest for caving into George and his fears. She wanted no harm to come to John, but he had been adamant about helping the president in his way. They were too far short of time for anything else. Halloween was here, and they all knew that date was the tipping point for whatever was happening in Moreno.

Kennedy ignored further argument. He couldn't risk another of his friends' lives.

Jennifer watched without further comment as Gabe stuck the needle into John's arm.

"John, it's time to wake up," Gabriel said softly, leaning over Lonetree, as he placed the empty syringe on the table.

Jennifer took up John's left hand and squeezed. "Come on back; you've been under too long."

Lonetree's eyes stopped moving, and his breathing became deeper.

"Heart rate coming up and coming up fast," Leonard said as he studied the monitors in front of him. The small black man nodded at Harvey, who was watching Leonard move from monitor to monitor. "Blood pressure is also rising. He's coming around." Leonard leaned over to adjust the heart rate to get an accurate count on beats per minute when the laptops and monitors suddenly went blank. "What the hell?" he asked himself as he looked around the darkened room. "Hey, J. Edgar, turn on the overhead lights."

Damian stood and then walked to the wall and hit all ten of the old-fashioned switches. He looked up as the fluorescent lighting flickered as if coming to life and then went out. Damian hit the switches twice, up and down and then finally up.

Gabriel stood from his chair as the only lights they had on was the two small lamps on the table. He looked around and settled on Leonard, who shrugged. Sickles turned and pulled up the old-fashioned yellow roll-up blind that covered one of the main second-floor windows.

"The lights at the radio station are on. I even saw light from the first floor reflecting off the water in the street." A flash of lightning made Leonard flinch and step back from the glass. Harvey moved past him and then saw what had caught his attention just a moment before.

"Uh-oh," he said, "that damn K-Rave sign is on again."

"What's so mysterious about that?" Damian asked as he stepped up to the window and looked down into the storm. He saw the bright red gas-fed fluorescents glow.

"That damn light has been busted since the sixties. It doesn't even have a ballast for the damn gas. And according to old Bob and Linda, strange shit starts to happen when that light comes on. I didn't believe it until now." He turned away from the window. "I had this feeling in '65 when the damn Vietcong zapped us but good in the Ia Drang Valley. They chewed our asses up. There's something out there, and now I think I should have done what all the others did and gotten the hell out of here."

"He's coming around," Jenny said.

George felt relief momentarily settle his mind.

"Okay, let's—" Gabriel began but was stopped when the windows across the entire circumference of the second floor exploded inward. Wind-swept rain and glass inundated the entire area of the darkened floor. There was just enough light coming from the empty elevator shaft and the emergency stairwell they had propped open.

"NOOOO," came the deep and booming voice. It reverberated in their ears. Leonard forgot about the glass that had peppered his face when he became more aware of his eardrums about to burst. Gabriel bent at the waist, and Jennifer collapsed onto John in terrible pain. Damian fell to his knees, and Harvey hit the floor as if mortar rounds were striking inside his old firebase in Southeast Asia. "BRING HIM BACK!" the voice screamed in abject anger.

George felt the force as it took him by the throat and raised him to the thirteen-foot-high ceiling. He was taken so hard and so fast that Gabe actually lost sight of him. As he raised his head, still holding his ears from not only the explosion of glass but the booming voice that shook their world.

He and Jennifer, with a waking Lonetree, saw Cordero as he was slammed over and over again into the old, water-stained ceiling until his head was punched all the way through it. His legs were kicking for the briefest of moments, and then his body was released and he fell to the floor with a bone-crunching impact.

Gabriel was horrified as he tried to move toward the dark and still form of his friend. He made it in two steps when he hit the small table and the medication there went crashing to the floor. The empty syringes bounced once, twice, and then flew up. In the soft light, Jennifer screamed when she saw the four syringes spin in one spot for the briefest of moments and then shoot like darts at Kennedy. The first two struck him in the chest, the third near his collarbone, and the fourth in his shoulder with a force hard enough to send Gabriel flying backward over the still form of George Cordero.

Jennifer left John, who was trying to gain some sense of what was happening around him. He shook his head as he watched Jennifer run and then fall out of his sight. On the floor, she reached for Gabe's ankle as he tried to get his own wits together. His leg was ripped from her grasp, and then they all watched as Gabriel was smashed against the wall while grabbing at his throat, and then he went straight up as he was propelled into the air by the unseen force just as George had been a brief moment before. His shoes kicked holes in the old plaster as he was lifted. Damian and Harvey had recovered faster than they would have thought possible for being as scared as they were. For Jackson, this was not like the past six years chasing down hoaxers and frauds; this was real, and now he remembered how scared one man can be. Damian dove for the Gabe's kicking feet only to hit his heel, and then he went sprawling, sliding on the old tile floor until he impacted the wall with his head and shoulder. Harvey followed suit and missed completely, going headfirst into the wall that he never saw coming.

"*STOP IT! STOP IT NOW!*" came the booming voice that seemed to come from all directions. "*I DIDN'T NEED YOU FOR THIS! THEY ARE TO WITNESS WHAT WAS!*"

The old department store shook as if an earthquake had struck the area. The remaining glass flew from the window frames, and a crack formed in the tile-covered cement floor. It moved like an aggressive snake until it slowly stopped its run. Rainwater was pushed inside by the powerful wind that had tripled in strength in the past few seconds.

Suddenly, Gabriel released his hand from his own throat that was foolishly trying to hold off the choking fingers of the entity, and he felt himself falling. He hit so hard that he went out like a light. Damian was the first to him just as the overhead fluorescents flared to life, blinking on and off, and then settling into their steady, cold light.

John was finally able to sit up and stumble from the bed. He actually kicked Jennifer as he tried to find her. She was half under the bed.

"Ow," she said and then wiggled out of the tight space. "Go check George and Gabe!" she screamed.

"George is dead," Damian answered solemnly as he kneeled next to Cordero's broken body. Jackson flicked blood away that fell into his eyes from the gash on his forehead. "Are you okay, old-timer?" Jackson asked Harvey, who was sitting with his legs splayed against the wall.

His eyes moved first and then his head. Leach had several cuts on his face from flying glass and a rather good-sized bump on his head from his collision with the formidable wall.

"This town has seriously gone downhill," Harvey said as he stared at the large black man leaning over him.

John finally reached Gabriel, who was being held by Julie. She brushed some of his brown hair out of his eyes and then retrieved his glasses and slid them on his face. Lonetree stopped cold and stared down at his friend. Then his heart started beating once again as Gabriel moaned and then opened his eyes.

"Hey, we saw the lights come on and thought you might . . . want . . . some . . . coffee," the female voice said from the stairwell's opening as the newcomers saw the state of everyone. Bob and Linda stopped when they saw the devastation on the second floor, and then Linda dropped the tray of coffee and cups. They smashed on the floor at her feet.

Their eyes moved to Damian, Julie, and John as they assisted a bruised Gabriel to his shaky feet. They heard Jennifer crying as she sat beside the crumpled body of George Cordero. She had a hand on his head and was trying in vain to wipe some of the blood away. Leonard was standing in shock by his computers and monitors. He angrily turned and pushed two of his laptops from the table and then kicked at them.

"A lot of good this shit is against that!" he said, pointing at the top of the thirteen-foot-high ceiling.

Damian, Julie, and John got Gabriel to the chair. He sat as they tried to get a cut on the back of his head to stop bleeding. Jennifer found a dust cover and covered George's body with it. The entire time, Gabriel's eyes never left the scene.

"We can't fight this," he said, watching Jennifer wipe her eyes as she stared down at George.

John dabbed a washcloth at the six-inch-long gash in his head. "Yes, we can," he said, tossing the cloth down onto the floor. "I have to go back in."

Jennifer looked up. "Stupid red man."

They all turned to see her standing in a slouched position while eyeing George's still form at her feet. Then her head, barely inches from her chest, turned and faced Lonetree. By the stairwell, Bob and Linda wanted to turn and run but were mesmerized by what amounted to one wicked acid trip.

"I've been here watching you idiots fumble around with something that you have never encountered, and your deal here is not only going to get yourselves killed but Jenny also." She smiled and then moved a few steps closer to George's body. She looked down. "Ritchie Valens here was right. You're being led down the garden path, and he knew—or had a pretty good guess—that was the way of things. They wanted the medicine man here to keep dreaming, to witness what was done to her. And let me tell you something, guys and dolls—she has help, a lot of it. Help the likes of which you can never begin to imagine. They are strong; they were created to be strong. And now *she* is to the point that she can no longer control them." Jennifer smiled—or Bobby Lee McKinnon did. "They are out again, just like they were out that night, and we all know what happened then, don't we? You, Injun Joe, will get Jenny killed." Bobby Lee in the guise of Jennifer Tilden looked around at everyone in the room one at a time. "Only one of them is like me. Power from them feed her. They also warp her. She sees things they want her to see, believes things they want her to believe. Misreads intentions of love and hate."

Jennifer collapsed into a ball on the floor. "Ow," she said again as she sat up rubbing her head.

John was there in a flash. "You okay?"

"Yeah, this time, I was aware of everything he said. Bobbly Lee is terrified of what we're facing here."

"We got that point," Julie said, relieving Lonetree of Jennifer and leading her to the chair beside Gabriel. "Look, we've lost two friends here, but if you guys want to stay, I'm with you," the former reporter said as she sat in between Jenny and Gabe and tried to attend them both.

"You guys are out of your minds," Bob said from the doorway of the stairwell.

"We don't run," John said, pacing. "I know one thing here. We have a chance to find out what started all of this and what actually happened in 1962. All I need is a few minutes back inside. This thing thinks it can kill us and that we'll just accept that and run."

"We don't have George anymore," Jennifer said with tears in her eyes. "And Bobby Lee won't help."

"Something got mad that George and I brought John out of his dream-walk, that was for sure. But that same presence was angered that *something* else took things too far in its attack." Gabe looked over at John. "What lead did you learn from the dream that you say can give us an advantage?"

John walked over and gently lifted the covered body of George Cordero into his arms and faced Kennedy. "Julie, you spent three years at your network's Berlin bureau, didn't you?"

"Yes," she answered, looking not at John but the small body of their friend.

"You can read German?"

"A little, not much."

"I can read and speak it. Don't like to, but my mama was a war bride from Germany. She grew up in Nuremberg."

They all turned and looked at Harvey Leach.

"Does this have anything to do with that creepy Dr. Fromm? The man was a nut, always coming in before my ma died, thinking that they could be friends because they were both refugees out of Germany, but she never liked him. The man was bad, and she knew it from the get-go."

"I need to go back in and get something," John said. "It may be there, it may not be."

"Without George and his ability, we won't know what you find, and you can't read German. You can't take Harvey with you." All eyes turned to Gabriel, who dashed a few hopes with his obvious observation.

"That won't be a problem. In my dreamwalk, those two crazy kids found something in Dean's father's locked office. It was a journal of that man Harvey just mentioned, Dr. Jürgen Fromm. He and the founders of this town brought a souvenir back from the war; that's the key here."

Gabriel moved his head too fast and winced at the sharp stab of pain. He grimaced and looked over at Leonard, who was silently picking up the remains of two laptops.

"Is there any chance you can get those computers connected so you can get some dirt on someone?"

Leonard stopped what he was doing and threw the cover of one of the destroyed laptops against the wall.

"One of the feds' satellite phones, but not tonight. There's way too much electricity in the air. It would take forever to get online."

"Gabe, the only way we can get the information you need is in that damn black journal. If I go back in, I'll know where to find it. Gloria and Dean would never take it back to his house; they will stash it someplace. I can find that place if it still exists. I have to go back and find out what they did with it. It's the only way."

Gabriel watched John move George's body to the bed, and Lonetree laid him down, still covered in the dustcloth. He placed a hand over his chest and closed his eyes as he prayed for his ancestors to watch over his friend.

"Okay, if everyone is agreed."

"Yeah, for George," Leonard said as he tossed the remains of one of the laptops into a garbage can.

"Whatever it is, we can't let it do this to anyone," Julie said, looking at Jennifer, who smiled and nodded.

"All right. Mr. Leach, can we ask you to brave a little bit more of this madness until John can find what he is looking for?"

"I can't say I never felt like runnin' from a fight more than this one, but I can see you're hurting for your friend here. We lost a lot of good folks back in '62; maybe I owe them too, so running's not an option." Harvey looked over at Bob and Linda. "You two should skedaddle."

Bob opened his mouth to say something but closed it when Linda cut him off. "We have to stay and get what that damn company owes us, or we'll spend the rest of our lives broke and looking for work suitable for two old and broken-down hippies. Hell, we're not even hippies; I grew up in an affluent section of Marin County, and Bob is from Pasadena, for God's sake."

"Mrs. Culbertson, I will guarantee you receive what your contract calls for. You have my word. If they don't, I'll pay you and then take it out of someone's ass later," Gabriel said with the hint of a smile.

Linda looked at Bob and then over at Harvey Leach. She tried to smile, but her shaking legs said that would be a failure for the circumstance they faced.

"Harvey's our friend, just like Mr. Cordero was yours. Maybe we'll stay and help our friend," Bob said, wrapping an arm around Linda's shoulders. "Fuck it. We went through a rougher time throughout the sixties and the seventies. We faced down the Reagan years and trickle-down economics, and we still survived it all, just to meet each other through a shitty job offer to watch over this town. Wouldn't say much for us if the very first time Moreno needed us, we split. As much as we complained about it, it's been our home too."

"All right, thank you," Gabriel said, walking toward the door.

"What's first?" Damian asked, making sure his nine-millimeter was loaded and snapped into its holster. He winced as Julie applied a gauze bandage to his head. He looked comical as if he were wearing a small dairy girl's hat.

"We go down and warn the feds that all hell may break loose. And maybe it is time to get them and the president out of here."

"And you do remember that ghosts aren't very susceptible to bullets, Serpico?" Leonard said, struggling to contain his laughter over the silly-looking bandage on Jackson's head.

"Yeah, well, like all of you scientific types, I plan to test that bullets-don't-hurt-ghosts theory over and over until it does work."

"Well, it's past twelve. It's now Halloween," Julie said.

At that moment, just like the scene out of a very bad horror movie, the lightning lit up the room and the lights flickered. The thunder was distant but strong. The rain increased.

"For people who claim that hauntings are few and far between and that most of the claims are hoaxes, you sure were wrong about a few things. Maybe you should stop chasing the supernatural," Bob said as he and Linda started for the stairs.

John looked from Jennifer to Gabriel.

"We would, if only the damn things would stop chasing us."

18

Gabriel, Julie, John, Leonard, Jennifer, and Damian stood rooted as Lonetree said a prayer in his native tongue for his ancestors to guide the lost
and tormented soul of George Cordero to a place where he could finally be
happy. They all had their moments with the small clairvoyant through the
years, but they all knew because of his strange ability, George was always
mere inches away from suicide. He hated the fact that he could read people
and their darkest thoughts. He not only lost faith in himself but ordinary
people because of those thoughts. Now they hoped the man could find the
peace in death that he could never begin to find in life.

Bob, Linda, Casper Worthington, and even Peckerwood stood silently
by the doorway leading downstairs. They saw the hurt as they said goodbye
to Gabriel and the Group's friend.

Over the sounds of thunder and the flashes of bright lightning, Gabriel
heard the sound that ended the small prayer for George. He went to the
window that looked down onto Main Street and saw men running from
their hiding places. The unmistakable sound of helicopter rotors overrode
the power of the storm.

Gabriel turned away from the window. "Leonard, is there anything
on those worthless radios?"

Sickles hurriedly moved away from the group to his makeshift desk
and tried to listen to the walkie-talkie they had been issued. He listened

and then looked at Kennedy, shaking his head. Damian listened too, but heard nothing but static. He tried to call out, only to be answered by return static.

"This damn weather has screwed everything up. Even the satellite phone is out," Damian said as he leaned over and saw that Leonard had also checked the computer systems. He looked up and shook his head again. "We have nothing."

Gabe turned away from the window. "Okay, Julie, come with me. We'll find out what's happening." He had to speak loudly over the thumping of the rotors. It sounded as if the helicopter was coming straight down onto Main Street. "John, get ready. Jennifer, get our medical supplies organized. Prepare John's kicker." He turned back to Leonard and Damian. "This thing may think it's in control, but I suspect that its partner in crime is not amiable to that fact. Whatever wants us here is in direct opposition to something else that enjoys killing."

"Great," Damian said, wincing as thunder broke directly overhead.

Gabriel and Julie were met at the double doors of Newberry's by the lead field agent in charge, Haskins. The FBI agent was out of breath and was soaked to the bone. He had to shout to be heard over the storm raging over their heads and the large military-type helicopter that was hidden above them in the raging winds and swirling black sky.

"I'm ordering an evacuation for my people, the Secret Service, and the state authorities." The heavy thumping of the helicopter was starting to make a decibel gain on the storm sweeping the Southland. The agent leaned in closer to Kennedy. "We were finally able to get through to Washington an hour ago, and our earlier request was officially granted by a federal judge. The Justice Department obtained a warrant returning the president's care back into federal hands. Our dear First Lady can now go kiss another judge's ass, but he'd better be higher in rank than the federal judge in Los Angeles."

"When are you moving the president out?" Julie asked, trying to shield her face from the windblown rain.

"As I just told you, the warrant only made the move official; unofficially, we moved Hadley out of here an hour ago. He should be safe and under better medical care than he was here. His blood pressure was dropping dangerously low, and as you know, we are having trouble with communications."

Gabriel looked out at the men running down the sidewalks as they gathered on either side of Main Street. They were all watching the skies.

"My team wants to stick it out. We have work to do here," Gabriel replied. "I'll ask the townspeople to leave with you, but we have a job to do—not only for the president but because we lost people."

"Brave, but foolish. Get your people together, Professor; we leave in ten. Your group and the townies will be the first lifted out. Now get them down here."

"Look, we need—" Julie began.

"You need to get your people ready to move!" the agent shouted over the din. "The locals say this entire hillside could come down at any time. They heard reports of hills like these coming down in Chino and in Riverside. The whole damn state is being drowned. The water has no place to go!"

Gabe turned to Julie and nodded that she should go inside and warn the others.

"We'll lose our one chance at getting to the bottom of this!" she shouted back angrily.

"That's an order, young lady. Get yourselves and those townspeople out of here!"

Julie gave the agent a dirty look but turned and went back inside Newberry's.

As Gabriel was about to resume his protest against their leaving, several men—some FBI, some California Highway Patrol—ran into the main intersection of town from where they had been waiting on the sidewalks. One old-fashioned traffic signal hung suspended from thick cables centered in the roadway forty feet in the air. Several men tossed burning red flares into the road, where they were immediately swept up in the rush of water cascading down Main Street. They tried again, this time closer to the inundated sidewalks. Some stayed, and some were swept away. Soon they had both sidewalks bright red with burning flares.

"How did you get through to the helicopter?" Gabriel asked, realizing what the federal authorities were attempting.

"It was ordered in by the State boys earlier, just in case. Good thing, with every electronic piece of equipment being knocked out by this damn electrical storm. Our radios and satellite phones should not be affected this way. We have to assume they may be getting jammed, and that would mean an outside force at work. We can't take the chance any longer; the president has to be moved!" the agent shouted.

Kennedy ducked as a very distinctive *pop* sounded over the thunder. His eyes widened when he saw two men, one agent and one highway patrolman, shooting their pistols seemingly straight up into the air. Then Gabriel realized what they were doing. They were trying to shoot the cable that held the old traffic light in place over the intersection. Five bullets missed, the sixth struck the cable and produced the bright sparks of a ricochet. Both men took more careful aim and fired again. This time, the cable was hit dead center, and the traffic signal and its supporting cables crashed down into the street. Kennedy had to shake his head when the two gunmen high-fived each other and then ran for the sidewalk. Several more men came forward and started shining powerful lights into the air and waving them around in an arc.

"What in the hell is happening?" John said as he joined them under the Newberry's awning.

Lonetree heard the distinctive thump overhead just as a bright flash lit the sky. The large gray bird slowly descended as it chopped the falling rain to mist.

"The National Guard made a Black Hawk available," the agent next to Kennedy said to John as he shielded his eyes from the driving rain. "As soon as it's down, you people are out of here."

Lonetree, for no apparent reason, reached out and pulled Gabriel back and away from the sidewalk, shaking his head when Kennedy asked what he was doing. His eyes were not looking at the descending UH-60 Black Hawk but at the hills above Moreno. In a flash of chain lightning, Gabe saw what John was looking at. The ancient ruins on the hill.

"It's there, Gabe, I can feel it. It's watching us right now," Lonetree said. He looked at Kennedy with consternation. "They are there. It's driving me crazy! I go from one impression to another. One minute it's a single presence—the next, many." He stared at the hills and the ruins they protected.

"Maybe it will stop now that it doesn't have the president here," Gabriel said.

"What?" Lonetree said. "You mean Hadley's gone?"

"Julie didn't tell you?"

John continued to look up into the dark hills above Moreno and didn't speak at first. Finally, as the Black Hawk came close enough to the ground that the cascading river of Main Street was sent crashing into the walkway and into Newberry's and the other buildings facing the road, Lonetree turned and faced Gabriel and the agent in charge.

"Something is wrong. If Hadley has been evacuated, I don't think that thing up there would have taken it too damn lightly, Gabe. It's still playing the same game of cat and mouse with us." He faced the agent. "Have you confirmed that the president is safe?"

"Their communications are all down," Gabriel said as he also faced the FBI field agent. "They have no idea."

"Come on. This crap is done. You people don't know when to stop. Now get your people together, Professor."

The Black Hawk came down slowly, being careful that her tail rotor didn't strike any existing overhang from the buildings on both sides of Main Street. They were aiming for the direct center of the rain-pummeled intersection. The heavily built, four-bladed UH-60 Black Hawk created a powerful blast of wind, making the storm look meek in comparison.

Gabe, John, and the agent watched. Suddenly, all three men turned their heads at exactly the same moment when the red neon light inside the K-Rave window fronting the station flared to life. Then every radio in town, no matter what frequency it was tuned to, began playing a song. The volume for these radios was maxed out at decibel levels these encrypted systems were not capable of producing. Men reached for their radios on their hips but found they could not lower the volumes. Several were so shocked that they tossed their radios away when all of them recognized the old song being broadcast.

I . . . fall to pieces . . . each time I see you again . . . I fall to pieces . . . how can I be just your friend?

The dead lights in all buildings, regardless of powerlines that had been disabled since the seventies, all flared to life, again shocking everyone in the rain-soaked streets. To a man, they looked around in fear. The Patsy Cline hit from 1961 reverberated even over the rotors and thunder enough so Gabriel and John felt Cline's voice through the soles of their shoes.

"Look!" Lonetree screamed, pointing. Even the agent in charge saw it coming.

Darkness even blacker than the night was there. It stood between Elm and Jackson Streets. Everyone saw the shape as it stood as if examining the activity. It was enormous. The blackness moved, causing the rain to move with it. Gabriel knew the only reason they could clearly see the entity was because the rain outlined it perfectly. Rivers of water ran off the thing as it stood watching from a distance.

"What the fuck is that?" the agent called out as he moved to the street, drawing his weapon. The others turned and saw what was watching them, and they too advanced on the black shape.

"Get your men back and wave off that damn helicopter!" Kennedy shouted as he grabbed the agent and spun him around.

Lightning flashed as the Patsy Cline song grew still louder. The black thing moved fast. Three agents were hurled out of the way as they watched the giant hand and arm swing out. The agents, Secret Service, and highway patrolmen slammed into buildings to the right and to the left, falling to the street dead or severely injured. The blackness came on toward the intersection.

Lightning flashed and streaked across the skies. Gabriel followed it and saw the glow of light from down the street. His eyes widened when he saw a whole and intact marquee of the Grenada Theater as it flashed its fancy wares to the world. Then the neon lighting blinked out, and the form of the marquee was no longer there. Kennedy couldn't believe it. The town was also reacting to the entity's presence.

The Black Hawk pilot must have seen something, because he tried in vain to take the massive bird back up. The tail dipped as the four main rotor blades fought the air for purchase. It slowly reacted. Rain was pushed aside so brutally by the powerful twin turbines of the Black Hawk that the water striking Gabriel and the others stung as if bees had been set loose on them. It climbed a hundred feet before the blackness struck.

They were helpless to stop it from happening. They stared up at the twenty-five-foot-tall swirling currents of black in a human shape. The entity lifted free of the water-covered ground and simply passed through the Black Hawk. The electrical systems failed, and the powerful anticollision lights flared in brightness and then failed. The helicopter hung in the air for a moment, and they could see the panic high in the air of the crew fighting dead controls. The tail boom of the National Guard helicopter spun without the power of her twin engines to keep her in the air. The tail swung, and the tail rotor struck a light pole, shearing off the rotor and five feet of aluminum housing. The main four-bladed rotor of the Black Hawk tipped precariously toward the tall structure of Newberry's. The Black Hawk overcompensated and went over onto its left side as the pilot tried to miss the fourth floor of Newberry's but struck it anyway. The rotor sheared away as the main body of the bird spun out of control. The helicopter, with its three crewmen, slammed to the earth in the intersection where it had been trying to land just a moment before. The fuel tanks ruptured, and then as they all watched in horror, the helicopter exploded.

The remaining agents, patrolmen, and Secret Service personnel slammed themselves into a protective ball as they hit the water-covered streets and sidewalks.

Gabriel and John recovered quickly as burning debris filled the rain-swollen air around them. In the confusion, they saw the darkness speed past them, hesitating for the briefest of moments, until Gabe thought the sloth-like form was going to conclude its business with them right then and there. But for a reason Kennedy thought as arrogant, it moved off.

Lightning flashed and thunder exploded over their heads as men ran to the burning helicopter, the fuel-fed flames roaring high into the air.

Every light inside the town of Moreno instantly went dark. The music was cut off like someone had merely unplugged a radio.

The attack was over in a matter of three minutes.

The town of Moreno was slowly being hemmed in. The only way out was down Main Street and fifteen miles to the interstate.

In the eastern sky, they couldn't see it, but the morning sun broke over the rest of the country, bringing on the new day—that day was Halloween, the thirty-first of October, fifty-five years to the day Dean Hadley and Gloria Perry had accidentally unleashed hell onto the earth.

19

The six survivors of the Supernaturals assisted in collecting the bodies of those killed. Two had looked as if they would make it only to die inside the darkened interior of the old Pacific Bell telephone exchange building. They would join the three helicopter crewmen and three of their brothers inside the makeshift morgue of Pacific Bell. John was the last one through with the covered body of George Cordero. He said another Blackfoot death prayer over all the bodies and then angrily turned away.

It was now eight in the morning. The sun was out somewhere, but not in Southern California.

The survivors kept looking at their watches and shaking them on their wrists. Not one of them was working. With the black skies overhead, they could not tell the difference between the current time and midnight the night before.

Gabriel didn't care. He was exhausted and sat down in the water where he thought the sidewalk began. He was in hip-deep wetness when the agent in charge lifted him from the river that threatened to catch him and send him to Huntington Beach.

"Come on, Professor. Get out of the water," Agent Haskins said, patting him on the shoulder as he stood Kennedy up.

Gabriel blinked and looked at the agent. He shook his head as he stumbled toward the awning fronting Newbery's. The agent followed and was joined by Lonetree returning from Pacific Bell.

"Okay, Professor Kennedy, you made your point."

"Oh, you mean that wasn't a Russian or Chinese black mass that knocked a four-and-a-half-ton military helicopter out of the sky? I'm glad we were able to convince you," Lonetree said as he attempted to turn Gabriel away and get him inside to pump him full of coffee. John's eyes lingered on the agent for a moment, and he was tempted to say something more, but Gabe shook his head.

"I recommend you evacuate your team, Professor. I do have the authority to make you leave for safety reasons. Washington says that's enough."

Both Gabe and John stopped and turned. "We're staying."

The agent in charge was about to argue when Harvey came through the doors of Newberry's wiping his hands and staring down the street.

"What in the hell?" Harvey said, stepping past all of them and running into the raging storm. He splashed through the water, and they all saw the man in the mud-covered suit as he stumbled down the street through knee-high water. As they reached for the him, it was the FBI agent who recognized the injured and battered man.

"Jesus, it's Bob Chapman, one of the president's protection team," he said, startled at Bob's condition.

They assisted Bob and made it to Newberry's, still splashing through ankle-high water. They made it to a booth and placed the Secret Service agent inside.

"What happened?" FBI agent Haskins asked as he leaned over the mud-caked man in the booth. Harvey hurriedly pushed a cup of steaming coffee in front of the man, who picked it up and drank.

"Let the kid get his senses about him, Hoover Boy," Harvey said as Lonetree pulled him back. He winked at the older man, and Leach mumbled something but backed off anyway. He joined Bob and Linda and an ever-curious Casper Worthington as they watched the mud-covered agent.

The hot liquid spilled down his face, but he didn't seem to care. The coffee mixed with blood and mud, and all three coursed down and off his chin. He finally put the cup down as the rest of the Supernaturals and a few of the federal agents gathered around.

"Buried, all of them," he said, his red eyes finally looking up. "The entire hillside came down on us."

Haskins leaned over, took the Secret Service agent by the shoulders, and lightly shook him. "The president?"

The man could only shake his head as a coughing spell hit and hit hard. It was Jennifer who stepped forward and then took the man's vital signs as the others waited impatiently. The coughing fit ended, and the man stared off into space as he tried to focus on what he was being asked.

"He's near shock," Jenny said as she raised the agent's eyelids and checked them.

"Damn it, man, is the president safe?" Haskins asked again, this time more forcefully.

"I couldn't dig them out. I felt like I was trapped for days. I . . . I—"

"The president?"

"Gone." The man looked up and into Haskins's eyes and held steady. "Did you think I would leave him there? I finally managed to find the med unit. It was on its side. Only the driver's compartment was above the mud. The driver and the other one were dead. It took me so long to move them. The mud kept caving in, and water was flooding inside."

He went into a second coughing fit, and Jennifer knew he had swallowed enormous amounts of mud.

"I finally dug into the bay. Found two doctors, both dead. I couldn't dig out the three nurses. They were in like it was cement. The president's gurney was there, half-in and half-out of the mud. The president was gone. Just gone. I saw impressions in the mud and handprints on the side of the med unit. He had crawled out on his own through a foot-wide gap between the slide and the window. I don't know where he is." He started gasping, trying to hold back tears.

Haskins straightened, slapping his hand on the tabletop. "Get all law enforcement—now. I can't believe a man who was in as bad of shape as Hadley could crawl out of a mudslide. He's still in there," he said angrily, casting an accusing look at the Secret Service agent.

"He's gone . . . he walked away. The slide was so bad he had to come back this way." The voice was starting to drift away as the man slowly succumbed to shock. "We're trapped here."

The man slid forward, and Jenny, Julie, and Leonard took the agent and led him into the back where he could lie down.

"I want the hostage rescue team unit with me. They're better rested than the others. We'll go to the slide and dig the president out. The rest of the Secret Service and the State boys will start a search of the town."

"I'll get my people to help," Gabriel said as he slowly turned away.

"No, as you said, you have work you have to do. Do it and let's get the fuck out of here, Professor." Haskins angrily turned and left Newberry's with the other agents.

"Well, you heard him," John said.

Gabriel looked at Leonard, Julie, and Jennifer. Bob, Linda, Harvey, and Casper Worthington, with a wide-eyed Peckerwood at his feet, watched them and knew that this was going to be the longest day of their lives. As the agent said a moment before, they were now trapped and really had no choice. The thoughts were punctuated by a loud crack of thunder, and the lights blinked, dimmed, and then came back full in protest to the electrical assault over their heads. Every person wore the same face. That did not bode well.

Gabriel paced to the window as he was handed a cup of coffee by an admiring Casper Worthington. He laughed a shrill old man's sound. It was a laugh that caught everyone's attention.

"What are you cackling like a hen about, you old fool?" Harvey asked.

Casper turned and faced the remaining group. "I was just thinkin' 'bout the old factory up there," he said with a sly look back at Kennedy, who turned away from the window to listen. "In all your book readin' and such, what you people call *research*"—he looked at Leonard and back at Gabriel—"why didn't you ever ask the question you needed asking?"

"What question, Mr. Worthington?" Gabe asked, becoming intrigued.

"Well, several questions, really. Remember what we used to talk about after the big explosion at the plant when we both got out of the army after 'Nam, Harvey?"

Harvey Leach was silent as a familiar memory came to him. "Dean and Gloria were asking the same questions that very day, weren't they? Those strange questions about mercury."

"Yep," Casper said with a twinkle in his old eyes. "The first question to you ghost people is, why would the gov'ment finance building a plant in a hidden-away spot like Moreno? Yeah, we know the old story about how the natural elements that made up the formula for mercury were in the ground here, but come on, we all knew even then that was a lie. There was never any digging going on around Moreno. There were no mines. They always said they needed massive amounts of mercury for their products, the gauges and meters, for the aerospace industry. The second question is why, when they had contractors already in place all over California that supplied McDonnell Douglas, Hughes Aircraft, Lockheed, and such with the very same gauges and meters?"

"Could you please tell us what's running through that head of yours?" Bob said, growing frustrated.

"Third and most important question is, why did the comp'ny always have a hundred times more mercury on hand than they were ever capable of using? As far as I know, it's a rather expensive heavy metal. Dean Hadley and Gloria Perry thought to ask. Why not you folks?"

Gabriel and the others didn't know what to say. Leonard opened his mouth to say something but closed it. He would never hear the end of this from Damian, who was giving him an "I told you so" look.

"How do you know all of that?" Damian asked when he thought Sickles had enough guilt thrown his way.

"He knows all of that because Casper's daddy was the second-shift foreman at the plant," Harvey said as he now remembered it all. He moved a few steps as he thought. "I never could figure out why those two were so interested in that damn mercury."

"Wait, did you say your father had been the second-shift foreman at the plant?" Gabriel asked.

"*Was*, yeah. He was blown sky-high with the rest of those good people. With my daddy dead and all, I got angry when I was old enough to think about it. Why did they have so much mercury stored there when it was so damn dangerous?"

Gabriel Kennedy looked at John and raised his brows. "Now I guess you have your duty spelled out for you. You now have a starting point besides the journal you saw."

John nodded as he looked at Jennifer. She was anxious about his next foray into the dreamworld of Moreno but was ready for him to do it.

"And you came up with this mercury question all on your own?" Leonard asked.

Casper Worthington cackled again as he looked at the small black computer genius.

"I watch *Doctor Who* on the BBC on the cable TV. He's a genius, you know?" He looked sad for a moment, and Peckerwood ventured over. Casper picked the small Yorkie up and hugged him. "No offense; I'm sure your show was pretty good too," he said as Harvey placed an arm around the old man's shoulder and they walked into the kitchen.

The Supernaturals exchanged looks of wonder.

"Well, it's simple enough," Damian said as he stood and followed the two men as they laughed and walked away. "We'll just call in Doctor Who."

20

The figure was moving from alley to alley. The broken form eased into a sitting position near the back entrance to the empty shell of the Bottom Dollar Bar and Grill. His weakened body slid down the graffiti-covered wall until he collapsed fully into the seven inches of water that lapped at the rear of the building. His head fell toward his chest as he closed his eyes. His gray hair was soaked, and the hospital gown provided little warmth or comfort. He was a shell of who he had been at eighteen years old. He was scared, wet, lost, and confused. He knew he had to be somewhere, but since his harried flight from the accident, his memory had failed him. He tried to raise his head and failed. He collapsed face-first into the pool of accumulated rainwater. He curled up into a fetal position and cried in frustration for his inability to remember who he was and why he was in this place. He did know, however, that if he didn't remember soon, she would die.

Former president of the United States Dean Hadley lay in the cold water and begged for forgiveness. For what? His mind failed to explain. Lightning flashed across the sky, and the earth under him shook. He raised his head and leaned against the rough brick of the old building. He opened his eyes, trying in vain to keep his body from shivering as he took in his surroundings. He squinted into the driving rain and tried to focus on the metal sign screwed into the chipped brick. He opened his mouth to try to say the name, but nothing came out. He tried to focus his eyes once more.

"Royal Cr . . . own . . . Cola," he managed to say as the strength in his neck gave out and his head once more fell to his chest. He felt the pain there, and then with waning strength, he tore at the hospital gown until the collar ripped. He tried to focus, failed, and then tried again. He tore away at the tape and gauze and saw the wounds he had received in Virginia. He shook his head and became scared. He tried to pull the gown closed again but could only get it to cover his shoulders. He collapsed again.

"You're home now. Do you remember where you can find me?" came the voice into his ear.

Hadley once more raised his head.

"You should remember; you left me there, left me there for eternity."

"No, no," he said in answer to the melodious voice that seemed to whisper into both ears at once. "Dad . . . Dad . . ." His head went down and his body fully collapsed.

As the rain whipped in between the two buildings hard enough to make the Royal Crown Cola metal advertisement flap with an irritating squeak, Dean went out with a frustrating memory that ate away at the edges of thought and memory.

Sleep for now. I have waited a very long time to see you again. We have time left, but you must be here before the others learn their true power over this world. I can no longer control them.

"Gloria," Hadley said as his eyes closed. He knew he was home.

The team was upstairs. Bob, Linda, and Casper, with a brave Peckerwood yapping in the kitchen, would stay on the first floor to monitor the search for Hadley.

Jennifer was in the corner near the bed that was now covered in a fresh sheet supplied by Harvey. The medication had again been laid out and placed where Gabe could get to it quickly. Julie made ready with her notepad, since everything that needed power, either battery or from the outside power grid, could not be trusted. Damian and Leonard were still trying to discern why the satellite phone wasn't supplying a link for the online help they needed.

"Without George, we won't have any idea what he's going to face until he faces it. No warning, no help. He'll be totally on his own," Julie said quietly so as not to upset Jennifer again. The small anthropologist had named all the dreamwalk's hazards, mentioning them until the dangers seemed lessened somehow. Julie didn't want to start that over again.

Gabriel remained quiet as he readied himself and the few devices he had that could help Lonetree in his walk. He'd never felt this helpless. He looked up at Julie and found no voice to agree or disagree with her fears. Julie caught the drift of worry from his silence and nodded.

Gabriel sat down harder than he wanted in the chair next to the bed. There were three of them. He would be center of Julie taking notes and Jennifer helping John when he needed it. They had found that Jenny could occasionally contact John through speech.

Kennedy lowered his head, and it wasn't until John poked him on the shoulder that he finally looked up.

"Thought you were taking this dreamwalk instead of me."

"Sorry," Gabe said as he stood and faced his friend. "I've been thinking about this entity."

Lonetree slowly lay down on the bed. "I am truly happy to hear that. Believe me, I've been thinking on that very subject myself," he said, trying to get a rise out of Kennedy. He had never seen his old friend this disconcerted about what they did for a living.

"Do you want to hear this or not?"

"Okay, tell me how dangerous this thing is for the hundredth time."

"John, I don't think that thing outside this morning was the real power here."

"Gloria," John said. "I figured it was something like that. Like you, every time an attack happens, no matter how brutal it is, I get the sense of remorse."

"My theory is a little more direct. I think something happened that was even more devastating to this place than this so-called disaster. I think we are dealing with a betrayal on a massive scale. Not by Hadley's old man or Frank Perry either. Even that entity that attacks so fiercely is not the root cause of this. Oh, I think it has everything to do with what happened to the town, but not to Gloria."

"You think Dean Hadley killed her?" John sat up on his elbows as Jennifer finally joined them.

Gabriel lowered his head and nodded.

"We've known each other since college, Gabe; trust me when I say that boy that I've seen in my walking state could not have harmed that girl. It's got to be that thing, those others that caused all of this."

"I guess it's time to find out for sure," Jennifer said as she tried to smile at Lonetree but failed miserably.

"I hope I'm wrong, because if I'm not, you may see something even more unpleasant than what happened to this town fifty-five years ago."

"And I won't be able to stop him from killing Gloria anyway. One thing you didn't think about, Gabe, is the fact I could end up watching that beautiful young woman die anyway." John leaned over and fixed Kennedy with an intense look. "Mark my words, if I can keep her out of that theater, I will. I know I can't, but for my sanity's sake, I have to try."

Gabe patted John on the knee. "Hell, bring her back if you can," he smiled as he picked up the syringe of Demerol. "We could make a fortune with that voice of hers. Imagine what she could do on *American Idol*?" Gabriel eased the needle into John's arm just above the elbow.

"I want both of you to know I intend to try to get into both Gloria's and Dean's heads. Between the two of them—a survivor of that night and one who was killed—I should be able to get most of the story. And if the journal is still in existence, I'll find out where it is." The few words trailed away as John's system absorbed the Demerol kicker. The dose was close to the limit Lonetree could take.

Jennifer held John's hand as his head finally sank back on the bed that had held George Cordero's body only hours before. For Lonetree, that was not a totally uncomfortable thought to drift off to. Finally, Gabriel reached out for Jenny's hand. She hesitated but finally released John. She knew that her touch would hinder his connection with whatever he was to face. Gabe smiled and then he eased the dark glasses once more into John's hand. He closed the fingers over them and then closed his eyes as he willed Lonetree to be careful. He finally let go as John's eyes settled in just before he went deep under with the Demerol.

"Watch your ass in there."

The words, along with the world, went black for Lonetree.

The sounds were the first to come. John felt the length of the long tunnel was too much of a distance to travel to get to the pinhole dash of light that seemed miles away. He couldn't see in the blackness but moved forward over air toward the sounds that slowly began to have a familiar ring.

He heard the heavy bass guitar and then cocked his head as he felt the speed of his journey begin to pick up speed like a train. His eyes picked up brief flashes of light of varying colors. The music was now recognizable.

You don't remember me . . . but I remember you . . .'twas not so long ago . . . you broke my heart in two . . .

John tried to slow his pace through the blackness of the space, but his mind and spirit moved faster toward the renown sound of Little Anthony and the Imperials, a doo-wop group from the fifties.

Tears on my pillow . . . pain in my heart . . . caused by you . . .

For the first time inside his dreamwalk state, John felt cool air on his face, and then just as suddenly as he had entered this world of the past, it blinked into existence. He closed his eyes and felt himself rise into the air. His mind shifted from trying to observe just one life to many. The music became louder, the world was now visible, and John was now there to see it.

The two sat in uncomfortable silence as Gloria realized she had fallen asleep to the rain hitting the ragtop roof of the Corvette. She felt Dean quickly turn away and realized he had been watching her sleep. She swiped at her mouth and then she felt her face flush.

"God, I'm sorry. I wasn't slobbering on myself, was I?" she asked, facing Dean's direction.

The teenager laughed as though that had been the funniest thing he had ever heard.

"I'm so glad you find me so amusing," she said in a huff as she pulled her sweater closer to her chest.

"Sorry, no, you weren't drooling on yourself." He laughed again as he pounded the steering wheel. "I couldn't picture that if I wanted to."

Gloria stuck out her tongue and then angrily turned the Corvette's radio up. "I happen to love this song."

If we could start anew . . . I wouldn't hesitate . . . I'd gladly take you back . . . and tempt the . . . hands of fate . . . tears on my pillow . . . pain in my heart . . . caused by you, you, you, you, you.

Dean stopped laughing as he concentrated on her face in the soft glow of back porch light of the Bottom Dollar Bar and Grill. The rain had recently stopped, and the sun was down. Little Anthony and the Imperials played on as Dean studied Gloria's face. She was even more beautiful to him in the soft darkness than she was during the brightest of days.

Dean watched her red lips move with the soft words of "Tears on My Pillow" from the yellow glow of the exposed light bulb. The alley was small, and the only business it backed was the Bottom Dollar. They had been hiding there since early afternoon after escaping the close call with his father and the theft of the journal. Suddenly, Gloria reached out and turned down the radio as she realized something.

"How long was I asleep?"

"It's seven o'clock now—about two hours."

Once more, Gloria pulled her sweater across her chest and then turned her head. She had an angry glare about her that sent pleasurable chills down Dean's spine.

"You'd better not have—"

"Relax, Donna Reed, your honor is still intact. Sheesh, what do you take me for?"

Gloria's left eyebrow went higher than the rim of her dark glasses, and Dean knew she was giving him the evil eye. She relaxed and then yawned.

"Thank you for watching over me while I slept."

"I guess you're the type that isn't used to narrow escapes, are you?"

"I don't know what kind of life you think blind people lead, but running from parents after break-ins isn't normal." She faced him fully. "What now? This Halloween report seems like such a distant memory now; I think maybe we should let this go. You're already in big-time shit with your dad."

"Yeah, well, he's used to cleaning up my messes—one more won't hurt."

"My father says he's so hard on you because he's got big plans for his little boy," she said.

"Yeah, well, did it ever occur to anyone that I may have plans for my-self?"

"What plans?" she asked, with a large smile on her face and leaning in with rapt attention.

"Does it shock you that I even have a plan?"

She placed her chin on her hand as she leaned on the center console. She waited patiently.

Instead of answering her, Dean quickly leaned in and kissed Gloria on the lips. It was just a split-second peck, but it was enough to make him feel as good as he'd ever felt in his life. His head sprang back and he closed his eyes, just waiting for the sharp-tongued girl to rip loose on him. When nothing happened, he opened his eyes and slowly turned. She was still leaning against the 'Vette's console with her head resting in her hand. She hadn't moved an inch.

"You call that a kiss?" She finally shook her head and then sat back in her seat. "Oh, boy, I can see why all the girls throw themselves at your feet, Fabian."

"All the girls? You listen to too much gossip. Why, if you knew the truth—"

Gloria leaned over as suddenly as a springing cat and had Dean wrapped in an embrace. Her lips met his like two crashing cars on Dead Man's Curve. His eyes widened as he felt her soft lips on his own. His heart skipped five or six beats, and he felt his entire body stiffen. Dean even felt her small right hand as it caressed the back of his head, and he felt the slight tickle of her tongue just before she released him. He watched her as she eased back into the seat and then smiled as she faced straight ahead. Dean felt his heart start once more as he leaned back. The radio was turned up, as Gloria knew the silence wasn't as uncomfortable as she thought it would be. Her mouth was now set in a permanent grin as she had closed the intimidation gap in their budding relationship. She was the victor, and Dean, well, he was now a mere slave to those blind eyes and red lips. He felt himself melting away sitting right next to her.

"Okay, that was Little Anthony and the Imperials, 'Tears on My Pillow.' The time is seven oh five in the one hundred block of Moreno, USA. Happy Halloween! You're with Freekin' Rowdy Rhoads for the duration. Let's get out there and kick up our heels and celebrate the fact that we will all still be beboppin' around this old world for a few more years, thanks to the president. Now let's go out there tonight and show the commies how we rock and roll! Now my assistant, Roberta, will be here for the next hour as I get ready to go remote from downtown Moreno. It's Halloween, and we are going to *par-tay*! Now it's spooky, it's terrifying, it's the Five Satins and 'In the Still of the Night'!"

The doo-wop hit about the darkest part of the night began. Dean looked over at Gloria once more.

The tap on the driver's-side window startled him out of his moment in the sun. Dean slowly turned his head and saw the white apron of the Bottom Dollar's bartender and Gloria's piano player, Charlie. And as Dean's full attention went to the man's companion, he could see the gun belt. He closed his eyes as he lowered the window. Gloria turned down the Five Satins.

"Gloria, come on. Your father's looking for you," Charlie said as he went around the front of the car toward the passenger's side.

"And I'm looking for you, Mr. Hadley," the chief of police said, smiling in at Dean as he leaned over so the boy could clearly see his face.

"Look, Chief Thomas, my dad's—"

The door opened, stopping Dean's words as he was taken by the arm and gently pulled from behind the car's steering wheel.

"I haven't even called your pa yet, boy. I figured I'd get your story first."

"How can I be arrested for breaking into my own house?" Dean said as he angrily pulled back and grew even angrier when he saw Gloria was also being removed by Charlie's careful hand.

"You wish it were breaking and entering. I'm arresting you for assault, boy."

"Assault?" both Gloria and Dean said simultaneously.

"Did you or did you not beat up the Weller boy and his two friends this morning?" Thomas said as he pulled Dean away from the car.

Realization hit Dean as one of the punches he had received that very morning. It would seem that Jimmy Weller, Sam Manachi, and Steve Cole got the best of him anyway in this morning's brawl. He felt his bravado deflate inside him like air escaping a balloon.

"He did it to protect me!" Gloria said as she was pulled away from the car.

"Come on, son. I'll book you in and then call your father at the plant," the chief said as he thought about the handcuffs in his hand and then placed them back in their holder on his belt. "Come on, Marciano," he said.

"Stay at the bar; I'll find you," Dean said as he heard the back door to the Bottom Dollar open and Gloria was taken inside.

"I don't think you'll be doing much meeting tonight; your father's been calling me since this afternoon. It seems he may already be aware of your fisticuffs this morning."

Dean knew that was not the reason his dad was looking for him. He could only thank God that Gloria had the foresight to make him hide the journal.

John was taking all of this in with many eyes. For the first time ever, he was able to view many moments in time from differing points of view. He suspected that Gloria—the spirit, at least—was helping him to achieve this. He felt his body split, and parts of him went in different directions. A small speck of consciousness remained behind on one of the main characters in this haunted tale of the past.

As Dean was led down the side of the alley, a man with a dark jacket and fedora stepped from the shadows, and instead of following Dean and the police chief, he eased back into the shadows and then waited for a moment before inching to the front of the building.

Dr. Jürgen Fromm, a man thought gone for many years, avoided the yellow glow of the lights in the alley as he crept along with hands deep in his coat pockets. He followed Gloria inside the Bottom Dollar.

He had plans on concluding his life's work in this, the last night in the one-decade-old small town called Moreno.

21

The candles placed around the room flickered. Both Leonard and Damian were in the far corner near the computers, and they flinched and watched the flames of the closest candle flicker slowly back to life after being nearly extinguished. They looked at each other with wide eyes. The flashing lightning and the sound of the rain slowly ate away at the veteran investigators' nerves.

Everyone in the large second-floor space jumped when they heard a rending of metal near the front wall near the large windows were. Damian and Leonard shot to their feet as the candles blew out.

"Oh, come on," Damian said as his eyes adjusted to the total dark.

The sound of metal on metal echoed on the empty floor as Gabriel and Jennifer tried to see John in the darkness but could only discern a vague outline on the bed. Suddenly, the overhead lights flashed and then went out. They all had fine red dots dancing in their eyes as if they had been surprised by a bright flash of a bulb in a camera. Then the fluorescents buzzed to life, and then just as quickly went out, and then came on and steadied. They all heard the hum of electricity as it once more coursed through the once-busy department store.

"I sure as hell hope that's Harvey screwing around downstairs," Leonard said as he looked around nervously.

Gabriel moved toward the noise, and Damian fell in step with him as they made their way to the front of the second floor. Gabe flinched at the extreme brightness of the lights and shielded his eyes as he looked up. He could actually feel heat coming off the tubes in waves.

"Okay, now this is fucked up," Damian said as he came to a sudden stop.

Gabe lowered his hand, and his eyes widened. "Not a very clinical observation, but I must say that I concur, that *is* fucked up."

The escalator, looking as if it had just been repaired and cleaned, was running as smoothly as the day it had been installed late in 1958. The rubber handrail slid along silently as the steel stairs folded into one another.

The lights flickered once more and then came on, making them all flinch in the sudden brightness. When they looked up, the escalator was there as it had been for the past fifty-plus years, broken and silent.

"Uh, guys, you may want to see this," Leonard said from the front of the floor. He was staring out into the night and was silhouetted by a bright flash of lightning.

As Gabe, Damian, Jennifer, and Julie gathered by the thirteen-foot window next to Leonard, they saw the lights of Moreno flickering, first one side of Main Street and then the other. Even past Main they could see lights flare to life in the old abandoned tract homes that had been built for Hadley's employees and hadn't had power supplied to them since 1965. It was a brightly illuminated kaleidoscope of lights that reflected off the rain-soaked streets.

"What's happening?" Julie asked, her eyes reflecting the strange light show being staged for them. Sparks exploded from long-dead electrical transformers and fell into the water coursing down Main Street.

"John's having some kind of effect. Whatever this thing is, it's reacting."

Leonard looked over at Gabriel. "Is that good or bad?" he asked, hoping for an answer he was prepared to hear. Gabriel didn't answer.

At the pounding of feet coming up the empty stairwell, they turned as one and saw Casper, Peckerwood, Bob, Linda, and finally Harvey as they came through the door.

"We can't get out of here," Harvey said as he immediately walked to a window and raised a chair up in the air. Gabriel and the others watched wide-eyed as he threw the chair as hard as he could at the window. The foldable steel chair hit the glass and rebounded back into the room. "It's the same thing on the first floor."

"Look!" Julie said as the newcomers to their little party moved over to where they stared out of the front set of smashed windows.

Down on the street, they saw two men in blue windbreakers as they made their way hurriedly down the street toward the FBI's new command post inside the old Pacific Bell phone exchange. Before they reached the door, the man on the left was lifted into the air, and his body was thrown as if he weighed nothing at all. They watched in horror as the body flew through the air right at them. The man hit just below the windowsill and then slowly peeled away to fall the thirty feet to the street below. Everyone observing tried to move away, but that didn't stop them from seeing the end result.

"You people done pissed something off!" Casper said as he reached down and picked up the trembling Yorkie. Peckerwood shook in the old man's arms.

"Leonard, we still don't have communications with the search teams outside?"

"Nothing; it's like our phone service is cut off."

"This ain't no God doing this, at least the kind we used to believe in," Harvey said as he stepped away from the glass.

"Damn it, that's about enough of this crap," Damian said as he stepped back from the window and pulled his firearm. He took aim and fired three times into the top portion of the window's crown. The bullets ricocheted off, making all duck and cover.

"Whoa, Quick Draw," Leonard said as he finally removed his hands from his ears.

Damian cursed as he placed the nine-millimeter back into its holster.

"Look!" Jennifer said.

All eyes went back to the street. They saw the second man standing and staring their way as if he could see them all perfectly from two hundred feet away. Even beyond him, a few more of the other agents from inside the phone exchange were watching and pounding on the glass window trying in vain to get the FBI agent's attention as he stared at them.

"What's he doing?" Julie asked as they too watched the man standing on the sidewalk after his companion had just been tossed to his death. The agents inside were still pounding on the glass desperately trying to get the man to enter the exchange.

They saw a small child with a shaved head and ragged clothing walking through the rain right down the center of Main Street. The water was up to the child's ankles and was rising steadily.

"Harvey, who in the hell is that?" Damian asked. He pounded on the glass as the agent standing there staring up at them smiling as the child approached. "Are there kids left in this town? I thought you said everyone was gone."

Harvey's eyes widened as he saw the child move with intent toward the unsuspecting agent. The agent was transfixed on the Newberry's building across the way.

"There is no one in town and especially no children. The last family moved out yesterday; I told you that."

"That's not a boy; it's a little girl, and she has company," Jennifer said as she pointed out the window.

A bright streak of lightning brightened the darkness that had gathered in Moreno. Down the alleyways and the cross streets came several more children; Gabriel quickly estimated there were at least twenty of them, all with shaved heads and dressed similarly in ragged clothes.

"Leonard, get to your job!" Gabriel admonished the small man, who stared wide-eyed at the scene below.

Damian tossed Leonard the camera, and the computer man rapidly took pictures, the flashes bouncing blindingly off the glass.

The small girl whose bare feet seemed to step on the running waves instead of being submerged by them stepped onto the sidewalk. She looked up at the agent and then turned their way. Julie gasped as another flash of chain lightning illuminated the child's blank and blackened eyes. The girl smiled and turned away. She tugged on the agent's leg, and he looked down, his smile never leaving his face. He leaned over, and she whispered in his ear. He nodded, turned to look at his fellow FBI agents inside the building, then turned back to face Newberry's. He reached into his jacket and pulled out his service weapon. Without losing the creepy smile, he raised it to his temple and pulled the trigger.

Linda and Casper screamed as the man collapsed into the gutter and then was partially washed away. The agents tried unsuccessfully to break the glass fronting the exchange. They were all helpless as they watched the small child join the others as they gathered at the center of Main and Jefferson Streets and watched the town. They were in a circle, and as they faced the buildings around them, Leonard continued to shoot photos of them.

"Good God, Gabe, what is this?" Jennifer asked.

"I don't know, but we have to be prepared for anything until John comes back."

"Whatever those things are, they've come back to finish what they started back in '62," Casper said, Peckerwood barking in agreement.

"I seen them kids before," Harvey said as he finally managed to turn away from the awful scene outside.

"What do you mean?" Gabriel asked.

"That night, we saw them kids. We thought they were all from out of town here to trick-or-treat. They were everywhere. The movies, standing on porches with other town kids. Not harming anyone but also not carrying bags for collecting candy neither. They came in the store. They were at the Grenada Theater. They were everywhere."

"Why didn't you mention this before?" Damian asked, cursing the old man's memory.

"That's right, that's right," Casper said. "They was standing on our porch that night. You're right, Harve, they was everywhere."

"You too?" Damian asked.

"I swear, I didn't remember until just this minute. It's like it was erased from my mind and then there it was." He looked at Gabriel. "Doc, that's the thing that killed us that night."

"You mean *things*, don't you?" Leonard said as he finally lowered the camera after getting his fill of the strange and haunting children below.

"No, in the end that night, they were one. They were one when they knocked that helicopter out of the sky. They were one when those federal boys were attacked last night. Now they're split again." His eyes were haunted as he looked confused. "That thing didn't want us to remember until it was ready for us to."

"Well, it sure as hell seems like they're ready now," Leonard said as his eyes went back to the storm-tossed night and their creepy new company.

"Leonard, keep trying the radio, the computers, anything you can. Warn the other agents out searching to stay out of the town until this thing has done what it came here to do."

"Okay, Prof, I'll see what I can—"

The lights went out for the last time.

John Lonetree was not in a normal dreamwalk as he had been a hundred different times since childhood. He knew he was not in control. He was firmly of the belief that either Gloria or something far worse was his tour guide. Instead of being scared, he was fascinated with the images of a split town and his journey through it. Part of him was with Gloria inside the Bottom Dollar, part with Dean inside the police station, and part was somewhere he never expected to be—the factory on the hill. He was now in the same room with the two men he most wanted to hear from.

The plant conference room was empty with the exception of a lone form. He sat at the head of the long conference table and stared out of the window

at the rain that was slowly coming to an end. The lights of the town he created were bright from down below. From the plant's high vantage point,
he could see the neon display of the Grenada Theater as the lights played
brightly on the shiny sidewalk where teenagers were lining up for the
Monster Mash spook show later in the evening. His thoughts were on his
son. He pushed the phone away from him after the call from Chief
Thomas—another of his club of friends from the war. His men were everywhere in the town's government, as he always liked to have full control of
Moreno. He was about to leave for the police station when the conference
room door opened and a familiar face stared in at him.

"Well, how did your trip to LA go? Find any interesting new music
groups?"

Former captain Franklin Perry entered, being sure to close the door
behind him. It didn't go unnoticed by Robert that Frank reached behind
him and then flicked the lock. Evidently, this was a business meeting.
Robert eased himself back down into the large chair.

"I'm sure your cronies in the system informed you where I was at since
early this morning."

Hadley remained quiet. He raised that right brow of his and that
infuriated Perry more than anything. He remained standing as he faced
his former friend.

"How long have you known?"

"Known what, Frank?"

"You know damn well what I'm talking about. Our good Dr. Jürgen
Fromm was never deported back to Germany."

Hadley remained silent as he took in Frank. He shook his head
sadly.

"Do you think we would allow him to go back to Germany, or even
deport him to Israel to stand trial for war crimes, and then sit looking like
fools as he explains where he has been the past seventeen years?" Hadley
laughed. "What he has been doing at the behest of the United States government?"

"You tried to eliminate him, didn't you?" Perry asked, placing his
hands on the back of a chair. By the way his knuckles turned white, it was
clear he was angrily expecting the truth from his former colonel.

"Me? No, not at all. After the agency stopped funding the doctor and
his work, I couldn't have cared less what they did with him."

"So, you're saying Washington authorized his official removal from
life?"

"That's about the way of it." Robert watched Perry, whose hands did not relax.

"Why didn't you tell me about any of this?"

"You chose to end your partnership on that day in 1958. You wanted nothing more to do with this madness, so why should I ask advice from a disloyal former officer?"

"Disloyal, because from the very beginning I was against involving us in this nightmare?"

"You seemed to have come off almost as well as the rest of us. Or don't you like the easy life that very same project provided you with?"

"We're cursed for doing what we did. This entire town is tainted for it." He leaned forward, his hands still pressing into the back of the chair. "We're as guilty as that German maniac for hiding the truth of what he did."

Hadley stood from his chair and faced Perry. "It's all over, Frank."

"Yeah? Well, here's something you didn't know. Fromm is alive and well and running loose in this country again. It seems your agency friends failed to do their jobs. The crazy bastard escaped and is here somewhere. I've seen him on more than one occasion."

"That's absurd; I would have been informed."

"Yes, since your friends in higher power have always been so forthcoming in that regard. Don't you see? We were as evil as that bastard for funding his work and supplying him with work space. A whole town founded on this man's evil intent! This factory"—he gestured around him—"all for him. We've supplied him with mercury to keep that evil alive, and now he's back."

"I don't believe it," Hadley said, staring at Frank.

Perry slammed the chair into the table as he turned away in anger.

"I will say this: it is perfect timing on your part, Captain."

"What do you mean by that?"

"It seems my son and your daughter have been poking around where they shouldn't. They came into my house and took the one piece of evidence that could get us all—and I do mean *all* of us—hanged."

"That goddamn journal. You kept it, didn't you?"

"I was instructed to keep it. Now they have it. Your snooping daughter and a boy that I have plans for. This could not only ruin his chances for him to be who I think he can be, it could turn him against me. You need to get your head out of your sanctimonious ass, Frank, and talk to that girl of yours. She has designs on my boy, and that will never happen. He needs more than a blind girl on his arm."

"Why, you son of a bitch!" Frank said as he moved toward Hadley.

"You don't want her involved with Dean; you hate him as much as I despise your arrogance and deep-seated tendency to righteousness."

Perry stopped his advance.

"My boy's waiting in a jail cell because of what he did to protect that daughter of yours. This I cannot have. I will get with the parents of the boys who have pressed charges against him and settle that little score, but you need to get to town and explain to Gloria why it's in her best interest as well as yours to give back that journal. My boy would never have had the inclination to do something like this if she hadn't influenced him. Now I suggest you go get that journal, or we could be in for some embarrassing questions about our postwar activities."

"We all should have stopped this back in 1945 when you suggested it after finding Fromm in Yugoslavia. We knew the atrocities he committed in the name of science, and still we all saw a chance to make some money after the war. But we never thought about what was in those vaults and the reasons they existed in the first place." He turned for the door. "Maybe we deserve what we get."

Hadley watched him leave. He picked up the phone and connected to the police department. "Thomas, keep Dean there until I arrive. Then I want you to canvass the entire town. It seems Dr. Fromm isn't as dead as we were led to believe." He hung up and sat heavily into his chair.

He knew the big plans he had for Dean were close to becoming a moot point. The scandal alone would isolate him and his son from the world for the rest of his life.

"Goddamn you, Fromm, and your little ghosts. You may have just gotten us all hanged."

Police Chief Thomas hung up the phone, wondering just what sort of trouble was brewing on the busiest night in Moreno's history. This wasn't shaping up the way the colonel had planned at all. The chief and several other founding fathers of the town had been assured that Jürgen Fromm and his experiments would vanish forever. He shook his head as he faced Dean sitting in a chair next to his desk. He looked dejected and angry. He went to the wall and removed a large set of keys.

"Okay, the colonel said to lock you up until he gets here." He made a gesture toward the teenager, indicating for him to get on his feet.

"Anything the man says, right, Chief?" Dean said as he stood up and straightened the letterman's jacket.

Thomas didn't answer, taking Dean by the elbow and leading him to a door. Dean saw the three jail cells and made up his mind. The chief opened the first cell, stepped aside, and gestured the boy in. Dean stepped up but stopped short of entering.

"We know what you and the others have done, you know," Dean said as he slowly turned toward Thomas, trying to make his bluff seem as plausible as he could. "We know about the ruins. We know about Dr. Fromm."

That was it. That was the total package of everything he and Gloria had discovered from his father's office. It was enough to make Thomas stop cold and allowed his true facial color to appear. It was white.

"You don't know crap, kid. Anyone as rich and spoiled as you can't know anything but girls and cars and how much Daddy gives you in allowance." He leaned in and started to push Dean into the cell.

"Sorry, Chief," Dean said as he took a quick step back, snatching the ring of keys, and then with his left hand reached for the chief's gun and with his right pushed him into the cell, where the man stumbled and fell face-first into the unmade bunk. Dean quickly closed the door and then just as fast placed the .38 revolver on the floor across from the cell along with the keys, out of reach Thomas's reach.

"Boy, you don't want to do this," Thomas said as he quickly gained his feet and reached through the bars. Dean easily stepped back out of reach.

"I think I just did it, Chief," he said as he reached for the door handle and left the cell area.

At that exact moment, a sliver of John's mind was following Dean, and another part of him was inside the darkened Bottom Dollar Bar and Grill.

Gloria sat far back from crowded dance floor and the busy bar. She could feel Charlie's eyes on her, and she slowly raised her right hand and flipped the bartender the finger.

"How does she do that?" Charlie said, eyeing her a moment longer before passing the extra bartender they had on for Halloween and heading for the storage room.

Gloria cocked her head to the right and listened. She heard a sound familiar from the past years of helping her father in the bar. She heard the storeroom door open and then close. She moved quickly, assuming it had been Charlie who entered the storeroom, as he would never trust their part-time bartender to get in with the stock. She started moving in between tables that had yet to be occupied. She cursed herself for not having her cane with her, but it was inside Dean's car. She braced herself as she moved dangerously fast. She managed to only bump three tables as she made her way toward the back door that led into the alley. She didn't stop to listen for Charlie; she went straight to the door and pushed it open. Before she could take a step, she felt her nose crash into something unyielding. She knew she had been caught.

"Hey!" said a voice as Gloria rebounded away and was starting to turn in the opposite direction to make another break for the front door when two strong hands grabbed her.

As she was turned, she brought up her right hand and punched outward. She felt her knuckles connect, and then she heard, "Ow!"

"Oh, God, Dean?" she asked as she covered her mouth with both hands.

Holding his nose with one hand, he reached out and took Gloria by the hand with the other and pulled her free of the Bottom Dollar. He started running with her flying behind him.

"They took the keys to my car," he said, his voice strange after the blow to his nose.

"Stop running. I know where we can go to hide. They won't think of looking for us there."

Main Street was packed. Children, as tradition called for, started their trick-or-treating by hitting all the businesses first. The stores stayed open late for the event, and busloads of children invited by Moreno from out of town came to share in the joint celebration of Halloween and the ending of the Cuban Missile Crisis. Costumed kids dragging their parents by the hand made for a good cover as Dean and Gloria walked down Main without attracting attention to themselves. Dean kept glancing at the police station and was relieved not to see his father's Caddy parked out front. That meant his break had yet to be detected.

Gloria stopped just as they reached the Grenada Theater. Dean looked at the long line of teenagers just starting to get tickets from the box office. Several of them called out to Dean, but he turned away as if he hadn't heard them. Three boys at the end of the line, however, took notice. Jimmy Weller punched Sam Manachi on the arm to get his attention as he pointed out the new arrivals.

"They'll show up here later; everyone does eventually. We can take that bastard then," Sam said, not very interested in revenge at the moment.

"He'll never see it coming," Jimmy said as his eyes bored in not just on Dean but Gloria also.

Dean looked around as Gloria leaned in to him. He looked at the marquee high above his head.

> Halloween Monster Mash
> The Tingler—House on Haunted Hill—The House of Wax
> Starring Vincent Price
> Hosted by K-Rave Radio and Freekin' Rowdy Rhoads—Tonight, 9:00 p.m.

The red plastic letters were bright and coupled with the flashing neon were damn near blinding. They saw the K-Rave step van out in front as teenagers crowded around Freekin' Rowdy Rhoads as he unspooled a reel of microphone wire. Freekin' Rowdy looked up from his adoring and very irritating teenybopper fans and saw Dean and Gloria looking none too good after their flight. He got a curious look on his face as he took the two in. He finished with his wire, winked at Dean, and raised his hands up in a boxer's stance, jabbing at the air. Dean gave him a dirty look.

"Come on. We can cross now. Hurry—I feel eyes all over us."

"Maybe that's because everyone sees us," Dean said as Gloria angrily pulled him into the street.

Again, they failed to see the man in the dark trench coat and fedora follow at a discreet distance.

As the two-man security team moved past the broken south wall of the old winery just below the shattered and ancient remains of the Spanish mission, the boy held the girl tightly. Gloria felt his strong arms on her as he lowered her to the dead grass surrounding the old ruins. She felt the chill go through her as the butterflies rose from her stomach. She was beginning to feel anticipatory chills when Dean touched her, and she found herself liking it. She cursed her weakness at the thought of having this stuck-up, snobby boy enthrall her so much that she could nearly swoon at his mere touch. She shook her head, his arms holding her in place as the security team moved past. It would be a cold day in hell—her father's favorite saying—before she ever admitted that weakness to him, or anyone else, for that matter. She shrugged his arms from her back.

"Okay, Troy Donahue, they're gone."

The boy looked over at Gloria in the rising moonlight. Although her words were sharp and harsh, he could detect a hint of a smile on her lips. He shook his head.

"Don't call me Troy Donahue; the guy's a phony, just like his pals Kookie Byrnes and Fabian—a disgrace to rock and roll, if you ask me. Now how in the hell can you tell if they've moved past us or not? I'm beginning to think you're not blind at all."

Gloria tilted her head and smiled as she faced Dean. "*Blind* doesn't mean *deaf*. They're still wearing their raincoats; they squeak."

"But they were sixty feet away," Dean said as he took in her face in the brief flash of moonlight clearing the dark clouds above. Even tumbled and tossed, the girl was beginning to dig a deep trench in his soul.

"Come on," she said as she stood from the grass and placed her hand on the broken wall. "Give me a boost."

Dean shook his head but cupped together his two hands nonetheless and hefted her light body up until she vanished over the low-slung adobe wall. "Blind, my ass," he hissed as he quickly checked where the two security men were and then deftly and athletically followed Gloria.

She was waiting for Dean, and she held out her hand. He stared at it a moment and then looked around the abandoned winery and mission one last time.

"Come on. I can do a lot of things without sight, but running isn't one of them."

Dean took Gloria's hand in his own and ran toward the mission's front entranceway. He stopped and looked around the parking area, and when he was satisfied the two security men were in their guard shack, he pulled on her hand once again until they had run all the way across the gravel surface as quietly as possible. He saw the doorway and hoped it wasn't locked as they ran up the thirteen steps and then without hesitation opened the door and entered. He pulled her against the wall and listened.

"I've never been here after dark," he said as he gripped her hand tighter.

"I do it all the time," she said, trying to catch her breath.

Dean shook his head as he caught himself watching her chest rise and fall in the small security light just inside the doorway.

"You mean you come here and get around security on your own?"

Gloria smiled as she pulled on *him* this time, leading him to the steel door that led to the subbasement of the ancient Spanish winery.

"Oh, you thought you were pulling off something impossible? Sorry to ruin your high-handed opinion of yourself."

"Look," he said as she stopped only a foot away from the steel door, "we can stop this right now. I can talk my father into most anything, even taking the police chief prisoner. We may never be able to prove your little ghost story anyway. We can stop right now and go back to what we do best."

"What? Bebopping around town in your hot sports car, impressing all the admiring girls?" Gloria removed a set of keys from her sweater pocket and handed Dean the ring.

"Yeah, something like that," he said. He used one of only two keys on the ring, guessing wrong in the first attempt. He tried the other key, and the lock popped free of the steel hasp. As the door opened, Dean looked down a long, very dark staircase, and he swallowed. "Of all the people I could have picked to fall for, I get Nancy Drew."

For some reason, Gloria got mad and shook her head.

"What?" he asked as she angrily stepped by him and entered the stairwell.

"You can play games with the other girls in school, but don't try to bullshit me, Dean Hadley. How many girls have you fallen for this month alone? Five? Six?"

"You don't know me at all. Maybe if you could see instead of just hear the gossip, you would know I'm not like that. Most of the time anyway."

"Well defended, Sparky," she said as she started down the darkened stairs.

Dean stood rooted to the spot, as he had never in his life heard a girl talk like that before. He closed his eyes and shook his head. Is that what he got by declaring he had fallen for her?

Gloria hesitated at the bottom of the stairs and turned toward Dean, her dark glasses covering angry eyes. "Are you coming, or do you want to make peace with Daddy?"

"I'm sorry I opened my mouth. When we're done, you can go back to hating the world, and I'll go back to making my plans to get the hell out of Moreno and away from my father," Dean said as he shook his head for the hundredth time that day. He turned on the light switch and saw that the stairwell was almost new in appearance. His nerves took a nosedive; something was wrong with this place.

He joined her at the bottom. Gloria used her hands in the darkness that was her world and made her way to a second door. This one was thick and extremely cold to the touch.

"Turn off the lights until we go inside." She waited until she heard the click of the light panel.

"This so-called vault is in there?" he asked as he examined the door with a small penlight.

"Would you turn that off until we're inside?" she said harshly under her breath as she grabbed the keys from his hand.

Again, Dean was amazed at her unseeing prowess. He watched her deftly place a key into a deadbolt locking mechanism. The door clicked.

"Are you sure there's a vault in here?" Dean asked as he nervously turned and looked up the darkened staircase. "And we're sure this has something to do with my father and yours?"

"Your father and my father installed the vault back in 1948," she said with a grin as she stepped into the room. She was angry at her perception that Dean was playing games with her. She was quickly finding out that she was indeed capable of getting hurt by a boy.

"Look, this poor little blind girl act is getting a little—" Dean closed his eyes as the harsh lights inside the deep and dark basement flared to life, successfully stemming his insult about her blindness and his monetary disposition.

"Welcome to Alcatraz South," she said as she stepped aside and allowed a full view into the basement. She moved quickly to the L bend and then vanished. Dean, looking at the strange equipment mostly covered by drop cloths, followed nervously. It reminded him of the old Universal film *Frankenstein*.

He stopped when he saw Gloria standing at the bend in the room with a large smile on her gorgeous face. Dean admired her momentarily until he saw what she intended for him to see.

The vault was as large and impressive as she'd said it would be. The lines running to it had deteriorated through the four years the lab had been shut down, but the tanks sitting atop looked new.

"This is the prison cell that holds the mysteries of life," Gloria said, smiling widely as Dean's silence told volumes about his amazement.

He gaped as he took in the tiled floor, the stainless steel desks, and the vault that dominated the room. Along the walls were many pieces of scientific equipment he had never seen before, all covered in a thick coat of dust. Oscilloscopes, x-ray machines, and other systems he could never identify until he saw them on television years later. Gloria left him standing with his mouth agape and returned to the large steel door. She closed it and stepped back until she heard a familiar hissing of air.

Beyond the bend in the room, Dean felt the pressure in his ears increase and then relax once the seal was made when Gloria started the air pumps in the back. The room, as she had claimed, was now completely soundproof to the outside world. She returned to Dean.

"What in the hell are our fathers up to placing this thing down here?" he asked as he moved ever closer to the giant stainless steel vault. "This is what they and that Nazi doctor were hiding?"

The vault was dead center of the back portion of the immense basement. It was a twenty-by-twenty-seven-foot rectangle and was reminiscent of a shoe box made of thick, hardened stainless steel. This advanced research lab was hidden from the small town and its occupants.

"I take it that your report would have centered around that thing? What's in there?" he asked nervously as Gloria rejoined him. Dean looked down at the girl he had gone through the last four years of school with but had never exchanged two words with before last Friday's afternoon class.

"Not riches, not gold, not the nuclear launch codes for the president to use against Nikita."

"Then what?" he persisted as he took in the vault and its sliding windows covered in darker, thicker steel.

"Look, do you want to see this or not?"

Dean looked from the vault to an angry Gloria. "Yes, but you do know that this has little to do with a school report now, don't you? I hate to break it to you, but this jive stuff is not right. We're into some serious trouble."

"Maybe I never really intended this to be written down in a school report. Maybe I just wanted to tell someone, anyone. Then you came along. Who better to tell than the son of the man responsible for placing it here?"

"May I remind you that my father wasn't the only one to hide this thing down here. Your dad isn't exactly above all of this."

"I didn't know that for sure until today." She bit her lip and angrily shook her head. "No, that's a lie; I knew it all along. You're right; they are all involved, and we probably *are* in some serious trouble."

Gloria felt her way to a dark corner where he couldn't see what she was doing. He heard her shuffling things around, and a moment later, she reappeared with a small box. He watched her place it on the floor at the vault's giant door. She placed a hand on the cold steel and patted it lovingly as she opened the top of the small portable phonograph.

"Oh, are we going to listen to records now, just the two of us? I think the kids in school will gossip about this."

"Look, I'm sorry for acting like a bitch to you, but please don't insult my intelligence by declaring undying love. I don't like being hurt."

Dean stepped up to her and gently touched her shoulder. As she stood, he kissed her. Gloria remained frozen as he stepped back. Then she reached out and pulled him close, and they kissed deeply. They finally parted.

"By the way, if you're lying to me, I'll haunt you for the rest of your life."

"Deal," he said with a winning smile. His stomach did backflips as Gloria knelt beside the small black box. "I doubt there's anything in there that will save us from our fathers' wrath."

"Oh, ye fools of limited imagination," she said mockingly. She cranked the handle on the small phonograph, winding the interior spring. "I started with a battery-operated player, but I was going through batteries until my dad thought evil things about me." She giggled, and Dean didn't understand her advanced and bawdy humor. He was starting to believe he knew nothing about this girl until his mouth fell open as he finally caught the joke, smiling despite his growing concern at the way she spoke outside of the classroom.

The seventeen-year-old senior hesitated before lifting the needle to the spinning record and looked up. Her face was magical to Dean. It was as if he were seeing her for the first time in clear daylight. Gloria was one of the most beautiful things he had ever seen. His buddies in school would never believe it, even after he beat the crap out of them that very morning. They had never seen beyond her walking cane and dark glasses before this week had started. He cursed the wasted years.

She went to the facing of the vault and placed a hand on the cold exterior just below the large combination tumbler lock at its center. Dean watched as she leaned her cheek to the door and, with a hand splayed lovingly on its surface, proceeded to scare the hell out of him. "Alley?" she said in a normal tone of voice.

"Alley?" Dean said curiously.

"Yeah, Alley Oop. That's not its name, but I get the impression its very, very large, so maybe it's a caveman. Who knows? I just call it Alley Oop. Sometimes it speaks as one person, and other times many of them. Maybe as many voices as twenty or more. I can never be sure. When it's angry or put out, it's always one person. When calm, many. At least that's what I think."

Dean just pursed his lips, silently admitting to himself that little

Gloria might be nuts. Beautiful, but very much off her rocker. He still smiled at her as though he had never seen such beauty before.

"If we could have understood what was written in that journal, we wouldn't be guessing at what it is; we would *know*," she said.

"Let's just hope that damn ticket seller doesn't find it before we get it back."

"It'll be safe. It's under the ticket machine."

Dean watched the vault's facing. "Maybe your friend, or friends, aren't home tonight."

"Alley, come on. We have someone here who wants to meet you."

Dean shifted from foot to foot as he thought about what could be inside. "Uh, I don't know if I do. Don't you need air in those things in order to, like . . . breathe?"

A curious look came over Gloria's features. "For people, yeah," she said in her irritatingly smug tone. "Alley?"

"For people?" he asked nervously.

Frustrated, Gloria returned to the small record player fronting the vault's giant door. Gloria lowered the old-fashioned needle to the spinning forty-five vinyl record. "Can't Help Falling in Love" by Elvis began playing. Dean's brows rose as he watched the strange events unfolding before him. He involuntarily took a step back, his black tennis shoes squeaking as he moved. Gloria ignored Dean's fear and went to the vault's door once more.

"I bought this for you. I thought you might like it," she said, fogging the stainless steel door as she spoke. The song droned on, and Gloria felt her face flush somewhat. "Come on, Alley." She half turned toward a wide-eyed and fearful Dean. "Believe me, he doesn't bite. He's a spoiled jerk for the most part, and he's mean at times, but when you get to know him, he's—" She again faltered. "Well, he's not like his daddy. I kind of like him."

Dean was about to say something when a loud and very clear thump sounded through the steel door. It was loud enough that Gloria pulled back and looked at the vault with her unseeing eyes.

"It doesn't care for your father—or mine, for that matter. It expresses itself like that. I don't think it's a friendly sort of acknowledgment."

"Look, Gloria, I don't know what's in there, but nothing can live in a sealed vault," he said, trying hard not to doubt her.

The song on the record player finished, and Gloria gave her school-mate a look that said he needed to be a little more open-minded.

"I never said it was alive, did I?"

"You have to be nuts to think that."

"I've been coming here secretly since 1958. Believe me, Mr. Skeptical, it's in there." She again leaned into the door and listened. Dean knew that it would be impossible to hear a voice or anything else on the other side of ten inches of stainless steel.

"Gloria, listen to yourself; you're talking to an empty box. Not only that, but you're admitting to talking to it since 1958. People will think you've gone on the long sea cruise to insanity."

Gloria pulled her ear away from the vault and looked toward Dean blindly through her dark glasses. Her confident look faltered for the first time.

The boy saw the hurt look. "Hey, I didn't mean that, but there has to be some other logical explanation for what's really in there." He stepped tentatively forward and took her small hand. "Sorry."

"It's in there," she insisted as Dean hugged her.

Neither one of them noticed the bright fluorescent lights overhead dim when they made contact. Gloria leaned into Dean and felt his warmth and even his fast-beating heart.

"This whole thing about the report was to prove to myself that I'm not insane."

Before he realized what he was doing, he kissed her. Gloria's stomach was doing backflips as he very reluctantly parted their embrace. She knew that the two were meant for this. She also knew that she had fallen hard for him.

Dean swallowed as he took in Gloria. She was standing still, unmoving, unseeing. She closed her eyes behind her dark glasses as she took a step back. Her hands tried to find a chair, but instead her left foot hit the phonograph. The needle jumped, and the turntable turned and Elvis picked up in mid-song as Dean reached out and caught her. He was just pulling her toward him to kiss her again to take the subject as far away from the strange basement as he could when the vault door rattled in its airtight frame. Both he and Gloria jumped and stared at the vault. Dean placed his arm around her shoulders as another loud bang sounded from the vault's interior. This time, the combination dial spun and then flew off the center of the door and rang sharply off one of the steel tables. They both jumped again as this time the door bent outward.

"You don't think Alley's the jealous type, do you?" Dean said as Gloria became frightened for the first time since starting her sojourns to the old winery years before when she was twelve.

"I don't . . . this has never happened before," she said.

They waited for the action to continue, but the vault and its internal activity ceased. Dean held Gloria tighter.

"The fools did not believe me. I knew you were the key, but they refused to listen."

Dean and Gloria felt their blood go cold as they turned to face the German-accented voice. The man was wearing a black trench coat, and he was just removing the wet fedora with his free hand. In the other, he held a Colt .45 semiautomatic aimed at the two.

"Whoa," Dean said as he maneuvered Gloria behind him. "Why the gun, Pops?"

He felt Gloria stiffen behind him.

The old man looked from the two teenagers to the gun he held. "Yes, rather dramatic, I know, but there are certain men in this town that would like to do me harm. They have tried before, you know? Therefore, the gun."

"Dr. Fromm?" Gloria said as she tried to step from behind Dean, but he held his ground and kept her at bay.

"Yes, I am he. I also know you, my dear. I've watched you for four long years." He kept the gun pointed their way as he moved to a small box on the side of the vault. With darting, nervous looks toward the two startled teens, he lifted a small hatch, and then a roll of paper fell free. He tore it away, making sure his gun hand never wavered. He smiled as he studied the readout.

"Man, you want to lower that gun? You're scaring the girl," Dean said with as much bravado as he could muster.

Dr. Jürgen Fromm smiled again, the bright fluorescents flashing off his gold bridgework. Dean envisioned the creep in a Nazi uniform or at least the evil white coat seen in movies.

"You stand only feet away from the greatest discovery in world history, something that, if loose, could devastate any enemy on the planet, and you're afraid of a little gun?" He laughed aloud. "This graph says that for the four hundred and thirty-sixth time, our little blind girl has received a reaction from the interior—an accomplishment we have not been able to achieve since we moved operations from Europe. I must know what attracts them to you."

Gloria wouldn't be held back any longer. She removed Dean's restraining hand and then faced the doctor.

"You say *they*? There is more than one, isn't there?"

Dean did his best to concentrate on the gun aimed their way and consider how he could get them out of there without getting shot like Liberty Valance.

"Oh, yes, my dear, more than one indeed. There are twenty-seven, to be exact."

"Then why do I get the feeling there is only one most times?"

"They are stronger together. I documented this many years ago, back when they were active for us. When they are frightened or angry, they come together as one. Very powerful." Fromm became thoughtful. "It all started out as a high-altitude experiment, you see." The gun moved right along with Fromm as he walked toward a control panel.

"High altitude? What in the hell is that?" Dean asked as he continually watched the man before him, awaiting an opportunity.

"The Luftwaffe, or what you would know as the German Air Force, financed my work in the hopes of fighting off high-altitude disorientation for their bomber and fighter pilots. Two groups of subjects in the final test—that's what is in there, young lady." He flipped a switch on the control panel, and the sliding door on the farthest end of the vault opened with a soft hum. He kept the gun on them and then waved it toward the vault. "You can see the results of high-altitude sickness inside section two."

Gloria turned her head and for the first time was nearly grateful for being blind. She nodded at Dean, who stepped up to the vault and climbed a small boxlike step and looked inside just as Fromm turned on the interior light. He fell back so hard that he stumbled and crashed to the floor. He couldn't catch his breath as Gloria reached for him in the darkness of her world.

"Hard at first, is it not? But necessary."

Gloria ignored Fromm's words as she tried and failed to lift Dean from where he sat trying to catch his breath. Finally, he managed it, and his anger showed on his face as Fromm again smiled.

"You're a butcher!" Dean finally managed.

"No, no, no, my American friend; I'm a creator. There were only butchers in camps that killed for no gain. This"—he patted the steel vault lovingly—"is for science and knowledge, not the slaughter of life for no other reason than to kill over prejudice. Science is exacting and has no room for emotion. No, not a butcher, but a creator of life. That in there is life."

"All I see are dead people," Dean said as he began to lose the cool demeanor that he had practiced over many years.

Gloria straightened. The look was directed at Fromm. "Bodies?"

Dean finally managed to stand on shaking legs. This was not how he saw his Halloween night unfolding.

"Yes, bodies. These subjects were older. They were the parents of section B. In a chance experiment before shutting down the project near the war's end, we decided to induce stress on the last test. We filled one compartment with parents of . . . of—"

"Jews," Gloria said angrily.

"No, not at all. As I said, young lady, it doesn't matter the test materials; it only has to do with the results. Purely by accident, but we most assuredly had results. No, not Jews, but families taken in whole from the cities of Czechoslovakia and Yugoslavia, minor folk who would never be missed. We didn't need Jews, whose fear of death was muted by their treatment and also their knowing that death was as eventual to their kind as the rising of the sun. Their complacency would have skewed the results. No, just families."

"What did you do?" Gloria asked with tears welling up under her glasses.

Fromm hit a second switch, and the gentle hum of a motor returned. This time, a small view port at the front side corner opened. Dean could see the light from inside. He watched Gloria and knew he had to finish this thing. He stepped quickly to the metal step and peered inside. His hand went to his mouth, and then he quickly leaned over, dry-heaved, and stumbled free of the step and rested his head on Gloria's shoulder, trying to stop from shaking with fear and loathing at what Fromm and his Nazi backers had done.

"What's in there?" Gloria asked with a whisper.

Dean finally got his breathing under control. He swiped at a tear in his eye and faced Dr. Jürgen Fromm.

"You sick bastard. What did you do?"

Fromm reached out and flipped both switches, and then the two viewing ports closed.

"Dean, what have I been talking to in there?" she asked, not knowing if she wanted to really know.

"Children, a lot of them. All dead, decayed." His lips trembled. "They look as if they tried to claw their way through solid steel. I saw small scratches in the steel where they tried to get out."

"As I said, twenty-seven, to be exact."

"Why?" Gloria asked as she took Dean into her arms.

"As I said, the discovery was all an accident. To place maximum stress on the test subjects, we had seventeen families, some with one or two children at prepubescent age. At seventy-two thousand feet, the parents, inside section A, were deprived of oxygen, and if you don't know the pain involved, I can assure you it is extreme. During this process, we wanted to see what the stress level was on younger subjects at altitude, so we opened the main viewing port between sections A and sections B housing the children. As their parents in the next room fought for life, dying in the most horrid way you can imagine, the children were witness as their own oxygen depletion was started. Can you imagine the horror a child faces when watching a parent fight for life? Then that terror turned to pain and agony for themselves. The emotion inside these compartments caused a most unusual result. While the parents inside died, the children fought— oh, how they fought to live. We observed not fear in the end but pure hatred—hatred in its purest form. Rage. Magnificent rage." He gently tossed Dean a pair of heavy, bulky glasses and then threw the switch for section B once more. He adjusted the light setting and gestured for Dean to place the glasses on. He did. "Now see the result your fathers saw in 1945."

Dean stepped onto the steel step and, with a nervous look back at Gloria, he looked inside the dark compartment.

The green-tinted images were all staring at him as he looked inside. Their eyes were dark and their clothing ragged. The ghostly images stood near their physical bodies where they had fallen in agonizing death throes, their greenish skin riddled with pressure breaks in the arms and legs. Their faces were stretched and hung loose on the nearly invisible frames. Still, they watched Dean as if they were curious as to his intent. He removed the glasses and then threw them at Fromm, who simply moved out of the way as they flew by him and hit the control panel. Several lights went off as the glasses broke against the steel.

"You created ghosts?" he said as he once more placed a protective arm over Gloria.

"A remarkable feat. Accidental, mind you, but very satisfying." Fromm moved away from the control panel, but the gun never left the area of Dean's belly. "Can you imagine terror so complete, hatred so palpable that the spirit refuses to die? The anger that has the power to manifest in a physical form? Needless to say, your army wasn't that hard to impress; they saw remarkable prospects for a weapon that could infiltrate an enemy stronghold without notice. No, your fathers were quite impressed with my work."

"What went wrong?' Gloria asked as she took Dean's hand and held it tightly.

A saddened look came to Fromm's face. "They ceased their activity five days after transferring the vaults from Eastern Europe. There wasn't one documented case of spiritual activity at all. Until you," he said as she took several steps toward Gloria. "You are the key, as demonstrated tonight. They have an affection for you. They react. Now you will demonstrate what you do for your fathers so I can get my project back. It took me four years to get to this point. The federal authorities finally believe I am dead, and for the first time since they tried to eliminate me, I am here, and now they will see I was right."

"That day four years ago, when you caught me down here, that was the day Dean's father shut you down, isn't it?"

"Yes, after your father, Captain Perry, forced him to. But that was also the very day you initiated contact with my children. Now with my journals and with your demonstration, we can move forward with my children."

"You have no right to call them that," Gloria said angrily.

"I have every right!" he screamed, and Dean pulled Gloria away. Fromm stepped forward and without warning hit Dean in the head. As he collapsed, Fromm placed the .45's barrel against the back of Dean's skull. "Now we will have cooperation when your fathers arrive, or our little spoiled friend here gets a bullet. Do we understand each other, Gloria?"

When she glared up with hatred behind her dark glasses, Fromm became unhinged and slapped her across the face with his free hand. She didn't cry out, but Dean made to attack as his vision returned from the blow he had received. Fromm once more hit Dean as he dove and missed. Dean sprawled on the cold floor as Gloria crawled to him.

"I asked if we understood each other."

"You son of a bitch, leave him alone!" she said as she threw her body over Dean's.

Jürgen Fromm began advancing on the two intruders when he saw something that froze him in place. Silver-colored fluid was spewing all over the top of the vault. The main lines of mercury had been closed, and the pressure behind them exploded into them. The change was so sudden, the old steel-reinforced hoses gave way. Mercury went in all directions as Fromm panicked. He looked around him and then saw what had happened. When Dean threw his glasses at him, they had missed and struck the purge switch for the mercury containment system.

"My God!" he cried as he ran to the console to reengage the lines, but it was to no avail.

"What is that?" Gloria screamed over the noise of the escaping mercury.

"It's the only thing that keeps my children at bay. Mercury is a natural defense against their force. It will eat them away if they touch it. Even being near it makes them weak!"

The ten-inch-thick vault door suddenly bent in its reinforced frame. This time, a weld broke somewhere with the sound of a shotgun blast. Dean and Gloria backed away on the floor toward the door leading to the outer room.

"Jesus, we're all alone here," Dean said. "Everyone's either at the plant working their second shift or at Newberry's or the spook show at the Grenada. Fromm, do something! Get Gloria out of here."

Bang! The frame rattled again, and this time, they saw the upper-left corner of the vault being pushed outward. Dean saw the thickness of the steel as it was wrenched forward by something on the other side of the thick door.

"Alley, stop it!" Gloria shouted above the noise of escaping mercury and air and also of the horrid wrenching of hardened steel.

"I don't think it wants to be in there anymore, Gloria, and frankly, I don't want to wait around to meet your buddy Alley." Dean stood with renewed strength and pulled Gloria to her feet. He turned and stared at Fromm, who still had the gun pointed their way. Then, as if he knew what was coming, Fromm turned from the startled teens and ran for the door.

Gloria spun on her saddle shoes and pulled Dean's hand as she turned for the inner door to the basement. The roar of a caged and enraged animal sounded as the bent section of steel thrust forward even more.

"Alley Oop is pissed!" Dean said as he and Gloria broke through the door and made for the stairs, close behind Fromm.

Behind them, they heard the ten-inch steel door explode outward and smash into and then through the reinforced inner wall of the basement.

Gloria and Dean knew beyond a shadow of a doubt that hell had just escaped from its confinement and wanted to avenge a brutality that had occurred during a distant war.

John wanted to stay and see the entity. He found he had less control of what he saw. Even though the entity had been explained by the nutcase Fromm, John was not at all convinced that this threat was the only one the Dean of the future faced. He felt his body was being dragged through the lower basement just as the entity made its first appearance. Now he knew the importance of mercury to the town of Moreno; it was meant to protect, and that was the reason for the abnormal amount the factory went through. It was for electrical fencing that enclosed a nightmare. His body was now flying past the laboratory at great speed as events started to pick up.

Behind him, the entity was free and was now roaring its pleasure. The old winery shook, and pieces fell from the ancient adobe walls and ceiling.

Halloween was now rockin' and rollin'.

22

Gabriel tried to get some light onto the second floor, but every time someone lit a match or flicked a lighter, the flame would just die as if the oxygen were being sucked out of the room. Damian stood apart from everyone to keep an eye on the street below. Thus far, he had counted twenty-seven children ranging in age from a few years old to twelve or maybe thirteen. Their black eyes never left the second floor of Newberry's.

The statement Harvey and Casper had made earlier about their sudden remembrance of the strange trick-or-treaters that night in 1962 played heavily on all their minds. For Damian, this was a far worse scenario than even Summer Place had been. At least there, it was confined to a house; here, it spanned not only time but had conquered an entire town. He wiped away some condensation from the window and peered into the night, trying to see if the agents that had been trapped inside the telephone exchange had made any progress in escaping. He saw the same frightened faces as they too watched the strange crowd of children.

The lights inside Moreno were restricted to the buildings in the downtown area now. No longer were the lights shining inside the old tract homes that circled Moreno. The old and fallen marquee of the Grenada Theater that lay in a heap near the sidewalk was flashing her brightly colored neon as if the old girl was showing her best films from a bygone era.

"Are you thinking what I'm thinking?"

Startled, Damian took a deep breath. He shook his head as Gabriel stepped up to the window. The dark eyes of the children adjusted to him.

"My thought processes abandoned me right around the time we lost George," he said as he again faced the window.

"I mean the theater. Did you notice anything in the past hour?"

Damian turned his head and tried his best to peer down the street toward the Grenada. Thus far it had only been the flashing of her neon that could be discerned. The rain and lightning didn't help him any.

"I only noticed because the only thing of the Grenada we could see from this floor was the remains of part of the marquee that lay on the sidewalk. Remember when we toured this town we had to step over the debris to move down the street? Now that debris is gone."

"What are you saying?" the former state police detective asked.

"Don't try to see the theater from here; just look across the street at the building there. I think it's the old TG&Y Dollar store. The reflection, see it?"

Damian adjusted his view and then froze. *What the fuck?* he thought. The marquee was fully functional and back in its original place atop the theater entrance. Damian could even see the AIR-CONDITIONED FOR YOUR COMFORT banner flapping in the storm. The box office, at least from their poor vantage point, looked new and open for business. Harvey Leach joined them at the window to report that all attempts to get light had failed. Damian pointed out what they had discovered. Harvey's face went slack. The bright plastic magnetic lettering was plain to see and read even through the thick rainfall.

"Goddamn Vincent Price," he said as he quickly stepped away from the window.

Gabriel saw the terror in his eyes and reached out to steady the old man. "Hey, take it easy," he said as he became worried about a possible heart attack.

"My pa let me out of work early. I waited in line to see them movies, but I went more for the same reasons we all did back then. The girls would be there. I wish I had worked that night." He left the two men standing there as he walked away and sat heavily into a chair next to John Lonetree. Jennifer was there and took pity on the old guy and handed him a bottle of whiskey. Casper came to offer him a glass. Harvey waved away the glass, taking a long pull from the bottle.

Gabriel turned to face Damian. "That theater is a key part in all of this. The heaviest death toll outside of the factory explosion was right there, at least a full mile from the plant. The same goes for the Bottom Dollar. Exploding mercury covered most of the town, but only the theater and the bar were directly destroyed by it. There has to be a reason for it."

"What are you suggesting?" Damian asked worriedly.

Gabriel smiled. "I'm suggesting we go and see what in the hell is so important about those locations."

"What's this *we* stuff, Bwana?" said Jackson only half jokingly. "In case you haven't noticed, it looks like we have the cast of *Children of the Corn* out there."

"Yeah, but they haven't moved since they killed those two agents. If we wait too long, the rest of the rescue team may come back and walk right into this nightmare with no warning."

"You know they are just feds, right?"

Gabriel smiled as he realized Damian agreed that they had to go. He always joked when he was scared.

Outside, the lightning flashed, and Gabriel noticed that half the children had vanished while they had been talking. He decided to keep his observation to himself for the sake of Damian's piece of mind.

In the darkness of the room, they heard John's voice for the first time since he went under with the powerful dose of the Demerol kicker. The single word did nothing for anyone's confidence as his deep voice cried out. The whiskey bottle slipped from Harvey's hand and crashed to the floor.

"*Run!*"

The single word echoed in the nearly empty space of the second floor.

As they hit the steel doorway, Dean froze when the handle refused to turn, and then he let out a girlish yelp when the handle was suddenly pulled from his hands. Gloria clung to Dean as they came face-to-face with the two security men who had come to investigate the horrific sounds coming from a supposedly soundproof basement. The roar of something not of this world sounded behind them. This spurred Dean forward, crashing into the first guard and knocking him into the second. Both men went down.

"Come on!" Dean said as he pulled a stunned and frightened Gloria forward on and over the two downed men. Still, Gloria shouted for Alley Oop to stop behaving like it was. Dean tried to set her straight as they made the staircase. "I don't think your friend in there is what you think it is."

As they went up the steep stairs, they heard the security men gaining their feet. One was in pursuit, and the other was left to face Alley Oop all on his own. The security men were told many years ago that the thing they had been guarding was long since gone from this ancient wreck of a mission and its adjoining winery.

"Hey, you two!" the first security man shouted as Gloria and Dean gained the upper level of the staircase.

The second security man was almost to his feet when a sudden stench blasted into his nostrils. It was if he had entered an old and filthy slaughterhouse. The entity consisting of swirling dust and moisture from the damp and filthy basement stood before him, coalescing into an almost solid form and then breaking apart as if the strength to hold the vision together was too much to maintain. The blackness shed a shiny material from its form, and then the image reconstituted itself once more, gaining strength every time the mercury was dispersed.

The security guard's eyes widened in shock as the breathing came unbidden into his ears. His heart was beating so fast that he was surprised he could hear any external noise at all. He had been through the invasion of Saipan as a younger man, so he very much knew what fear was, but this thing standing over him was something altogether different. It wasn't of this world. The man tried to scramble back on his haunches, but he immediately saw and then felt the enormous foot come down on his lower half. His eyes widened, and his pain sensors shut down as he watched everything from his hips to his ankles condense as the weight of three elephants came down to stay his retreat. The man couldn't even scream as the swirling blackness momentarily took full form. The security guard's heart exploded in his chest as the entity casually stepped over his thrashing form and took the steps, bending and grinding them as it moved upward toward freedom.

The beast was free for the first time in more than twelve years, and Gloria's childhood friend, comically nicknamed Alley Oop, was about to descend upon the small and unsuspecting town of Moreno, California.

The quest for vengeance from an artificially created entity was just beginning.

Frank saw the man again in his quest to find Gloria. This time, it was a fleeting glimpse. He saw the shadowlike form duck in between buildings, and he was sure that it was Fromm. Frank slammed on his brakes, and his Dodge pickup fishtailed and then came to a stop. He jumped from the truck and began the chase. The old man was swift. It was as if something from hell was on his tail. Perry lost him somewhere near Rackley's hardware store. He knew that Rackley's was the only store not open that night for the benefit of the trick-or-treaters. The old man who owned the store was the bah-humbug type who never participated in town functions and hated children as much as a commie hated Yankees.

Frank grew mindless with anger at Robert and himself for what was happening. He searched the alleyways and the rear of the store but finally gave up in frustration. He needed to find Gloria; he knew she was in trouble. As long as she was with Dean, he feared for her safety, because he wasn't exactly sure what the colonel was capable of to keep his little secrets. He ran back to his truck.

Dr. Fromm watched from behind a Dumpster as Perry roared off. With a tentative look around, he moved to the back of the hardware store. Using his elbow, he smashed the rear window and then braced himself for a ringing alarm to sound. He didn't know it, but old man Rackley was as cheap as he was hateful of all children. There was no alarm.

"I will make sure the world knows of what I have done. You won't be using its weakness to stop it."

As he unlocked the door by reaching in through the broken glass, Fromm found what he was looking for almost immediately. His smile grew as he saw the metal locker lining the far wall. The cabinet was well marked by bright red lettering. The lock that secured it was old and easily broken.

It warned that the metal cabinet contained construction explosives.

Fromm snarled in German, "You won't be able to hide or harm my children now, you bastards!"

Dean and Gloria had eased over the alley fence behind the Mighty-Fine Donut Shop and eased toward the street after their flight from the winery.

"What now?" Gloria asked.

"Whatever that Nazi creep invented is out here somewhere. You're friends with Alley Oop; you tell me."

"I didn't know what was inside there. It never once gave me pause not to be its friend. Until today, it had never done anything to scare me. It was always kind and gentle."

"Hey, take it easy." Dean looked around the dark alley and saw that thus far all the Halloween activity was still centered on Main Street. "Maybe if I had paid attention in life, you wouldn't have had to go seek monsters for friends."

Gloria laughed and grabbed her stomach.

"You know, now's not the time to go all Anthony Perkins on me."

Gloria finally got herself under control as she placed her small hand on Dean's chest to steady her shaking legs. "I'm sorry, but this is so damn

Twilight Zone that I expect Rod Serling to step out of the darkness and look into a camera and say, 'Submitted for your approval, the small town of Moreno, California, one quaint and full of charm, now the epitome of hell itself.'" She laughed again.

"*The Twilight Zone*? I knew you were strange," Dean said as he pulled off his leather-armed Chino letterman's jacket and then tugged at the remains of Gloria's sweater. "Here, try this on; people might get the wrong idea of me if they see you only half-dressed." He watched her as she tore away the last of the knitted green sweater. She eased her small arms into the jacket and pulled both sides together for Dean's warmth that still lingered in the jacket. She raised her head and then half smiled. It faltered and then she looked down at her muddy saddle shoes.

"Does this mean I'm your girl now, Rebel without a Cause?"

Dean smiled when he saw the embarrassment come to her face from the weakened light coming from the street. He knew the tradition in high school of giving your girlfriend your letterman's jacket and class ring, the latter of which would inevitably be wrapped in yarn, or maybe angora, if the love was that serious. He could see that Gloria had never expected to get either a jacket or a ring maybe in her entire life. The thought of her isolation and of basically being ignored by him and everyone else made him sad. He slowly reached out and took her into his arms, and she in turn buried her face into his white shirt, sobbing. He decided not to comment on it since she would only step back and try to punch his headlights out. He just held her and was happy for the respite of being chased by monsters and madmen. It was normal, and right now Dean and Gloria needed a lot of normal.

Finally, he parted and held her at arm's length. "Yes, you are my girl, at least until you murder me for being stupid or something. And by the way, Perry, I am now a Rebel *with* a Cause." They started for the street and as many people as they could get around. The noise of the Halloween festivities was a welcome one.

A quarter mile away, looking down from its high vantage point over Moreno, the darkness gathered its form. The image looked like a blur of deeper, sparkling blackness highlighted against a dark sky. With the lights of the town to guide it, the entity moved toward the activity below. Many small voices, jabbering excitedly, were barely audible as they moved down from the hills.

As John Lonetree watched, he felt his hold on the dreamwalk slipping. He was losing his ability to see into multiple memories from differing subjects. He tried to concentrate as he watched Dean and Gloria move toward Main Street. His attention was drawn to the speeding pickup he recognized from his walk that morning. It was Frank Perry, and his Dodge truck sped recklessly down Main Street, barely missing several onlookers and bystanders. He saw the pickup truck speed past the very alley that Dean and Gloria slowly stepped from, and the chief of police was right behind him. John closed his eyes and thought deeply about Frank. The next thing he knew, part of his mind came back to the two kids and the other half sped after Frank.

He had a feeling that everything he searched for was about to be uncovered.

Gloria's father knew after he had discovered the two dead guards that Dean and Gloria had been where they shouldn't have. He saw the mangled men— one at the bottom of the stairs inside the old winery, the other torn to pieces on the gravel drive—but the footprints in the soft mud concerned him even more than the bodies. He found two sets of prints with a flashlight toward the back of the fencing that surrounded the winery and mission, and then a moment later, the one set of larger prints next to them. He knew without a doubt that Jürgen Fromm was definitely here in Moreno, and he knew about his daughter. He had a gut feeling that he knew where Fromm was going.

He had sent his pickup halfway onto the sidewalk and ran into the police station next to the courthouse and public buildings. He could only shake his head in anger when he found Chief Thomas sitting on an unmade bunk in the cell area. He released him and ordered the chief to go with him.

The truck once more slid into the parking area of Hadley Corp Gauge and Meter Company, screaming past the startled guard at the shack, even crashing through the yellow barrier gate that had never been raised. The police car was soon to follow, making the guard jump clear as its rear tires barely missed him.

Frank saw Robert's slim form stop and stare at him and the police chief as he walked toward his parked Cadillac. Perry slammed on his brakes, and the truck almost slid right into the black Caddy, making Hadley drop the case he was carrying and jump back, falling onto his expensively covered backside. Frank was out before the colonel picked himself up from the wet asphalt.

"I told you that son of a bitch was here!" Perry said as he took Hadley by the lapels and shook him. The colonel angrily tore Frank's hands away and looked from him to the chief of police.

"Did you see him, Chief?" Hadley asked Thomas as he came up to them, out of breath.

"No . . . I . . . uh—"

"No, he was too busy sitting in one of his own jail cells."

"Yeah, and I wouldn't have been there if it hadn't been for your two brats. Your son drew a gun on me!" he said, pointing a finger at his former commanding officer in the army.

"What are you talking about? You phoned me and said you had him in custody. Now you're saying Dean is out there somewhere?" Hadley said, fearful for his son and looking from the chief to Perry. He knew the captain was telling the truth. Fromm was here; his gut told him so. Now all he could think of was his son running into that crazed doctor. "Come on," he said to both men. "If that bastard's out for revenge against us—or me— there's only one place he can exact it, and that's right here. He could poison half the hills in the valley if he wanted to."

"I knew when we shut down Operation Necromancer we should have had all that mercury trucked out of here, but you were too cheap! You wanted to keep it on hand!" Thomas said in anger. "We've been following your orders for so long we have become blinded by your bullshit! We should never have—"

The slap across the chief's face stopped him cold. "If you had done that, you wouldn't be sitting pretty on that little nest egg I gave you. Now shut the hell up and earn your bloated paycheck for a change!" Hadley said, spittle flying from his mouth. He turned and started for the double doors of the plant.

Frank grabbed him, stopping him cold in his tracks. "Don't you want the rest of the good news, you son of a bitch?"

"What are you talking about?" Robert said, shaking Perry's hand off his arm.

"It seems the crazed little butcher wasn't lying; those things inside that cursed vault are still viable!"

"You're insane!" Hadley stepped back from an insane-looking Frank Perry, the man who had been against their grandiose plan since they first discovered Fromm in 1945. "The last activity recorded from the vault was in April of 1947. Those things are long dead, or deader, however you want to look at it."

"You think this is a joke?" Perry said, taking a menacing step toward his former commander.

"Then the two dead security men inside the winery, they just were torn apart by Fromm. And I mean *torn apart*!" Frank tried to regain some calm. He placed his hands on his hips and looked at Hadley. "That thing is after our kids!"

This seemed to have the desired effect on Robert. He froze as he tried to see the lie in Perry's statement. It wasn't a lie—just cold truth.

"You'd better hope that thing hasn't grown immune to mercury, because if I estimate its size correctly, it could take all forty-five hundred gallons we have on hand to stop it." Hadley swiped angrily at the blood coursing from his nose, he was grabbed again by Frank and turned him so he could see down the hill. He gestured to the bright lights beyond. "That nightmare you brought here has only one place to go, and that's right down there!"

This time, Hadley did move. He started running for the plant's front doors and the monster-killing mercury stored there.

In the darkness and without being able to warn anyone, John Lonetree saw the dark form of a man enter the back through the loading dock area.

Gloria clung tightly to Dean's arm as they stayed on the opposite side of the street from the Grenada Theater. They paused by the brightly illuminated window of the doughnut shop as kids came out in full costume with freshly baked goodies. Dean pulled Gloria close to him, and they tried to look as normal as they could. Still, they garnered enough stares that they knew they must look a sight. Gloria never felt more helpless in her life, not knowing what was happening around her. She had always been hesitant to depend on anyone outside of her father. Now she relied on Dean, a boy who had never paid her any mind, for protection.

"Music is everywhere," she said as she brought a hand up to her ear and pressed.

"Freekin' Rowdy Rhoads is right across the street, broadcasting live. Everyone has their radios on. It just seems loud." He held her tighter. "Come on; the line at the Grenada is gone," he said as he watched the area across the street closely, making sure Chief Thomas wasn't lurking nearby. "I'd feel safer over there and farther from what's behind us. Maybe it will stay away from this many people."

Dean saw a break in traffic and then eased Gloria into the crosswalk with about thirteen children and their escorting parents. A little girl of about ten looked up at the disheveled teens. She wore a Sleeping Beauty costume, one of those cheaply made sets that came complete with a plastic mask that had the creepiest eyeholes Dean had ever seen. As they moved slowly across the street, another child came up from behind and took Dean by his free hand. He stopped when the smell hit him. Gloria stopped with him and tilted her head.

"What's wrong?" she asked, not liking the fact that she felt the traffic all around her.

The small child who grabbed Dean's hand smiled up at him. He quickly shook his hand free and grabbed Gloria and stared at the kid. It was dressed in a ragged bag of a smelly dress, and her head was shaved. It was cut to the extreme so much so that he could see the scars from where she had been nicked by whatever it had been to cut her hair. It was the eyes. They were blank and dark. He couldn't see any pupils, only blackness. The child had no shoes, and her skin was whitish in color. Her teeth were broken, and her nails were gone. She smiled up at him again right there in the middle of the crosswalk as drivers honked horns at the slow-moving teens and the children now gathering around them.

Dean didn't answer as he pulled Gloria away without saying anything. What good would it have done? He looked back and then slowed as he saw that the child was not there any longer. The crosswalk was clear.

A horn blared, and Dean looked up to see man leaning out of the window of his 1952 Chevy. "Get the hell out of the road, you little punk!" The car screeched and swerved but made it around the startled couple, who made it to the relative safety of the sidewalk. They tried their best to blend into the many trick-or-treaters on Main Street. He pulled Gloria into a small alcove in the jewelry store next to the theater. He took a deep breath and tried to get his heart rate under control.

"Are you going to tell me just what in the hell has you so scared, outside of something from *Forbidden Planet* chasing us?" Gloria asked.

"Nothing. I guess all these Halloween costumes are getting to me." He watched the kids as they walked by in front of them, searching for any more of the realistic ghoul makeup he had seen a moment earlier.

"One thing you should learn, Mr. Hadley—I can smell a lie a mile away."

"I'm just trying to think," he said to buy time.

"From the hills overlooking Moreno to the dairy cows in Chino, this is Freekin' Rowdy Rhoads coming to you live from Spooksville, USA."

The sounds were coming from radios the business owners had placed near their doorways so all who were partying that night could hear the live remote they had paid K-Rave for. Dean and Gloria stood motionless, tucked away in the alcove on that side of the street. The speakers on top of the K-Rave remote van pumped out the sounds of rock and roll for the men, women, and children strolling the streets looking for treats. Dean saw Freekin' Rowdy look once more their way.

"Now here's one dedicated to Dean and Gloria, who have had the day of days in Moreno. This is for you, my haggard friends—Paul Anka from 1959, 'Puppy Love.'"

The song began, and Dean had the distinct feeling that everyone out that night was aware of what Dean and Gloria had been doing. He held her close as the song played and Freekin' Rowdy smiled at them.

"He plays the best music, but that man can be so irritating," Gloria said as she embraced Dean even tighter just as the second refrain from the Paul Anka hit began.

And they called it puppy love . . . Just because we're seventeen . . . tell them all, oh please tell them . . . it isn't fair to take away my only dream . . .

Freekin' Rowdy smiled even wider as Roberta handed him a cup of whiskey-spiked coffee. The smile remained even as Dean shot him the bird.

"We have to get off the street," Dean said even as his eyes remained fixed on Freekin' Rowdy.

"Where are we going? We can't even get the journal until they close up the box office. Without that, no one will believe us." Gloria swiped at a tear and turned away angrily. She was feeling far more helpless than she ever had just being blind. She was scared.

Dean held her and felt horrible seeing her only vulnerable moment. It brought out something inside him he hadn't even known existed. He felt empathy for Gloria . . . and also love.

"Let's hang out inside the Grenada. There, at least, we can dodge someone who's looking for us, and we can get you cleaned up some. Right now, you look like something that washed up on the beach in a Frankie and Annette movie."

"Thanks a lot!" Gloria said, only half-angry as she realized she must look terrible.

Dean looked around and saw that there were still too many people nearby to move without being further noticed. He saw the same emaciated little girl he had a moment before. She stood across the street just in front of the doughnut shop, and she was looking right at them. He wanted to jump when he saw she was joined by more of the ragamuffin-looking children. They stood in a group, and he saw that he wasn't the only person seeing them. Parents with their children in hand walked past them with looks of bewilderment. Some of the mothers instinctively drew their kids closer to them as they tried to avoid the look and smell of the strange-looking children. He quickly counted six of them and then he saw twelve more coming down the same alley they had used earlier.

"Oh, shit," Dean said only loud enough that he thought wouldn't be heard, but of course Gloria had.

"What?" she asked, far louder than she had intended.

"Either someone brought in a busload of kids with the best costumes I've ever seen, or we have company fit for that nutcase Rod Serling you admire so much."

"Children?" she asked.

"Yeah, and I don't think they look that damn friendly."

His heart skipped for just about the nine hundredth time that day as he saw another group of the children enter Main Street from the side of the Pacific Bell telephone exchange.

"I think now is a good time to see how the Monster Mash is going."

"The spook show?" she asked as he pulled her along. "Oh, yes, that will settle our nerves."

The children of the dead flowed onto Main Street and moved into the crowds and the neighborhoods surrounding Moreno.

All Hallows' Eve was up and running at full power as the entity spread its wings.

23

Gabriel stood still with Damian close by his side as they stared out of the double doors of Newberry's. They watched as the children watched them. The tallest of these was a boy of near thirteen. He stood much taller than all the rest but looked far more disturbing. Both men noticed the fingers of both his hands were worn down to the last knuckle on each. Every time lightning flashed, the brutal fate of these children became apparent. Each was ragged in dress, and each had exaggerated features. They were more of a charcoal rendering of humans rather than flesh and bone. It was surreal to the point they thought they may be looking into the darkest depths of the darkest of minds. Damian was in line with this sentiment as he swallowed.

"Now we know what Edgar Allan Poe saw in his worst coked-out nightmares."

Gabriel could not agree more as he opened the door only to have the rushing wind snatch it from his grasp. The door rebounded so hard that it slammed into the sidewall and shattered. Both men jumped back. The children, however, never moved. The three agents watching from the Pacific Bell telephone exchange cringed and shook their heads, thinking these two men were nuts in braving the gathering of the dead waiting for them outside. Gabriel gathered himself and took a step into the stormy night.

They were inundated with rainwater as they tried in vain to shield their faces from the worst of the windblown storm. Gabe pointed to his left, and Damian nodded as he pulled out his nine-millimeter from its shoulder holster. He pulled up short and grabbed Gabe's arm, gesturing ahead of them. Standing in front of Red Goose Shoes was the tallest of the children, now across Eucalyptus Avenue, staring at them. As they watched, he raised his right hand and gestured at the two men as if telling them it was safe to cross. Kennedy started to move, but still Jackson's hand held him in check.

"Look," Jackson said before the wind and rain could snatch his words.

Far beyond the teenage entity was the brightly flashing marquee of the Grenada Theater. Gabe saw the strobe-light effect as the lines of neon swirled and eddied into curlicues and ribbons of light. The buildings next to it were in the same shape as they had been before. Each was still a wreck of disuse and ill repair. The only difference was the Grenada; it was brand new in appearance. As they studied the change in the atmosphere of Moreno, the blue banner that hung under the marquee announcing that the Grenada was AIR-CONDITIONED FOR YOUR COMFORT flapped in the heavy wind, popping every time the wind struck the hardest. It was like it was also indicating an invitation.

"Whoever is producing this one knows how to add the little effects that make it real, don't they?" Damian said, trying to joke his way to being brave.

"Well, feel like touring one of the great movie palaces of the past?" Kennedy shouted as he started walking across the street even as the federal agents trapped inside the phone exchange started pounding on their window to stop them. They froze when one of the smaller apparitions, a girl of about four years, turned and shook her head at them.

As the two men approached the cement fronting the theater, they saw the brightly lit pagoda-style box office. It was empty. The banner flapped as they drew closer, and the teenage entity stood there and pointed toward the eight-doored front entrance.

Chain lightning flashed brightly across the entire length of Moreno, making Gabriel and Damian duck. The rumble of thunder was immediate.

"The storm is breaking right over Moreno!" Gabe yelled as loudly as he could. "Come on, Damian! Let's at least get out of the rain!"

"If I ever hear anyone that starts out a story with 'It was a dark and stormy night,' I swear to God I'll shoot them right between the eyes."

Damian followed Gabriel, holding his fedora tightly to his head, and they ducked under the relative safety of the giant marquee. Kennedy looked back and saw that the entity had vanished. He chanced a look a block back and saw that all the children had gone. He looked both ways and saw the deserted town and its dilapidated buildings—like the caesura before the main musical act, the pause before the big reveal. This wasn't lost on either man. Gabriel thought the analogy would even have pleased Bobby Lee McKinnon.

He and Damian turned, and a quickly moving force slammed into them. The object hit so hard they thought they were under attack, and Damian, convinced at the very least that the creature from the Black Lagoon was at hand, managed to get a shot off. The assault quickly ended when Gabriel grabbed the offender.

"Goddamn it!" Damian said when he saw what was in Gabriel's hands.

"Nice shootin' there, Black Bart," Gabe said as he held the object up so Damian could see the still-smoking hole he had placed right into the chest of the life-sized cardboard cutout of John Wayne, a lobby advertisement for his 1962 African adventure film, *Hatari!* Gabriel shook his head and then laid it down on the indoor-outdoor carpet.

Damian had nothing to say; he shrugged and looked smug, proud that in his haste he was still able to shoot old John right in his chest.

"Let's go see if we're late for the coming attractions."

Damian followed Gabriel inside to the smell of freshly popped popcorn and the sound of a distant movie playing in the auditorium.

It was now showtime at the Grenada.

Freekin' Rowdy Rhoads stood in front of his step van and watched the kids and parents as they strolled by, all of them curious about the live remote. Freekin' Rowdy thought these rubes would be fascinated by cockroaches racing across a hot metal plate. This burg was anything but sophisticated. Roberta was handing out candy as the kids came up to the K-Rave live event. Freekin' returned to his small portable desk and the one turntable they had dedicated to this night. He started another record and watched it spin as he calculated the time he had for his intro into the song.

"From El Monte to Pomona, from Chino to San Berdoo, this is K-Rave 106.5 on your dial coming at you with fifteen thousand watts of ghoulish power. The festivities have just officially started in Moreno, and by the looks of it"—he watched as a small girl in a poor man's Depression-era raggedy dress walked by while looking at the gathering by the van—"we have a lot of out-of-towners on hand, so come and join the Halloween fun. After all, with the Soviets letting go of their dream of a Cuban missile base down the block from Miami Beach, why sit at home? Get out and live!" He looked up and saw Roberta handing a piece of candy to a child wearing the most disturbing Halloween makeup he had ever seen. He cringed as she looked back at him with wide eyes, took the candy with absolutely filthy hands, and silently walked away, joining the amazed pedestrians who stepped aside as she approached.

"Now here's an oldie but a goodie, a man who was in on the start of it all, Mr. Bill Haley and His Comets, let's 'Rock Around the Clock,' people!"

One, two, three o'clock, four o'clock rock . . . five, six, seven o'clock, eight o'clock rock . . . nine, ten, eleven o'clock, twelve o'clock rock . . . we're gonna rock around the clock tonight . . .

As Bill Haley played on, Rowdy failed to see the strangely dressed and filthy children as they emerged from the hidden alleyways of the town and roamed the streets in force.

"I don't know how much more excitement we can wring out of this," he said as she turned to face Roberta, who was still upset about the small girl from a moment before. She didn't say anything but grabbed the bottle of whiskey she had on hand for Freekin's coffee and took a long pull to the gasping horror of two passing women in tent-sized dresses.

Freekin' watched the strange children as they stepped past the box office and the sickened ticket seller and walked straight into the theater. He noticed Gloria and Dean as they ducked into the first-floor auditorium. His eyes went to the kids, who once inside just stood there in front of the snack bar, where fifty teenagers were trying their best to order snacks as the harried concession workers struggled to keep pace.

"Man, this weird shit really makes you homesick for Chicago. I always heard that Californians were really out there, but damn!" he said as he quickly snatched the bottle of Wild Turkey from Roberta while giving her a dirty look. He was about to drink when he saw a dark cloud seemingly pass before his eyes. Many of the children who had joined the crowds on the street had gone. The passing wind of the darkness indicated it was heading down Main Street toward the factory. Freekin' shook his head, turned his back to the onlookers, and took a long pull from the bottle.

The speakers atop the van blared out "Rock Around the Clock" as the streets filled with revelers and trick-or-treaters alike. Freekin' Rowdy let the image of the dark cloud fade from his mind as the warm whiskey absorbed all unwanted thoughts of dead-looking ragamuffins wandering the streets of Moreno.

The stab to the heart of Moreno would happen in exactly one hour.

That assault would result in fifty-five years of horror for one man and a night of death for others.

The Monster Mash of 1962 was about to begin.

Gloria held tightly onto Dean's arm as they stood near the twin doors just inside the first-floor auditorium. She felt the excitement coming from the two hundred teenagers here and the one hundred and fifty upstairs in the balcony. This was only the second time in her life she had been in a movie theater without her father there to describe in quiet whispers what was being shown on the screen. Now all she heard was the voice of Vincent Price welcoming his guests to the *House on Haunted Hill*. What she heard primarily was the noise from the audience. She realized few were actually watching the movie.

Dean was amazed at the number of cardboard popcorn boxes being thrown toward the screen. It reminded him of bats flying through a darkened cave. He saw many couples necking in the seats in front of them. He shuffled his feet and shook his head.

"Look, it's too crazy down here. Let's go to the balcony."

As they moved to the lobby and then toward the right-side winding staircase, Dean flinched at every dark shadow exposed by the brighter lighting from the concession area. He shook his head, unable to get the sight of what he had seen not only inside the strange vault but what came out of it. He half expected the black mass to be waiting at every turn they had made since escaping the winery. The prospect of running into that maniac Nazi doctor wasn't that far removed from his mind either. He was beginning to think that they could never get this done without some serious help. He knew asking his father was out of the question, but if he understood what he learned today, Frank Perry might be the key. All he knew was he was slowly losing his nerve and the reserve of bravery he had unleashed for Gloria's sake.

They climbed the stairs and passed one of the ushers, who gave them a wary look. His flashlight was held like some sort of talisman against the evils of teenagers. Dean spied two seats just below the projection booth. They finally made it after squeezing past two couples trying for the world record for necking.

They managed to get to their spot and they sat. Gloria leaned her head on Dean's shoulder, and after only a second's hesitation, he placed his arm around her. Dean was content with the silence as his eyes saw the film but his mind rejected all images except for the image of Gloria. He looked over and kissed the top of her head and wished he was with her for other reasons than what they were hiding out for. He wanted this to be a normal thing, not one that forced feelings from her. After all these years, the teenage boy realized he was afraid of rejection—rejection from real people, not those of his father's variety.

Dean was relaxed, and Gloria placed her arm across his chest. His eyes started to slowly close as he felt the touch of her hand. He closed his eyes. The excitement of the day had finally caught up with them. They held each other and dreamed of nothing more than this moment.

Steve Cole jabbed Jimmy Weller in the side and nodded to the back. Jimmy looked, and in the briefest moment when the light from the projector dimmed and the theater was near dark, he saw Dean and Gloria sitting about fifteen rows up. He sat back and smiled.

The children moved up both sides of the winding stairs. The kids in the lobby for the most part stopped their yelling and ordering their snacks when they saw the procession of six kids dressed in rotten rags and another six dressed the same move away from the lobby and start up the staircases. Their filthy appearance made for nervous laughter from some but silence from others. Then the spell broke, and the shouting for speed from the attendants began in earnest. They didn't want to miss the best parts of the movie.

The entity from the vault sensed that the only living person that had shown them kindness was in trouble. That, they wouldn't have.

John became confused as both scenes from the past played out in fantastic speed. What felt like hours was actually only twenty minutes to his sleeping mind on the second floor of Newberry's.

He felt the end was near for both the small town and his ability to see what the truth behind the disaster really was. He mentally tried to picture the factory on the hill. He was now high above the plant, looking down. He saw the town in the distance, and it was still brightly illuminated, the ant-like forms of its citizens still in plain view. Then he felt himself start to sink once more. Evidently, when Dean and Gloria had fallen asleep, he had lost his connection with one or the other. It was Gloria, he assumed. Now that he had temporarily separated himself from the two teens, he was able to control his other task better. He felt his body and soul streak back to the manufacturing plant.

Frank Perry and Robert Hadley went through the back way through the loading dock area, sending the security man to round up the employees and keep them on the first floor. They were now searching for Fromm all on their own.

Ever since the government had cut funding to the project back in 1958, the plant itself had become the real moneymaker for Hadley Corp. The mixing and manufacture of gauges and meters was nothing compared to the mining of one of the world's most expensive heavy metals—mercury. The second-shift employees, under the supervision of Casper Worthington's father, were all on break downstairs as Robert and Frank made their way to the second floor where the storage tanks were anchored to the concrete floor. Forty-five hundred gallons of mercury were stored there after mixing on the third floor above them.

They met the shift supervisor, Went Worthington, in his office, and Hadley ordered him to get everyone from the third and fourth floors down to the first until they found what they were looking for, which they didn't tell Worthington about. As soon as the supervisor did what he was supposed to do and all employees were cleared from the upper heavy metal floors, Frank saw the motivation in not explaining to Worthington they had a nut on the loose. The Colt .45 had come out of Hadley's pocket before Frank knew what was happening. The overhead lights flickered but then steadied. Perry was the only one to notice.

"You want me to turn my back to make it easier for you?" Perry asked.

"That's a little melodramatic, isn't it?" Hadley said as he moved past Perry and went to the supervisor's door.

Hadley raced through the door, and Frank felt foolish for thinking the absolute worst about his former colonel, although most times he did not deserve the benefit of the doubt.

As they commenced the search of the heavy metal floors, the sounds of the live remote filtered through the air. The employees had been following the Halloween activities they had been missing. Freekin' Rowdy Rhoads was his vintage self as Connie Francis serenaded the empty floors.

Perry froze when Hadley held a finger to his lips and came to a stop near the containment vessels where the mercury was stored. The bright yellow warnings were marked no less than fifty times on each stainless steel tank. When Frank reminded himself what their use had been originally for, he shuddered.

"So, for the second time, you seek to murder me?" Hadley turned, but before he could shoot the figure standing only twenty feet away, he saw the twin of his own weapon pointing at him and Frank. "Lower the weapon to the floor, Colonel, or I will take the extreme pleasure of shooting you in your face. And you, Captain Perry, can join him." The .45 waved Frank over near Hadley as the colonel lowered his own weapon. "And to kill me on this night of triumph?"

Frank looked from the barrel of the semiautomatic weapon to Hadley. "I told you that even if this man is insane, his experiment is still very active. Those things are loose down there, and our children are in the line of fire."

"Very good, Captain Perry, a true believer. You have seen the power that I have created, have you not?"

"I've seen the results, you madman," Perry said as he lowered his hands but raised them once more when Fromm raised his brows in an invitation for him to try something dramatic. "Now if you want credibility, you'll help us contain this thing before more people are hurt or killed."

"Contain it?" He laughed. "Fools, I'm out to free it. Acknowledgment of my breakthrough is now no longer viable. I will die here tonight if I have to. After all, I've been dead since that day in 1958 when you decided to kill me at the airport in Ontario. But when it comes to predicting violence, it is always good to have the German point of view. Isn't that right, Colonel Hadley? You have taken what I gave you and have become a very rich man, but rich for all the wrong reasons. This experiment would have achieved things no military in the world could have fathomed before 1943. Now the world will learn another way. When I am finished here and my creation is no longer in danger from this town, I will send my journal to the newspapers. I know my life is over, but my work will continue, gentlemen."

Hadley smiled as he lowered his hands, knowing Fromm wouldn't shoot him until he said all he had to say. He had seen the two fire extinguishers at Fromm's feet, and he guessed at their nature when he saw the silver mercury running from the hose of one of them.

"So, you came all the way to my business to steal fire extinguishers?" Hadley asked with a hint of a smile.

Fromm glanced down at his feet. "Oh, I think you know what I have planned, Colonel; you have that devious mind about you. I must have proof even if I am no longer alive to receive the credit. After my creation rips this town apart, I will then contain our little friends from the vault. I will produce my journal, and I will finally have the evidence to prove to the world that Operation Necromancer was the supreme achievement produced for the war on any side."

He saw the smile on Robert's lips, and then he became concerned.

"You stupid bastard," Robert said as he took an arrogant step forward. "The journal was stolen. I don't have it. Your plans for making true believers of the world will never fly with just your word, or even that of Captain Perry here, so you may as well leave that mercury here."

"Colonel, I will destroy your new town. I will take from you the riches you have gathered from the sweat of my brow. Well, that has already been taken care of, and no matter what you do to me or my children, your town dies. Produce my journal, and I will tell you how this will be achieved. If not"—the smile grew—"my killing will truly begin. As I said, my sweat, your money."

"You mean the sweat it took to kill all those innocent people?" Frank said, despised by both men.

"Yes, that is what I mean. Those that made my experiment work were never innocents, Captain Perry; they were bugs to be examined." He looked at a pocket watch he produced. "In about five minutes, other bugs will be exterminated."

"What do you mean by that?" Hadley asked, finally becoming concerned about Fromm's confident demeanor.

"You will find out soon. Now the *journal*!" The last word was shouted.

Hadley was about to laugh in the scientist's face once more when his jaw went slack. His eyes moved beyond Fromm to something behind him. The former colonel of the OSS and United States Army stepped back, as did Frank Perry.

"I guess we may owe you an apology, Doctor," Hadley said as the gun in Fromm's hand faltered.

Eight of the many children stood behind the German. Hadley could see that the dripping, leaking mercury from the two pressurized cans kept them at bay.

"It's too late, Fromm. Your children are here," Frank said as he took another step back as well.

Finally, Fromm turned and saw the children. They were as he always knew them to be. They were ghostly white, and they had no eyes except for the reflection of the orbs that no longer saw the light of the world, only its darkness. They were unmoving.

The gun lowered. "My children. You must leave now. Go with the rest," Fromm said. With his free hand, he felt behind him for the two fire extinguishers. His hand hit empty air, and as he turned, he saw Frank with both extinguishers. The shadows from battery-driven emergency lighting made the children even ghastlier than they were.

Jürgen Fromm raised the gun once more but froze in sudden shock as the bullet struck him in the chest, sending him reeling backward and straight into the arms of the waiting children, who fell upon him like a pack of crazed wolves.

Frank turned. "Come on! We can still get those things contained," he said as his eyes fell on the gun pointed his way.

The sound of Fromm being torn to pieces was sickening. He had stopped his screams, and there was now only a gurgling noise from the pile of blackness covering him.

Perry raised the rubber hose on one of the extinguishers and depressed the handle. A pure stream of silver fluid shot straight out and covered the children as they screamed as if burned. They diminished in size and shape. Still Frank held the handle down. Finally, the blackness covering Fromm lifted and vanished. The overhead lights flickered and then came back on. Frank faced Hadley once more. The brightness of the return of light was nearly blinding.

"Robert, our kids, the people in town, we have to get that mercury down there and contain this before the whole world knows what we've unleashed."

"No matter what, old friend, they will never know. And as for our children, yes, that is my intent. Place the extinguishers on the floor, please, and back away." The gun moved menacingly. Frank did as he was ordered. "All of this was started by your daughter trying to get her little hooks into my son. My son!" he said loudly, as if the mere thought of Gloria being with Dean sent the man into a rage. "My plans for him justify what I will do tonight. I would sacrifice this entire town for my boy."

"Robert, you're as insane as Fromm. His children, your children—what is the difference?" His foot hit the pile of mush that had been Fromm, and he stopped moving back. "If you try to hurt Gloria, there won't be a place on earth you can hide, you merciless son of a bitch."

"I know your dedication, Frank, my boy. That's why"—the explosion of the gun sent the bullet straight into Frank's stomach—"I have to do this."

Frank went down to one knee and looked up at Hadley. The second shot caught him in the forehead, and he rolled over on top of the remains of Jürgen Fromm.

Hadley gathered up both extinguishers, and he turned, he tripped over something. He straightened, cursed, and then left the floor, taking the route they had used to get there.

If he had taken a moment, he would have seen the wooden box he had tripped over had the words EXPLOSIVES written in bright red lettering. The remains of the detonation cord were lying next to it.

Somewhere inside the expansive area of Hadley Corp Gauge and Meter Company, forty sticks of high-grade dynamite were slowly burning down to nothing.

Outside, the clearing skies clouded over once more. The death shroud was ready to be laid.

24

Gabriel and Damian eased themselves past the ghostly lobby. The scene was perfect, a true blast from the past. The red carpet covering the floor was no longer burned and scorched; it was bright with newness. The smell of freshly popped popcorn wafted throughout the lobby, and they even heard the rumble of a movie deep inside the auditorium. Gabriel examined the area and froze, unsure how to proceed. He looked at the winding twin staircases to the right and to the left of the concession stand. He shook his head.

"Well, what now, Doc?" Damian asked, his gun pulled free of its holster.

"I don't know."

"Maybe they have an idea," Damian said as he gestured to his right.

Children stood at the bottom of the stairs and near two doors labeled MANAGER and STORAGE. The tall child they had seen before on the street in front of Newberry's was pointing at the left-side door they could see through a red curtain.

"Another basement?" Damian asked, his eyes on the skeletal child in rags. Its blackened eyes were unmoving, as were the nubs of his pointing fingers. "Why does it always have to be a dark and dank basement with you people?" Damian wanted to turn and leave, but Gabe held him in place.

"If they wanted us harmed, I have the feeling they wouldn't have to do it in a dark basement."

"Oh, that's a good theory. Did you ever hear the nursery rhyme about the spider and her parlor?"

"Come on. It's either the basement or the dark and stormy night outside."

"Right now, dark and stormy looks pretty damn good."

They moved toward the door marked STORAGE.

The lightning erupted outside, and the dark and stormy night became even more so. The story was drawing to a close, and as the famous song said, the still of the night was close at hand for Moreno.

Freekin' Rowdy Rhoads was tapped hard on the shoulder as he sat on the edge of the portable table. He shook himself and looked at Roberta, who was starting to rival Freekin' on the number of shots in disguise she could consume. After only a moment of dead air, Rhoads slid back into his chair and placed the headphones on. One earphone was on; the other momentarily covered his eyes and nose. He angrily adjusted them and then gave Roberta a dirty look, but she simply stared at him. Still, he hesitated again when he saw two small out-of-town girls, maybe five or six years old, slowly sidle up to the remote van and look at them. Their heads were also shaved, and Freekin' could see the gouges in their scalps where their last hairdresser or barber had viciously cut them. They held hands and stood as if waiting for something. Others walked past with their store-bought costumes on, but after a cursory glance at the children and the radio van, they quickly moved away.

"Man, these kids are really starting to get to me. Did you notice none of them are actually gathering candy?" he asked out of the side of his mouth even as he tried to smile at the smallest girl. She stared back with those disturbing pools of blackness.

"Damn it, Rowdy, you know you're on the air?" Roberta snapped, pointing at the expandable boom mic.

He shook himself again and forced his eyes away from the two children, wishing their parents would start rounding the little critters up. He quickly drained the last of the coffee-whiskey mixture.

"Okay, that was Chuck Berry, and this is K-Rave. Now let's go somewhere exotic, maybe head on down to Cuba. This is Frankie Ford and 'Sea Cruise.'"

Old man rhythm is in my shoes . . . no use t'sittin' and a' singin' the blues . . .

Freekin's hand froze just above the spinning record. The children had moved forward a few steps and had stopped holding hands. Without warning, they turned and attacked anything and anyone near them. Mothers took up their children, and with candy bags flying, they ran from the many children who appeared as if from nowhere.

Freekin' Rowdy Rhoads fell backward and hit his head on the side of the van. Roberta screamed. The flight on the sidewalk became a stampede. Those who didn't see the assault start with the small and ragged children panicked because everyone else was. Cars screeched to a halt in the street as they tried to avoid the black shapes of small children jumping in and out of the street. Drivers tried to get by, but they hesitated in fear of running down the trick-or-treaters who were now all on the run. Rowdy even heard someone shout that there must be a fire.

As men and women ran with screaming kids, Freekin' Rowdy realized that Frankie Ford was still singing, but the volume had skyrocketed just as the streetlights and the illumination from the many buildings lining the street flashed on and off. The nightmare began in a split second. The music raised even higher in volume as Freekin' covered his ears.

So be my guest, you got nothin' to lose . . . won't ya let me take you on a sea cruise?

The punch to his belly was so hard that Dean lost his breath. Before he could even get his eyes open, he heard Gloria scream. He felt the movement of the others in the balcony as they were startled out of their heavy necking to see what was happening. Dean felt another blow, this one to his nose, and he felt himself falling backward. He felt his back hit the seat and then three more slams to his face in rapid succession. He was stunned, but still all he could hear was Gloria as she fought with someone.

"Shut up, bitch!" came the familiar voice of his old friend Jimmy Weller. Dean heard a slap, and then in between screams from the silver screen and from the audience, he heard Gloria curse at someone.

"Hey, man, I didn't sign up to hit on no girls," said Steve Cole.

There was a grunt, and then Dean felt the pressure come off him. He managed to get to his feet to see an amazing sight. Harvey Leach had come from nowhere and had managed to attach himself to the back of Jimmy Weller. He was trying desperately to hang on, but Jimmy was too strong and easily tossed him.

"Get help!" Dean shouted over the terrified screams of the teens watching the movie. On screen, a skeleton was rising from a vat of acid. It was the climax to *House on Haunted Hill*.

Dean managed to get a strike in when Jimmy grabbed for a fleeing Harvey Leach, missing by mere inches. Dean swung downward and caught Weller on the side of his head and then drew back to hit him again when a fist slammed into the side of his own head. He shook and tried to clear his thoughts when he heard a grunt of pain and then another, and then he was slammed in the head again. This time, he figured out the culprit.

"Oh, my God, are you all right? I thought you were someone else!" Gloria yelled when she recognized Dean's protest of pain. She stood there in the dark with her hands once more over her mouth.

Dean used the light from the screen to look around. He wiped blood from his nose and then saw Gloria. She was standing there with everyone else in the balcony looking at them. He quickly grabbed her hand, and then with a swift kick into the ass of a struggling Jimmy Weller, he pushed by a startled Steve Cole and an equally bruised Sam Manachi, and they ran for the aisle and the stairs.

"Don't just stand there like Martin and Lewis! Go get 'em!" Jimmy shouted as he picked his battered body and bruised ego off the sticky floor of the balcony.

The chase was on.

As the three boys gave chase, the children charged from the stairways leading to the balcony. Most kids attending thought it was one of those Hollywood gags that seemed to be popular these days—the buzzing chairs, the flying silk over the heads of audiences—real con tactics used to attract the younger crowds. Girls and guys alike from the main floor to the balcony began screaming as some of these character actors actually bit and scratched. Soon, they realized something was very wrong when most got a smell of the children. The panic began, and the aisles became unpassable.

Teenagers disgorged from the Grenada Theater like in the famous scene in the Steve McQueen horror flick *The Blob*. Freekin's eyes widened as he saw the rush. Girls were tripping, and boys thinking they were brave tried to help but then remembered what was in the theater and thought better of their chance at valor and ran. Roberta screamed as one of the children started toward her. She quickly rolled backward, and because she was drunk, she would never remember the brilliant maneuver as she slid right into the van and then quickly closed the sliding door.

With Frankie Ford screaming loudly about a sea cruise, Freekin' Rowdy

Rhoads pushed his way past the running trick-or-treaters and their fleeing parents. He entered the theater to see what he could do.

Inside, Vincent Price was heard. He was laughing that deep, dark, disturbing sound as the world went to free flight and the first feature of the spook fest called the Moreno Monster Mash, *House on Haunted Hill*, ended.

There wouldn't ever be a second feature.

Robert saw the children close-up for the first time, and now he realized what he had done. The town would never recover from this if he didn't get the entity back into containment. He looked at the two extinguishers and knew that they would be useless if he didn't have a way to get them back to the vault at the winery. He needed the steel enclosure for a trap. Unfortunately, the vault was two miles away on a hillside. He fought his way past the fleeing kids. He stopped just inside the lobby, not even sure if Dean was there, but then he spied him. He cursed when he saw he was still with Gloria Perry. He made his mind up and charged into the crowd.

"Dean!"

The boy stopped so suddenly that everyone behind him on the stairs slammed into him and Gloria. They both lost their footing, and down they came. Kids jumped over them as they ran by. The creepy children weren't even part of the plot of the Vincent Price vehicle.

"Dad!" Dean called as he tried in vain to gain his feet. He grew angry and frustrated when he heard Gloria shout out in pain several times. Finally, strong arms lifted him to his feet, and Dean watched as his father assisted Gloria up. Robert pulled them both aside and then thrust one of the fire extinguishers into Dean's hand.

Dean looked at his father as if he gone nuts. "It's not a fire, it's—"

"I know what it is; I'm responsible for bringing it here. We have to head them back to the winery; that's the only place they can be contained."

"They won't go back," Gloria said as she looked upon Hadley with hatred. "They'll never follow you or my father. You helped do this to them!"

Hadley looked up and saw the children as they once more gathered near the top of the stairs. "We'll discuss the right and wrong of it later, young lady. For now, we have to get them back into that vault you're responsible for letting them out of."

"Gloria didn't do anything but try to make friends with children that you had a hand in killing!" Dean countered, getting in between his father and the girl he had fallen for.

"Of course we didn't. But I cannot explain now. This is—"

"Mercury, we know—your little Nazi pal explained it to us. That won't work; the vault is too far and you'll never be able to get them in there again!"

"We have to try!" Hadley countered.

"Where is my father?" Gloria screamed above the din of shouts and panic.

"He's holding the doctor up at the factory. He wanted me to help get you out of here, but we can't unless we corral these damnable things. We need that vault!"

Frankie Ford was still going on a sea cruise as boys and girls ran by for no other reason than others were doing the same, screaming, "The Russians finally did it!" and "The damn government lied to us!" Most thought the missiles of that October had made their appearance just as Huntley and Brinkley had feared. The Cold War must have just turned hot.

"The old vault from the Moreno Savings and Loan!" Gloria shouted as she faced the two Hadleys.

"What vault?" Dean asked, taking Gloria by the hand and giving his father a defiant, challenging look. But Hadley Sr. played his role well; he nodded, indicating that he understood.

"When the new bank was built, they moved the old vault here. Remember, everyone was there to watch it being moved. My father described it to me."

Hadley wanted to kick himself as he remembered the fortuitous move of the old Savings and Loan vault to the only space in town large enough to hold it at the time—right there in the basement of the Grenada.

"Will they follow you, Gloria?" Robert asked.

"I don't know!"

Hadley pushed and pulled the two teens to the curtain-covered twin doors, and all three started down the wooden stairs. Suddenly, Hadley stopped.

"The extinguishers!"

"I'll get them!" Dean called out as he quickly leaned in and kissed Gloria on the mouth. Even during this horrid time, the girl smiled as they parted. "I love you!" Dean said as his words echoed in the half dark of the stairwell.

Robert watched as his son parted with Gloria. His eyes followed him until he had vanished through the door.

"Gloria, can you make it down the stairs to the vault without getting hurt?"

"Yes. Mr. Gallagher, the manager, and I used to practice music down there with the old organ that used to be installed upstairs."

"Good. I need to leave word for your father to join us down there; I'll only be a minute. The vault door is unlocked; just pull the dust cover off and open it with the latch."

Gloria nodded, frightened beyond measure without Dean by her side. She felt horrible for her new dependence on Dean, but she liked the feeling for the first time in her life. She started down the stairs and into the dark world of the basement.

Hadley watched her go step by step and then with a scowl he reserved for anything that disgusted him, he turned and exited the stairwell.

He met Dean a few steps outside the door. He was running in a panic as the children were walking toward him, struggling with the two heavy fire extinguishers as he ran. Robert saw his father, and then he doubled his efforts when he realized that Gloria wasn't with him.

"She's right in there waiting; we have to get something from the manager's office. Come on."

Dean followed his father, and instead of taking the left door and the stairwell, he opened the right. Robert was about to run in when he stopped and cried out a warning to his son.

"Look out!"

Dean turned and felt the sharp blow to the back of his head. He went down in a heap on the carpeted floor just inside the office. Robert stood over him with the barrel of a gun. He looked around quickly and then checked Dean. He was breathing as he lay there. Hadley moved some of his hair out of his face and then shook his head.

"What I have to do, you don't have the strength for, son," Hadley said and then stood. He looked up and saw a familiar face as the boy ran to the stairwell with two other boys. They were running from a few of the children.

"Harvey Leach!" Hadley called out loudly over the music.

Harvey came to a halt before hitting the bottom step with two of his friends from Newberry's.

"Mr. Hadley, Dean and Gloria are in trouble up there!"

"No, they're here." He stepped aside and gestured wildly. "Get him out of here! He's hurt pretty badly!"

Harvey's two friends ran over and got Dean to his feet.

"Where's Gloria Perry?" Harvey asked.

"She's safe with her father. Now get him out of here; I have to get these other kids to safety!"

Harvey did what he was told and assisted Dean out of the theater. Hadley turned, grabbed the mercury-filled extinguishers, and ran down the stairs to the basement. As he ran, taking the steps two at a time and almost falling several times, he turned and saw the progression of children as they started down the same stairs. This time, he stopped counting after twenty-two. He figured the rest would be close behind. They were sensing that Gloria Perry was in trouble.

The dynamite Fromm had planted underneath the largest of the mercury containment vessels detonated. The explosion ripped through the vats of heavy metal and then through the main gas lines. The resulting fireball pressurized into a gaseous sphere that expanded like a nuclear detonation, small but compact. Cars were blown out of the parking lot, and the guard shack flew high into the sky. The largest containment vessel blew skyward with most of the Hadley Corp roof. The roof went six hundred feet into the air and killed all the second-shift employees on the first floor. The walls then came down, leaving only two of the cornerstones standing. The fireball reached up into the overcast sky and reflected brightly off the dampened hillsides. Then the main gas line leading into the factory from the town below exploded in a chain reaction that started a run for Moreno a mile below.

Ten billion fireflies erupt from the sky and settled onto the town. Mercury covered the area like silvery snow.

Moreno was now a dead zone in more ways than one.

Robert made it down the stairs and then dropped the heavy extinguishers to the floor. He saw Gloria standing in front of the vault, with his son's jacket on. A fury filled him when he saw the way she stood. She had always been Perry's prized little girl. She could never become a true asset to anyone, much less the son he had such plans for. He started forward with determination.

Gloria tilted her head up. "Where's Dean?" she asked when she didn't recognize the footfalls.

"He thought it better not to be here. He said you can keep the jacket; he won't be needing it anymore."

"Where is Dean?" she repeated as if she hadn't heard him.

Hadley looked back and saw that the children were on the second landing; one more and they would be there with them. Hadley didn't expect a warm reception for one of their captors. He stepped up to Gloria, and she shied away.

"Get in the vault," he said.

"I want Dean." She stepped back until her foot hit the frame of the open steel door.

"I know what you want—to latch yourself onto my boy for a meal ticket. That isn't happening." He shoved her farther into the vault. "Dean doesn't have the guts to say what he needed to—you aren't good enough for him." He stepped inside with her. He felt the children behind him gathering now at the foot of the stairs.

The vault was much smaller than the original. It had no vents other than spots where old braces used to secure it to the wall of the old Savings and Loan. They had been sealed for the transport of the vault to the theater.

Gloria felt the tears well up and spill out from under her glasses. "Daddy," she said.

Angrily, Hadley reached out and removed her dark glasses. She flinched and cried out. He backed away. Hadley tossed the glasses out of the vault, where they shattered.

"Dean!" Gloria screamed.

Hadley hit her hard, and she went down, striking her head on the steel floor. She stirred a moment and then was still. Robert ran from the vault, took one of the fire extinguishers, and ran to one of the many storage lockers. On his way, he kicked Gloria's dark glasses away, where they slid under one of the cabinets. Hadley opened one of the taller ones, pulled out the old movie posters, and then squeezed inside, only closing the door partially.

Then the children were there. Hadley watched from the locker, his eyes roving from child to child as they remained motionless. Then in the silence of the basement, he heard the soft moan escape the vault. The children froze. With their black, gleaming eyes fixed on the vault, it seemed they were hesitant to move toward it. Then Hadley caught a lucky break. Gloria cried out loudly.

"Dean!"

The damn children of Jürgen Fromm turned as one and went into the vault. Hadley counted all twenty-seven of them before he charged out of the steel storage cabinet and quickly slammed the door closed. He spun the locking wheel and then reached for the first container of mercury. He quickly started spraying the entire stainless steel surface with silverish liquid.

He heard the screams of the children inside. He knew he shouldn't have been able to because of the thickness of the steel, but he could anyway. The sounds were satisfying to him on a base level. Then he heard crying, and that froze him until the now-empty extinguisher fell from his hands. He covered his ears, but he still heard Gloria's sobs as she felt the horror of what had happened. He could swear he heard not just her but the children as they pounded on the door, begging for freedom.

Hadley couldn't stand it. He knew Gloria would be dead in a matter of an hour as her air ran out, but listening to her die was something he could not stand. He ran.

As he reached the main floor, kids were running to get free of the new terror to strike.

As Freekin' Rowdy Rhoads sent five more screaming girls out into the night after picking them up from the floor, Roberta, who had sobered up quickly when the assault on Moreno had begun, grabbed him and pointed at the hill. The flames climbed high into the sky, and Freekin' realized that a disaster of massive proportions had just struck the town. They watched flaming material start falling from the sky. Pieces of burning wood and steel struck the town.

"We have to get out of here!" Roberta yelled. She pointed to Dean, who was laid out on the remote van's floor after being dropped there by Harvey Leach and his two friends.

"Where's his girl? She's blind!"

Roberta shook her head as she ducked sparks from the sky. "He keeps mumbling something about the balcony!" she shouted.

Freekin' turned and ran for all he was worth back toward the now-flaming front of the theater.

"No! Come back!"

"There are still kids in there!" Freekin' shouted as he ran back into the Grenada.

Moments later, the heaviest object ever to fall from the sky—with the exception of NASA space catastrophes losing their unstable orbits—crashed directly into the rounded roof of the Grenada.

The last containment vessel full of mercury slammed into the auditorium. Freekin' Rowdy Rhoads, late and great DJ of the Chicago music scene, stood next to several boys and girls, including three very woozy young thugs named Weller, Cole, and Manachi, when the entire balcony came crashing down, killing them all.

Outside, the town was burning as sirens from the surrounding towns wailed over the screams of terror. As Roberta bravely drove the K-Rave remote van away, a large section of brick wall came down and sent the beautiful marquee crashing to the sidewalk, killing three more trick-or-treaters and their parents.

John sat straight up in bed. He was unable to draw a breath. Harvey Leach came straight out of the chair he had been sitting in. The room was still dark, and all he heard was the large Indian trying to draw a breath. Jennifer, whose eyes were adjusted better to the dark because she had never closed them, sprang to John's side, and she tried talking him out of his dreamlike stupor. His hands were flailing, and he was slapping away her attempts to calm him. She saw his features in the semidarkness of the room, and they were a mix of terror and anger. His head rocked back and forth, and he shook uncontrollably.

"Harvey! Bob! Hold him down!" she shouted.

Both men sprang into action and tried their best to get John's flailing arms and kicking legs under control, but he was too much for them; Harvey was sent flying into a wall and Bob was kicked in the head. Linda threw her body on top of John to hold him in place.

Julie handed Jennifer the syringe, and without hesitation, she plunged the Adrenalin hard into John's thick forearm, but instead of waking him, it stimulated his efforts. Bob added his weight to his wife's, and they both bounced like cowboys bucked by an angry horse. Casper tried to help, and Peckerwood added his barking for support.

"John, wake up!" Jenny screamed.

Julie backed away when she saw the intensity on his face. Even Peckerwood stopped barking and ran under the bed, where the only cover could be found.

Suddenly, all went still and John lay easily back. He blinked several times as if he had just awakened from a ten-year coma. He looked around slowly and easily. Then he found he couldn't breathe. He saw three people lying on him, and the reasons for his breathing difficulty was apparent. He came eye to eye with Linda, who smiled as her face met his.

"Hi. Welcome back."

"Breathe . . . can't breathe," he managed to grunt out.

Suddenly, they realized that he had close to six hundred pounds on his chest. They quickly rolled off, and then he grunted again when Jennifer tossed her own weight on him. She kissed him several times as he tried to catch his breath. He finally managed to sit up when Jenny rolled free of his body. He took several deep breaths, and the air felt heavenly.

"What happened?" Julie asked as she tried to give John a bottle of water. He slapped it away as he tried to gather his thoughts.

"Murdered . . . them . . . all," he finally managed to say.

Bob, Linda, Harvey, and Casper moved away from the bed, but the haunted look never left Lonetree's face.

"Who?" Jennifer asked.

"Where is Gabriel?" he asked as he swung his head to the right and to the left, trying to peer into and penetrate the darkness. Lightning gave him a brief glimpse of only Leonard standing and watching from the window, happy not to be involved with bringing John back to the land of thought instead of dream.

"I need to tell him something . . . I don't remember . . . but it's important." Again, he tried desperately to sit up.

"Take it easy; your heart is going a hundred miles an hour. We had to use Adrenalin to get you back," Jenny said as John finally managed to place his feet on the floor.

"Well, I don't know how to say this, but I think Gabe's about to have a lot of company," Leonard said from the window. He was still staring out into the windswept storm. "All of them kids, the ones that look like a coked-out version of Wednesday Addams, they're doing something down there."

"Help me up," John said as he struggled to stand. Everyone, including Peckerwood from beneath the bed, offered support. He felt his brain go momentarily blank and his knees gave way, but with the assistance of all, he managed to stay upright. They moved through the darkness to the large set of windows where Leonard stood rooted to the spot.

"Glad to see you made it back from Neverland, Chief," Leonard said as he pointed down to the street. "It looks like you had some kind of effect on them."

As they watched, Linda gasped as the children all formed in a group in the center of the street. With one last look at the second floor of Newbery's, first one and then another of the black-eyed and soulless children started jumping. They hit in midair and re-formed, and others jumped into what now looked like a swirling mass of blackened rainwater. Each time one of the children jumped into the air, its form added to the tornado-type funnel. They did this until a solid wall of black on black formed. As the group watched from the windows, it stopped. Suddenly, what they saw made them jump back from the window. Across the way, the three agents trapped inside the phone exchange ran from their window to take cover.

The form was almost human in appearance. It stood at eye level with the second floor of Newberry's. Harvey and Casper felt as if they were seeing a repeat of an old horror film they had never wished to see again.

"It's happening again," Harvey said. Instead of being frightened, he became angry as the sight of the swirling mass in human form jogged his deepest buried memories.

The darkness was discernable because of the rain striking its form, almost as if the children were a solid more than a ghost when they were together. The children, in the form that made them formidable for their own protection, looked into the second-floor windows until they saw John. The large hand came up and steadied itself at the window, then lowered it, and the swirling blackness moved away. It was heading for the theater.

"Gabriel and Damian are in danger! That thing perceives them as a threat—not to them but to Gloria!" John yelled and then turned. "Help me get to the theater! I've got to stop them all. I have to tell Gloria what happened."

"What are you saying?" Jennifer asked, more confused than ever.

"The children aren't the real power here! Neither is Gloria!"

"You mean there's something else here more powerful that what we've seen?"

"Yes, trapped, but still the real power. Now help me, damn it!"

Leonard, though he didn't want to, left the window and assisted in getting John to the stairs.

"Not you, I want you to get to those agents in the search party and get me some explosives. The hostage rescue team unit ought to have breaching charges. I need them." John quickly leaned over and said something in Leonard's ear that only he could hear due to the tremendous shaking of thunder from outside. Leonard's eyes widened, but he didn't argue. John wasn't done. "Harvey, I need you and Casper to be brave for one more night. Bob, you and Linda can help. Get to the mission if the whole damn thing hasn't slid down the hill, and find me that original vault."

"No need for that," Leonard said as she reached the stairwell. "It's that big shiny thing that came rolling down in that last mudslide from the hill. The entire mission and winery are gone. But the vault is right out there, half-buried; it came down with the entire hillside as an escort." Leonard vanished down the stairs.

"See, things are starting to break our way," John said with a smirk as he sent the others on their particular assignments.

"If this is things breaking our way, why am I ready to shit my pants?" Casper Worthington asked just as they too vanished down the stairwell.

"Let's go and see if we can end this."

What remained of the Supernaturals started down the stairs in a harried flight. They had one final mission in them, and that was to save two of their own that were about to be meat for the grinder if things didn't work out the way John hoped.

The second death of the town of Moreno was now at hand. Halloween was almost over.

25

Gabriel had been drawn to the basement of the Grenada. The old theater was still decked out in all its antique glory. The walls looked freshly painted, the gargoyles sconces lining them looking as if a dust rag had been recently run across their scowling faces.

"It feels like an impression, like this is to make us feel more at ease," Damian said as he followed Gabriel. He leaned over and examined the candy on display in the half-circular concession stand. He saw the old standards—the hot dogs spinning bottom to top in the hot dog machine, the buns resting in a small doorway, catching steam from the hot dogs, the Jujubes and Junior Mints, the ice cream compartments displayed at both ends of the snack bar. But the popcorn smelled delectable. He even heard and saw a fresh batch being made—without so much as an attendant present. The magnetic lettering above the snack bar told them that the large boxes of candy and cups of ice cream were twenty-five cents. Popcorn was ten cents. He shook his head in wonder at the rate of inflation in this country. *That is the real horror*, he thought bravely just to get his mind off where he was. Then came the sounds from the auditorium. Damian turned and looked at Gabe, who stood behind him. He cocked his head, trying to place the jingle.

Let's all go to the lobby . . . let's all go to the lobby . . . let's all go to the lobby, and get ourselves a treat!

Gabe and Damian remembered the jingle from their younger years; it was the dancing soda cups and popcorn boxes showing their wares as if they were the Rockettes. As they smiled at each other, the distant music dwindled to nothing.

In the silence, they heard the door creak open. They turned and saw that the red curtain had been drawn back, and an open door was just finishing its swinging arc. The light switched on just inside the doorway.

"This is like being politely invited to join your own execution," Damian said as he watched Gabriel head for the open doorway. He followed only because he didn't want to be left alone inside the deserted lobby.

They went down into the basement.

The basement was clean and orderly. There was no water on the floor, and everything was upright. The smell was dank but not overpowering. As they eased past old chairs that needed to be reupholstered in the gaudy red of that golden era, boxes of cups, and folded popcorn boxes, they saw it. The vault. They knew exactly what they were looking at.

"The famous Savings and Loan bank vault, I presume?" Damian asked, not expecting an answer.

The lights flickered for the briefest of moments, and they froze, expecting the worst. But they steadied. Gabriel realized that this was it. Whatever was behind all of this wanted them to be able to see the end results of man's meddling where it should not have been.

They froze again when they heard movement from inside the vault.

"Oh, shit," Damian said. He never felt so helpless in his life while holding a powerful handgun. The barrel moved to the tarp-covered vault but was not in the least steady.

Gabriel felt the presence. It was right behind them. Somehow the children had come into the basement as they had been studying the vault. It stood there. It was massive. They heard the breathing of all twenty-seven children as the black mass stood by the bottom step and stared at them, unmoving except for the sparkling elements that swirled and eddied like a tornado flecked with gold. Damian and Gabriel jumped back as the black tornado moved past them, knocking them from their feet. It approached the vault, and then a giant hand reached out and pulled the tarp away. The jumbled mass of water, dust, and human life quickly stepped away with a roar of pain, and the mass started to come apart. First one, and then another, then another of the children fell free of the hurricane before them. One by one, they appeared out of the funnel cloud of motion. Each child stood and stared at them as they came back into singularity one soul at a time. The wind inside the basement picked up and then stopped as the last few children formed.

"Well, there goes your newest theory about how most hauntings are faked," Damian said, his bladder almost letting go as he watched the children staring at the two men. The smell was starting to get to them as well as the sight of their emaciated forms. The horror of seeing the skeletal bodies of mere children was enough to drive a good person insane.

"This isn't a haunting; this is something that has never happened before. The evil here isn't like what we ran into inside Summer Place—this is man. This was perpetrated on these innocents. Their evil is nothing but a reflection of us."

Damian half turned and looked at Gabriel. "Is that your professional opinion?" He snorted out of fear, not levity. "I see twenty-seven ghosts that appear very real."

"Ghosts? No, not ghosts. They're still with us because they are being kept here for some reason. As much as they want their freedom, they can't leave. Something is holding them here."

"Okay, that's it; you can't spend any more time with John. He's starting to affect you in some weird ways."

"Look," Gabe said as the children started raising their small hands. They were pointing to something. Gabriel bravely stepped forward, and the children stepped farther back. Gabriel stepped up to the vault's door. His brow furrowed when he saw what remained of the mercury that had been spread fifty-five years before from the fire extinguishers Robert had used to trap the entity back in 1962.

"Is that—"

"Mercury? Yes." Gabriel reached out and took a corner of the discarded tarp, wiping the offending heavy metal from the thick steel door just above the dial mechanism combination lock that had been missing since Hadley had it sealed days after the disaster in Moreno. His tracks had been thoroughly covered—or so he thought. When Gabriel had wiped most of it clean, he stepped back. The children still remained toward the far wall, glancing at each other and hoping for an answer.

"They don't know what to do. Their script in this nightmare has come to an end." Gabriel looked back at a frightened Damian.

The former Pennsylvania detective really wasn't concentrating on what these nightmare apparitions were confused about. All he knew was that the so-called innocents they faced had killed two of his friends and many others. The children turned their blackened eyes on the two men as if they expected help from them. Gabriel was nearly convinced that this was what they wanted all along. They wanted someone here who understood. These children had manipulated the natural order of things to end the nightmare they had been in since 1943.

Gabriel stepped to the door of the vault.

"No, she wants me," came the voice from the darkened area of the basement.

Gabriel and Damian saw the lightly formed shape of a man. He was frail, and he stumbled as he moved. The strangest part was the fact that the area the person spoke from was a wreck; it wasn't in pristine shape like the rest of the theater. As the form moved forward, so did the real appearance of the basement. The odor of mildew, rot, and rat droppings was prevalent. The basement itself was being brought back to a state of reality, not one of perfect preservation.

Damian jumped back when he saw the familiar shape of President Hadley step from the shadows and into the dimming light. His hospital gown and hair were filthy and covered in mud. His legs were scratched and bruised from surviving the landslide, and he was bleeding heavily from cuts that crisscrossed his body. Damian moved to assist him as the children parted for him. Gabe held the large detective in check before he could get too close.

"This is his show now," he said, making Damian flinch about the prospect of watching another man torn to pieces in front of them.

Hadley stepped up to the vault and stood still. The children all gathered at his back. The former president stood on shaky legs and lovingly reached out and felt the cold steel of the door. He fell to his knees and started crying.

"I failed her," Dean said as he kept his hand on the door. He stood with renewed strength and pulled on the lone handle of the vault until his strength gave out.

Hadley was suddenly thrown backward by an unseen force. The door bent outward as the occupant had decided that it was now time to make its move. The children came forward and added their power to the force inside. Damian and Gabriel heard the popping of heavy-duty bolts as the door loosened in its strong frame. It came free and was tossed aside, barely missing Dean's prone form. The children stepped aside and looked at Gabriel and Damian as if expecting something from them.

Gabe went to the vault, and Damian assisted Hadley to his feet. The man was sobbing uncontrollably.

"She has the right to my soul. I failed her," he said as Damian tried to get him under control. He nervously stood inside the gaggle of long-dead children holding the sick man up by sheer willpower. The large detective would rather have just dropped the man and gotten the hell out, but like Gabriel, he knew they had been brought to this point by the very entity that started everything.

Gabriel eased inside, taking a cautious step over the damaged threshold of the frame. His eyes quickly adjusted to the semidarkness of the vault's interior. His shoulders slumped when he saw the mass in the far corner of the vault. He felt a lump in his throat as he recognized a body in a fetal position. He had to grab the frame of the door for support as John's greatest fear had been realized; Gabriel knew he was looking at Gloria Perry. He had to step out of the vault when the smell of decades-old death hit his nostrils. The body was thin and almost deflated. The old letterman's jacket collapsed, as if all the air had been let out of a balloon. Then, before he realized it, someone was standing next to him. He smelled clean air. He also smelled perfume. He slowly turned, and his eyes went from the small body inside to Gloria Perry. She stood without her dark glasses, and she was whole. She tilted her head and placed her right hand to her eyes. Then she moved it toward Gabriel. Her hand caressed his face as she examined him. Her fingers ran from feature to feature. It was if she were seeing a face for the first time ever. She smiled. It was a sad thing to see, and Gabriel's heart reached out for the murdered girl. Then the expression changed as she turned and faced the children. She stepped away from Gabriel, who felt weak in his knees, realizing that Gloria had drained some of the strength from him while touching his face.

"Alley, you have been very bad." She stepped closer. "This shouldn't have involved anyone other than the person who left me to his father." She looked over at Damian, who was holding Hadley upright. Gabriel saw the look in the old man's face. It wasn't terror, but it was something he had seen before—it was longing. The man actually did love this girl, far more than even John hinted at. "It's now time to settle, Dean." She moved forward, and Damian felt his bladder let go as her face dripped and foundered on her bones. The hair came free in clumps, and her eyes fell back into her skull. Her right hand reached up for Hadley, who closed his eyes and waited for the thing that had controlled his life for over fifty-five years.

"Gloria," Dean whispered in a haunting voice as the rotting corpse came on. He closed his eyes as the skeletal fingers reached for him.

Gabriel and Damian felt the satisfaction of the children as they anticipated the justice of what was about to happen.

"Gloria!" came the shout from the bottom of the stairs.

Gabriel turned and saw John Lonetree being held up by Jennifer and Julie. He was staring at the apparition of the girl he had seen Dean become enamored with.

The deteriorating mass turned and looked at Lonetree. They all felt a change in the room as Gloria, or what had once been the girl, faced John. Lonetree saw the familiar turn and tilt of the girl's head as she tried to figure something out. Then her form started to come back to her young self again. She recognized Lonetree from her past. Before anyone knew it, Gloria was her old self again as she looked from person to person.

The children, however, looked agitated. They began to move as one toward the former president and Damian.

"Gloria, it wasn't Dean. Robert did this to you. The boy was stopped from returning by his own father. He did this to you, not Dean. He had nothing to do with his father's plan."

Gloria made no move. She stood there and looked at John for the longest time. She didn't even flinch when Lonetree tossed something that landed at her feet with a small tinkle of breaking glass.

"Dean's father knocked those from your face when he hit you that night," John said as everyone in the room saw the dark glasses at her feet. Gloria leaned over and picked them up. "I was there and saw it all. He can't hide behind the lies anymore, Gloria. You know I was there; you saw me," John said, almost begging the entity to remember.

Her eyes, the most beautiful blue any of them had ever seen, looked up from the dark glasses to face Lonetree.

"I watched you two fall in love. I saw how you felt about each other. You know that Dean never let you down. He's been paying for your death for his entire life. He has made his existence one of hatred and malice. He didn't deserve this any more than you did." John left Julie and Jennifer and stepped forward. He felt the hatred from the children as they advanced slowly on the newcomers. "Release them, Gloria. Get them to stop."

The girl looked at John, and then her eyes settled on the old man. Dean stood with the help of Damian, and then he gently pushed Damian away and stood on his own. He watched as Gloria advanced on him. He bravely faced his own death, a death he had wished for since 1962.

The Supernaturals all jumped when Gloria suddenly and inexplicably jumped into the old man's arms. They watched as fifty-five years of desperate hate dissolved into what it always was—pure love. Hadley began crying as he raised his frail arms and took Gloria into them and they embraced. She was on her tiptoes and crying also.

"Uh, someone isn't too damn thrilled with this lovely reunion," Damian said as the children advanced.

They could all feel the rage emanating from the twenty-seven souls murdered long ago. They were feeling betrayed by Gloria; Gabriel knew this as a fact. They had been her guiding influence since the day she had befriended them.

The time had come for their revenge against all.

Leonard started pointing as if he were crazed. Bob, Linda, Casper, and Harvey started digging into the pile of mud. Over fifty of the FBI and hostage rescue team that had been searching for the president earlier moved to assist. The fear that the people from town showed made them move all the much faster. Leonard only hoped John's theory was correct.

As lightning flashed and rain pummeled them, the vault was slowly uncovered. Men and women worked to free a large portion of the vault. Leonard let out a sigh of relief when he saw they had uncovered the correct end of the vault.

The rubble of both the old mission and the winery had been carried by the massive mudslide to the back door of K-Rave Radio. As the men and women fought to clear a spot, Leonard waved over the hostage rescue team explosives specialist and pointed down.

"Right there!" he yelled above the din of the storm. He watched as the man in black Nomex placed his breaching charges against the thick steel. "Will that be enough?" he shouted at the man as the FBI moved Bob, Linda, Casper, and Harvey away from the vault.

"No, the charges were never made to break through steel. These breaching charges are for doors and walls." He unwrapped a detonation cord and attached it to the six charges of explosives. He then attached a timer and looked up at Leonard. "I've placed them in what I hope is a soft spot. I think these were viewing ports of some kind. That should be the weakest spot. Now if I were you, I would get the hell back!"

Leonard watched the hostage rescue team explosives expert jump from the exposed corner of the vault. He quickly followed.

Overhead, the storm raged.

The children once again formed into the giant, swirling mass of hate and revenge. The giant moved toward Gloria and Dean, who stood the ground defiantly. The huge hands reached for the couple.

"God, anytime, Leonard!" John said as the others looked at him in confusion, helpless to stop the entity from tearing Hadley to pieces. They saw Gloria defiantly hold him as his death loomed above them.

The explosives detonated with a sound that drowned out the raging thunder. The hole was ripped into what Dr. Jürgen Fromm had once described as the viewing ports on section A. The vault then erupted in motion. The stored energy of seventy-five years was released into the storm-driven night. The cloud of fury exited the vault, knocking everyone within a hundred yards off their feet. The cloud of black, swirling hatred rose into the rain-filled sky and then shot off toward downtown Moreno.

"I think that thing's going to finish the job here in Moreno," Casper said as he watched the night over their heads explode into massive bolts of chain lightning.

"God, I hope this works," Leonard said as he turned and started running for town. The entire force of FBI and Secret Service quickly followed.

The mass of dead children formed into one and picked Dean up, tearing him away from Gloria in the ultimate betrayal. She reached out and screamed as Dean was once more snatched from her.

The basement erupted in bright light. The entity holding Dean stopped its assault as the room filled with swirling blackness that slowly became lighter and lighter. Then everyone saw it. There were dozens of people. They were dressed as the children had been. They were clearly older than them. The group stood surrounding not only the Supernaturals but also the black and swirling entity. Dean was released and fell to the hardened floor with a thud. The apparition that was Gloria ran to him and covered his still body.

Once more, the children dissolved into individual forms. They circled the adults that were in a state of misuse by the men who had tortured them to death many years before inside the borders of Yugoslavia. The children stood facing the parents they had been forced to watch die in the most awful experimentation ever conducted by the Nazis. The Supernaturals watched as the children ran to them. The room brightened just as Leonard came down the stairs, amazed at what he saw.

"That was the real power. Fromm never realized that the fuel that made this particular flame burn was not the children but the parents. Imagine the horror of knowing your children were going to die. That was the real power of the mind, not Fromm's experiment. It was the human ability to project the entire mind toward the things you hate or love. This was just like our entity at Summer Place. Like in Pennsylvania, this haunting was brought on by the mind and the fear of losing those you love the most in the world. The parents of the children had hate so powerful that even though their vault was sealed, they still managed to project that power."

Gabriel looked back at an exhausted John Lonetree. "I think you can have my job now."

"No, thank you."

Jennifer and Julie gasped when Gloria stood from her spot next to Dean. Her small frame was intact. She looked whole and young. She was crying, not tears of hate as she had done when Hadley Sr. had murdered her but a smile of long-sought contentment. She nodded and faced all of them.

"Thank you."

Gloria, with one last look at Dean, vanished.

The feeling of joy was felt by all of them as one by one the apparitions of the dead children and their murdered parents faded away to nothing. The lights flickered but remained steady as Jennifer and John checked on Hadley. Lonetree looked up at Gabriel and shook his head. Dean had died during the confrontation, but the look on his now soft features relayed to them in no uncertain terms that he too was now content.

Then the haunting ended. The lights in the basement went out, and it was Damian who broke first. He realized that when the lights went out, he had about the last nerve shocked from his system. The last they heard, he was pounding up the stairs without a word.

The group came out of the ruins of the Grenada Theater. They looked up at the clearing morning sky. The town was now useless to anyone. Mudslides now covered most of the old tract homes that used to house its citizens. Earth now covered most of the buildings on Main Street on the north side of town. Moreno was fading fast into California history.

"Wait," John said as the team stood just inside the debris field of the shattered marquee and box office. Lonetree dug through a pile of concrete and wood. The team watched him with interest. He finally stood, and with a smile, he tossed Gabriel a black book. It flapped in the stiff wind as Gabriel caught it.

"The journal." He looked up at Lonetree. "They hid it in the box office?"

"Yes, it seems that the old theater had everything to do with that night."

The Supernaturals stepped aside when the FBI and the Secret Service removed the covered body of Dean Hadley. They remained silent as the rescuers moved the former president's body to a waiting helicopter to be evacuated.

"What are we going to do with the journal?" Lonetree asked Gabriel.

"No one needs to know what happened to those innocent people. I have a friend in Nevada—at least I think he's still there. He is an archivist, from what I understand; he works closely with the National Archives. He'll know what to do with it."

"Who is this?" Lonetree asked.

"Oh, just a man I met many years ago. Name's Compton—Niles Compton. From my understanding, they're pretty good at unraveling the truth of things."

"Well, I hope this mysterious friend of yours has a strong stomach," Damian said as he kicked at the loose debris at his feet.

With that, the Supernaturals were finished inside the ghost town known as Moreno, California.

EPILOGUE

GLORIA AND DEAN

Blue moon . . . you saw me standing alone . . . without a dream in
my heart . . . without a love of my own . . .

—The Marcels, "Blue Moon,"
Billboard #22, 1959

Gabriel Kennedy, Julie Reilly, Jennifer Tilden, Leonard Sickles, Damian
Jackson, and John Lonetree were greeted as their limousine pulled into the
makeshift parking area atop the hill that once housed the oldest Spanish
mission and winery in California. The land was now barren. The hills were
still there, but that was all.

Bob and Linda Culbertson, Harvey Leach, and Casper and Peckerwood
Worthington shook hands with all of them as they faced the empty valley
that once sheltered the small town of Moreno. The land was now scraped bare
of all trace of human habitation. The off-ramp that led travelers to Moreno
had been closed, refusing access to the area. The old ruins of the Hadley Corp
factory had been erased from existence, and that hillside was also freshly
plowed under. New grass was starting to sprout where life once flourished.

The group was silent as they looked at the spot where Moreno once
stood. They remained so even when the black stretch limousine approached
and parked at about the spot where Newberry's once stood. Gabriel looked

over at Harvey Leach, who had a sad look on his face. Gabe knew he had been despondent when the federal and state authorities had arrived in Moreno the month before and handed him a court order to evacuate the town. He was informed that the entire area was now under a strict quarantine for mercury contamination. It was now something that was far beyond Hadley Corporation's ability to cover up. The EPA was now in charge.

"Shall we go down and see our benefactor?" Gabe asked Harvey.

Swiping a tear from his old eyes, Harvey nodded, and the entire entourage walked down to greet the guests to the resting place of a once-happy town.

They approached the stretch limo and waited. The driver stepped out and opened the door. Three men in expensive black suits stepped out. They were followed by the familiar form of Catherine Hadley.

"Okay, I'm here," she said as if she were the Queen of England. Gabe shook his head as he stepped forward. "I take it the settlement offered by my company wasn't sufficient for any of you. I gather you are assembled to take me to account?"

"Not at all, Madam First Lady." Gabriel gestured to Bob and Linda and then Harvey and finally to Peckerwood and Casper Worthington. They stepped forward and handed Gabriel several envelopes, which he handed to Catherine, who refused to accept them. One of her attorneys took them instead.

"What are these?" she asked as she saw the look of confusion on the faces of her legal representation.

"That is the generous offer you made to my team and these kind people. We cannot settle at this time."

"Settle what?" she asked with indignant arrogance. "This was compensation for property lost and an unsettled contract payment for the Culbertsons. I know your personal compensation was more than just satisfactory, Professor Kennedy."

Gabriel and the others watched the black SUV come from the direction of the old off-ramp to the interstate. Kennedy turned back to face the elegant former First Lady of the United States.

"Very satisfactory. However, our legal counsel, of which these kind people are now a part, have advised us to not accept the payments as offered. It may come to light that if we did accept said payments, we could be indicted on charges of conspiracy."

"What are you talking about?" the new widow asked with her smile deteriorating faster than her demeanor.

The black SUV pulled up, and two men in United States Marshals' windbreakers greeted the group. After showing their identification, they turned to Catherine. The taller of the two men started talking.

"Ma'am, you have our sympathies for the passing of your husband. However, our office has been ordered to serve you and your legal representation with this summons."

"For what?" the startled lawyer asked the marshals.

"Mrs. Hadley is now the sole owner of the Hadley Corporation holdings. The company is being placed into receivership for illegal dumping of harmful and toxic materials. You are now responsible for the cleanup of toxic waste in the town site formerly known as Moreno."

The first attorney opened the warrant and gasped, handing the paper over to Catherine. "Are you insane? The amount is ludicrous. The corporation doesn't have the assets to cover this. Fifteen point eight billion dollars!"

The U.S. marshal looked around the surrounding hills. "I guess the State of California and the EPA have differing views on how to clean up the land you poisoned with mercury. Thus, the company will be held in receivership until the courts officially rule." He nodded politely and then started for his car with his partner. "I hear they are rather unforgiving in cases like this. Just ask the power companies. Have a good day."

Catherine Hadley, who had just signed papers the past week to formally take over all sixteen companies of Hadley Corporation, stormed off to her car, followed by her frantic legal team.

"Well, I guess that's that," Harvey said.

"No, not yet," Gabriel said as he looked at John Lonetree, who moved to each of the old-timers. First to Bob and Linda. He gave them an envelope.

Linda opened it and staggered. "A hundred thousand dollars?" Linda asked as she felt near to fainting.

Then Casper opened his envelope. He felt weak kneed himself as he nodded in thanks for the property and walnut farm he lost. Last was Harvey Leach. He opened his white envelope, and he too smiled and took in the team of Supernaturals. Gabe held up a hand when they all wanted to talk at once.

"We're the ones responsible for you not being able to accept Catherine Hadley's settlement money. This is from our own funds. We won't need it. This was our last investigation as a team. Like you, we have lost too much."

With hugs and handshakes, the odd pairing of men and women separated, to never see each other again. They smiled as Casper and Peckerwood stopped and nodded, the dog barking a good-bye.

One month later, they stood in the spot where Newbery's used to stand. They could picture all the buildings of that long-ago town. Not a word was said by anyone. Even Damian, who had been adamant about not coming back at all, stood and admired the now-flattened land where Moreno used to be.

In the bright winter sunshine, they saw an amazing sight. The buildings from that long-ago place began rising from the earth. Streets pushed aside freshly dug earth, and the houses miraculously appeared. They saw people fill the streets around them. The town from the past was rising once more as they stood stunned, watching in silence. The buildings spiraled as they rose, shaking off the brown earth of the ancient hills. They were once more seeing Moreno as it was in far happier times.

"Wow," Leonard and Damian said, watching the magic come to life.

"Look!" Julie shouted with glee.

They all turned and looked in the direction she was pointing to. Standing on the sidewalk and looking their way was none other than George Cordero. He was smiling as he stood next to another figure. It was Kelly Delaphoy. The two lost friends had found each other. They were now a part of Moreno, and at least George had found that place he always wanted—his home.

They turned to the right and saw the familiar façade of K-Rave. Freekin' Rowdy Rhoads stood at the large plate glass window with his ever-present coffee mug in his hand. He raised it in toast to the people staring his way. They heard the music coming out of the building. The volume rose to a higher level as the Supernaturals listened.

Heart and soul . . . I fell in love with you . . . heart and soul . . . the way a fool would do . . .

They heard the old song by the Cleftones. They smiled as they saw the bright red convertible screaming down the street. It swerved and then centered itself again in the middle of the road. The car once more barely missed the sidewalk and then rebounded into the street. It came to a screeching halt before the startled men and women of the Supernaturals.

Dean shook his head as he smiled at the team. They saw Gloria was learning to drive inside their new world, and as she smiled at them, she mouthed the words *thank you*.

Dean looked as happy as anyone could ever have been. He nodded in thanks, and then his eyes went wide as the Corvette peeled out and almost smashed into K-Rave and a now-startled Freekin' Rowdy Rhoads. They heard the Cleftones singing about heart and soul as the Corvette vanished around the corner and disappeared.

The next thing the Supernaturals knew, they were standing on freshly plowed and smoothed-over dirt. The earth was ripe and rich to smell. They each exchanged looks of satisfaction.

The Supernaturals left each other without saying good-bye. Each man and woman had a decision to make, and that would be made without any help from each other.

After all, as George once told them, "We don't decide much in life. It has always been dictated to us by a force we will never understand."

The team known as the Supernaturals walked away knowing they had done the best they could. Perhaps someday they could all come to grips with themselves and decide that maybe the world really did need them.

Until that time came, they would wait.